BABY-SITTERS LITTLE SISTER®

KAREN'S WORST DAY

**DON'T MISS THE OTHER BABY-SITTERS
LITTLE SISTER GRAPHIC NOVELS!**

KAREN'S WITCH

KAREN'S ROLLER SKATES

ANN M. MARTIN

BABY-SITTERS LITTLE SISTER®

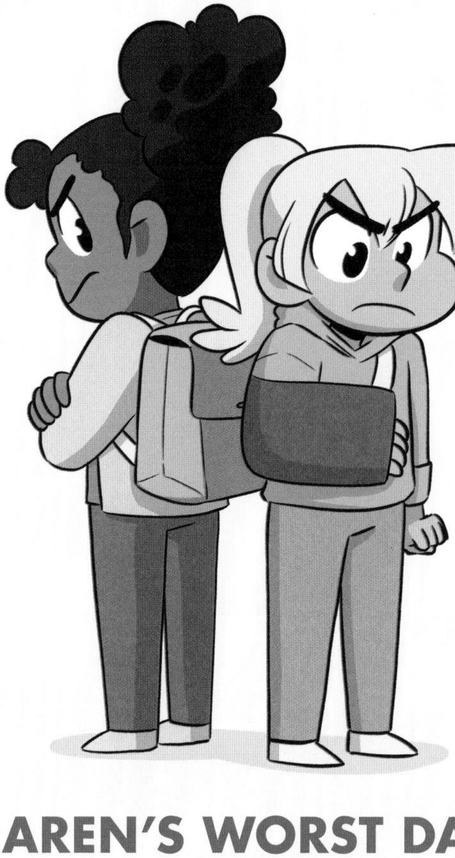

KAREN'S WORST DAY

A GRAPHIC NOVEL BY

KATY FARINA

WITH COLOR BY BRADEN LAMB

graphix

An Imprint of

SCHOLASTIC

This book is for
Read Marie Marcus,
Josh's little sister
A. M. M.

For Rian, my husband, who can turn my
worst days into my best days
K. F.

Text copyright © 2021 by Ann M. Martin
Art copyright © 2021 by Katy Farina

All rights reserved. Published by Graphix, an imprint of
Scholastic Inc., *Publishers since 1920.* SCHOLASTIC, GRAPHIX,
BABY-SITTERS LITTLE SISTER, and associated logos are trademarks
and/or registered trademarks of Scholastic Inc.

Library of Congress Control Number: 2019957367

ISBN 978-1-338-35619-9 (hardcover)
ISBN 978-1-338-35618-2 (paperback)

10 9 8 7 6 5 4 3 2 1   21 22 23 24 25

Printed in Malaysia   108
First edition, January 2021

Edited by Cassandra Pelham Fulton and David Levithan
Book design by Phil Falco and Shivana Sookdeo
Publisher: David Saylor

CHAPTER 1

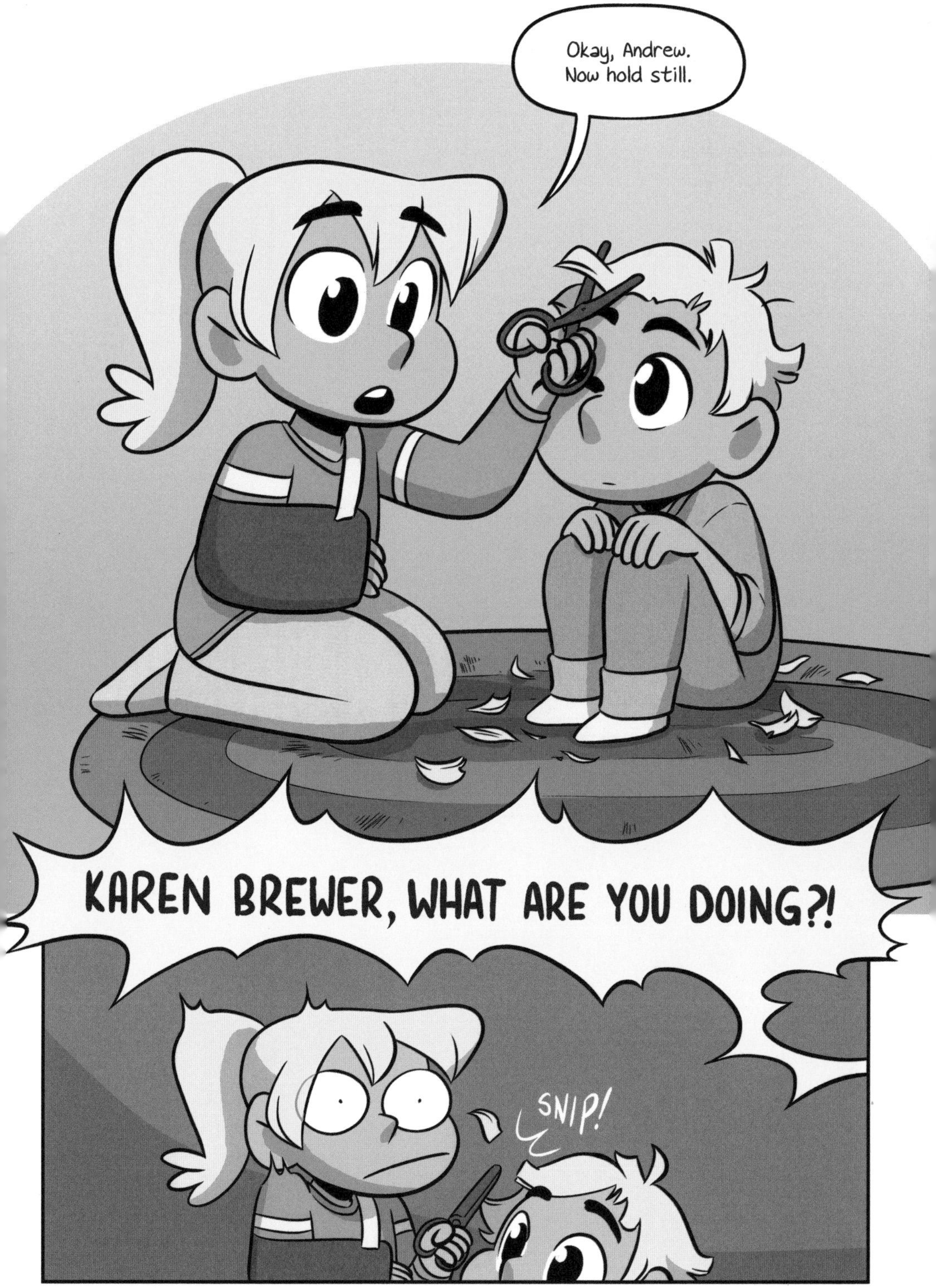
Okay, Andrew. Now hold still.
KAREN BREWER, WHAT ARE YOU DOING?!
SNIP!

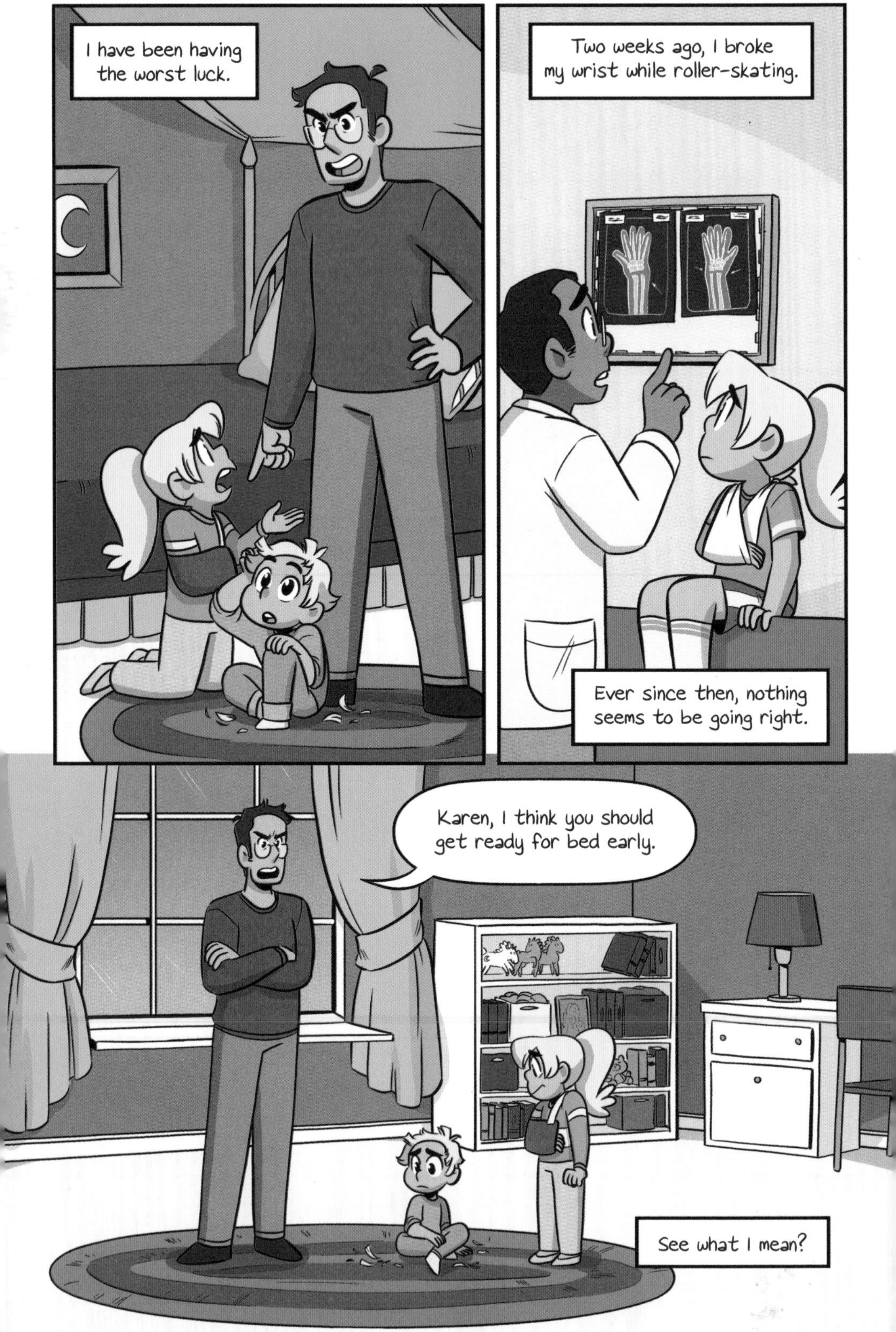
I have been having the worst luck.
Two weeks ago, I broke my wrist while roller-skating.
Ever since then, nothing seems to be going right.
Karen, I think you should get ready for bed early.
See what I mean?

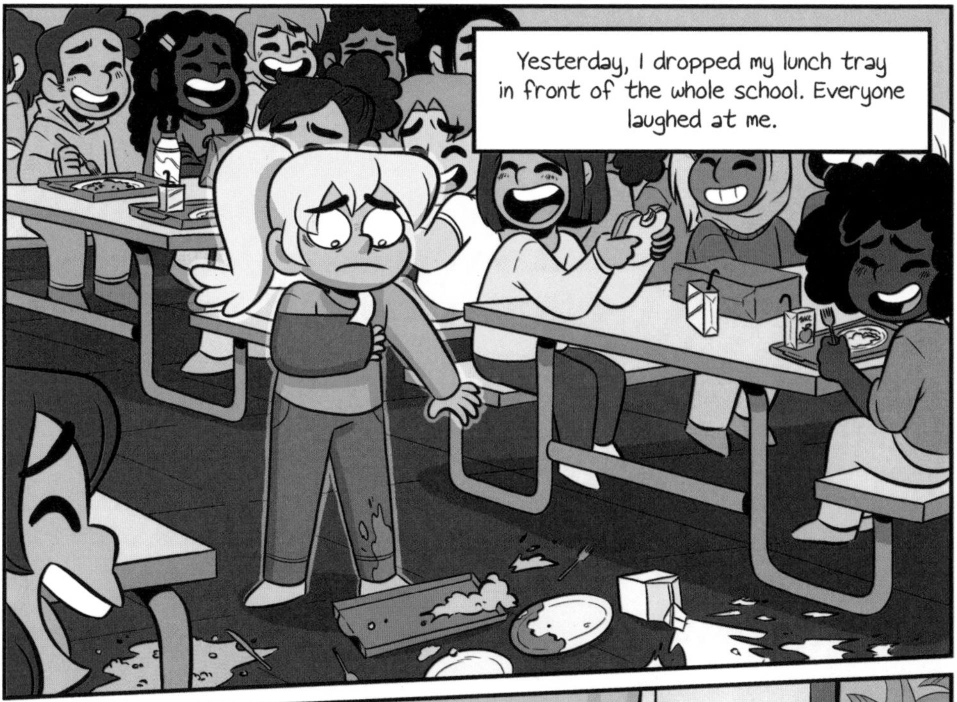
Yesterday, I dropped my lunch tray in front of the whole school. Everyone laughed at me.

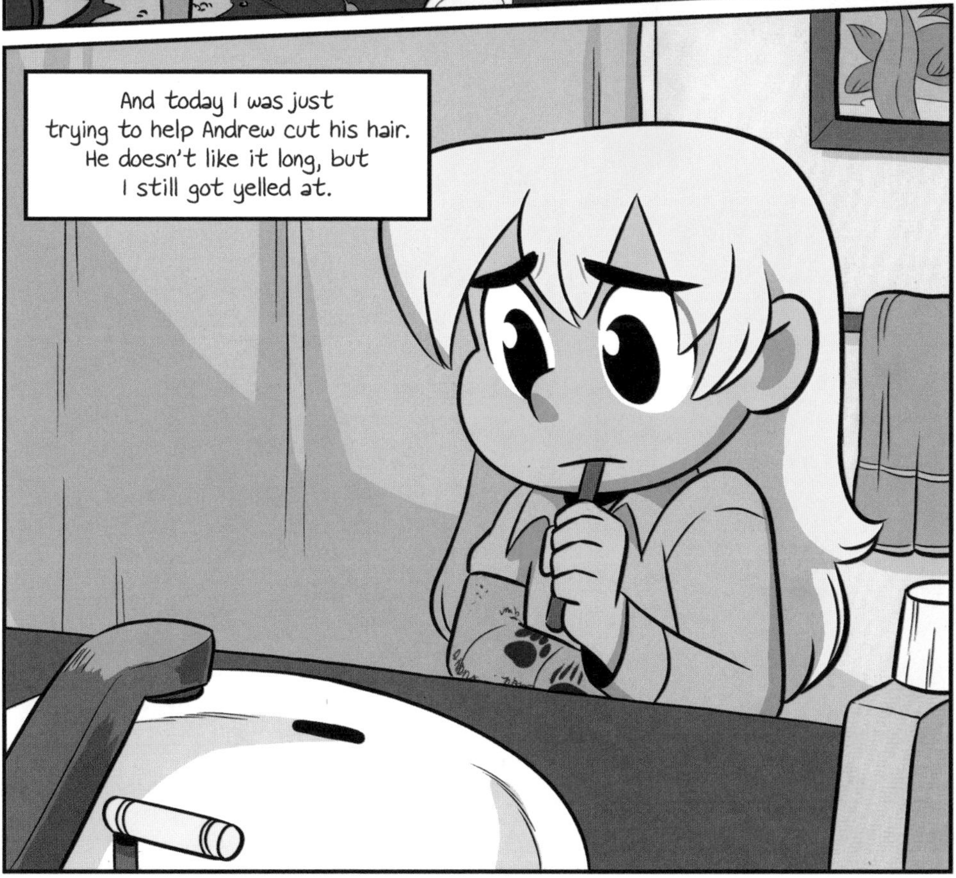
And today I was just trying to help Andrew cut his hair. He doesn't like it long, but I still got yelled at.

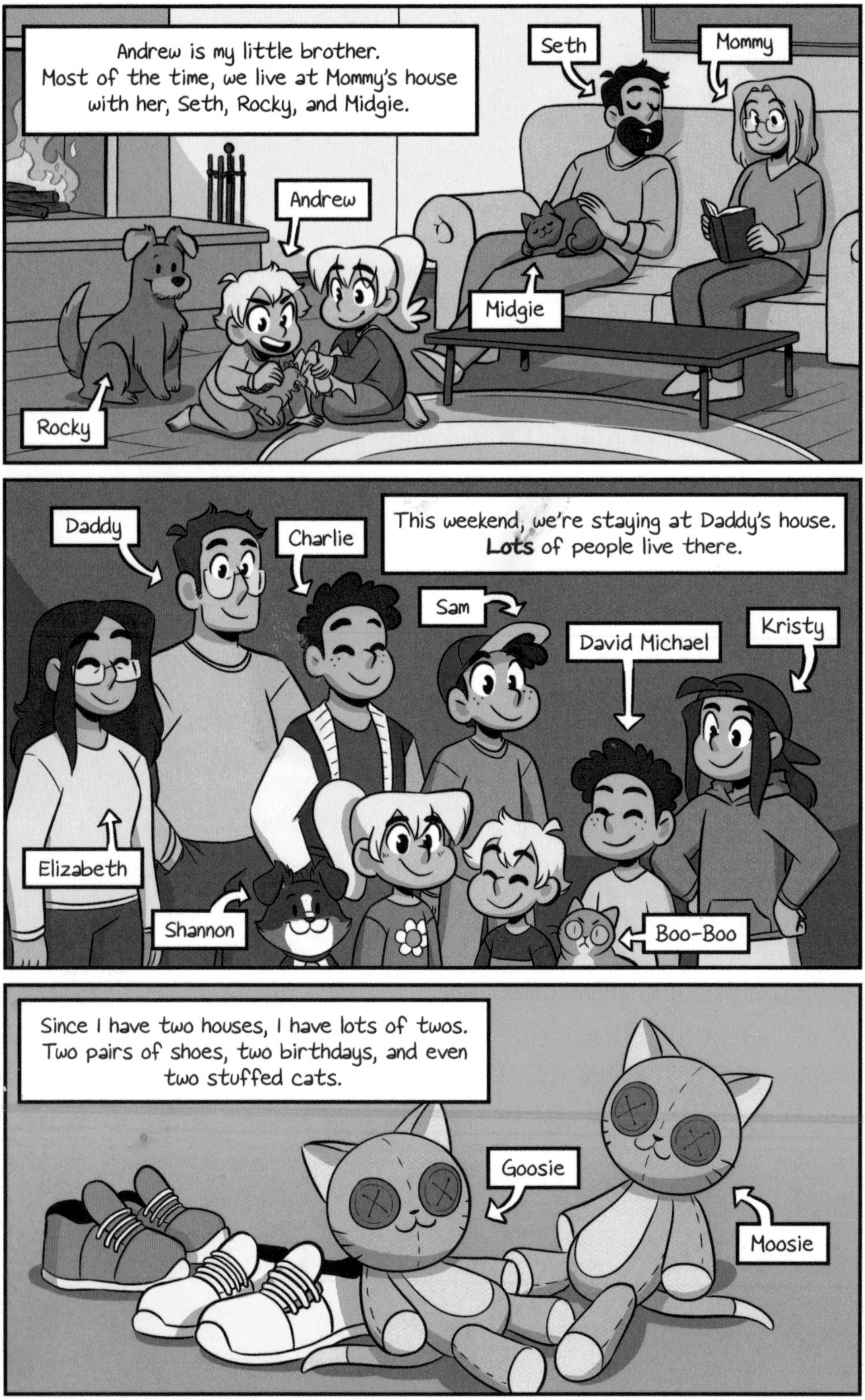
Andrew is my little brother.
Most of the time, we live at Mommy's house with her, Seth, Rocky, and Midgie.
Seth
Mommy
Andrew
Midgie
Rocky
This weekend, we're staying at Daddy's house. **Lots** of people live there.
Daddy
Charlie
Sam
David Michael
Kristy
Elizabeth
Shannon
Boo-Boo
Since I have two houses, I have lots of twos. Two pairs of shoes, two birthdays, and even two stuffed cats.
Goosie
Moosie

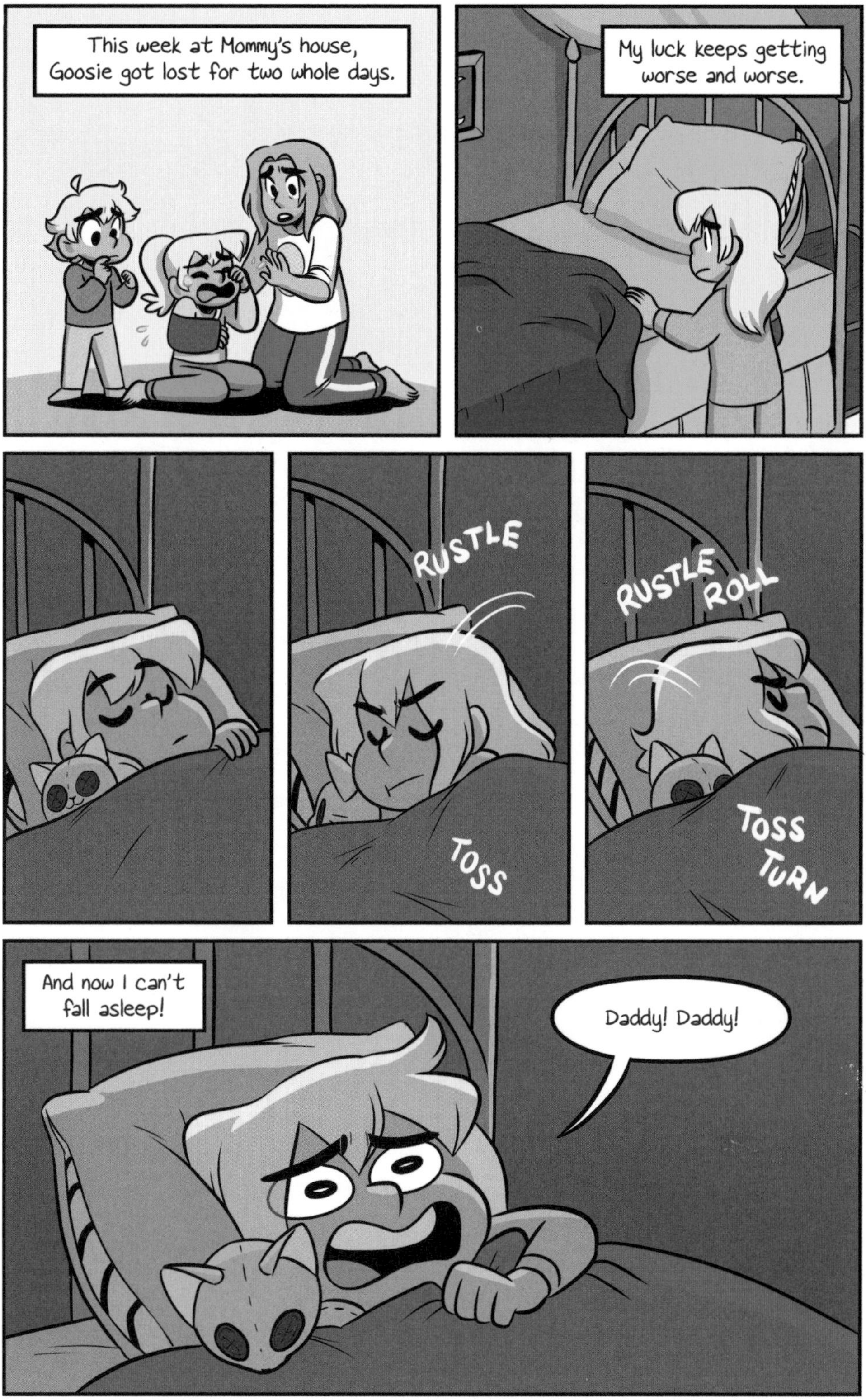
This week at Mommy's house, Goosie got lost for two whole days.
My luck keeps getting worse and worse.
RUSTLE
TOSS
RUSTLE
ROLL
TOSS
TURN
And now I can't fall asleep!
Daddy! Daddy!

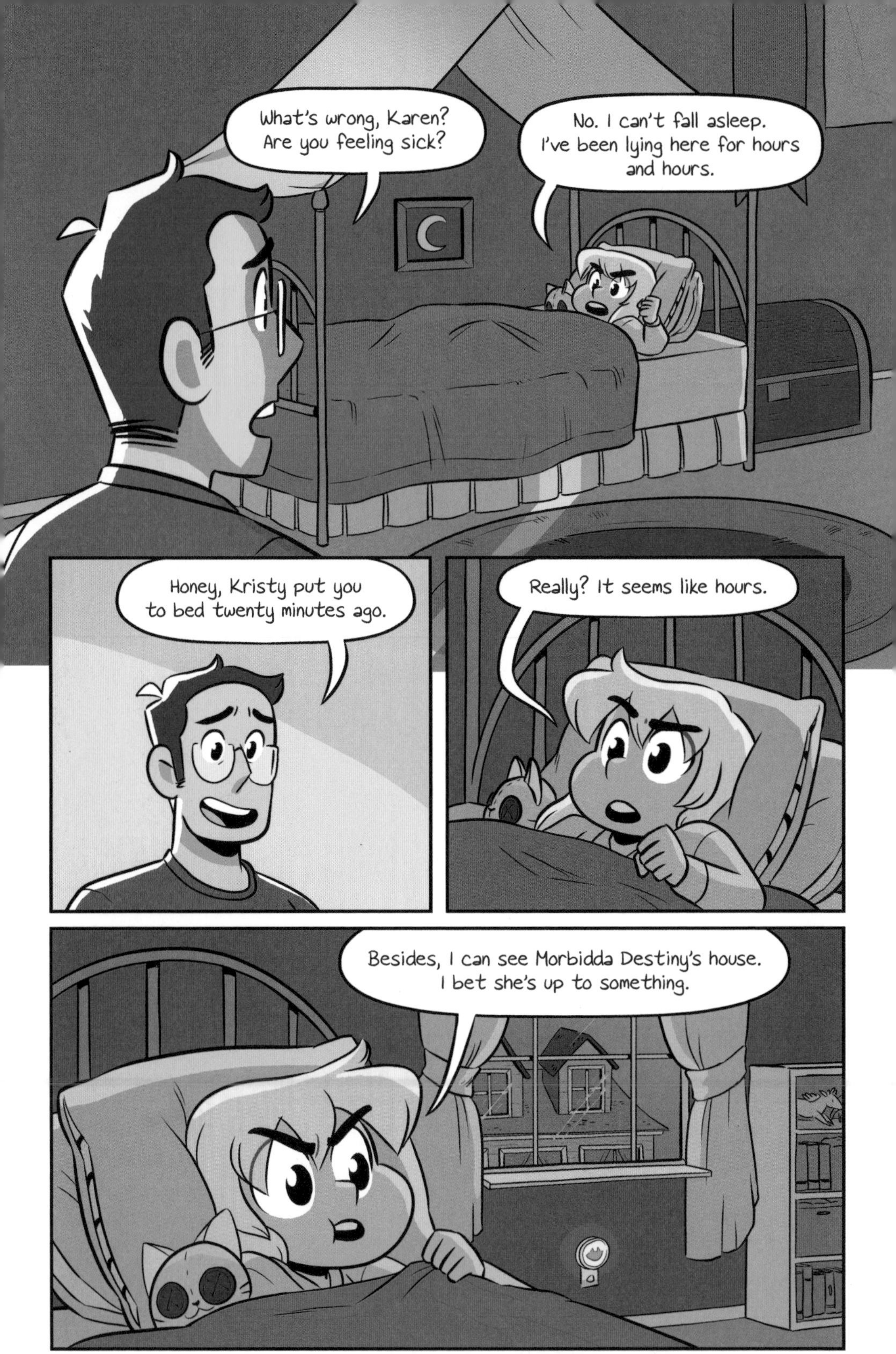
What's wrong, Karen?
Are you feeling sick?
No. I can't fall asleep.
I've been lying here for hours and hours.
Honey, Kristy put you to bed twenty minutes ago.
Really? It seems like hours.
Besides, I can see Morbidda Destiny's house.
I bet she's up to something.

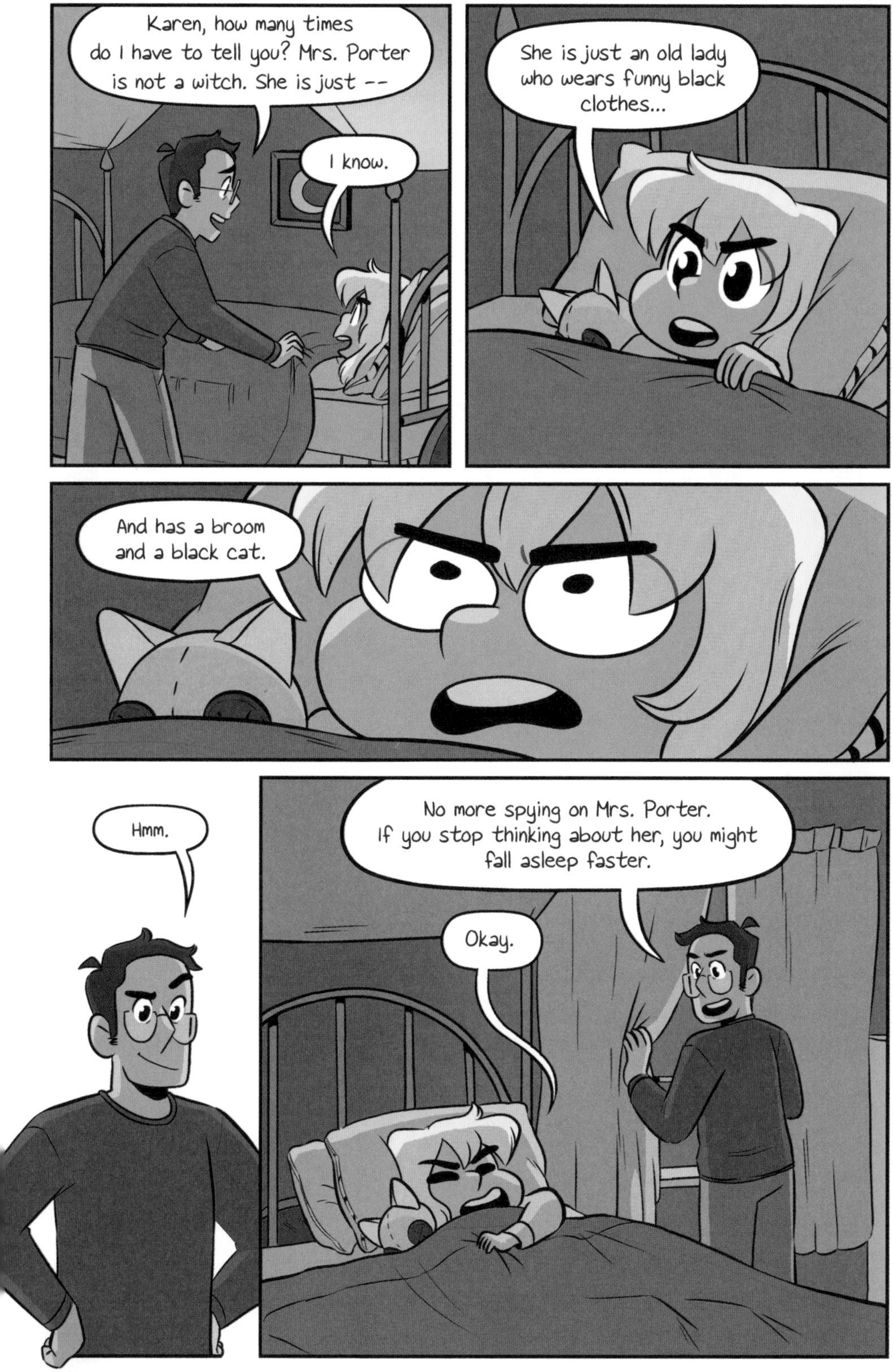
Karen, how many times do I have to tell you? Mrs. Porter is not a witch. She is just --
I know.
She is just an old lady who wears funny black clothes...
And has a broom and a black cat.
Hmm.
No more spying on Mrs. Porter. If you stop thinking about her, you might fall asleep faster.
Okay.

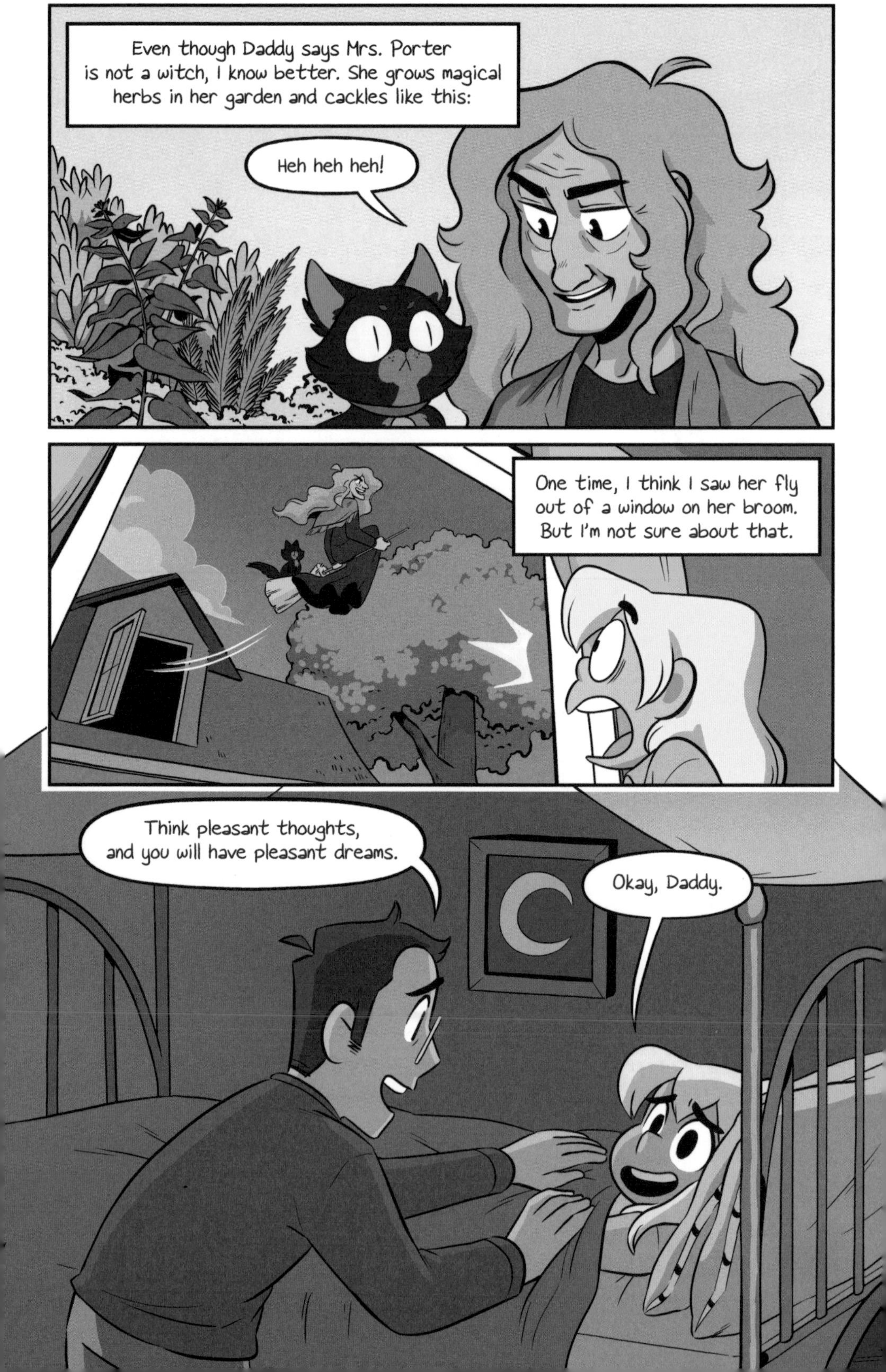
Even though Daddy says Mrs. Porter is not a witch, I know better. She grows magical herbs in her garden and cackles like this:
Heh heh heh!
One time, I think I saw her fly out of a window on her broom. But I'm not sure about that.
Think pleasant thoughts, and you will have pleasant dreams.
Okay, Daddy.

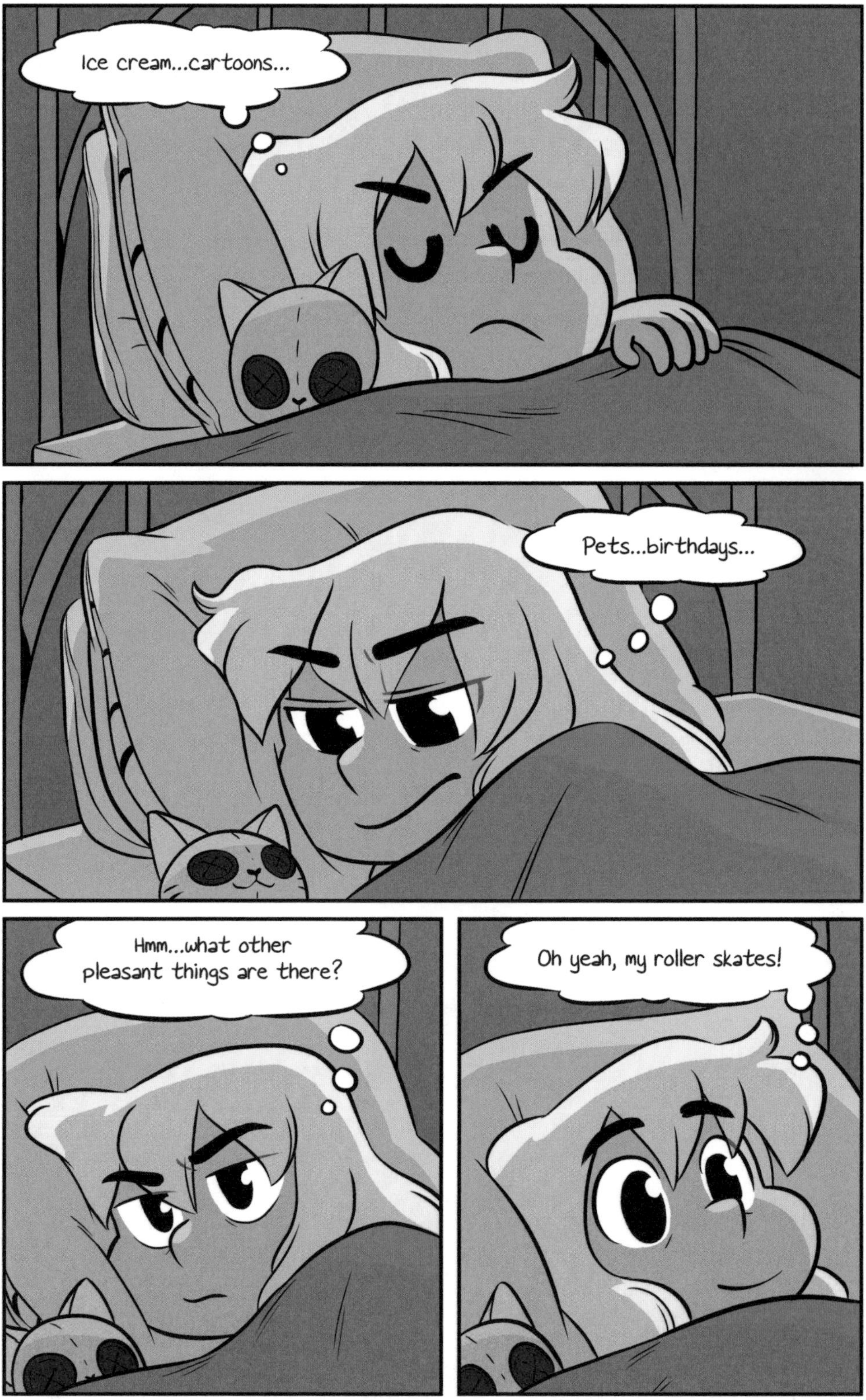

Ice cream...cartoons...
Pets...birthdays...
Hmm...what other pleasant things are there?
Oh yeah, my roller skates!

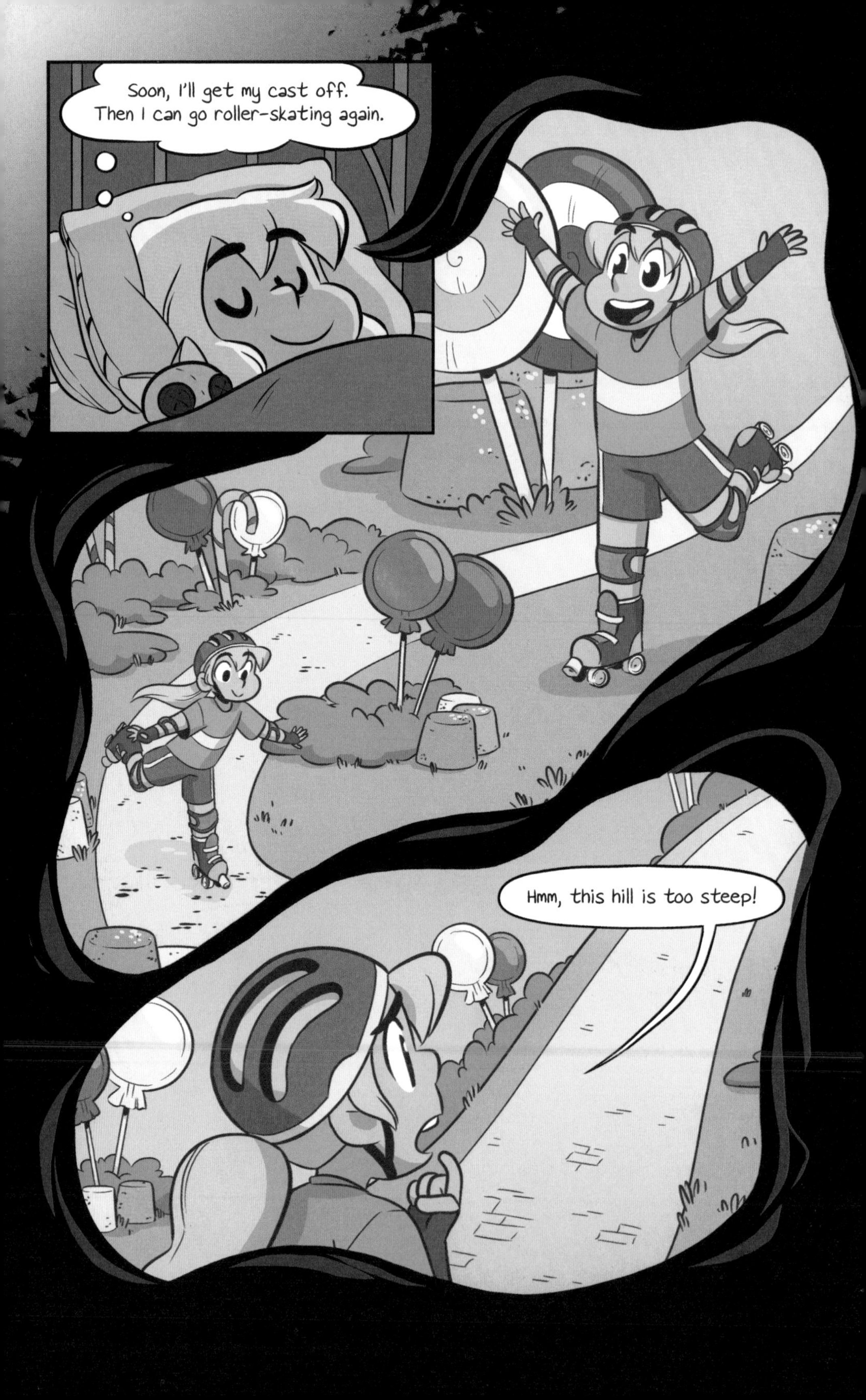
Soon, I'll get my cast off. Then I can go roller-skating again.
Hmm, this hill is too steep!

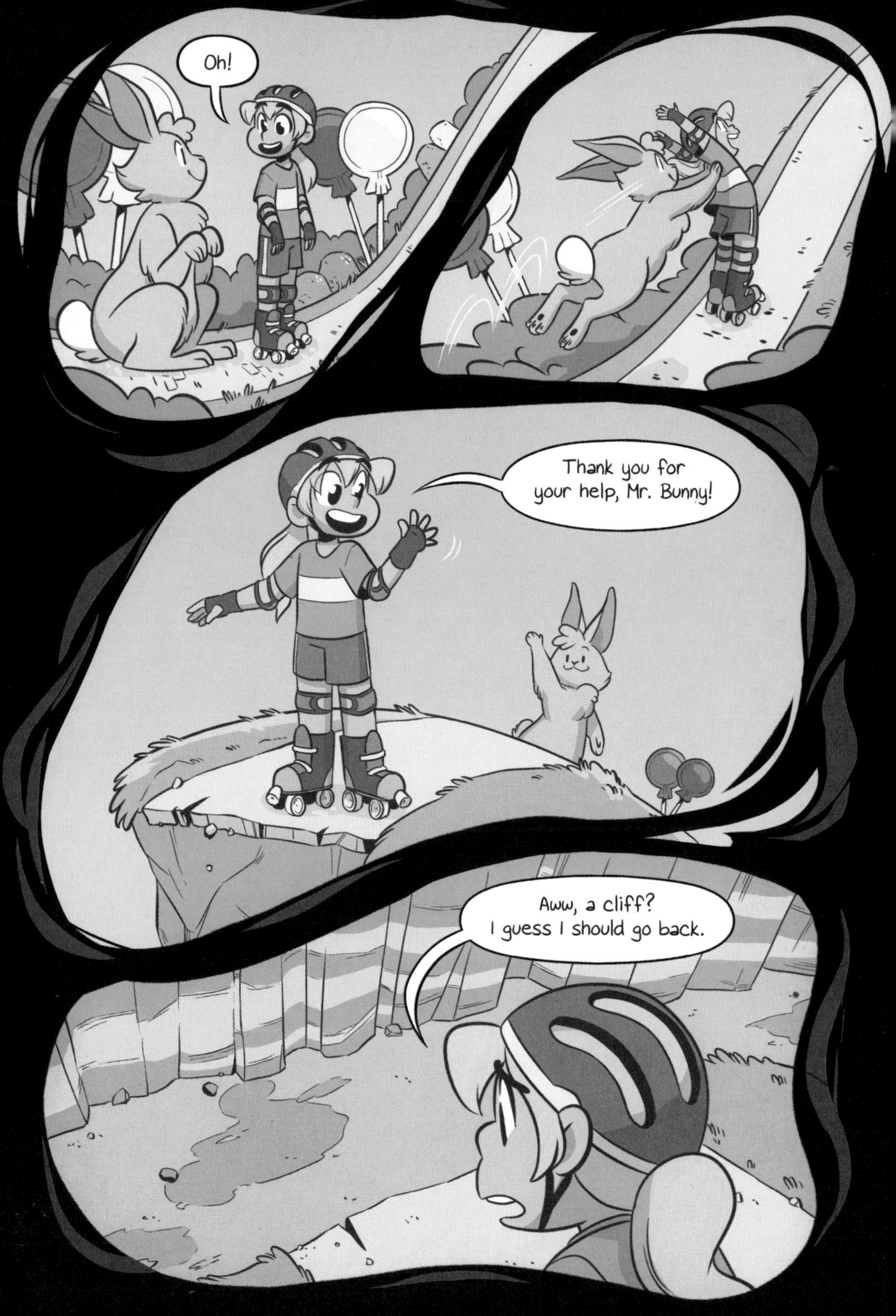
Oh!
Thank you for your help, Mr. Bunny!
Aww, a cliff? I guess I should go back.

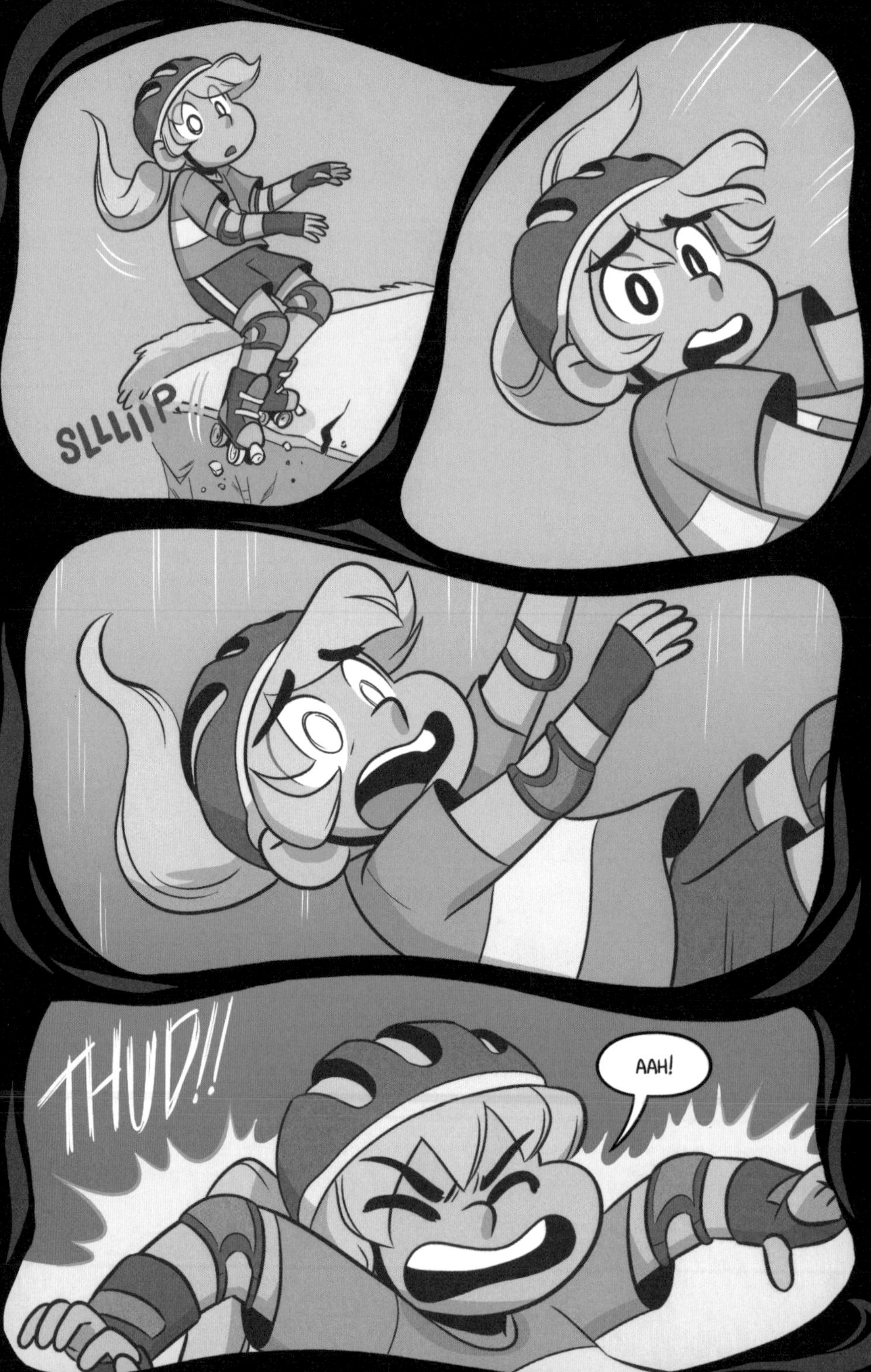
SLLLIIP
THUD!!
AAH!

CHAPTER 2

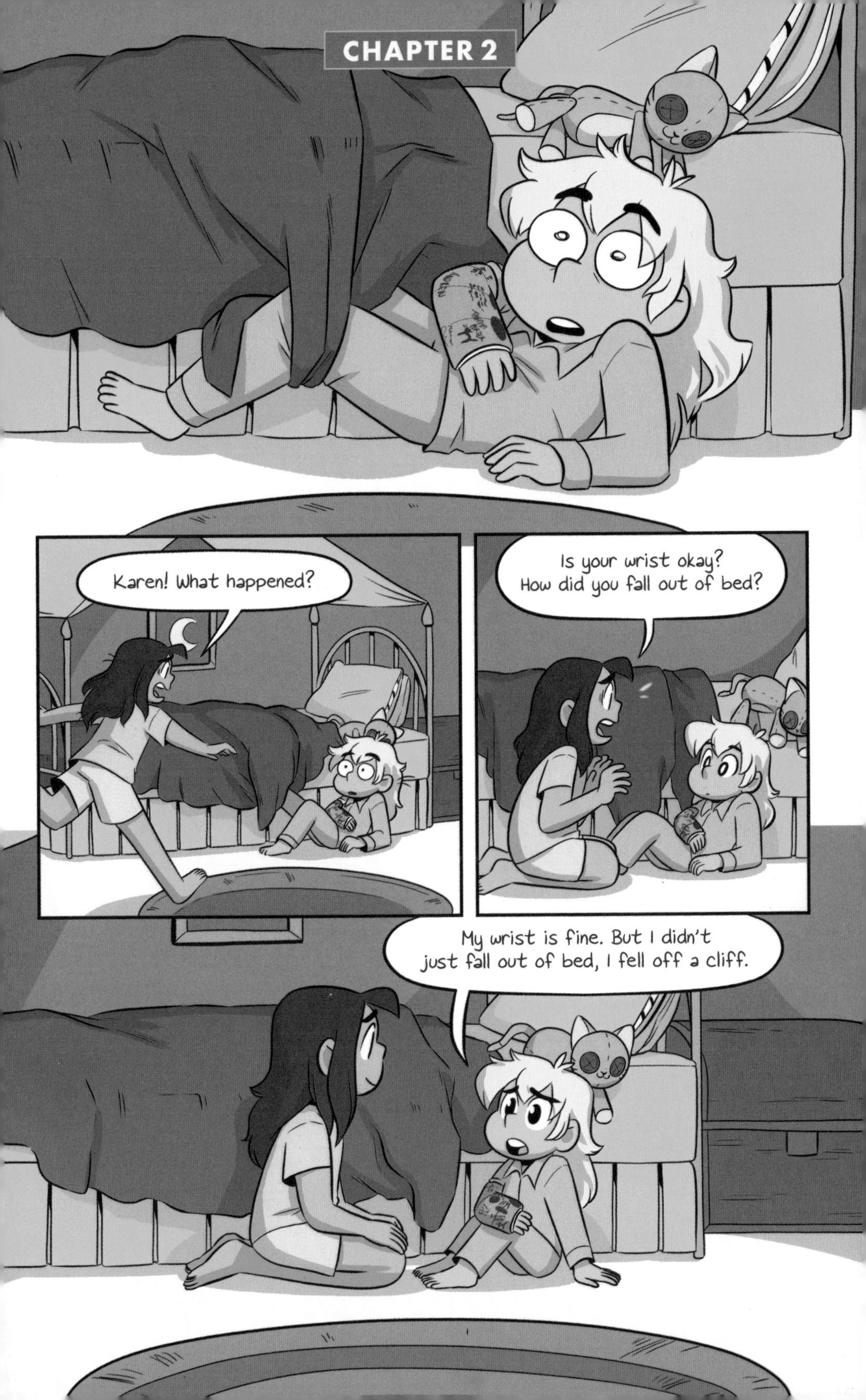
Karen! What happened?
Is your wrist okay? How did you fall out of bed?
My wrist is fine. But I didn't just fall out of bed, I fell off a cliff.

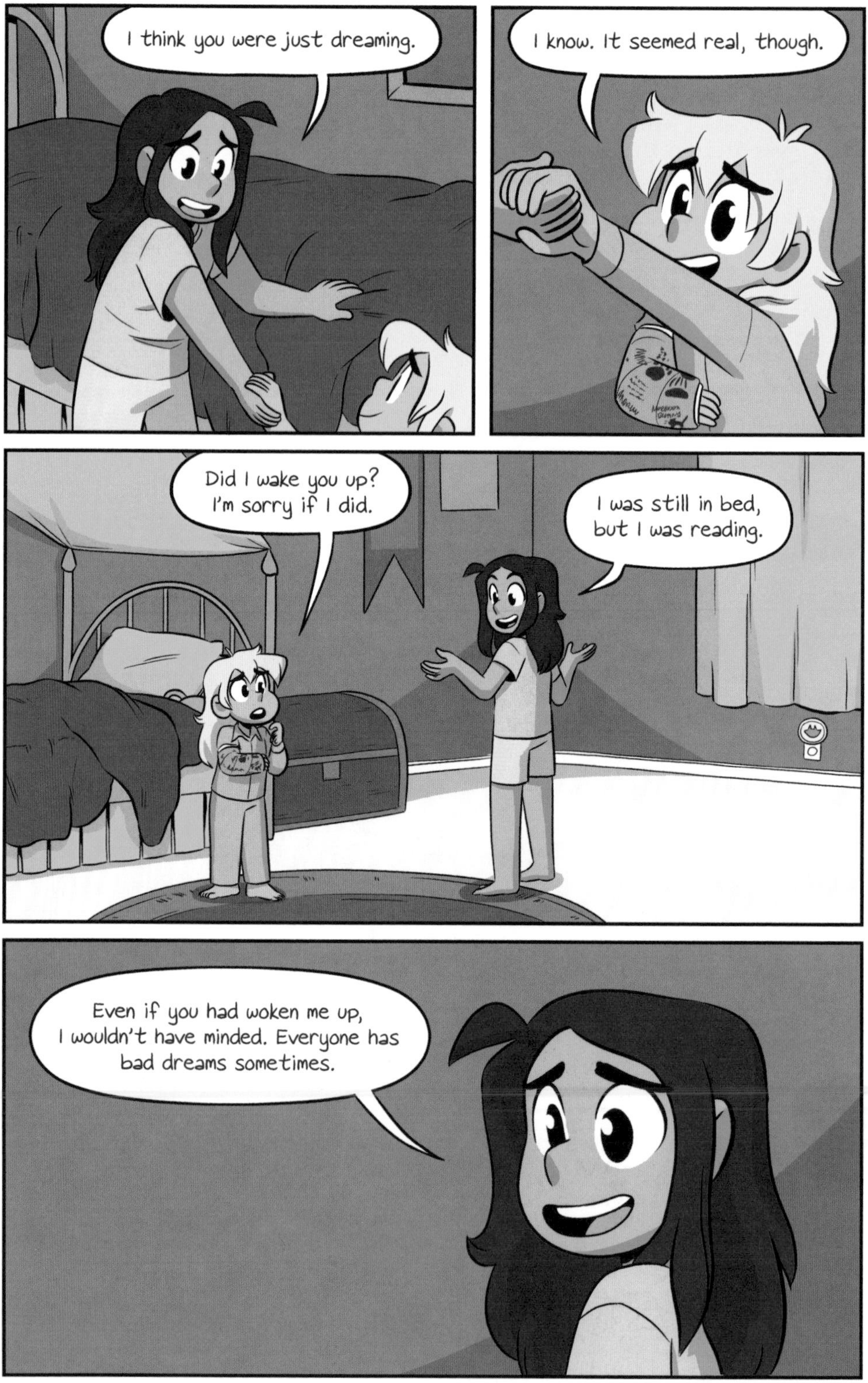
I think you were just dreaming.
I know. It seemed real, though.
Did I wake you up? I'm sorry if I did.
I was still in bed, but I was reading.
Even if you had woken me up, I wouldn't have minded. Everyone has bad dreams sometimes.

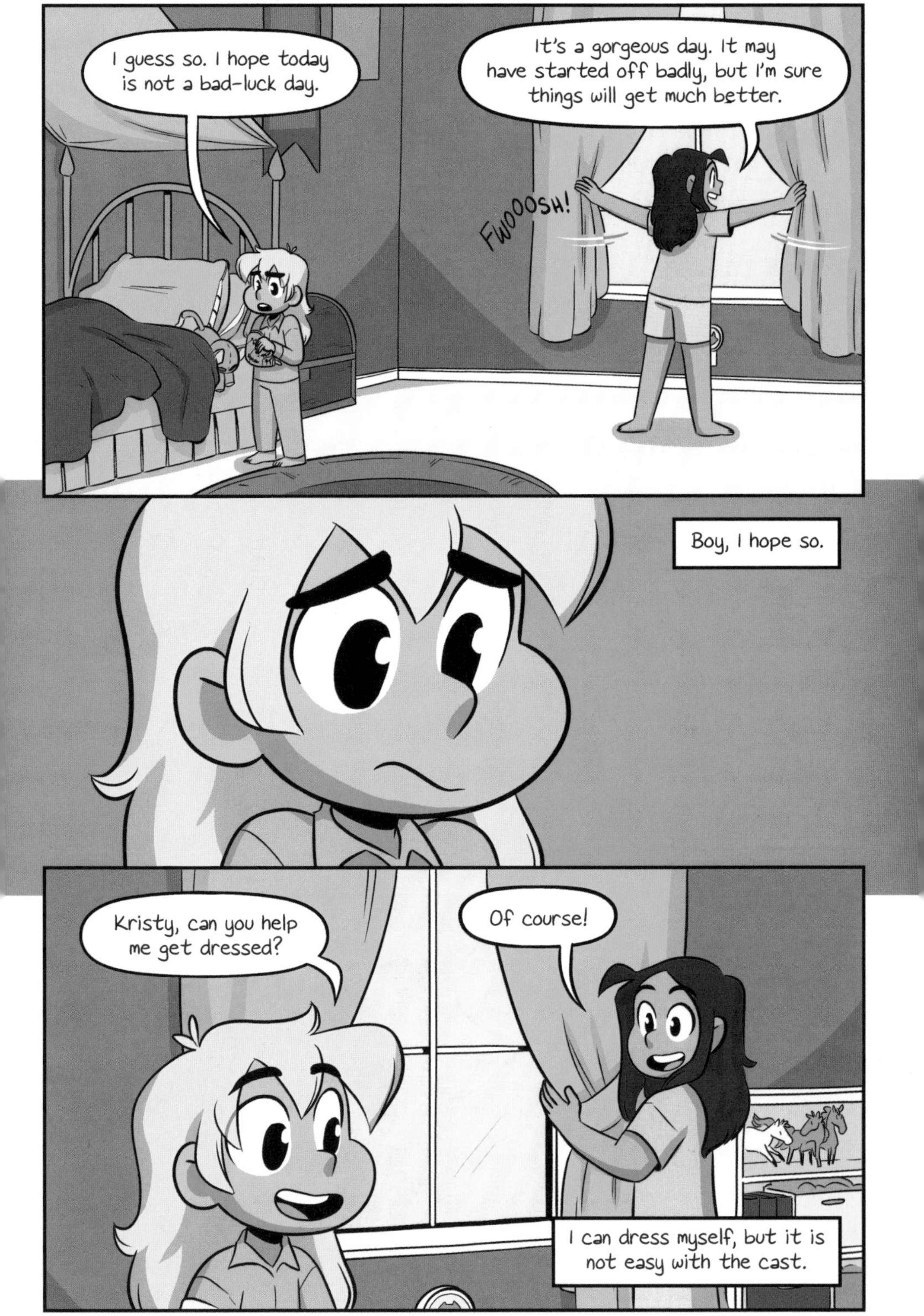
I guess so. I hope today is not a bad-luck day.
It's a gorgeous day. It may have started off badly, but I'm sure things will get much better.
FWOOOSH!
Boy, I hope so.
Kristy, can you help me get dressed?
Of course!
I can dress myself, but it is not easy with the cast.

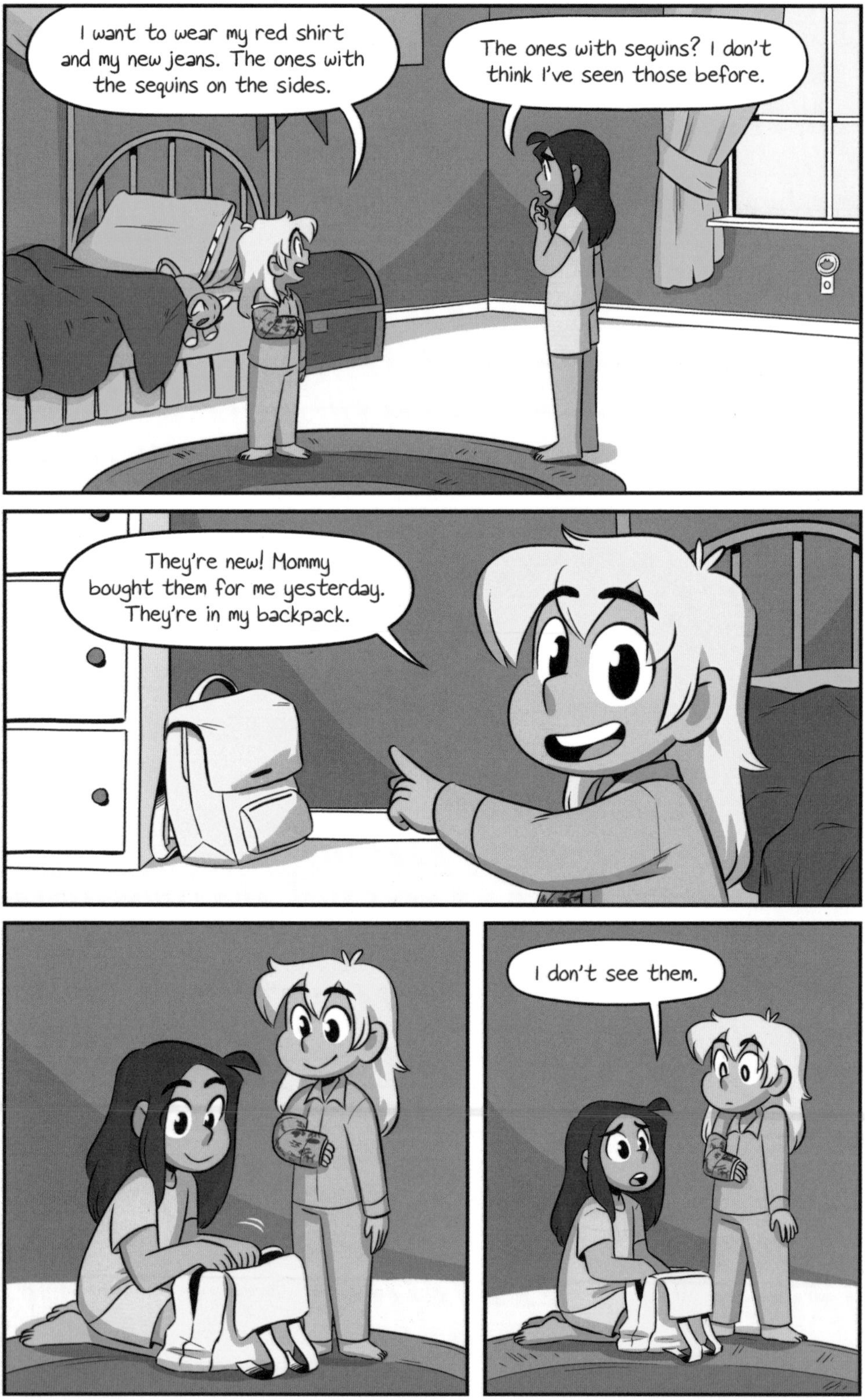
I want to wear my red shirt and my new jeans. The ones with the sequins on the sides.
The ones with sequins? I don't think I've seen those before.
They're new! Mommy bought them for me yesterday. They're in my backpack.
I don't see them.

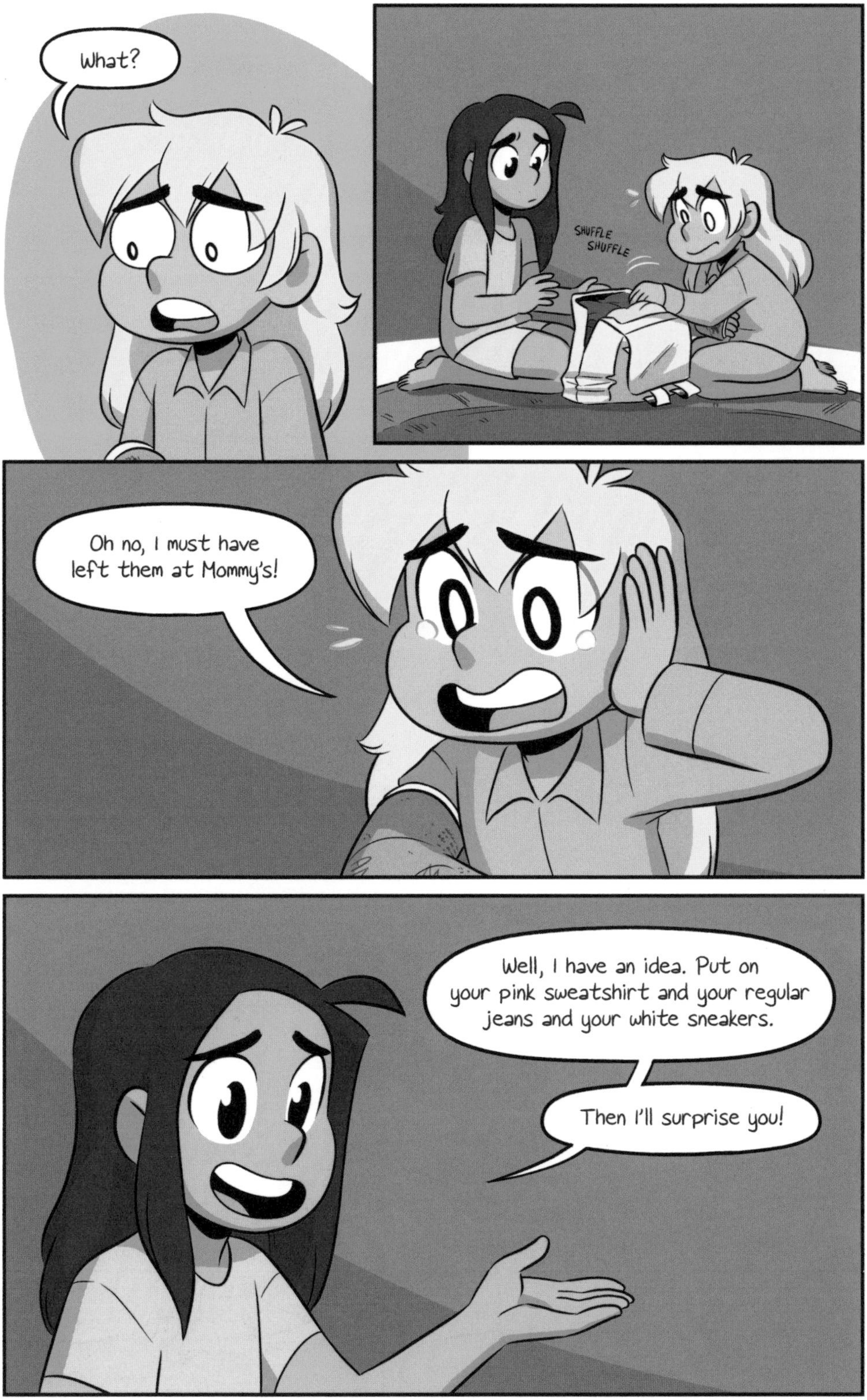
What?
SHUFFLE SHUFFLE
Oh no, I must have left them at Mommy's!
Well, I have an idea. Put on your pink sweatshirt and your regular jeans and your white sneakers.
Then I'll surprise you!

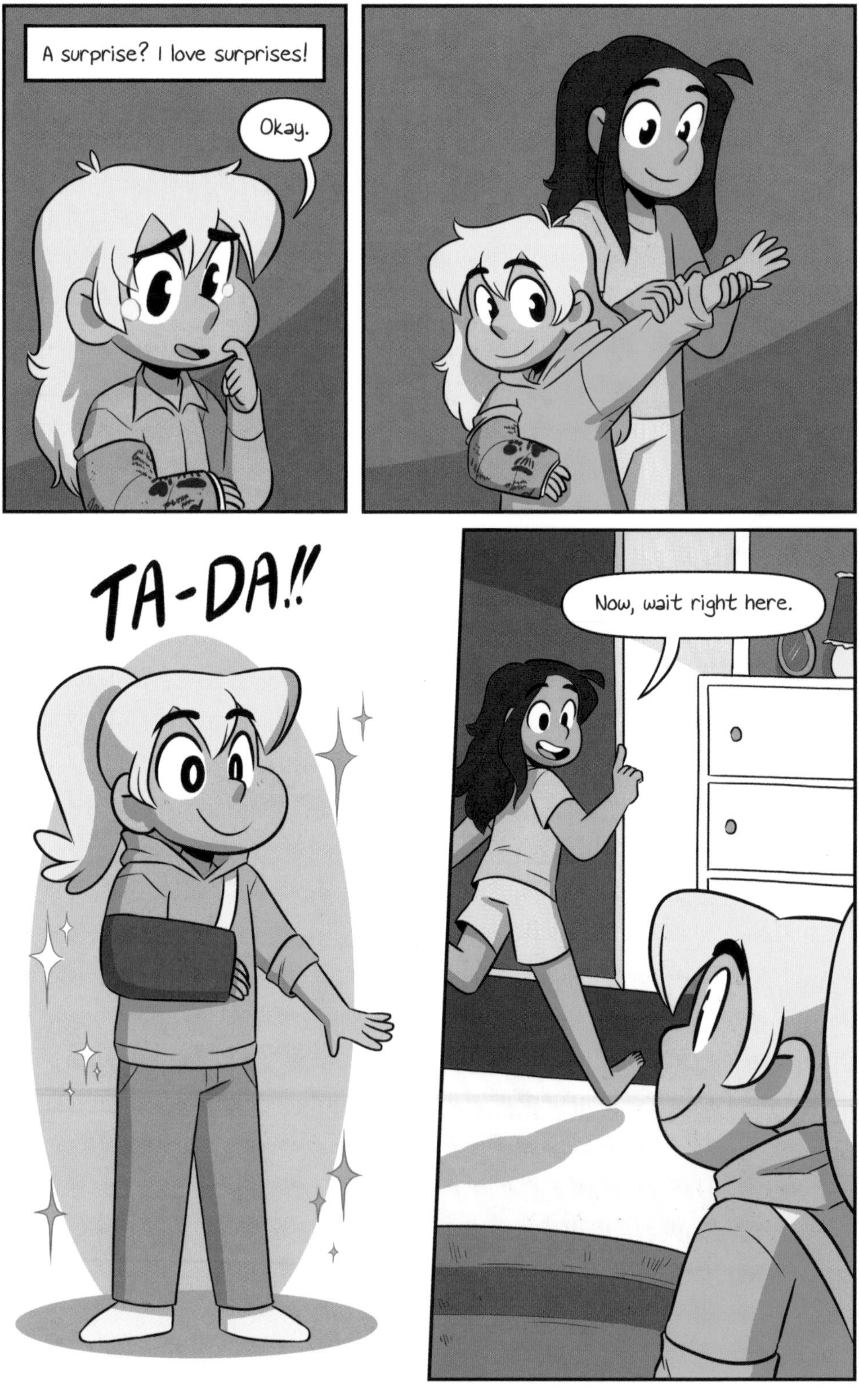
A surprise? I love surprises!
Okay.
TA-DA!!
Now, wait right here.

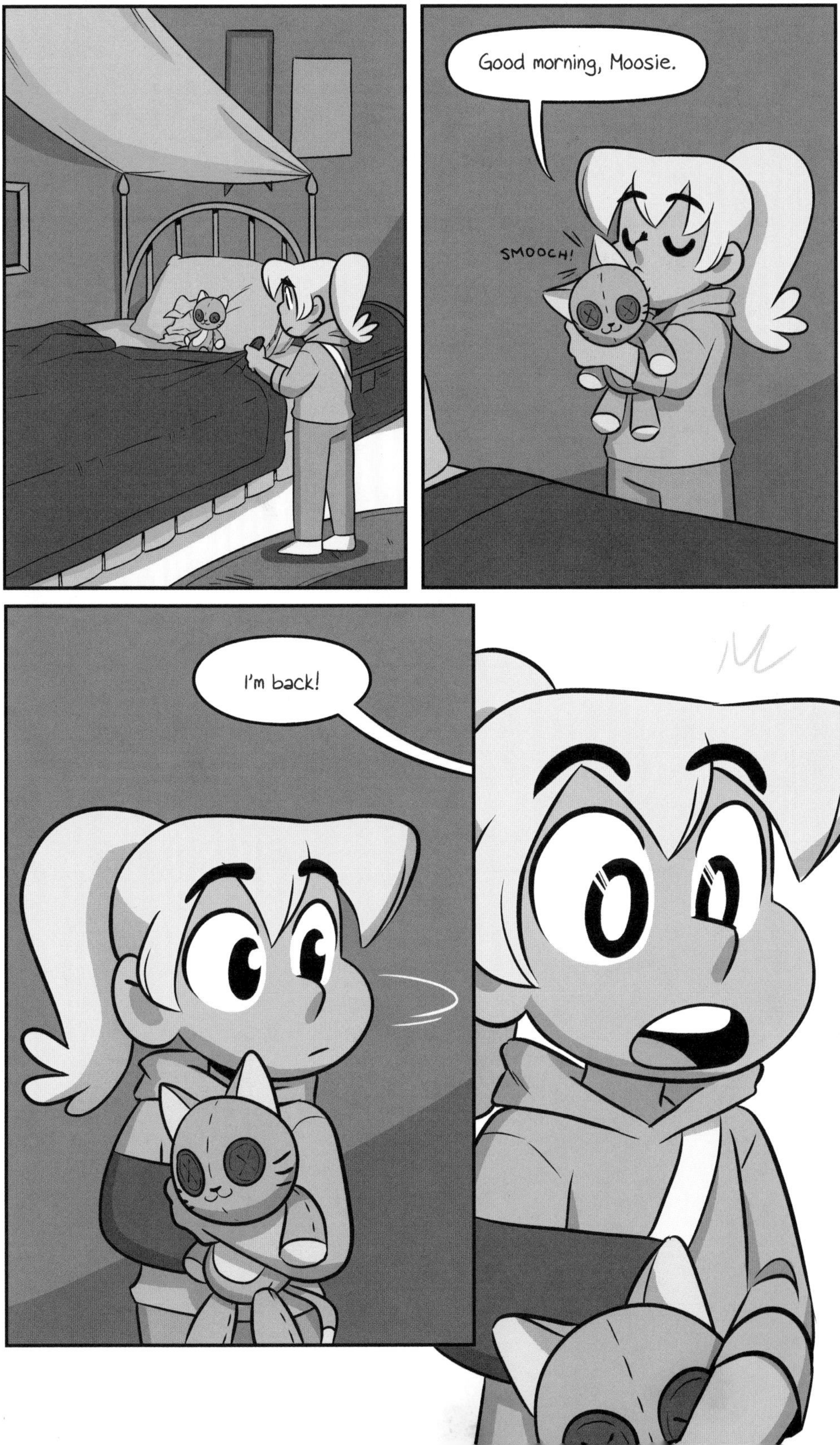
Good morning, Moosie.
SMOOCH!
I'm back!

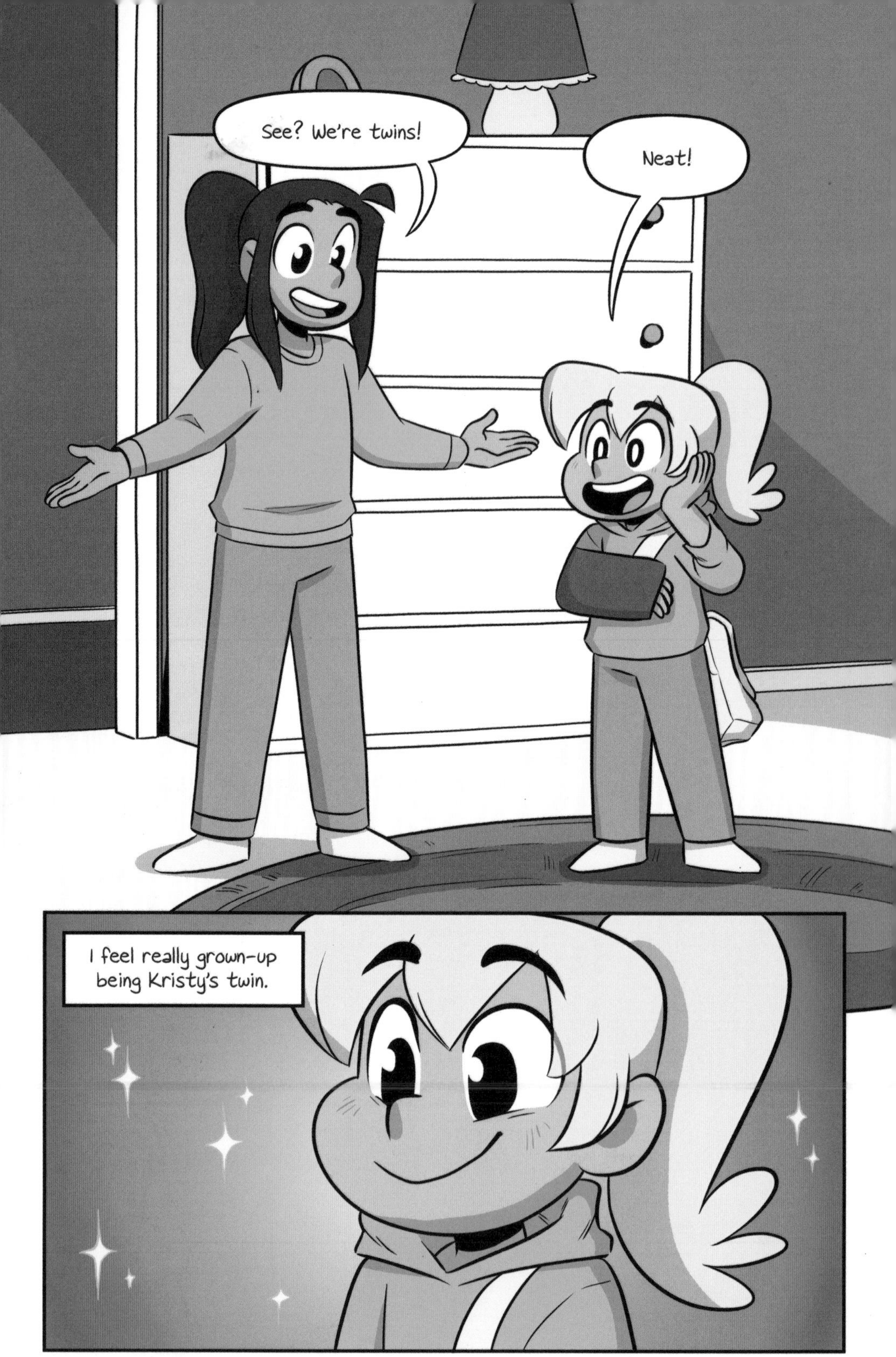
See? We're twins!
Neat!
I feel really grown-up being Kristy's twin.

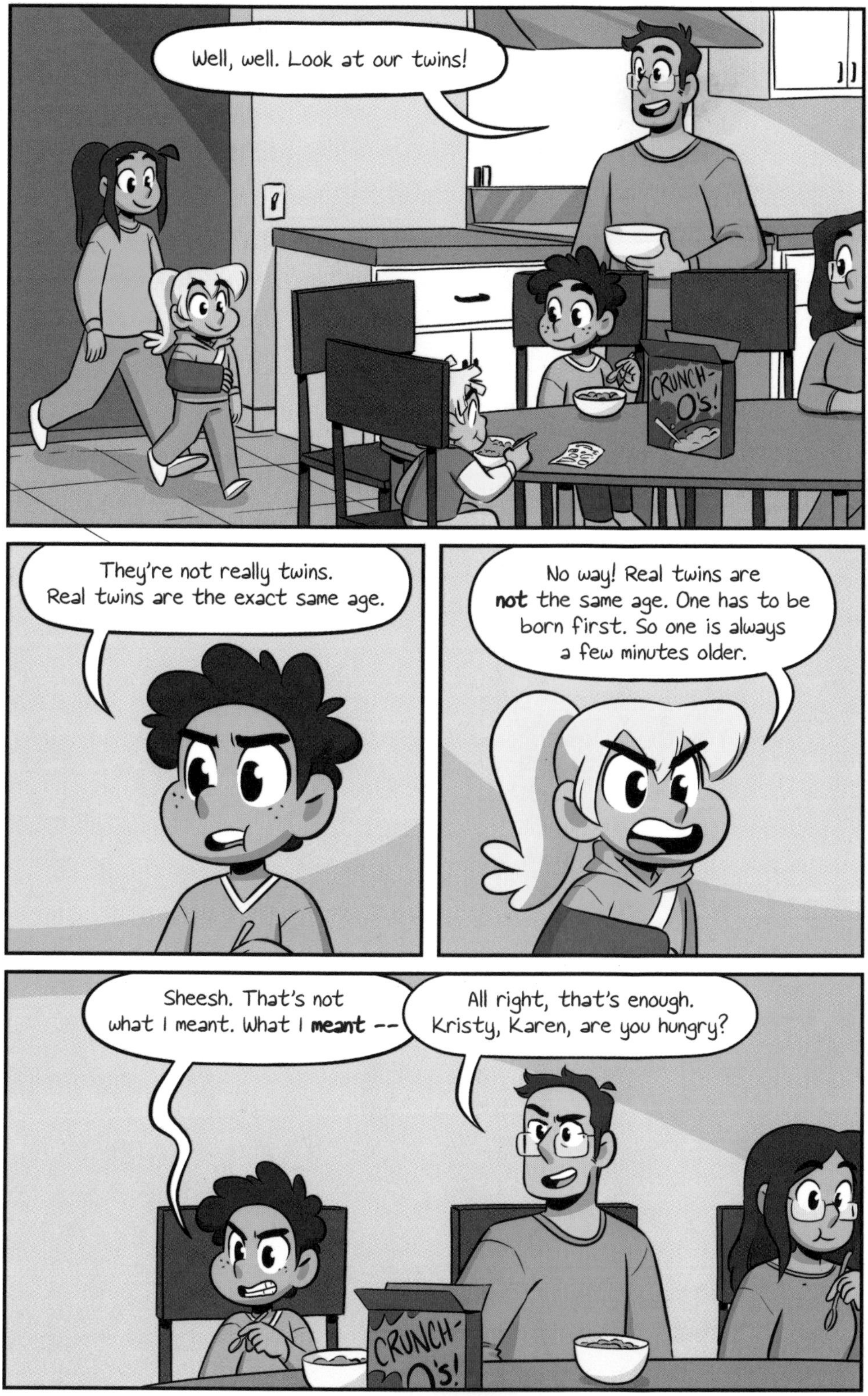
Well, well. Look at our twins!
CRUNCH-O's!
They're not really twins. Real twins are the exact same age.
No way! Real twins are **not** the same age. One has to be born first. So one is always a few minutes older.
Sheesh. That's not what I meant. What I **meant** --
All right, that's enough. Kristy, Karen, are you hungry?
CRUNCH-O's!

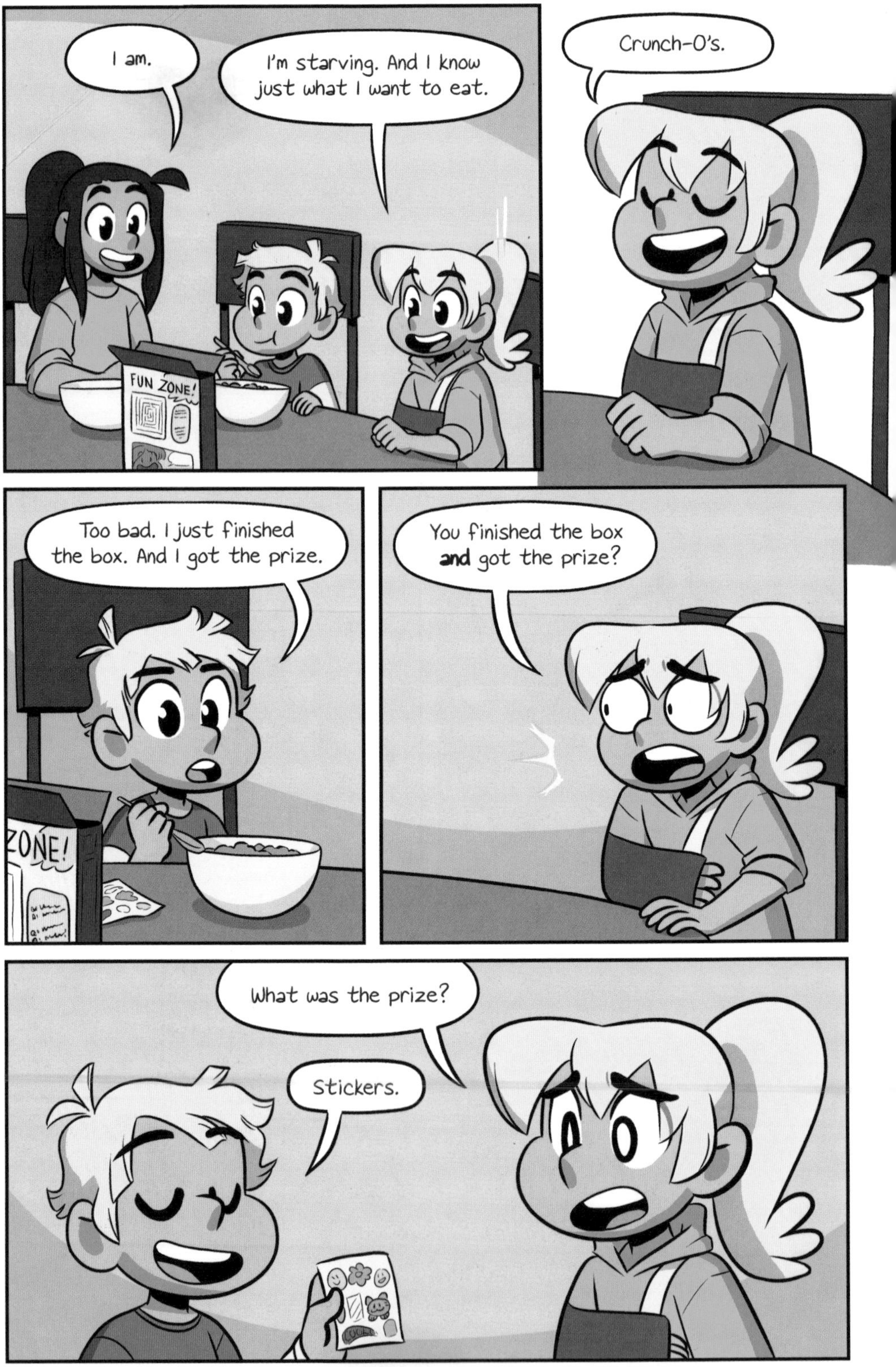
I am.
I'm starving. And I know just what I want to eat.
FUN ZONE!
Crunch-O's.
Too bad. I just finished the box. And I got the prize.
You finished the box **and** got the prize?
What was the prize?
Stickers.

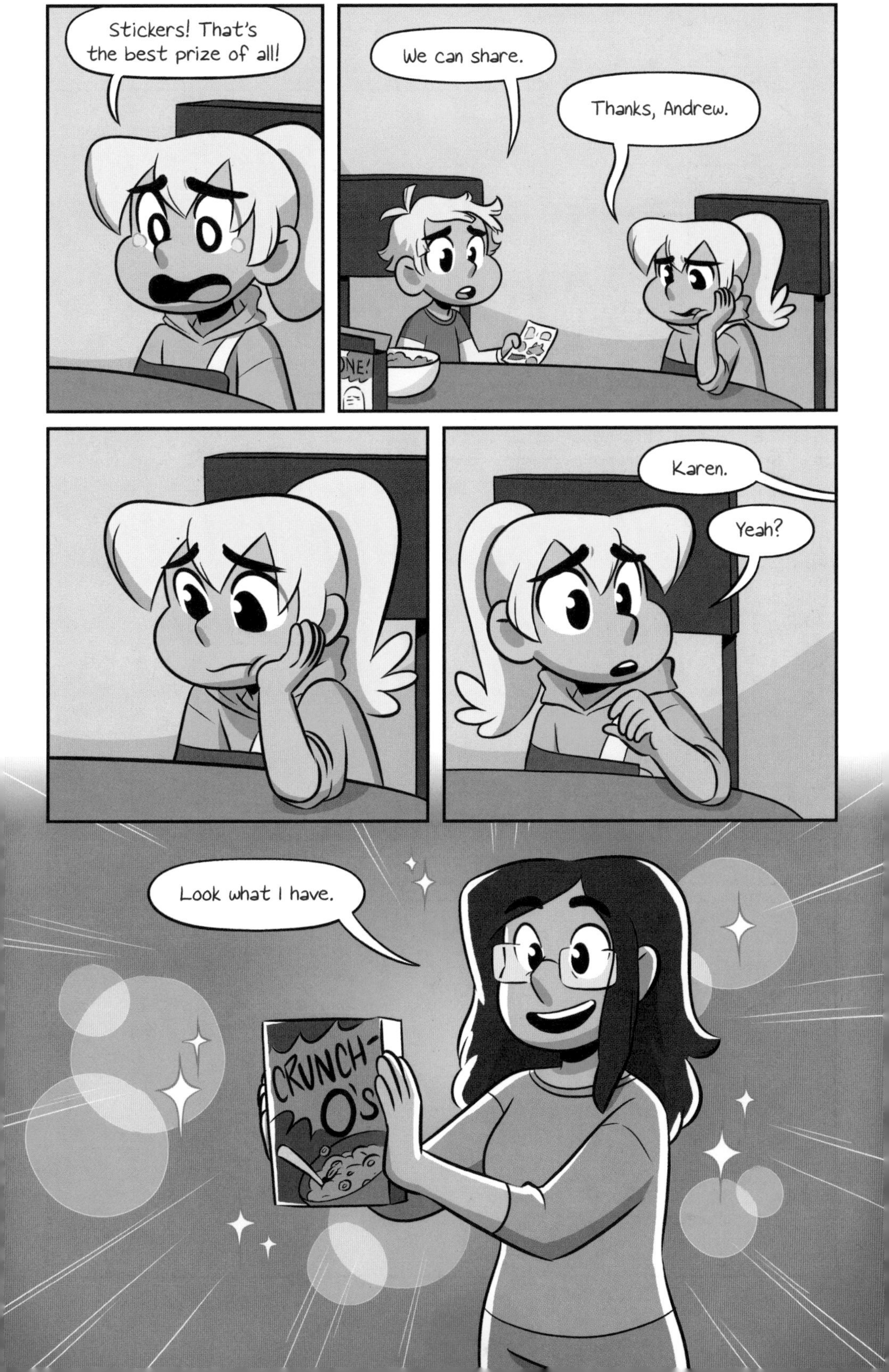
Stickers! That's the best prize of all!
We can share.
Thanks, Andrew.
Karen.
Yeah?
Look what I have.
CRUNCH-O'S

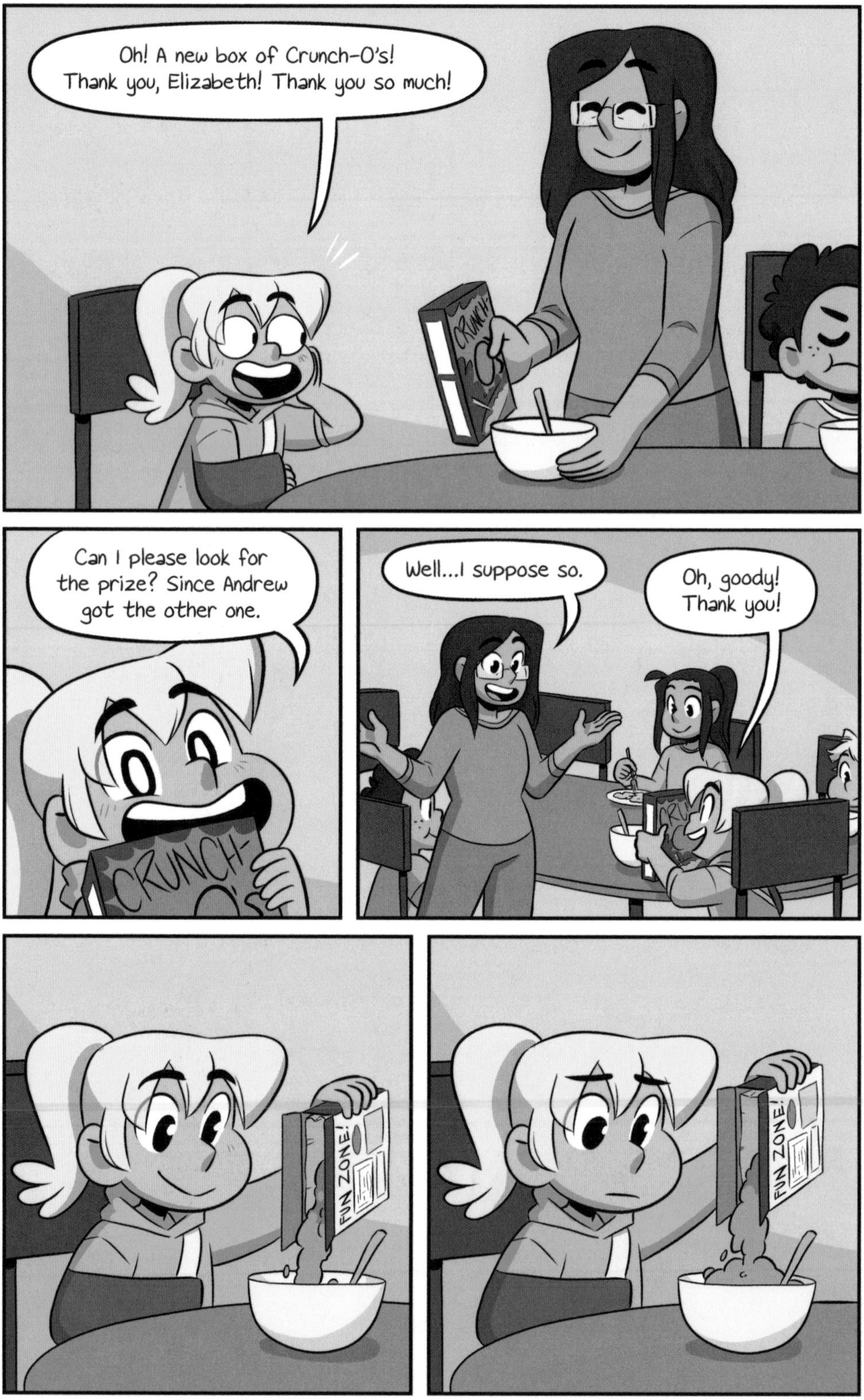
Oh! A new box of Crunch-O's! Thank you, Elizabeth! Thank you so much!
CRUNCH-O'S
Can I please look for the prize? Since Andrew got the other one.
CRUNCH-
Well...I suppose so.
Oh, goody! Thank you!
FUN ZONE!
FUN ZONE!

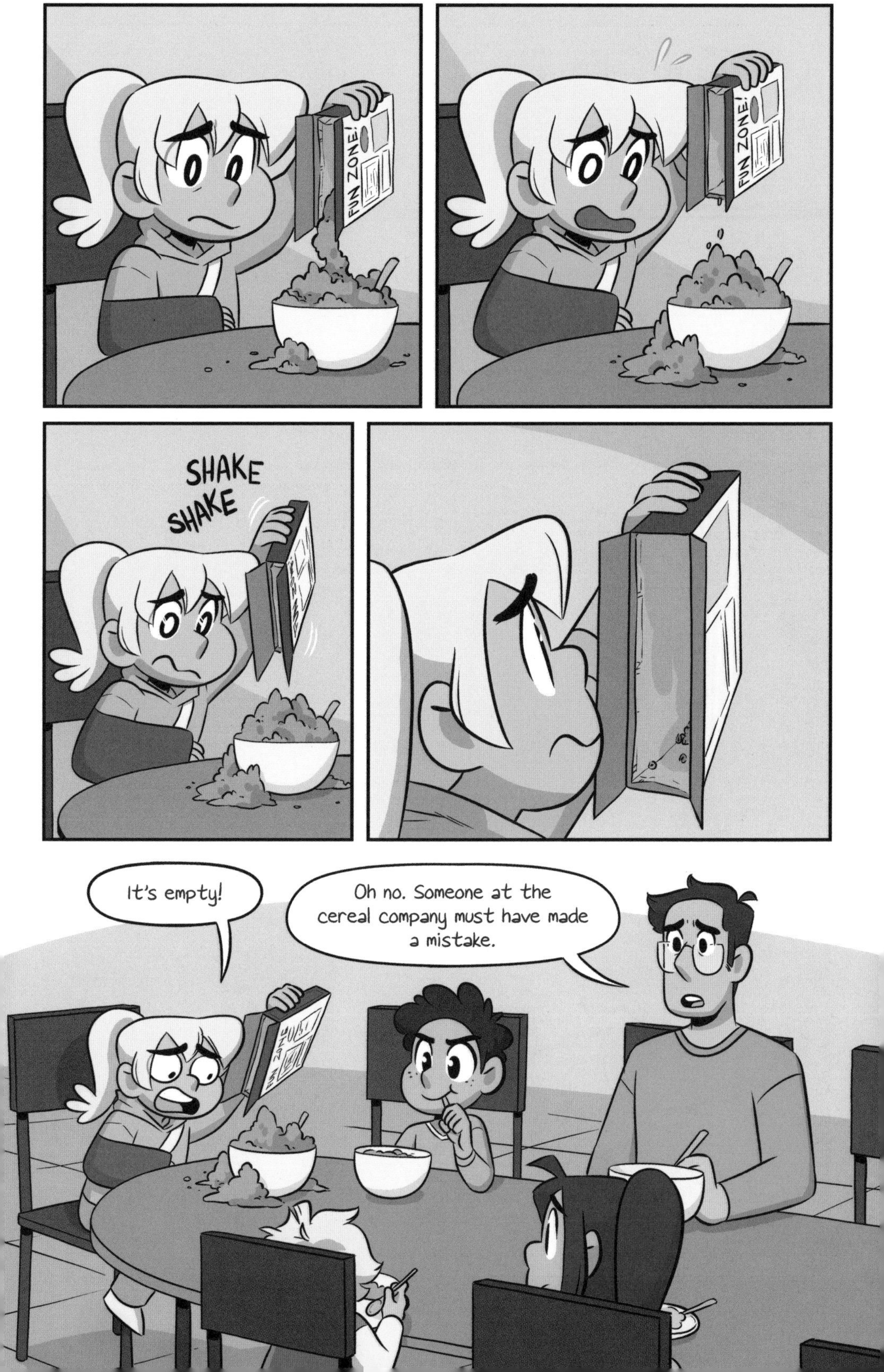
FUN ZONE!
FUN ZONE!
SHAKE
SHAKE
It's empty!
Oh no. Someone at the cereal company must have made a mistake.

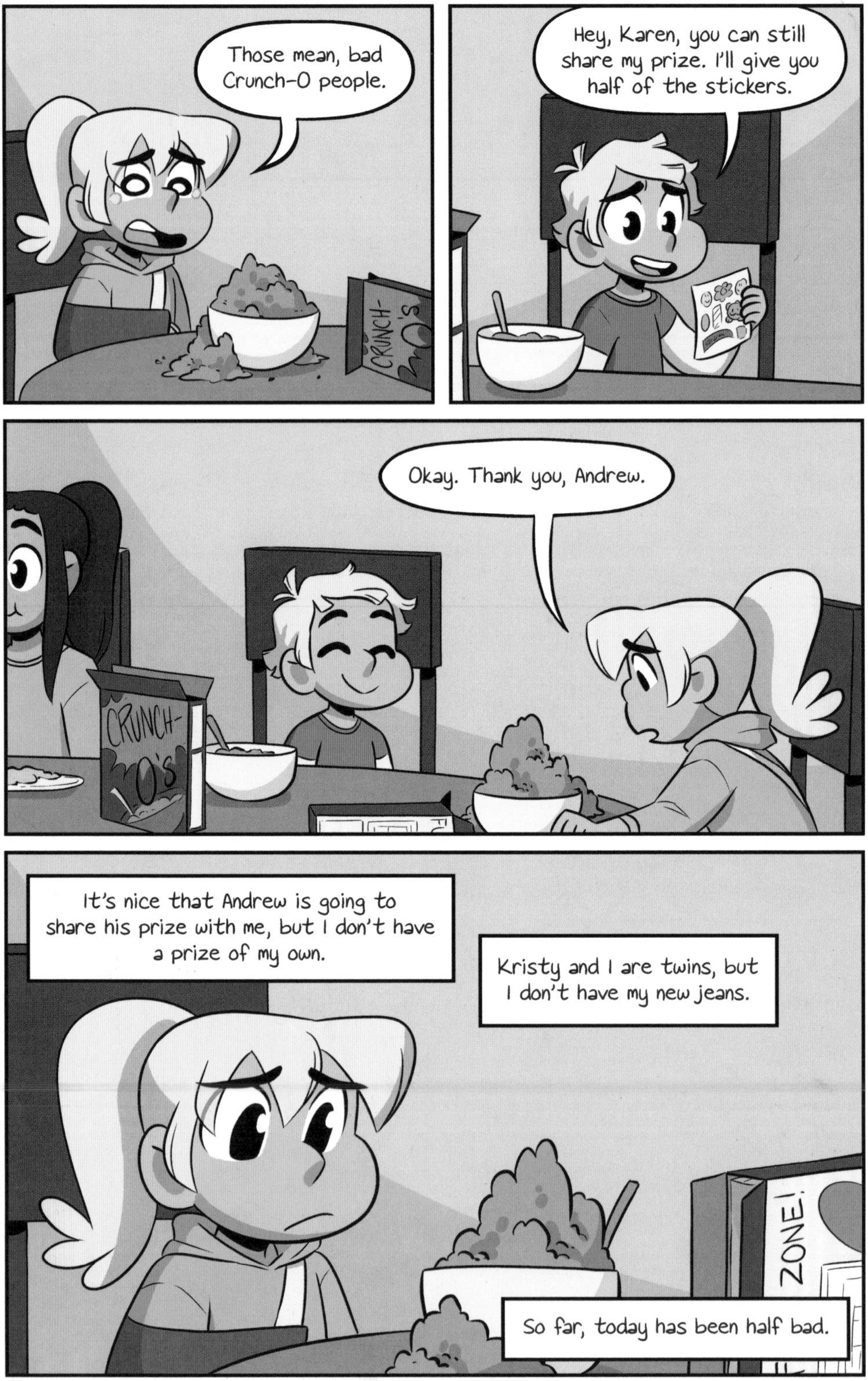
Those mean, bad Crunch-O people.
CRUNCH-O's
Hey, Karen, you can still share my prize. I'll give you half of the stickers.
Okay. Thank you, Andrew.
CRUNCH-O's
It's nice that Andrew is going to share his prize with me, but I don't have a prize of my own.
Kristy and I are twins, but I don't have my new jeans.
ZONE!
So far, today has been half bad.

CHAPTER 3

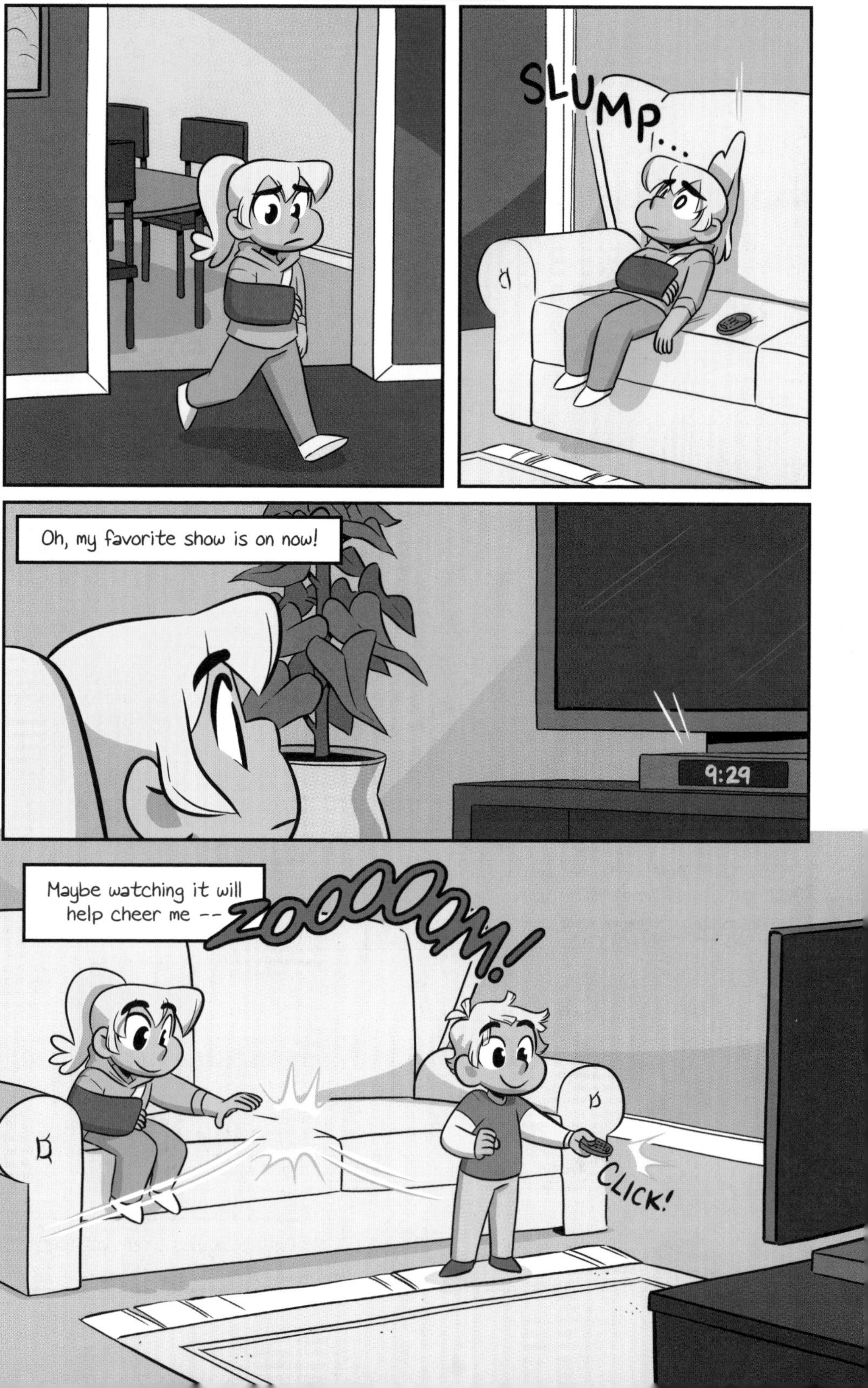
SLUMP...
Oh, my favorite show is on now!
9:29
Maybe watching it will help cheer me --
ZOOOOOM!
CLICK!

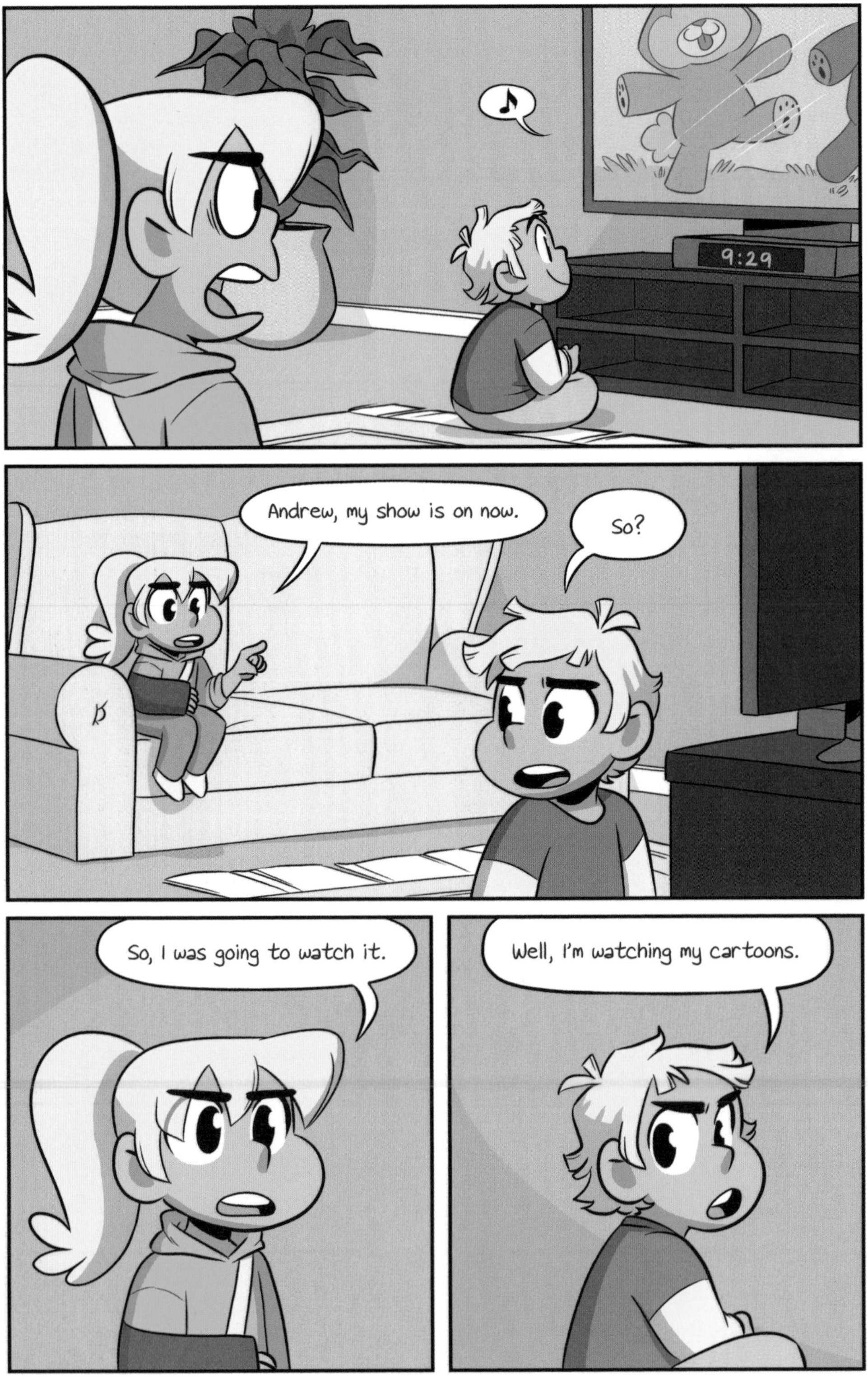
9:29
Andrew, my show is on now.
So?
So, I was going to watch it.
Well, I'm watching my cartoons.

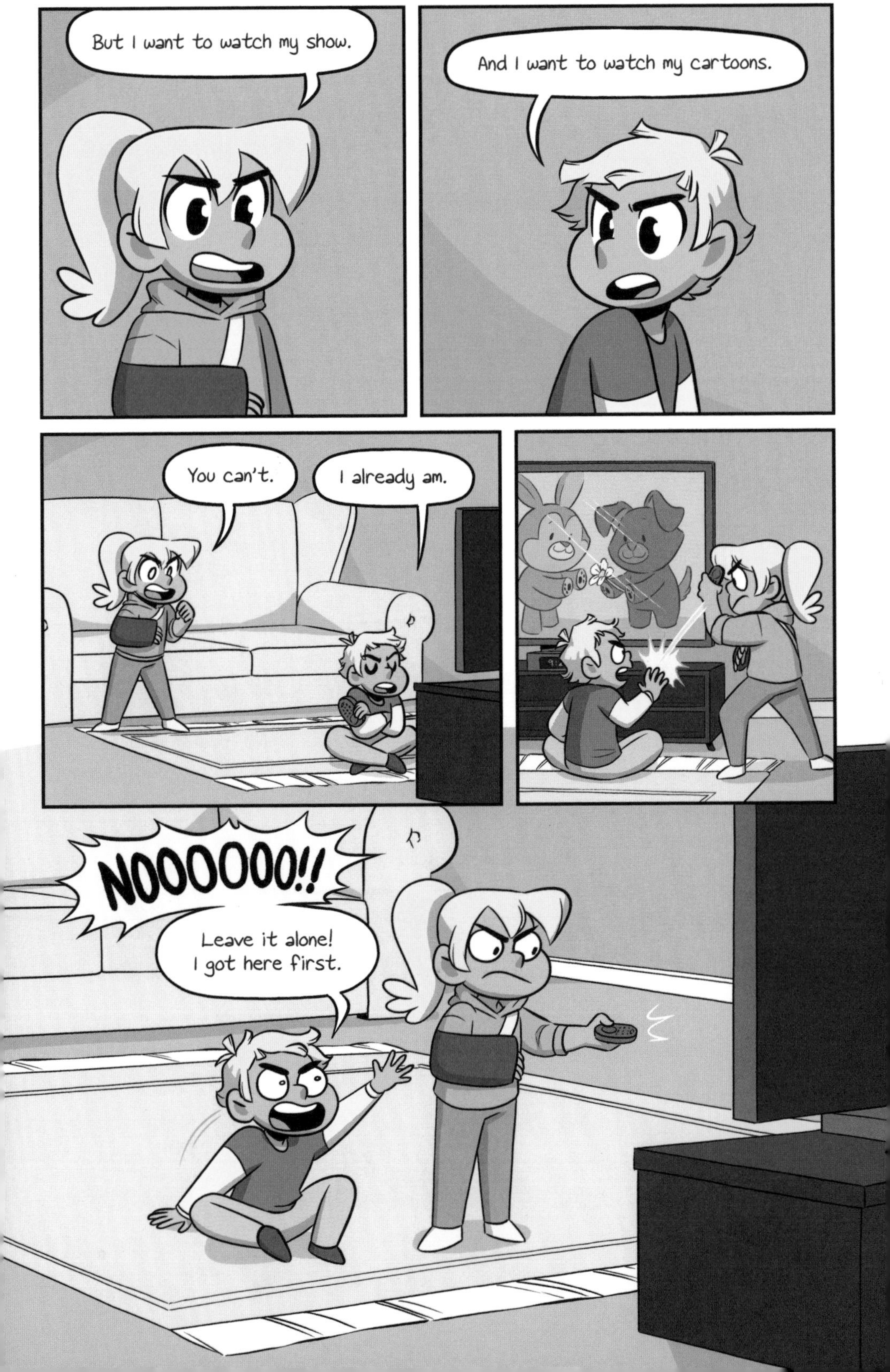

But I want to watch my show.
And I want to watch my cartoons.
You can't.
I already am.
NOOOOOO!!
Leave it alone! I got here first.

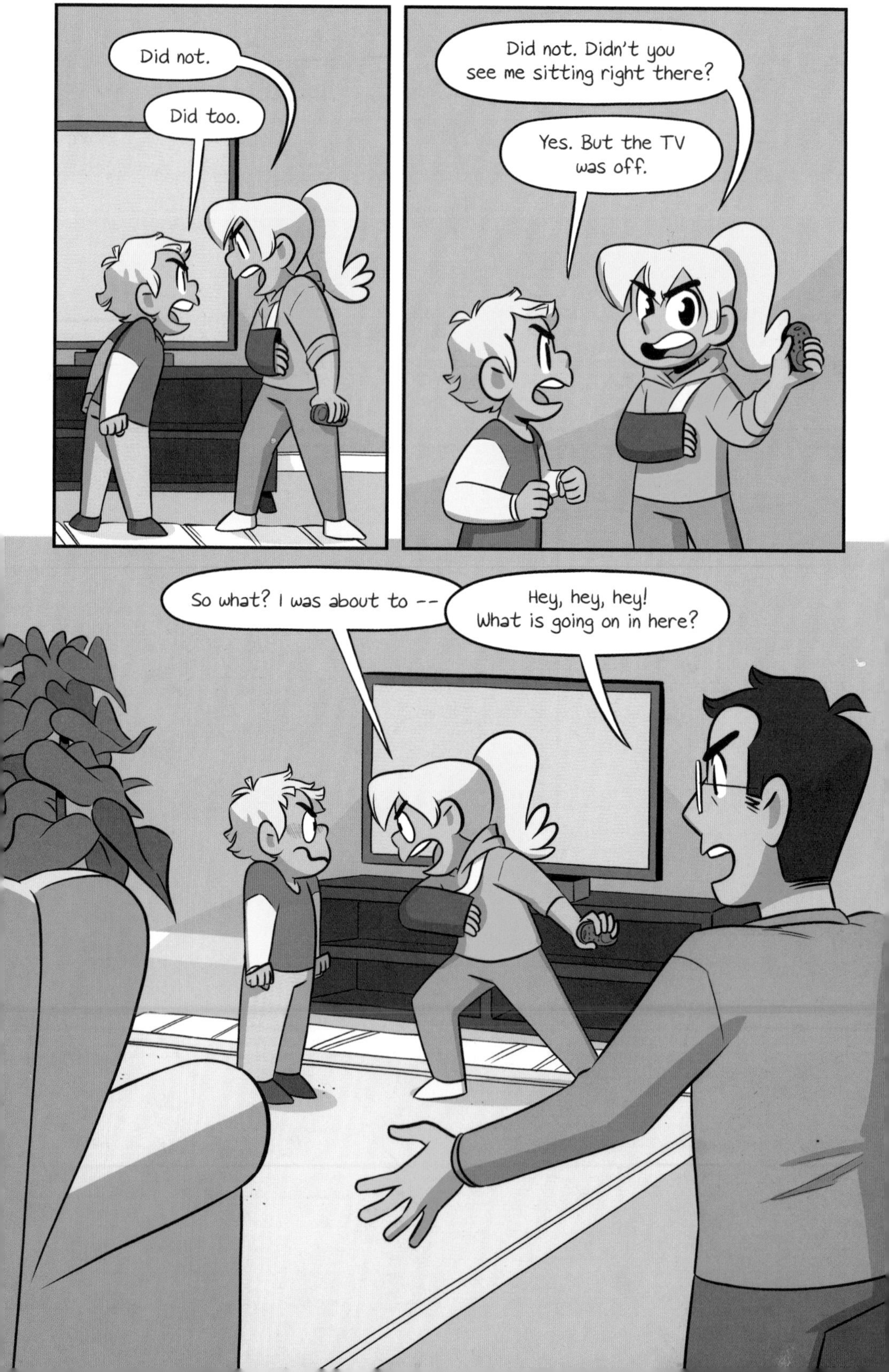
Did not.
Did too.
Did not. Didn't you see me sitting right there?
Yes. But the TV was off.
So what? I was about to --
Hey, hey, hey! What is going on in here?

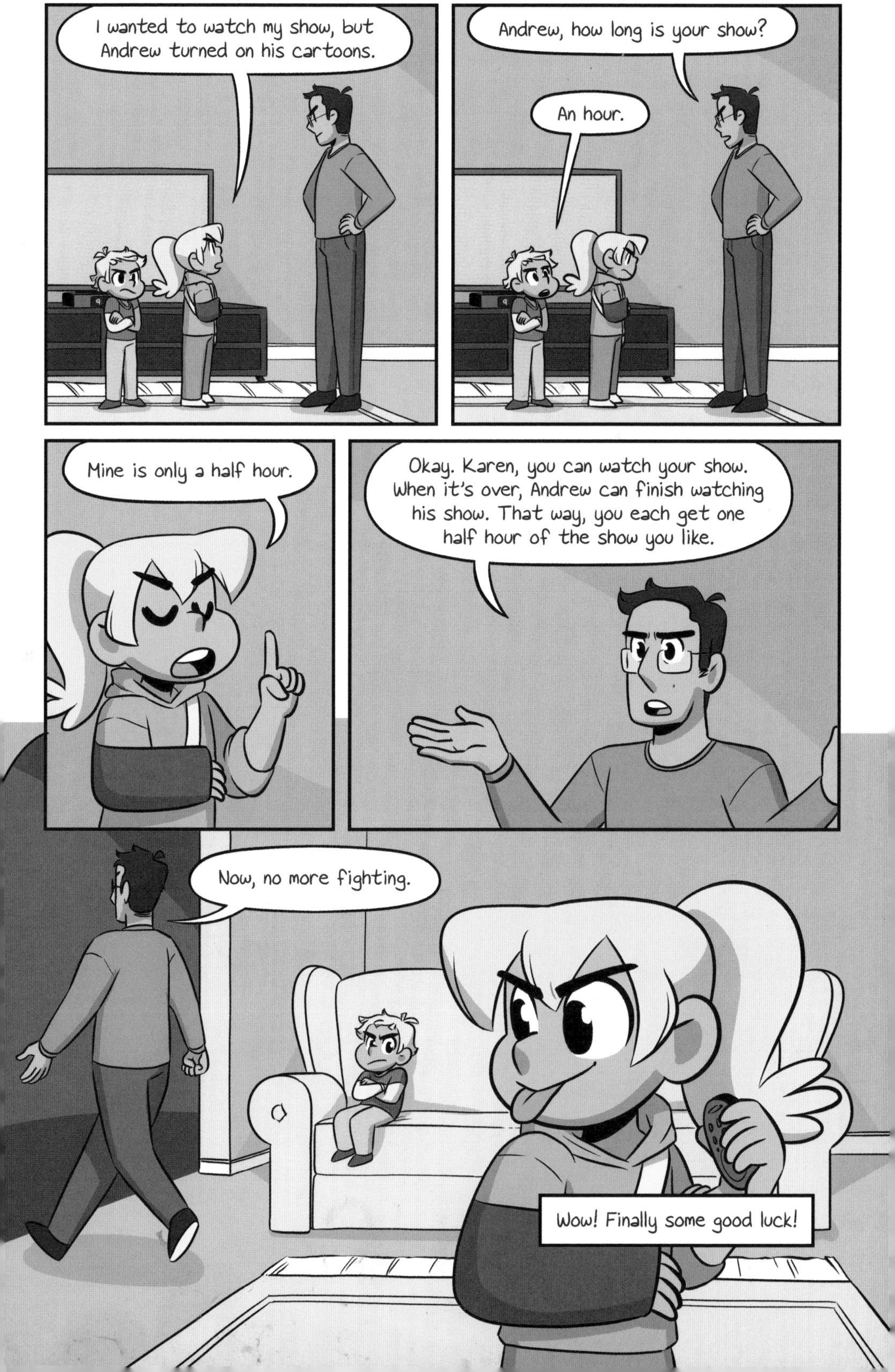
I wanted to watch my show, but Andrew turned on his cartoons.
Andrew, how long is your show?
An hour.
Mine is only a half hour.
Okay. Karen, you can watch your show. When it's over, Andrew can finish watching his show. That way, you each get one half hour of the show you like.
Now, no more fighting.
Wow! Finally some good luck!

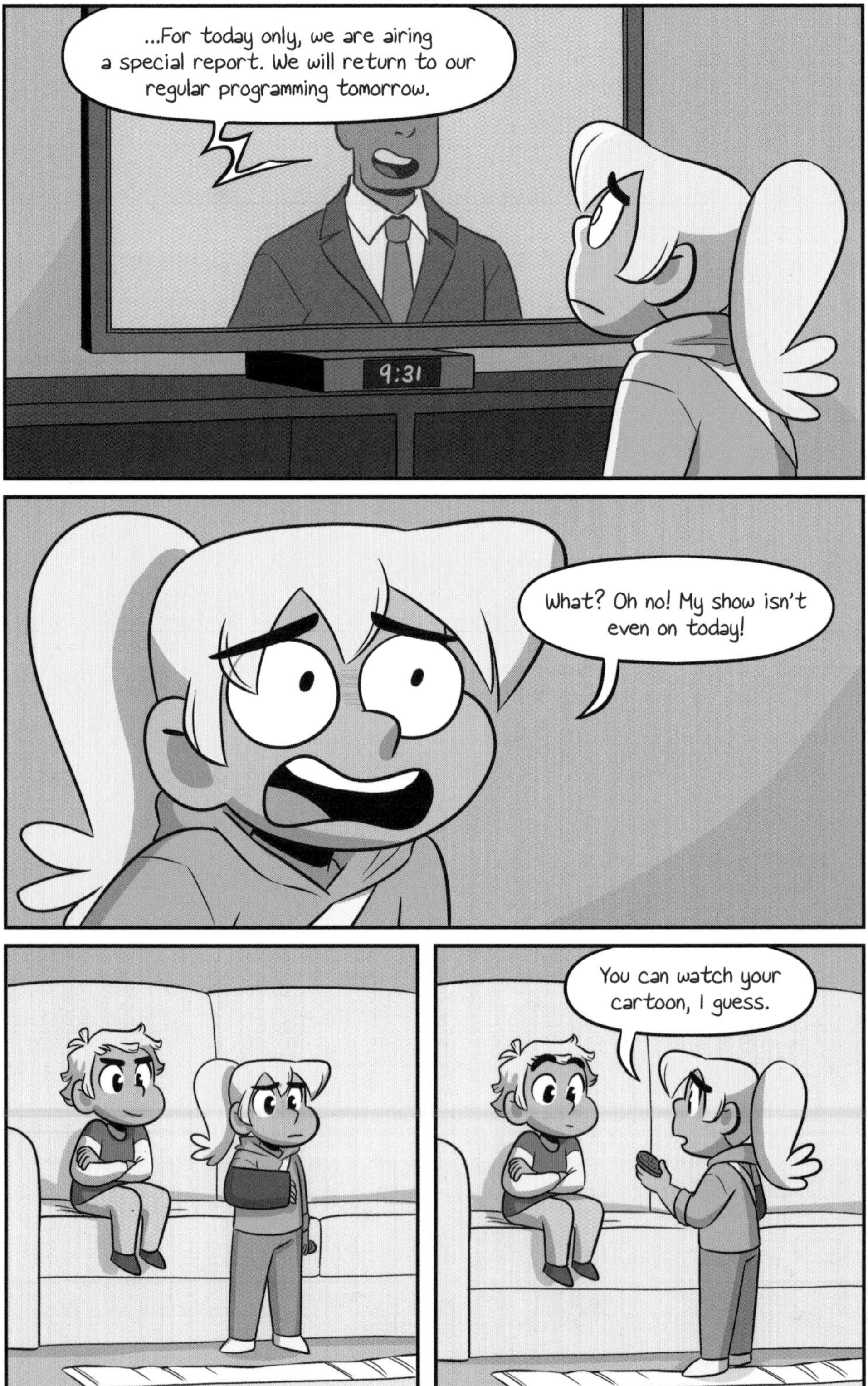
...For today only, we are airing a special report. We will return to our regular programming tomorrow.
9:31
What? Oh no! My show isn't even on today!
You can watch your cartoon, I guess.

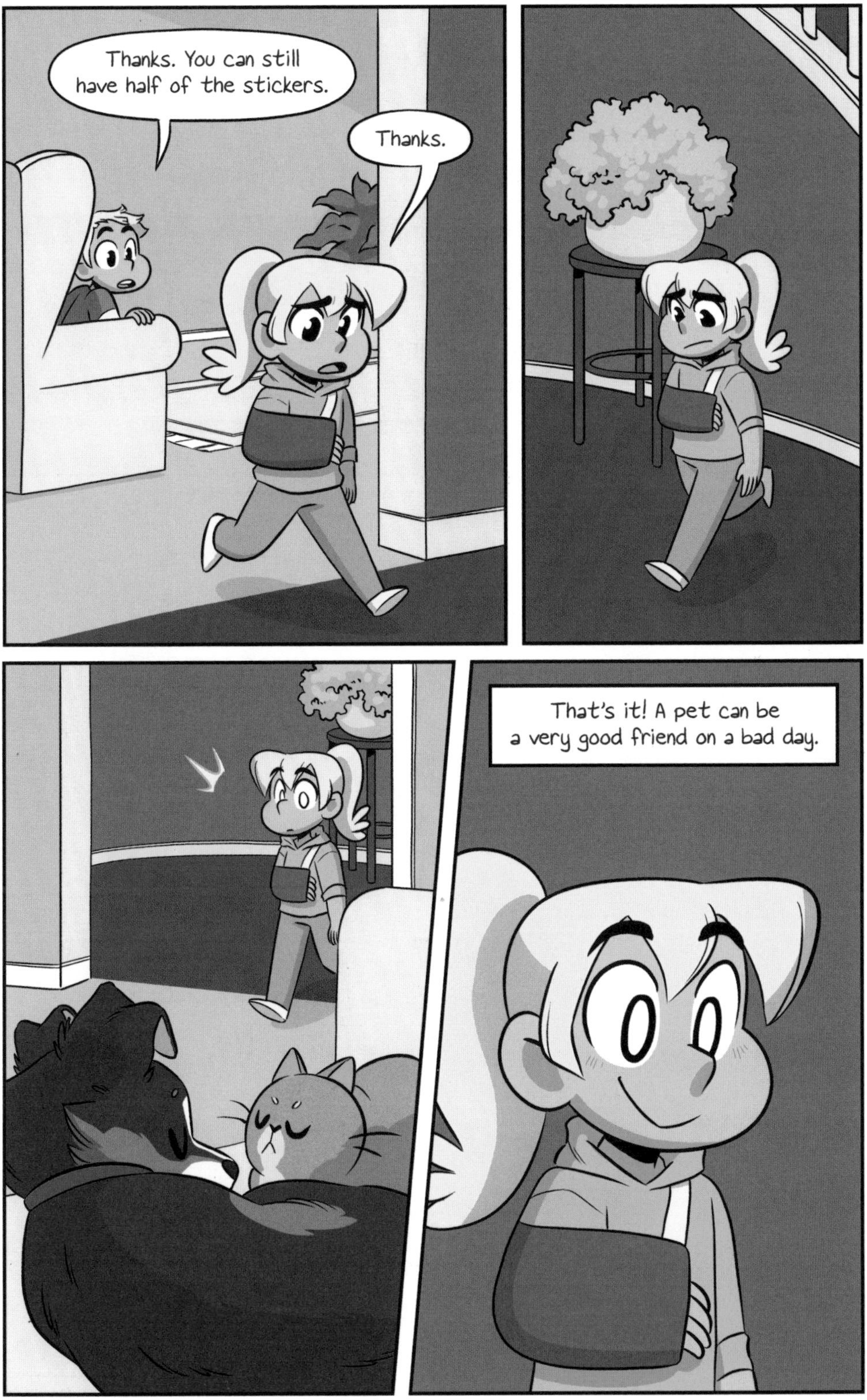
Thanks. You can still have half of the stickers.
Thanks.
That's it! A pet can be a very good friend on a bad day.

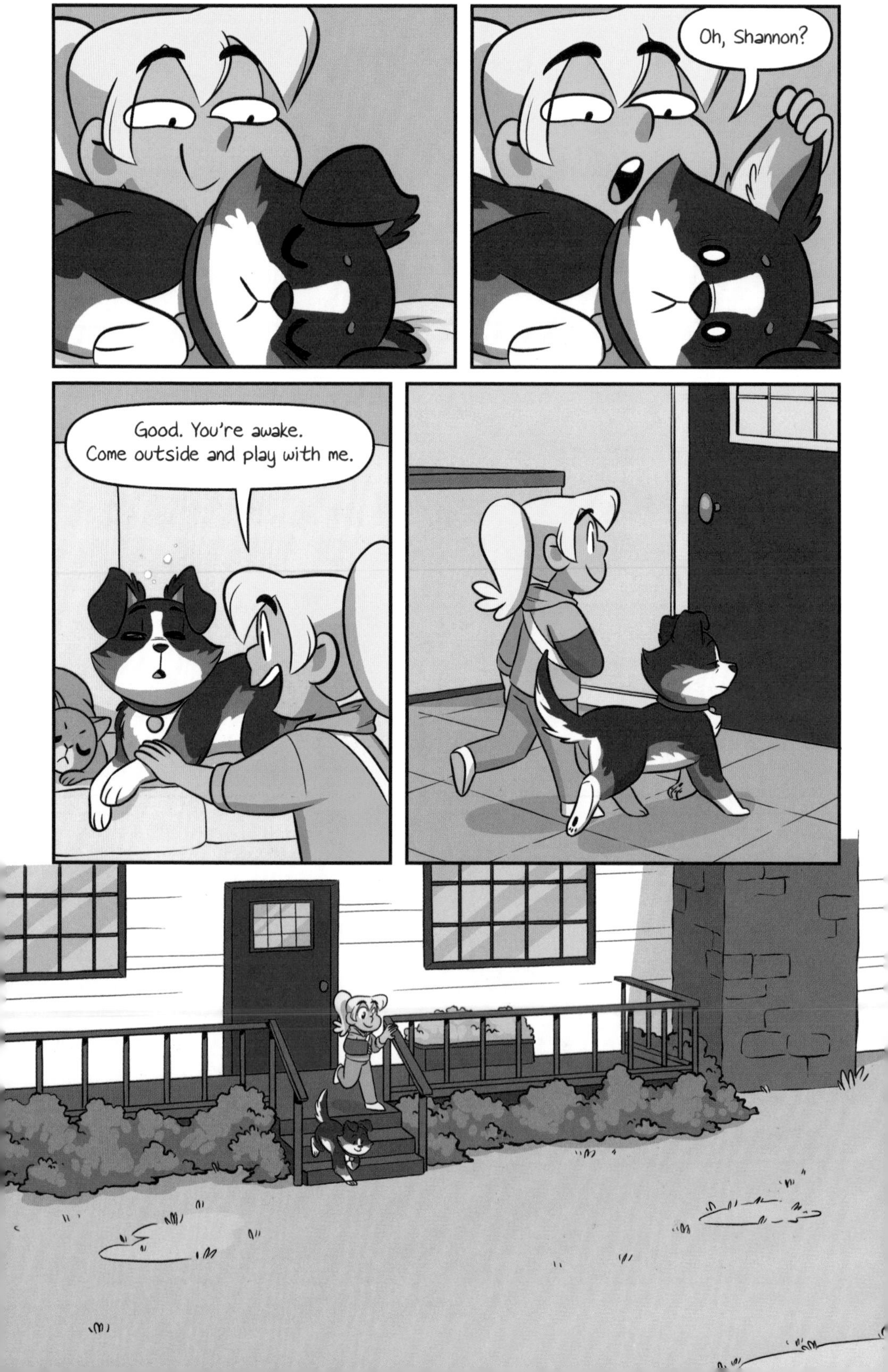
Oh, Shannon?
Good. You're awake.
Come outside and play with me.

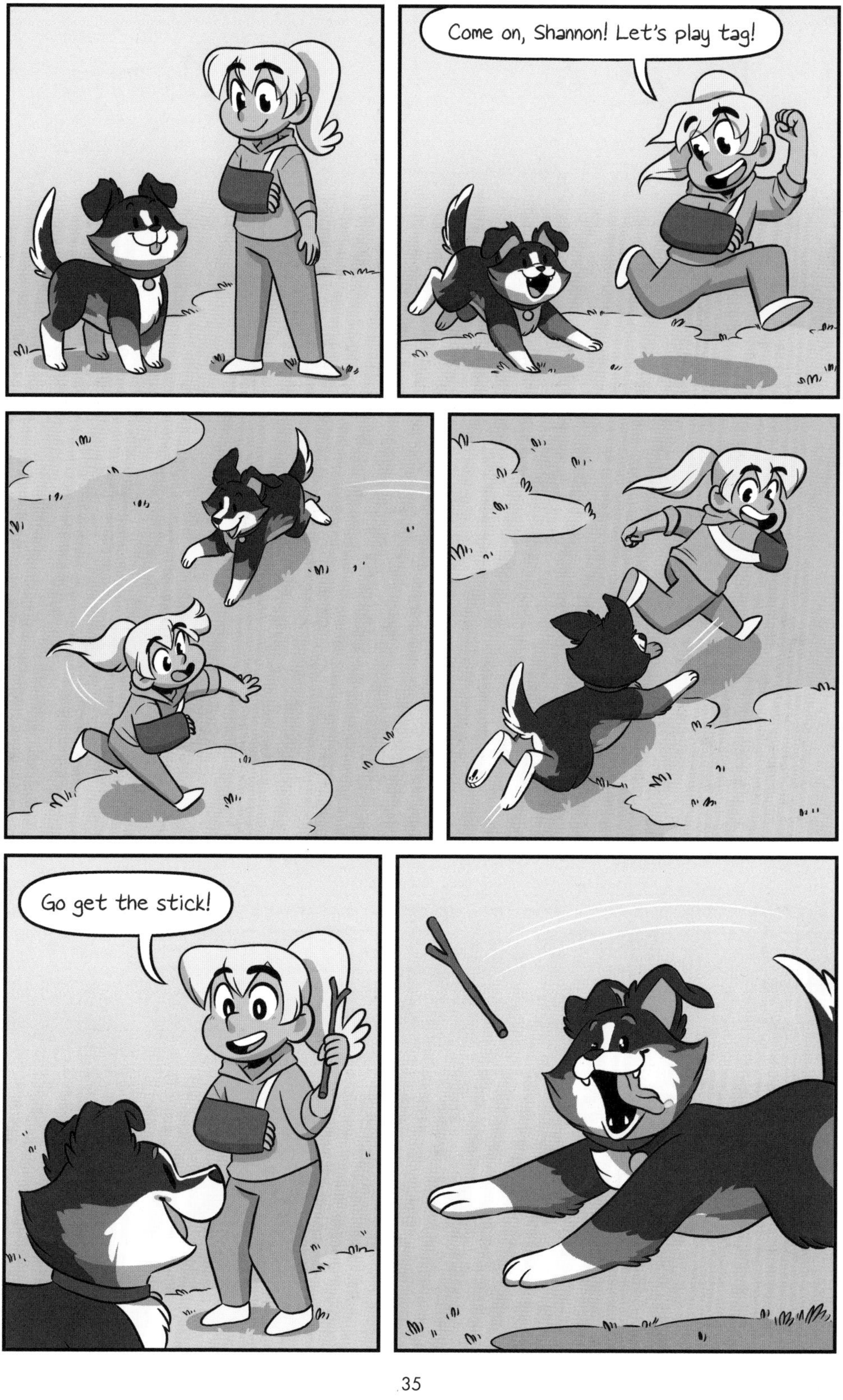
Come on, Shannon! Let's play tag!
Go get the stick!

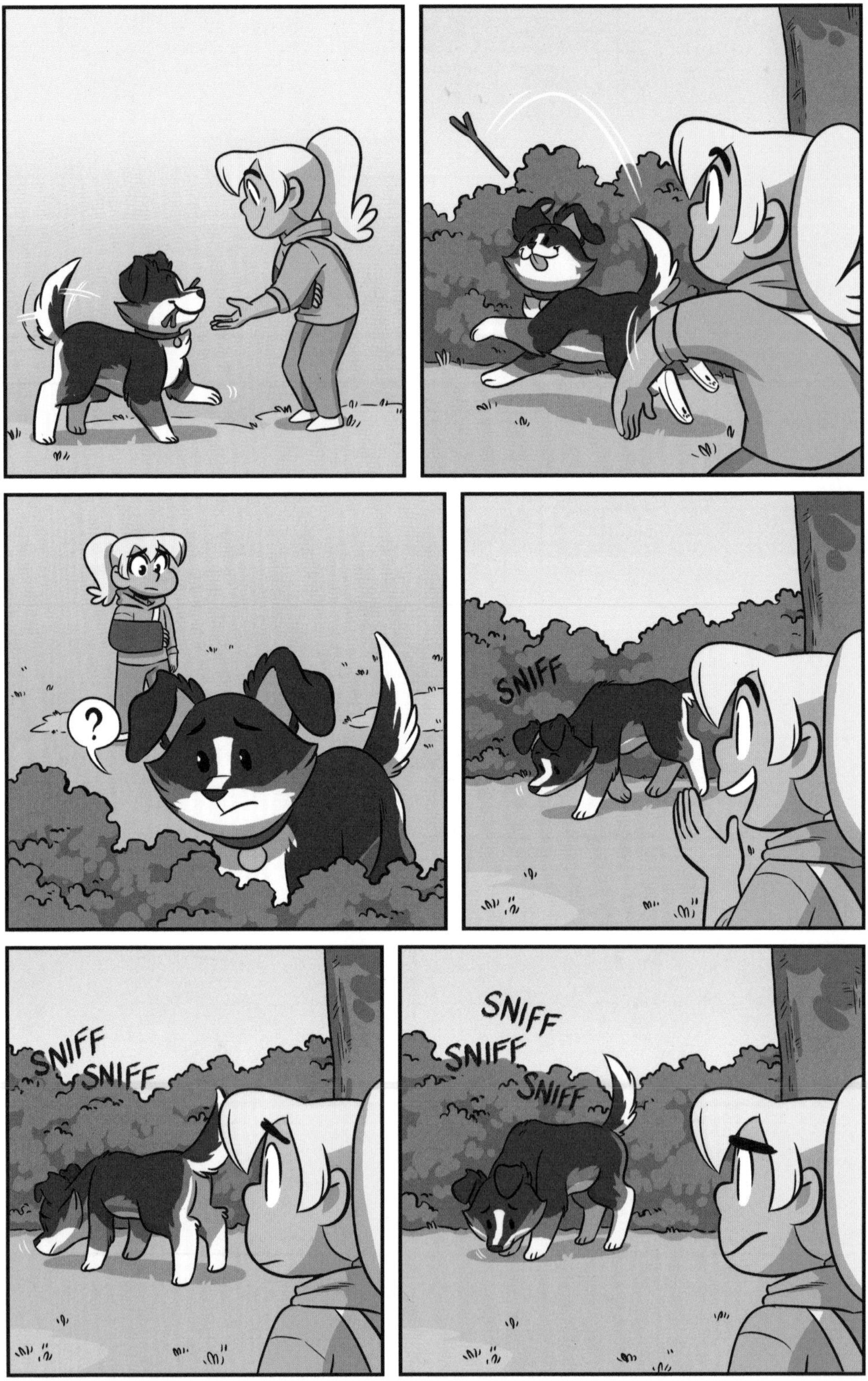
?
SNIFF
SNIFF
SNIFF
SNIFF
SNIFF
SNIFF

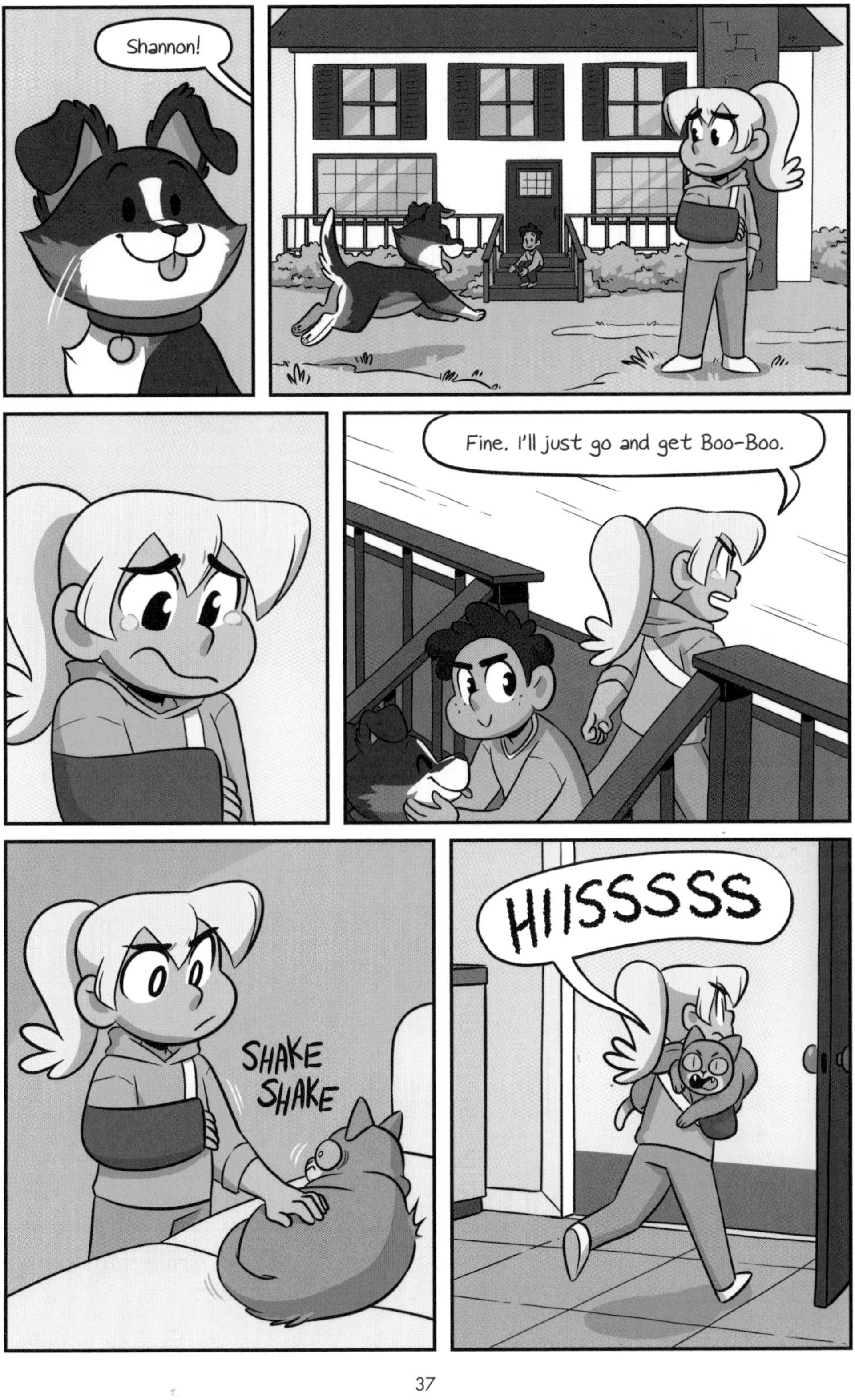
Shannon!
Fine. I'll just go and get Boo-Boo.
SHAKE SHAKE
HIISSSSS

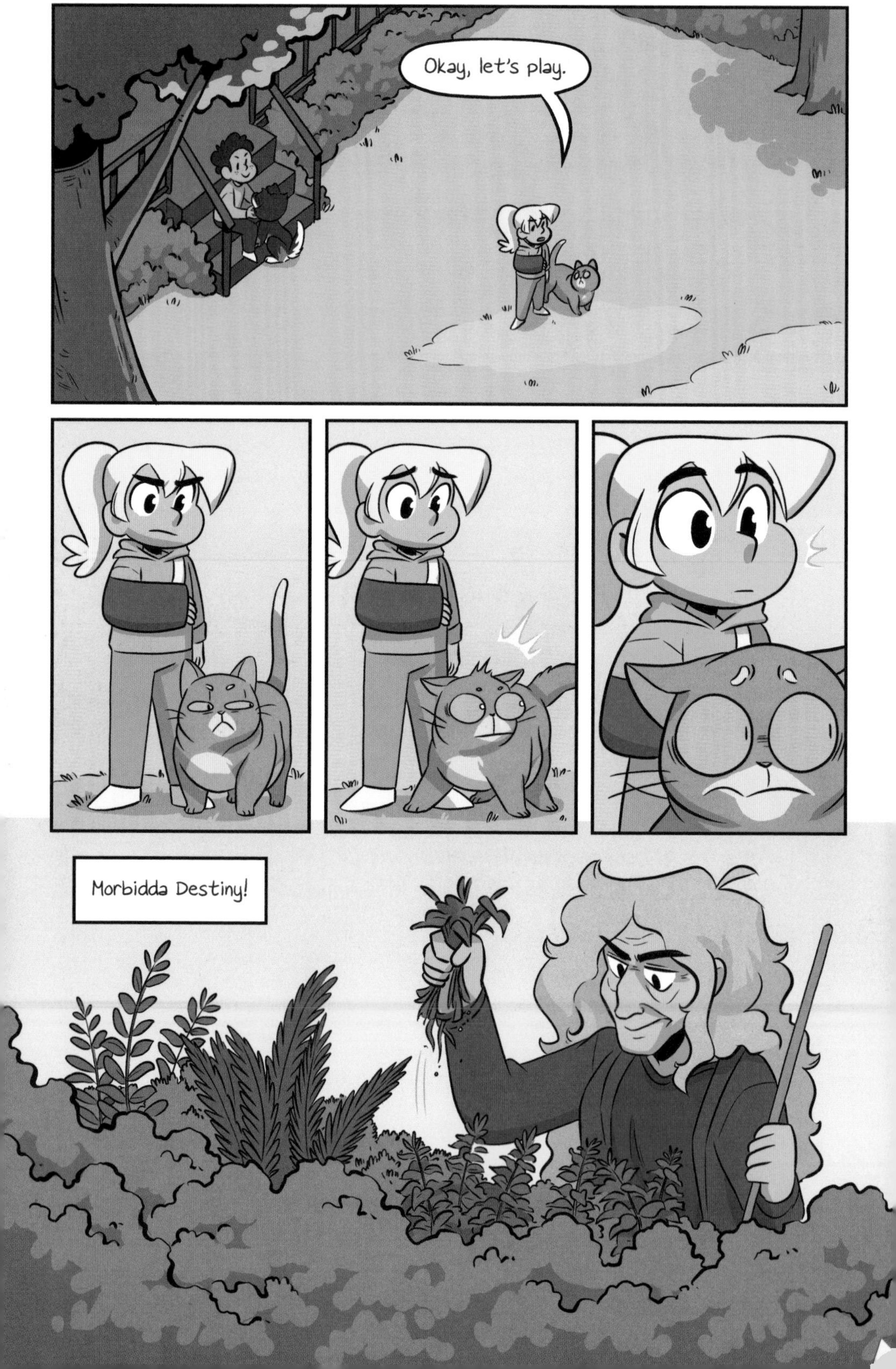
Okay, let's play.
Morbidda Destiny!

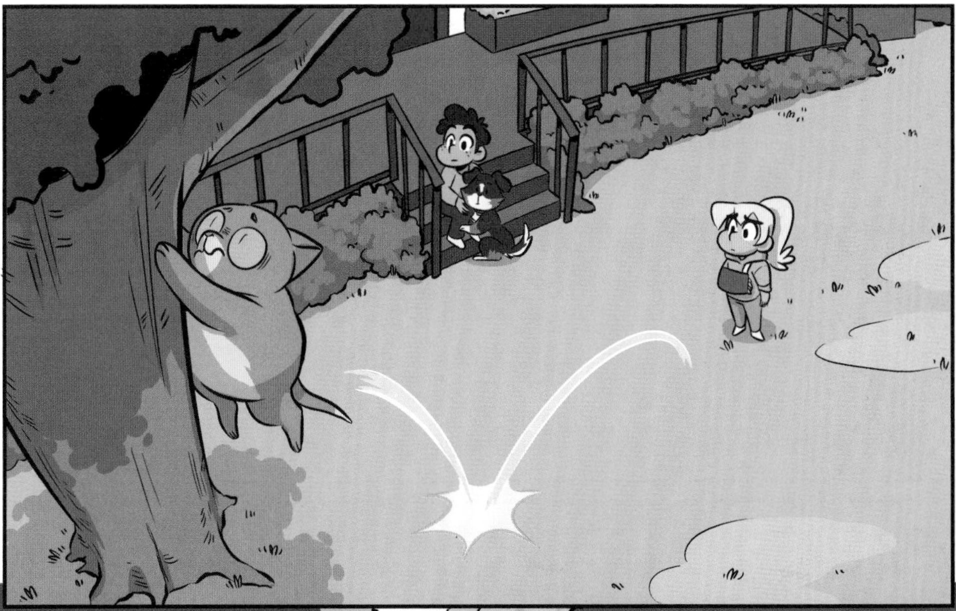

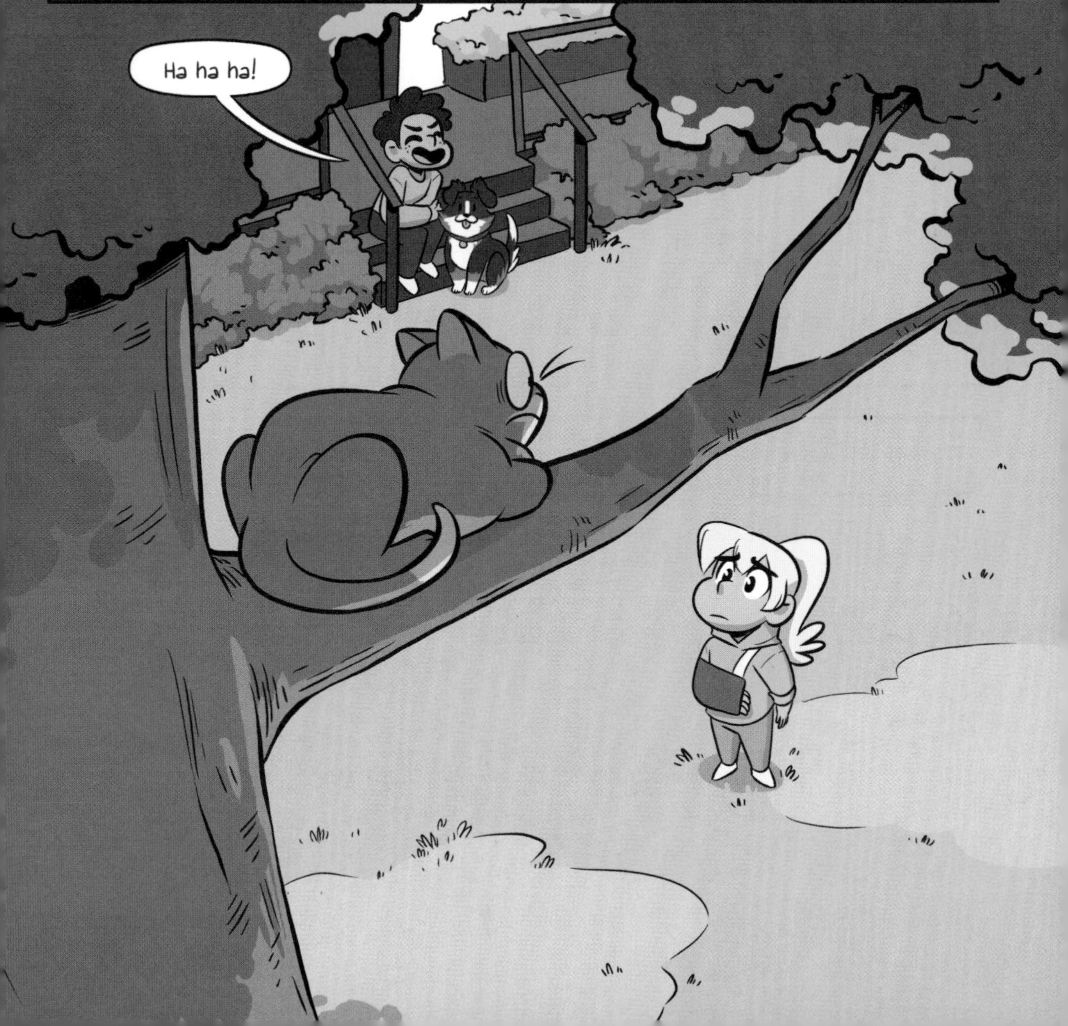
Ha ha ha!

CHAPTER 4

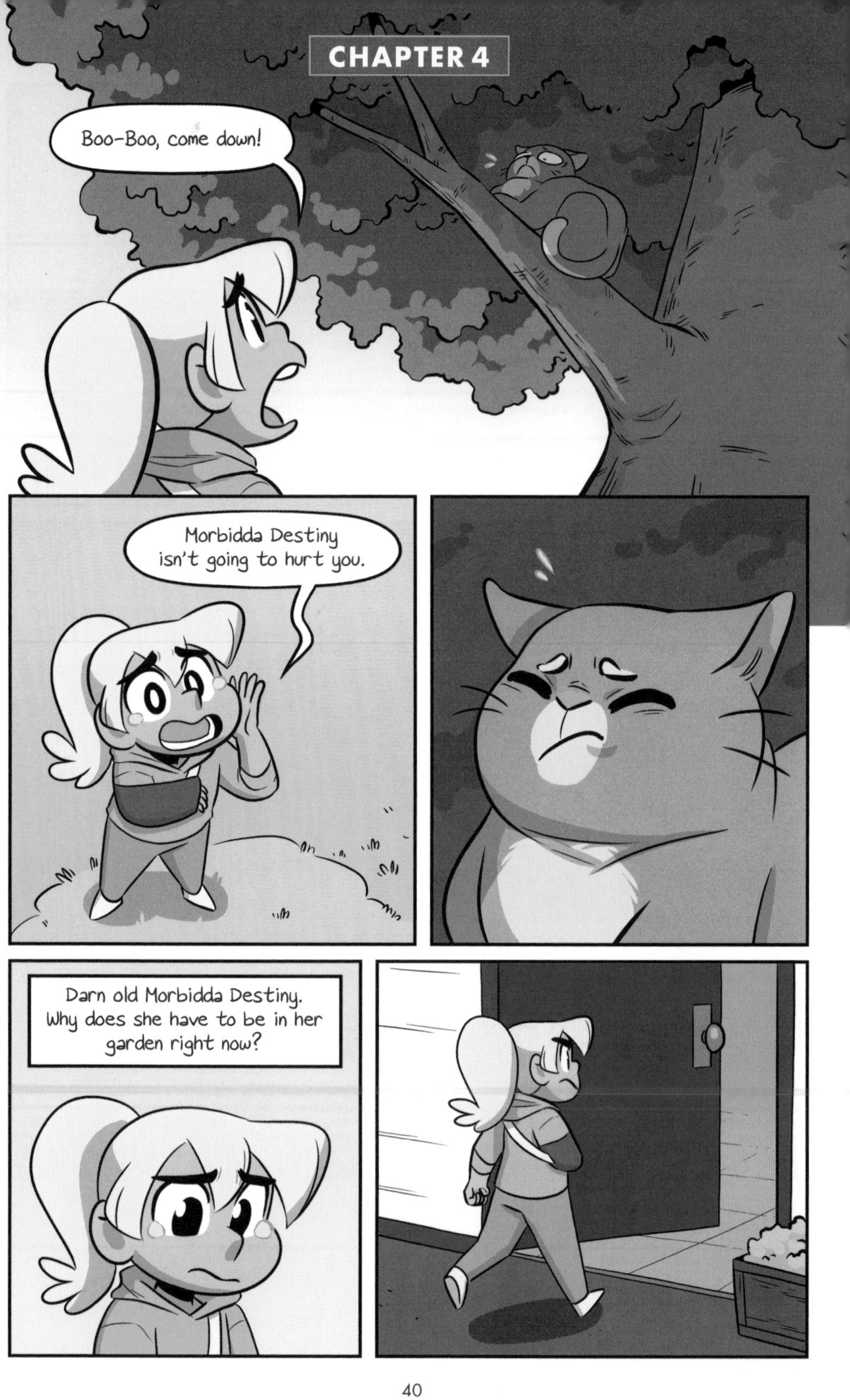
Boo-Boo, come down!
Morbidda Destiny isn't going to hurt you.
Darn old Morbidda Destiny. Why does she have to be in her garden right now?

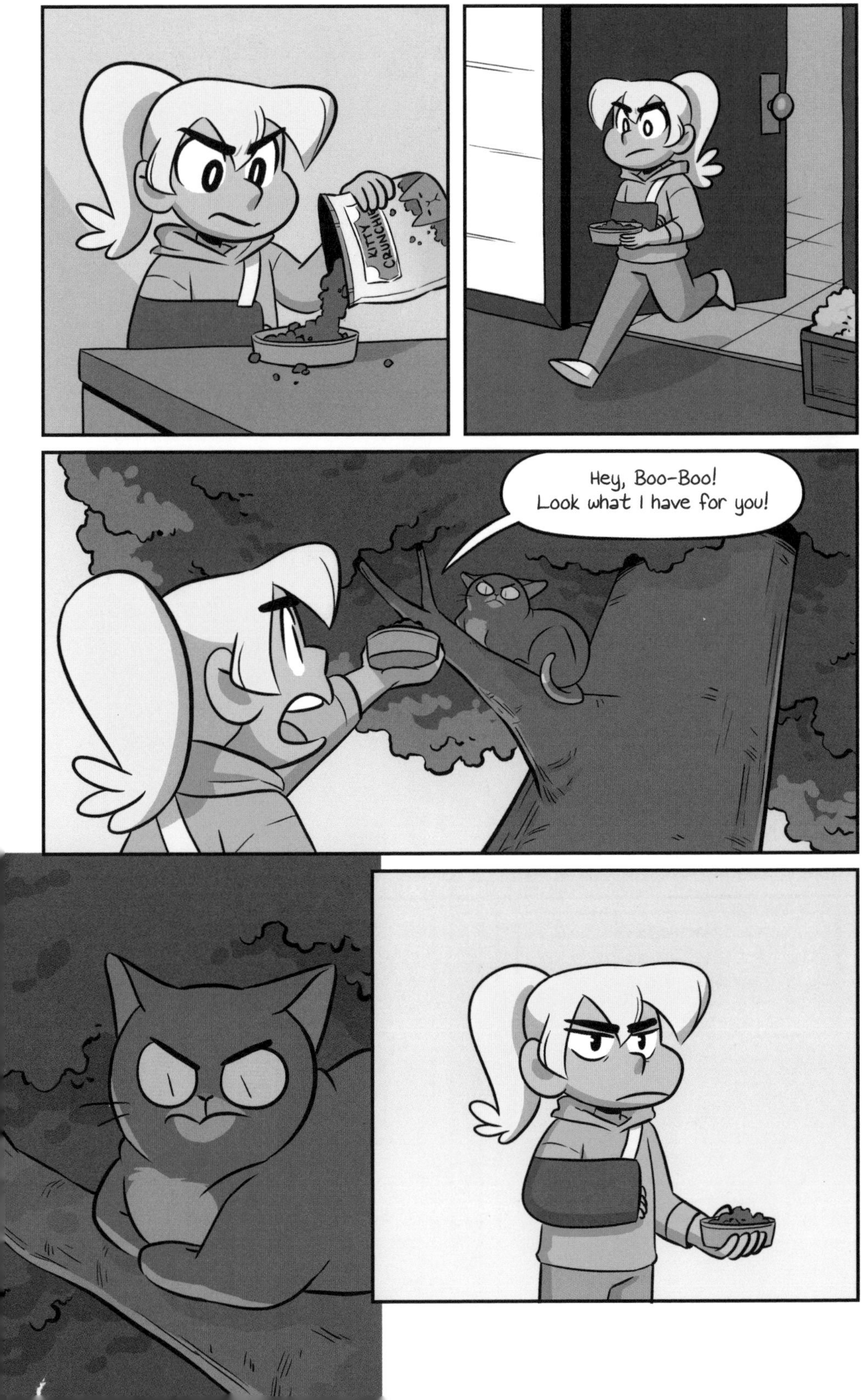
KITTY
Hey, Boo-Boo! Look what I have for you!

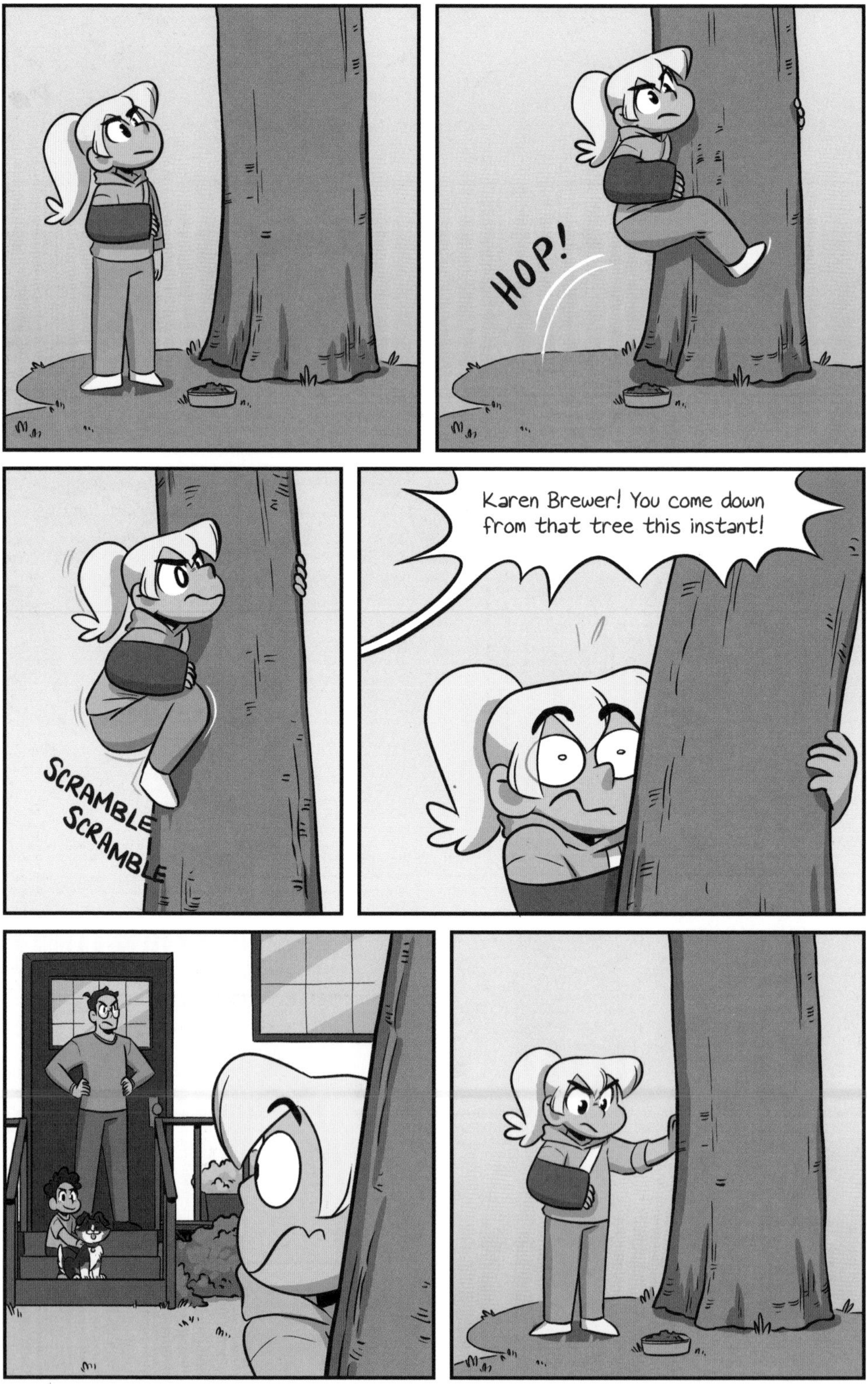
HOP!
SCRAMBLE
SCRAMBLE
Karen Brewer! You come down from that tree this instant!

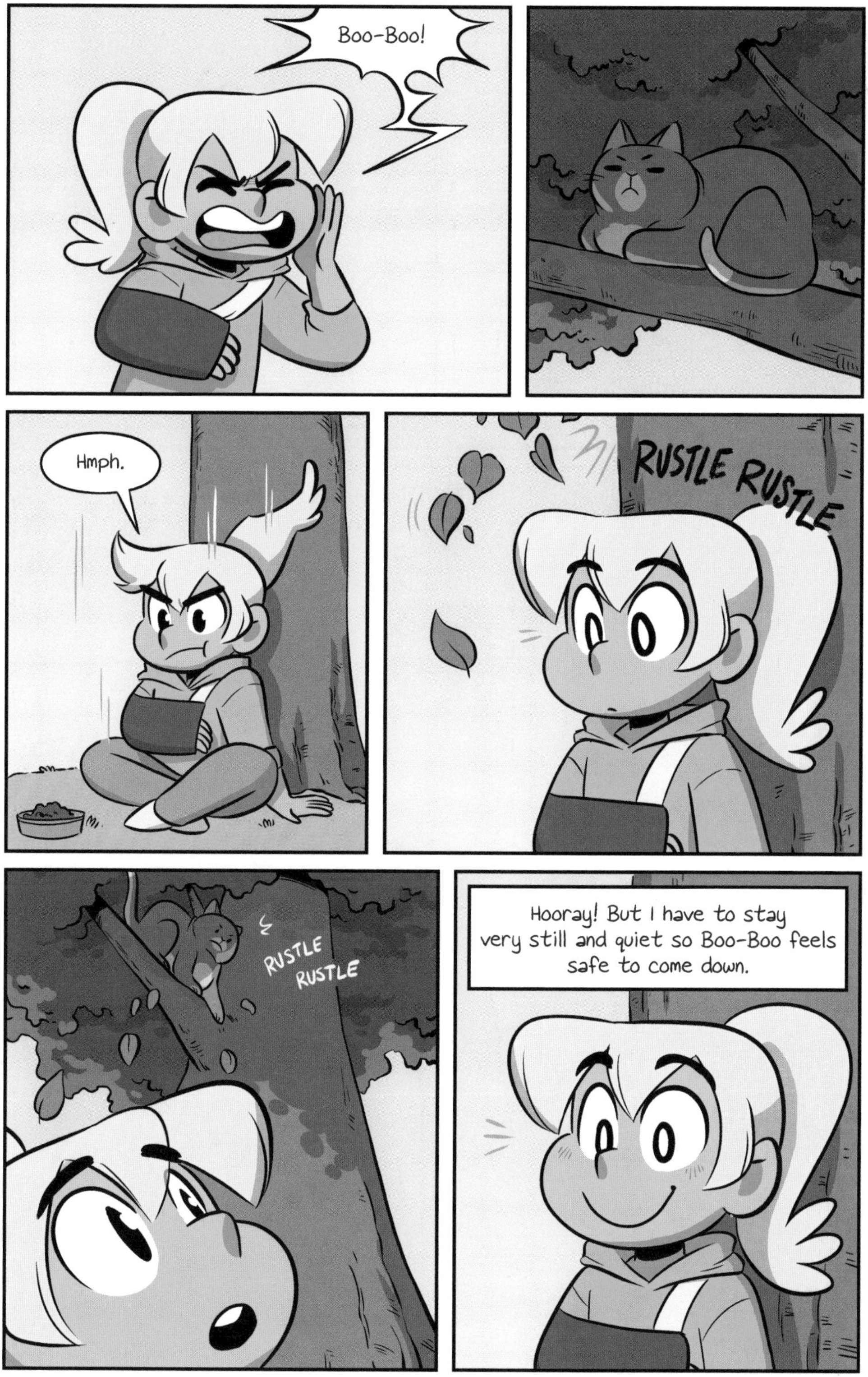
Boo-Boo!
Hmph.
RUSTLE RUSTLE
RUSTLE
RUSTLE
Hooray! But I have to stay very still and quiet so Boo-Boo feels safe to come down.

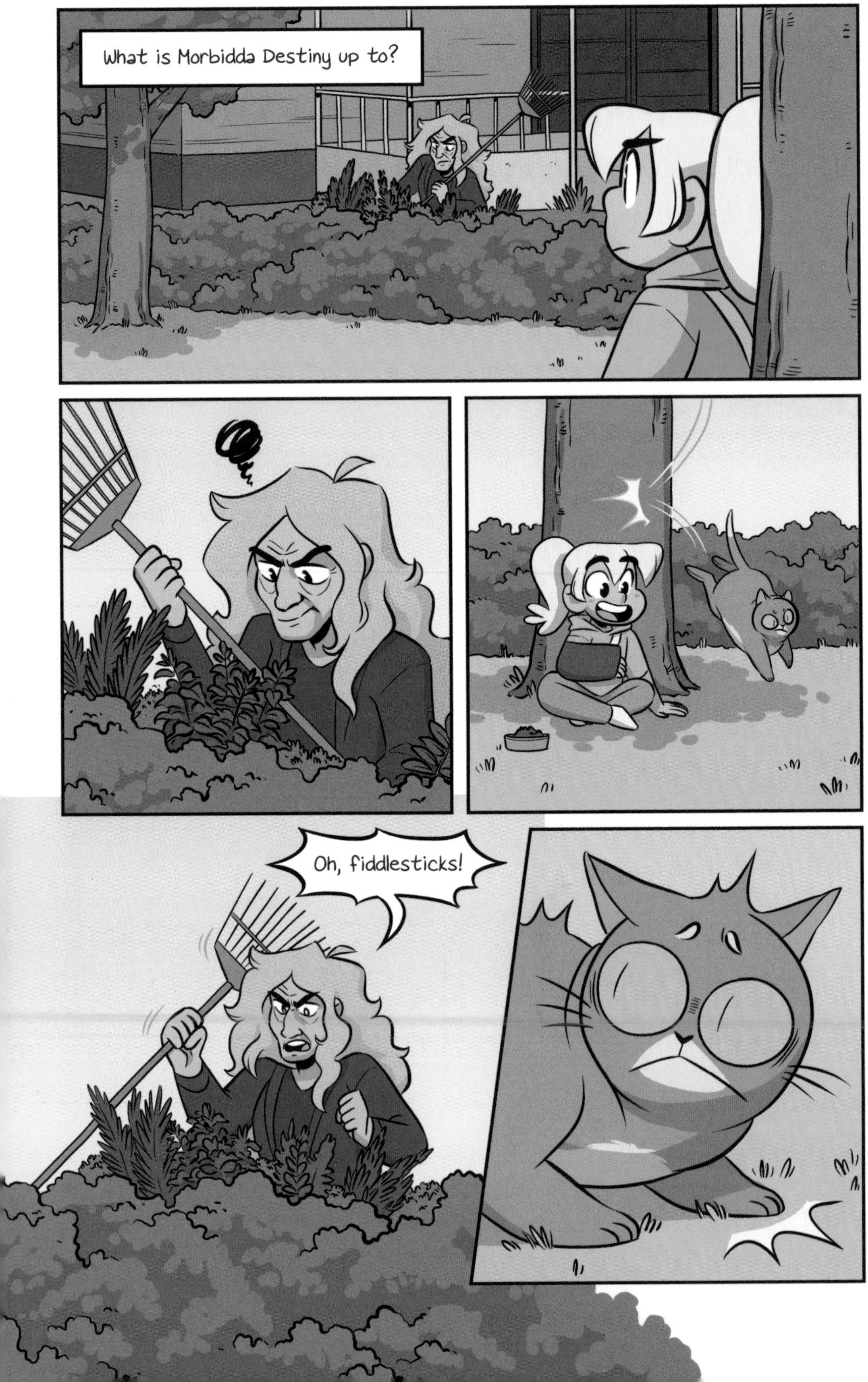

What is Morbidda Destiny up to?
Oh, fiddlesticks!

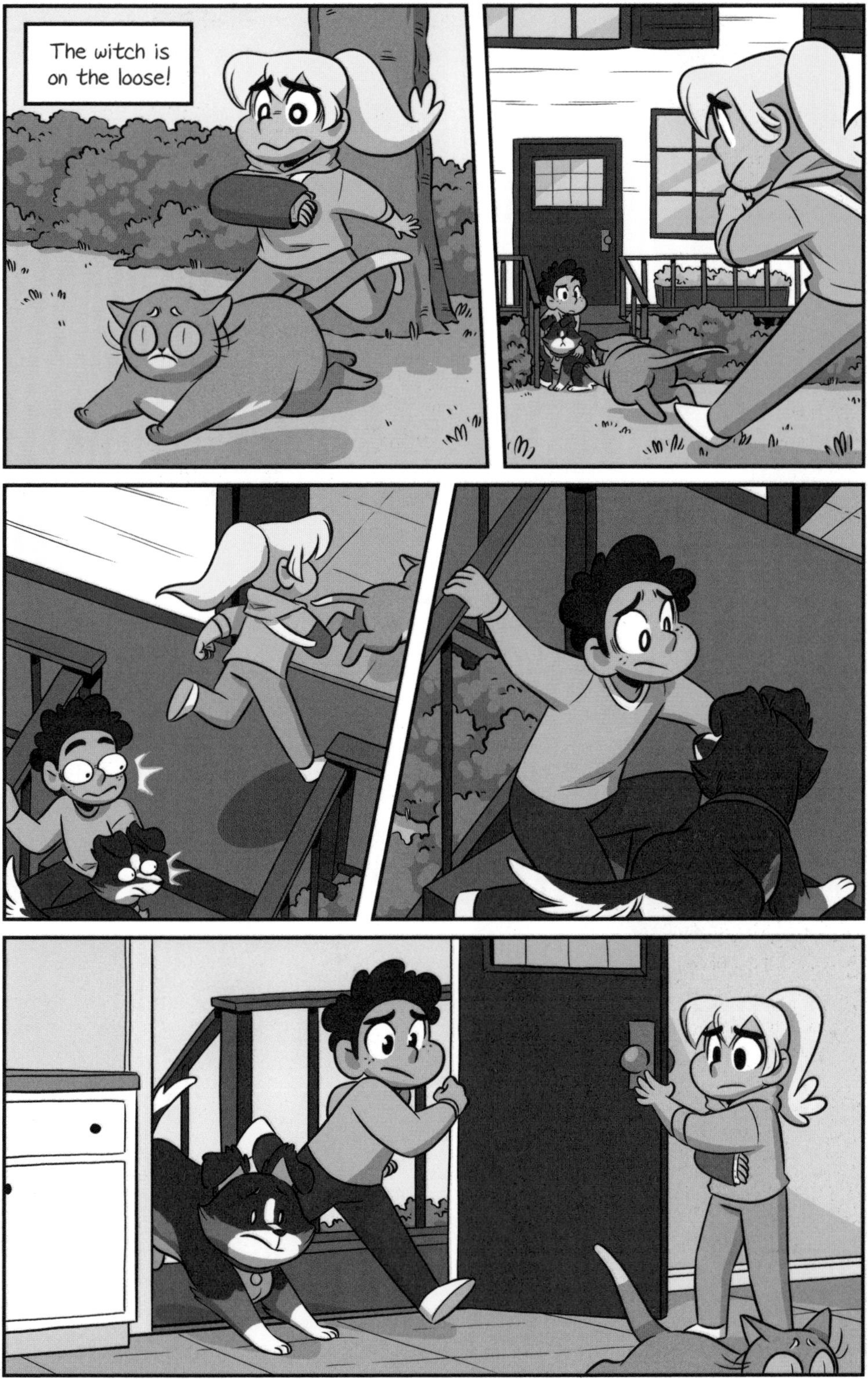
The witch is on the loose!

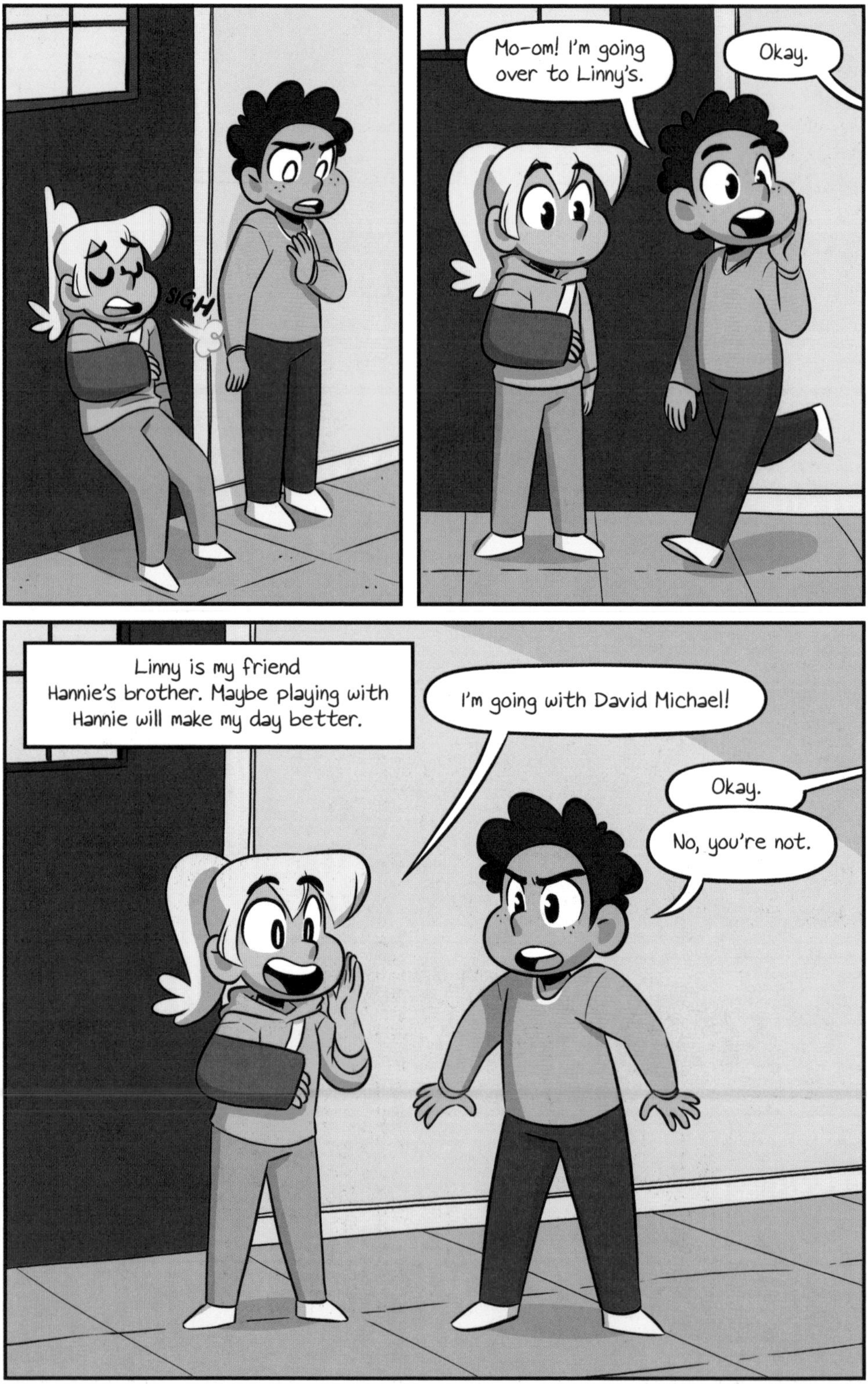
SIGH
Mo-om! I'm going over to Linny's.
Okay.
Linny is my friend Hannie's brother. Maybe playing with Hannie will make my day better.
I'm going with David Michael!
Okay.
No, you're not.

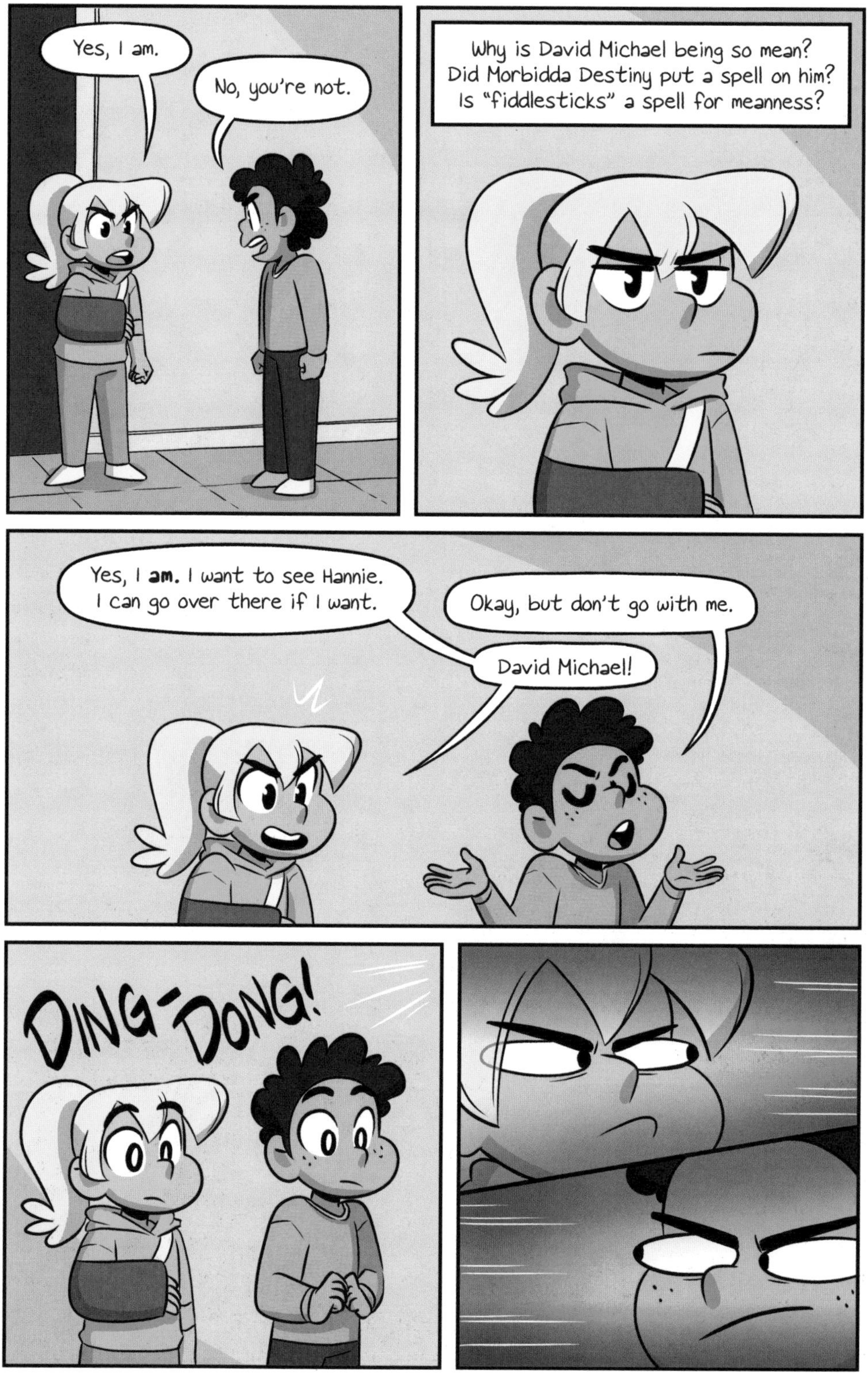
Yes, I am.
No, you're not.
Why is David Michael being so mean? Did Morbidda Destiny put a spell on him? Is "fiddlesticks" a spell for meanness?
Yes, I **am.** I want to see Hannie. I can go over there if I want.
Okay, but don't go with me.
David Michael!
DING-DONG!

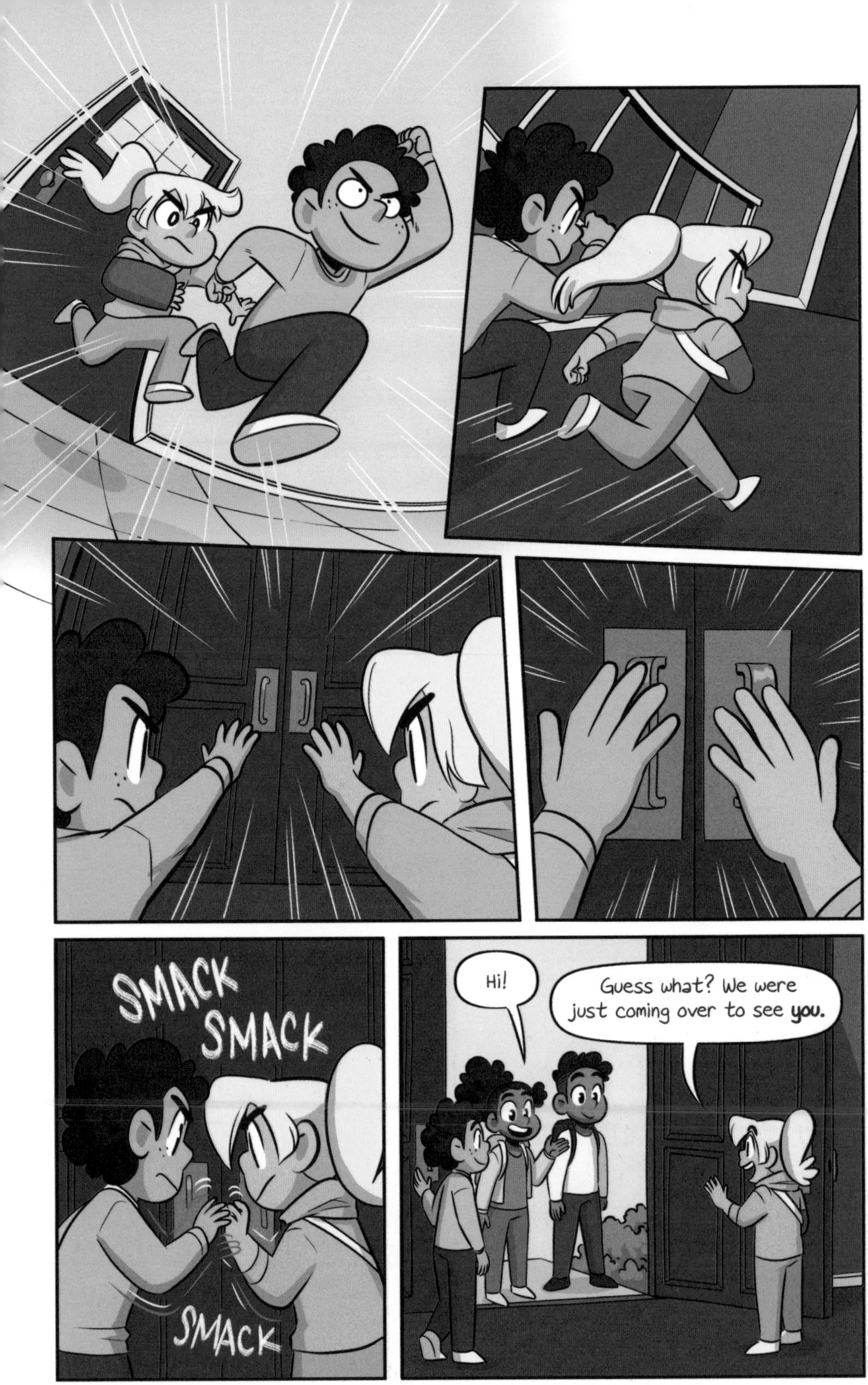
SMACK
SMACK
SMACK
Hi!
Guess what? We were just coming over to see **you.**

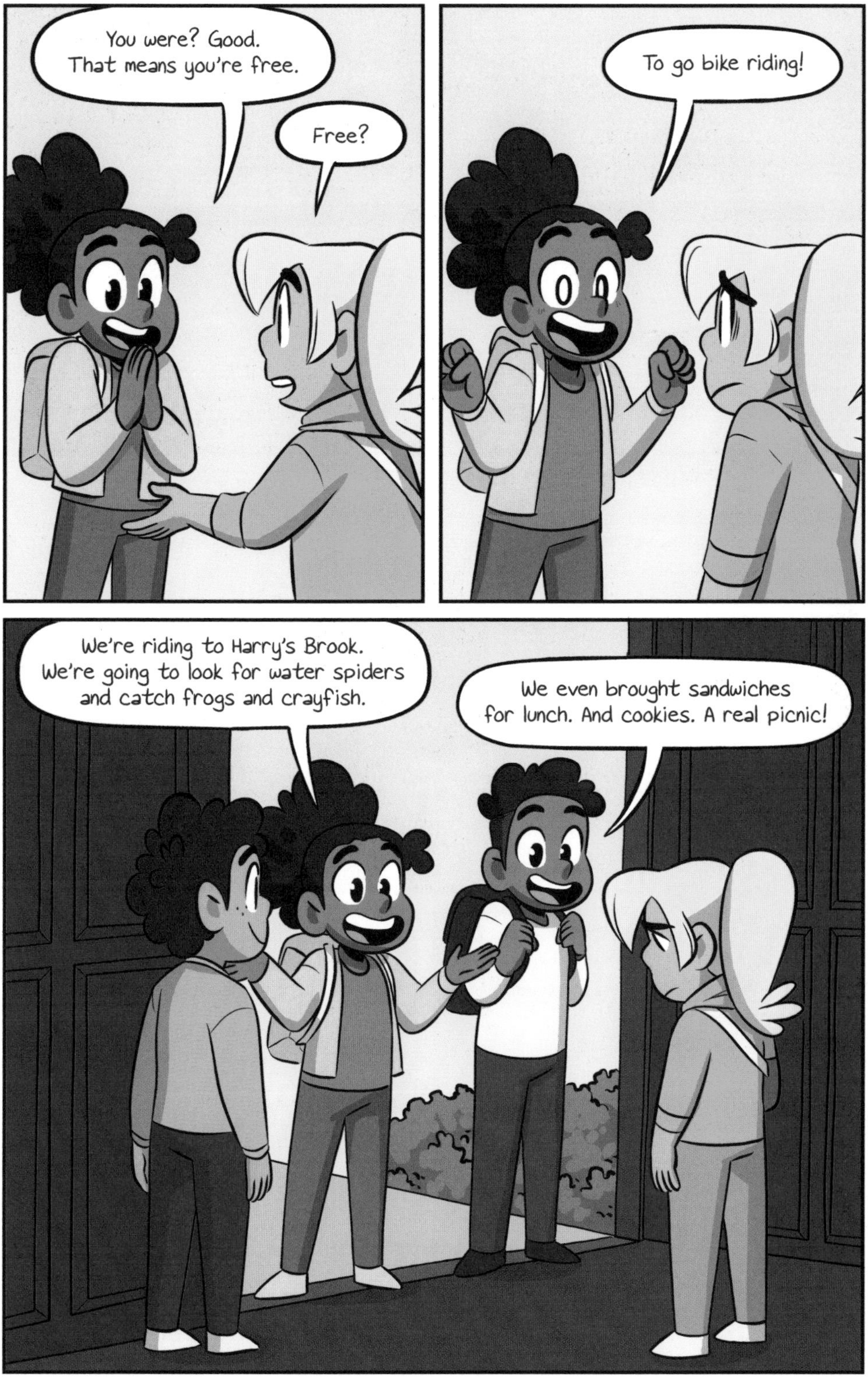
You were? Good. That means you're free.
Free?
To go bike riding!
We're riding to Harry's Brook. We're going to look for water spiders and catch frogs and crayfish.
We even brought sandwiches for lunch. And cookies. A real picnic!

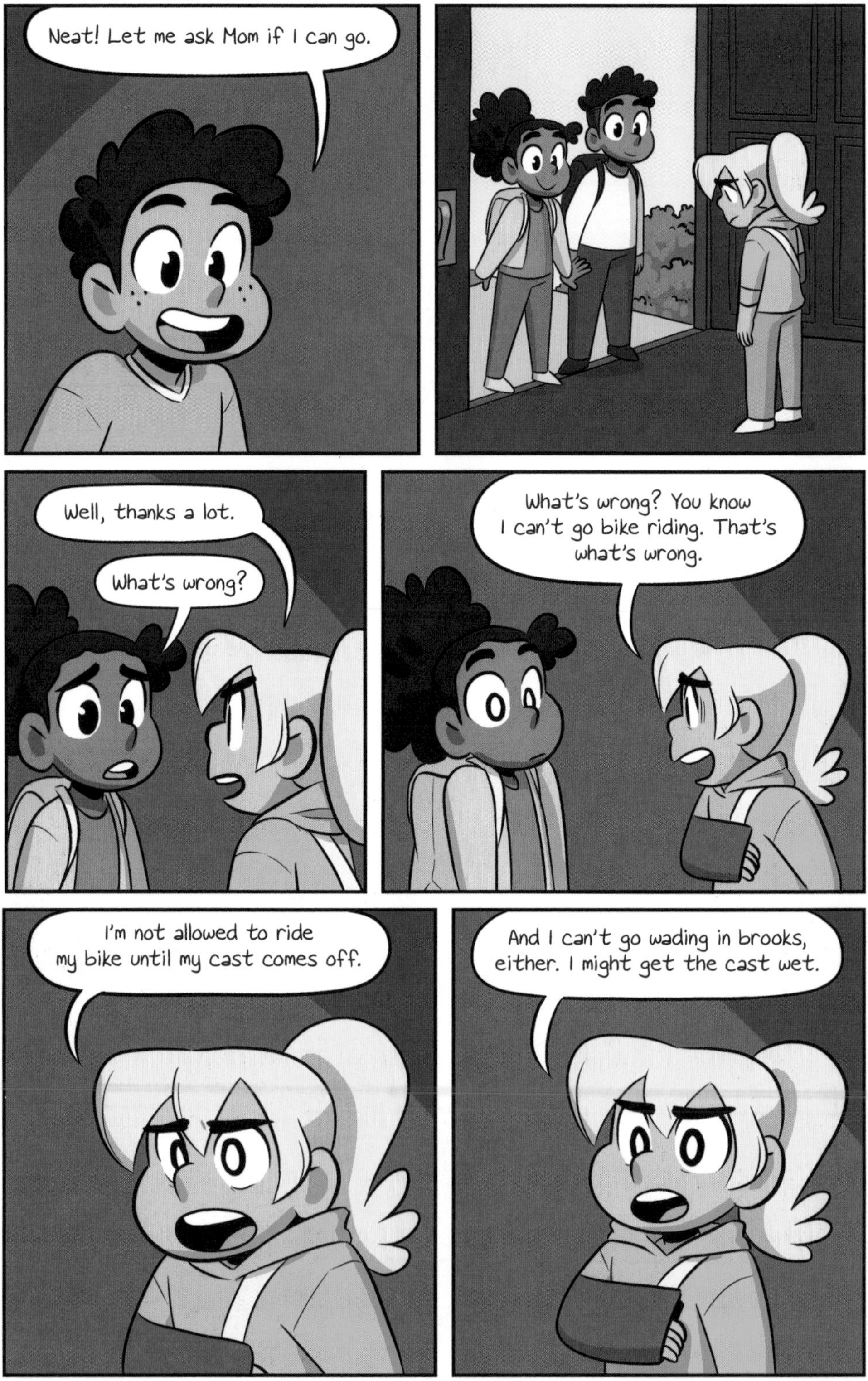
Neat! Let me ask Mom if I can go.
Well, thanks a lot.
What's wrong?
What's wrong? You know I can't go bike riding. That's what's wrong.
I'm not allowed to ride my bike until my cast comes off.
And I can't go wading in brooks, either. I might get the cast wet.

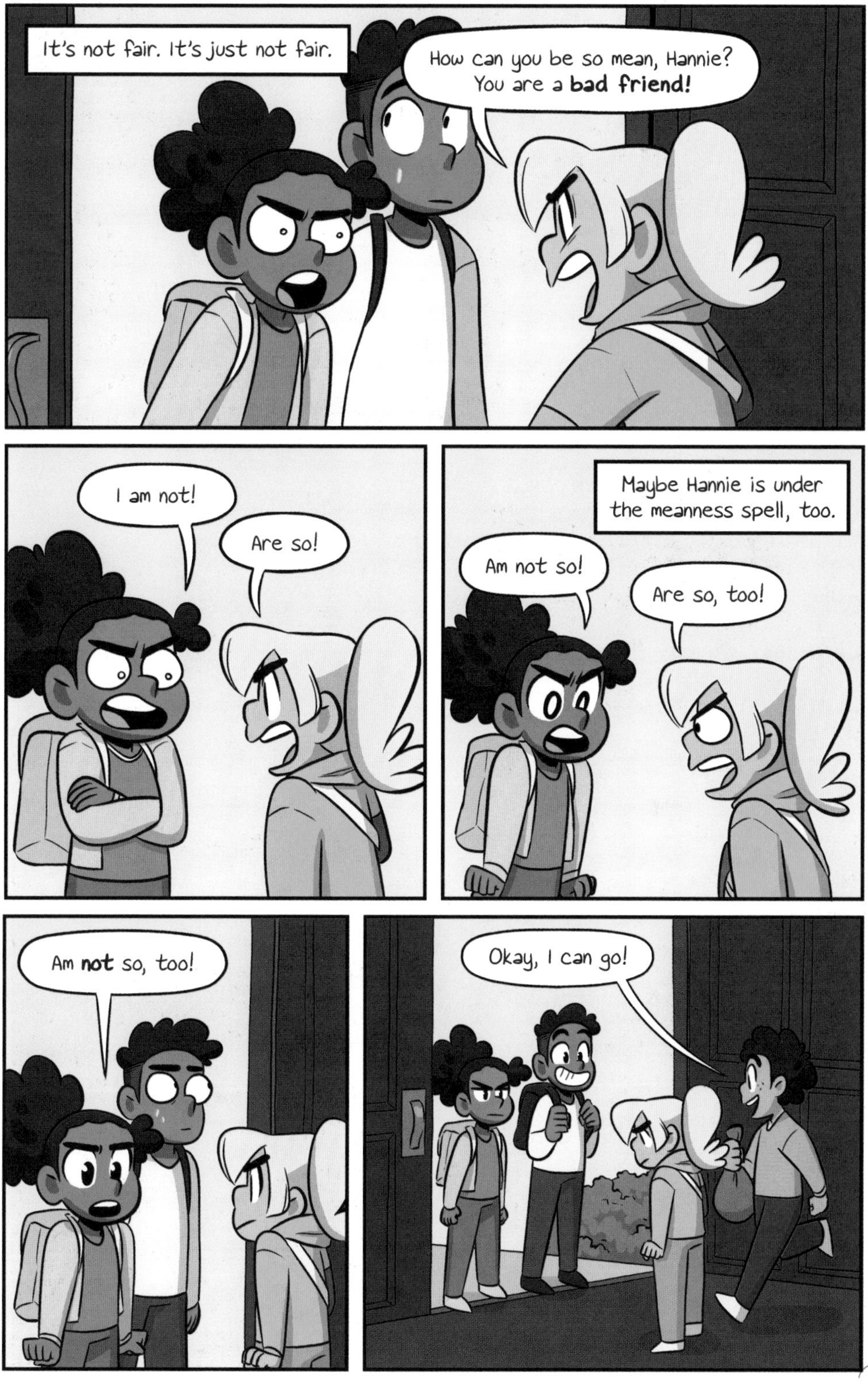
It's not fair. It's just not fair.
How can you be so mean, Hannie? You are a **bad friend!**
I am not!
Are so!
Maybe Hannie is under the meanness spell, too.
Am not so!
Are so, too!
Am **not** so, too!
Okay, I can go!

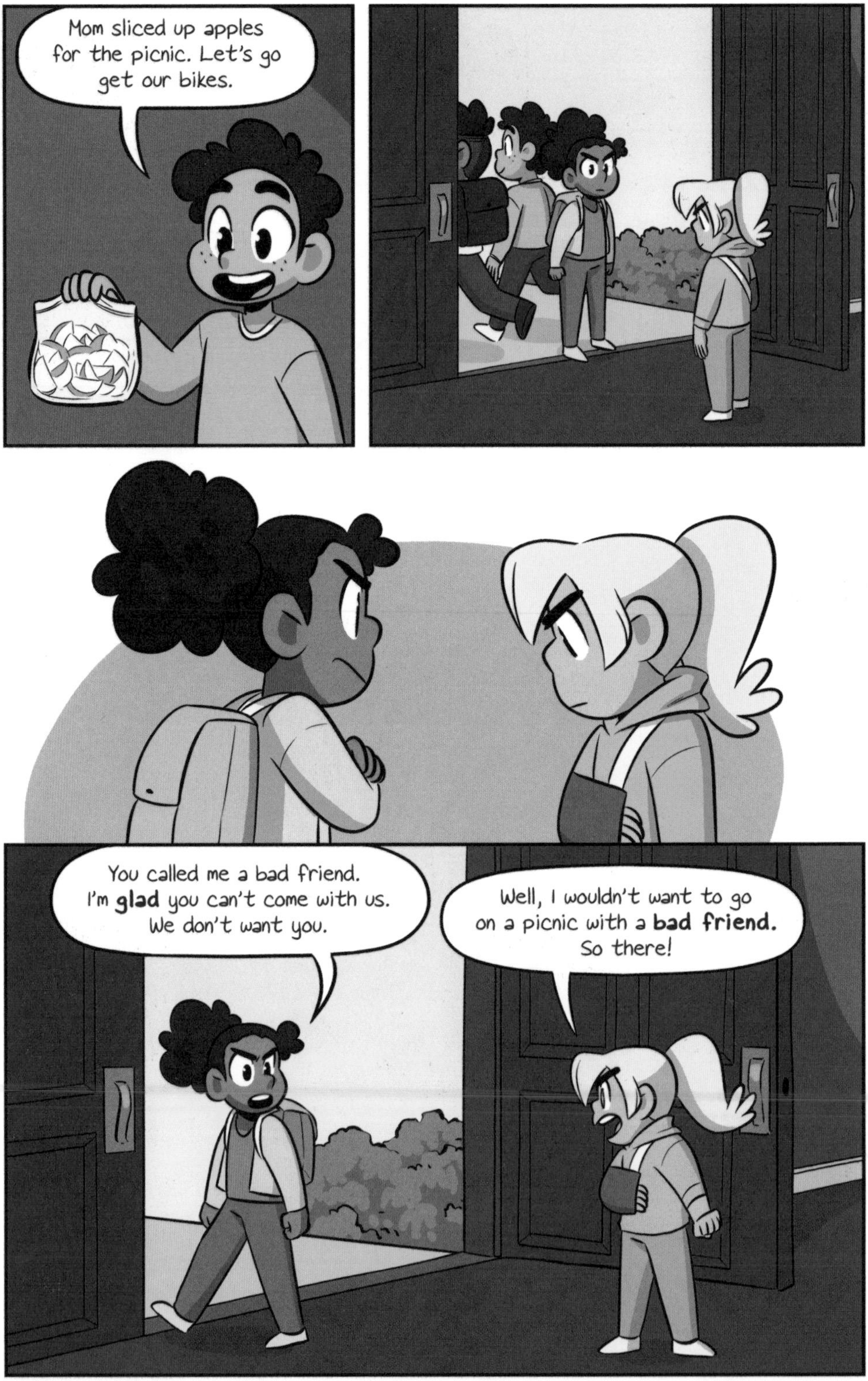
Mom sliced up apples for the picnic. Let's go get our bikes.
You called me a bad friend. I'm **glad** you can't come with us. We don't want you.
Well, I wouldn't want to go on a picnic with a **bad friend.** So there!

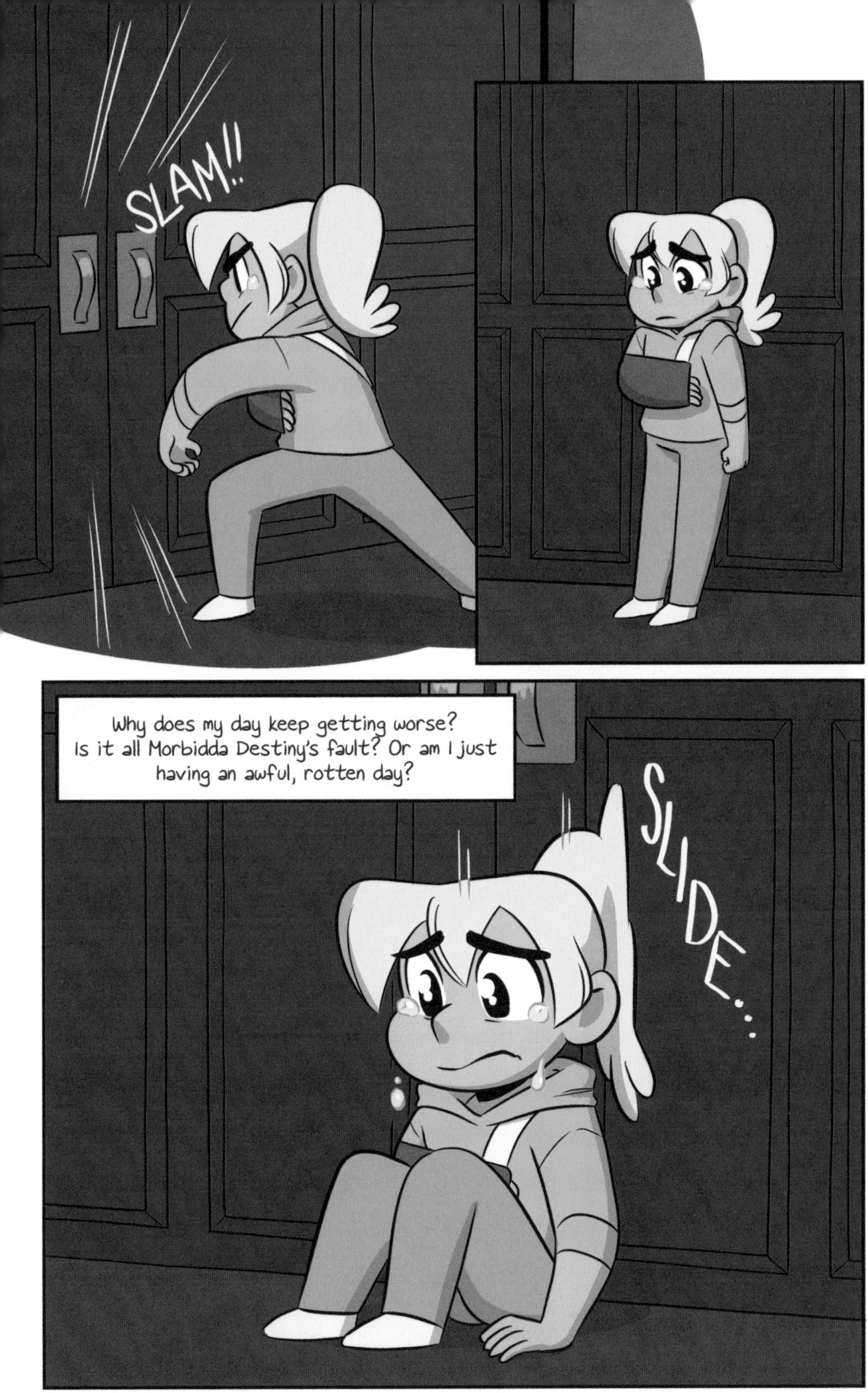
SLAM!!
Why does my day keep getting worse? Is it all Morbidda Destiny's fault? Or am I just having an awful, rotten day?
SLIDE...

CHAPTER 5

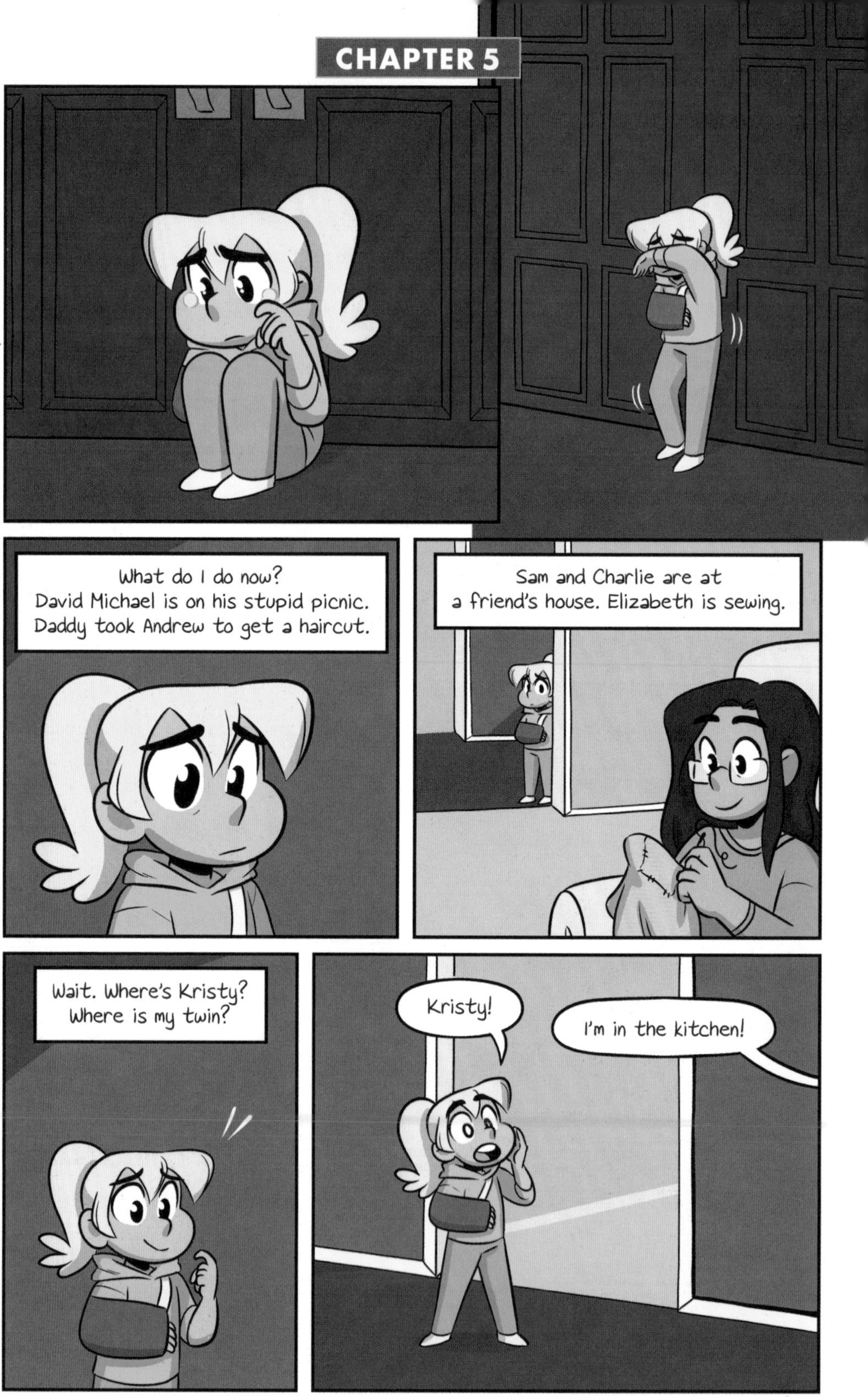
What do I do now?
David Michael is on his stupid picnic.
Daddy took Andrew to get a haircut.
Sam and Charlie are at
a friend's house. Elizabeth is sewing.
Wait. Where's Kristy?
Where is my twin?
Kristy!
I'm in the kitchen!

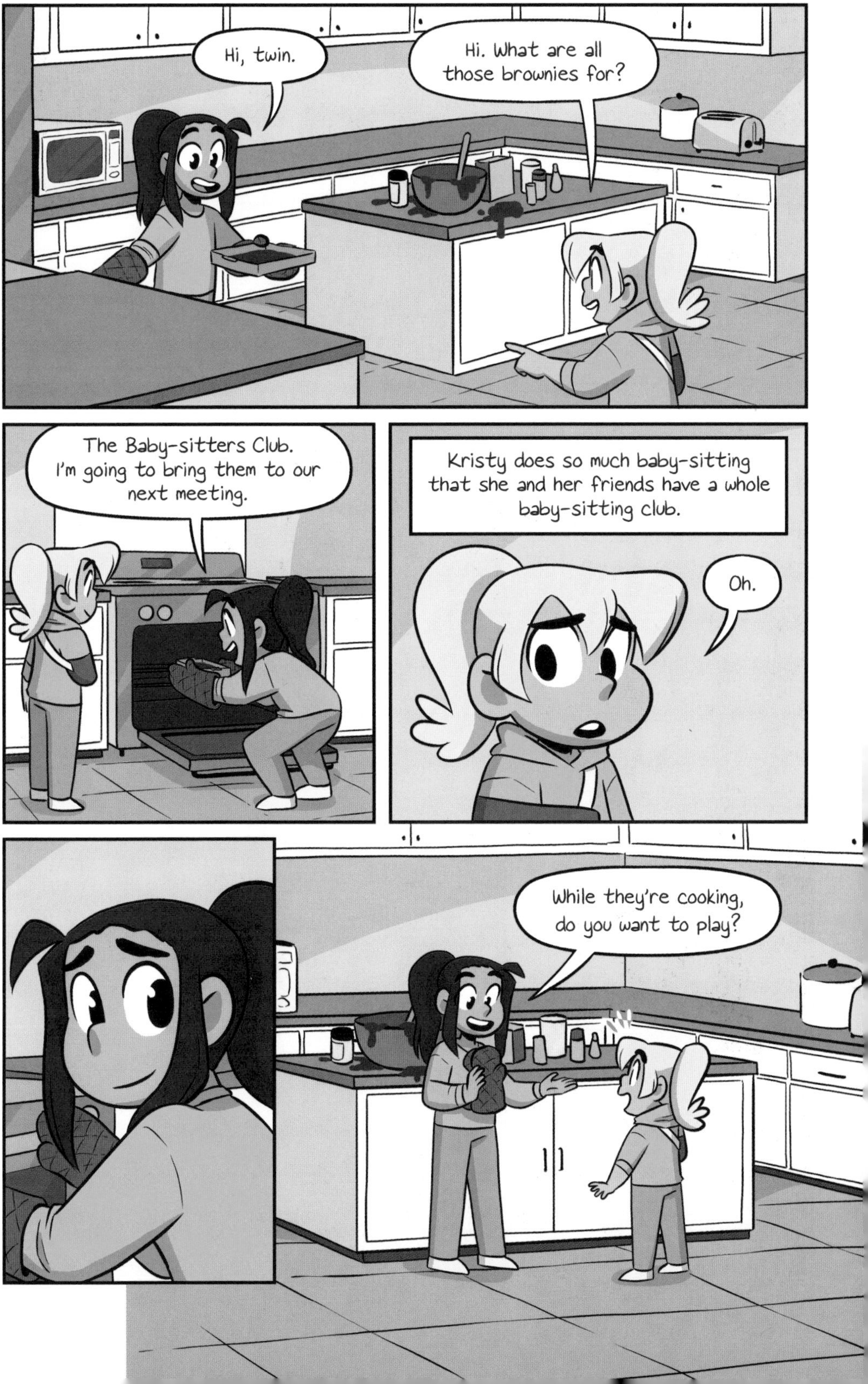
Hi, twin.
Hi. What are all those brownies for?
The Baby-sitters Club. I'm going to bring them to our next meeting.
Kristy does so much baby-sitting that she and her friends have a whole baby-sitting club.
Oh.
While they're cooking, do you want to play?

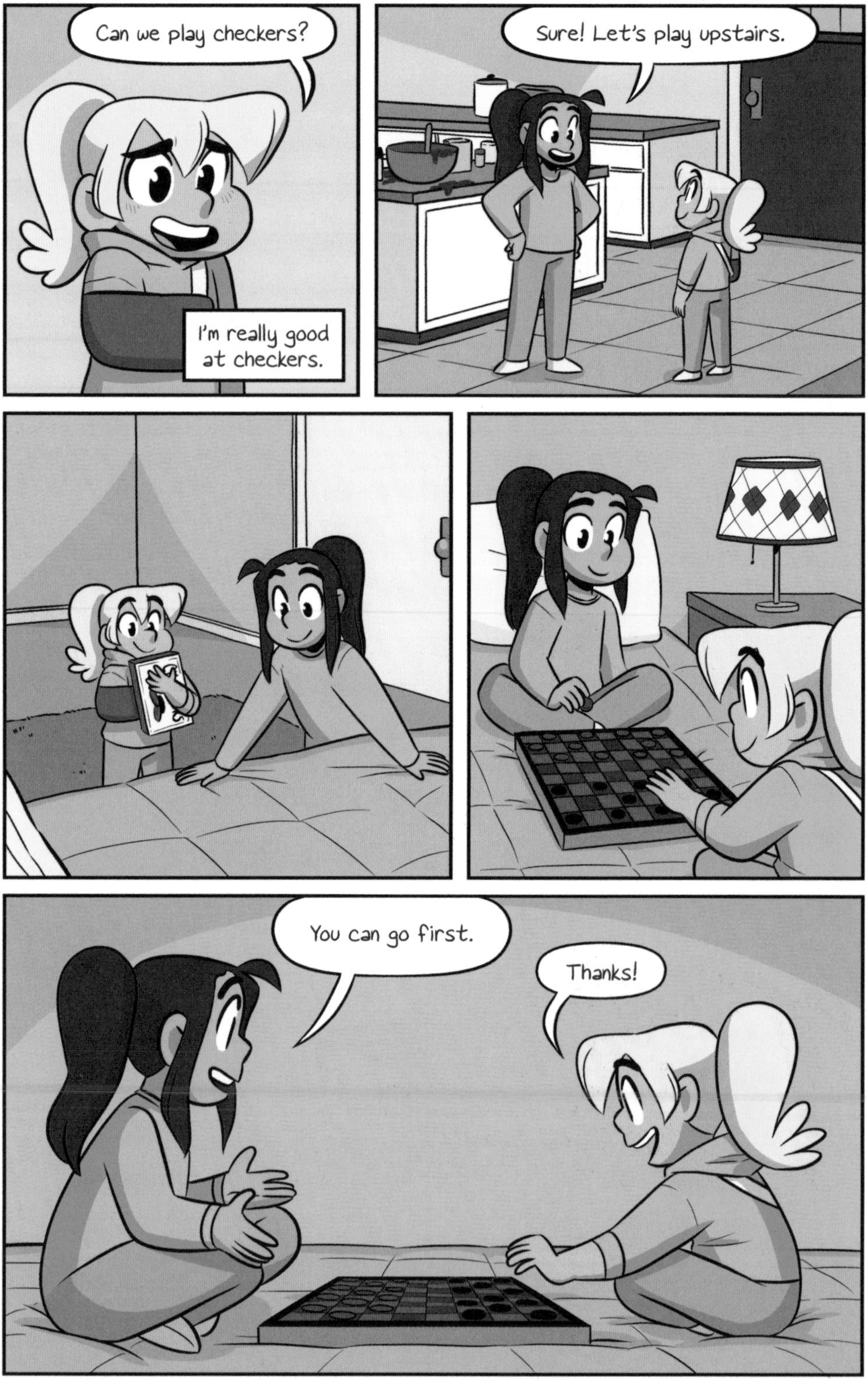
Can we play checkers?
I'm really good at checkers.
Sure! Let's play upstairs.
You can go first.
Thanks!

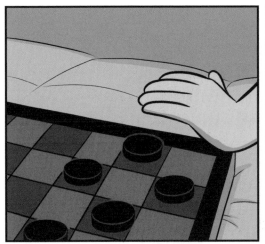

CLACK!

HOP HOP!

Now, don't **let** me win.
I hate when big people do that.

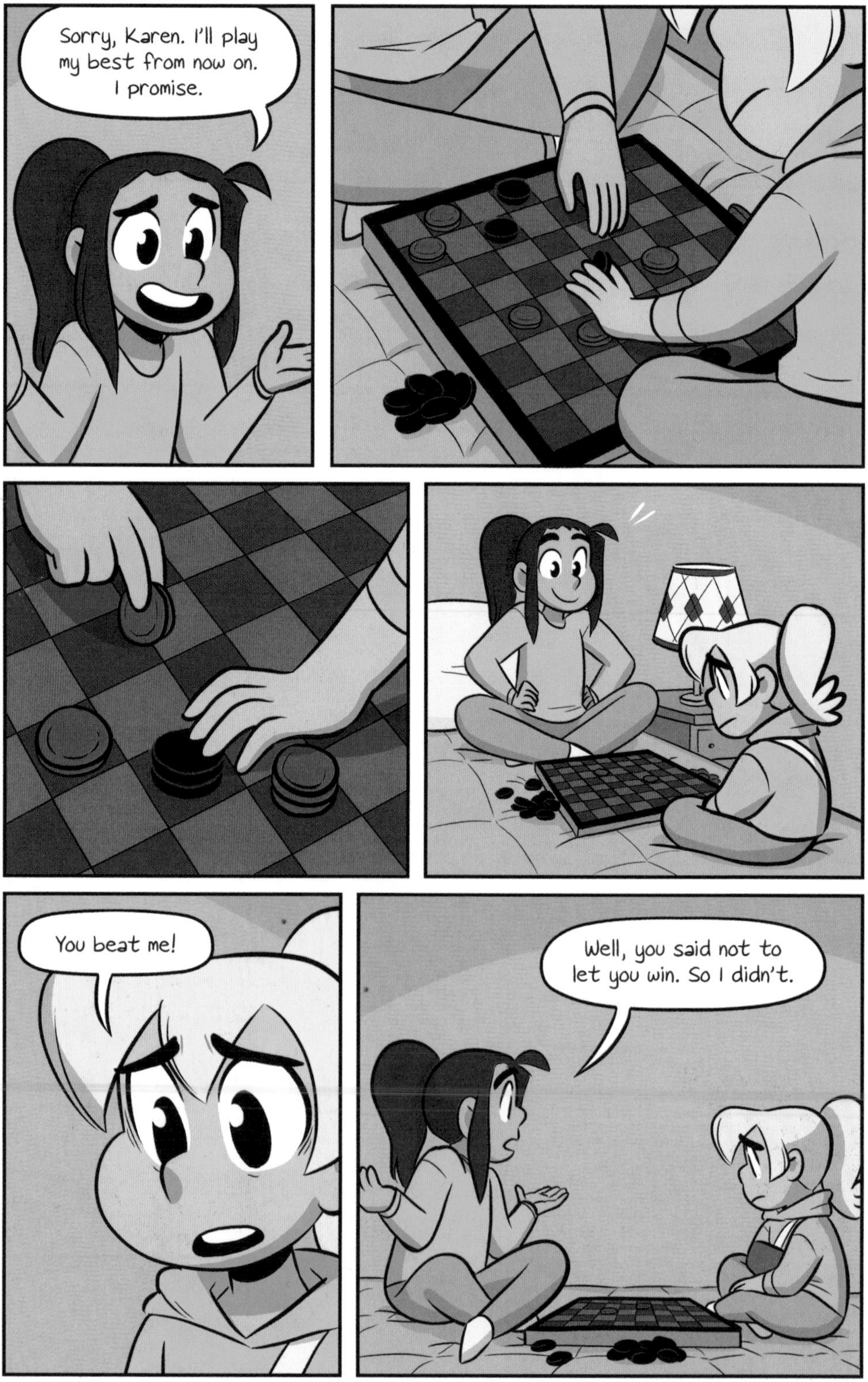

Sorry, Karen. I'll play my best from now on. I promise.
You beat me!
Well, you said not to let you win. So I didn't.

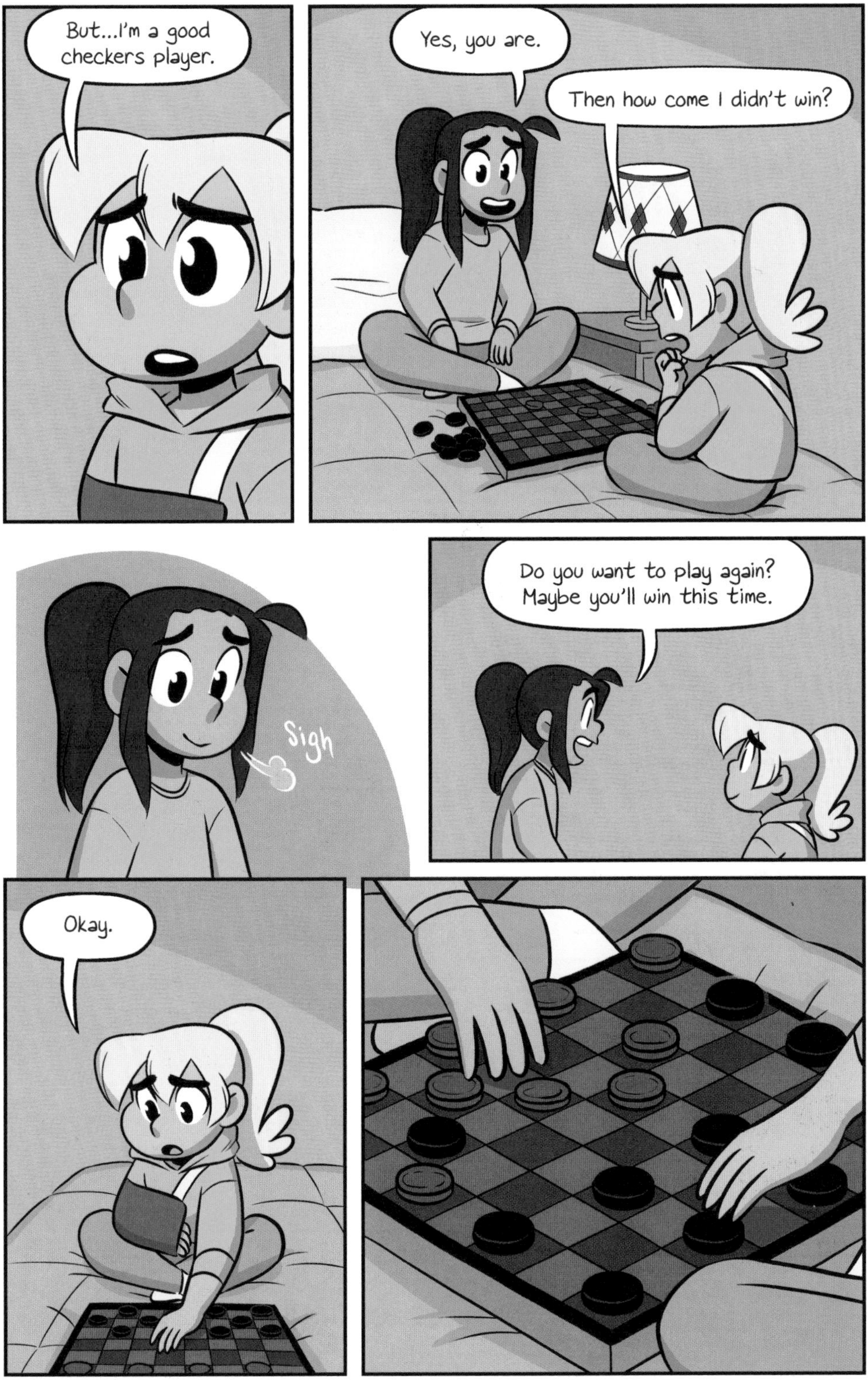

But...I'm a good checkers player.
Yes, you are.
Then how come I didn't win?
Sigh
Do you want to play again? Maybe you'll win this time.
Okay.

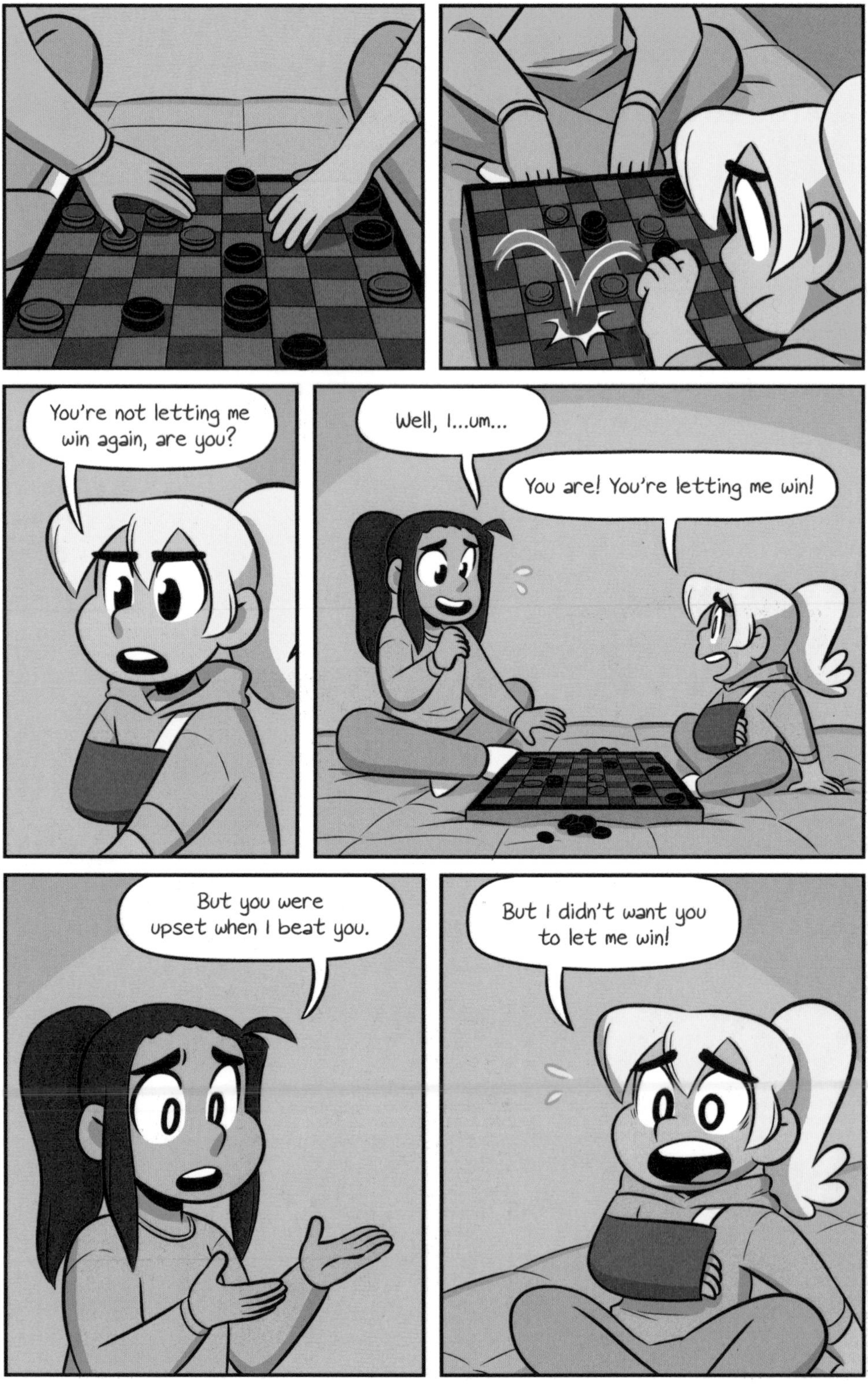
You're not letting me win again, are you?
Well, I...um...
You are! You're letting me win!
But you were upset when I beat you.
But I didn't want you to let me win!

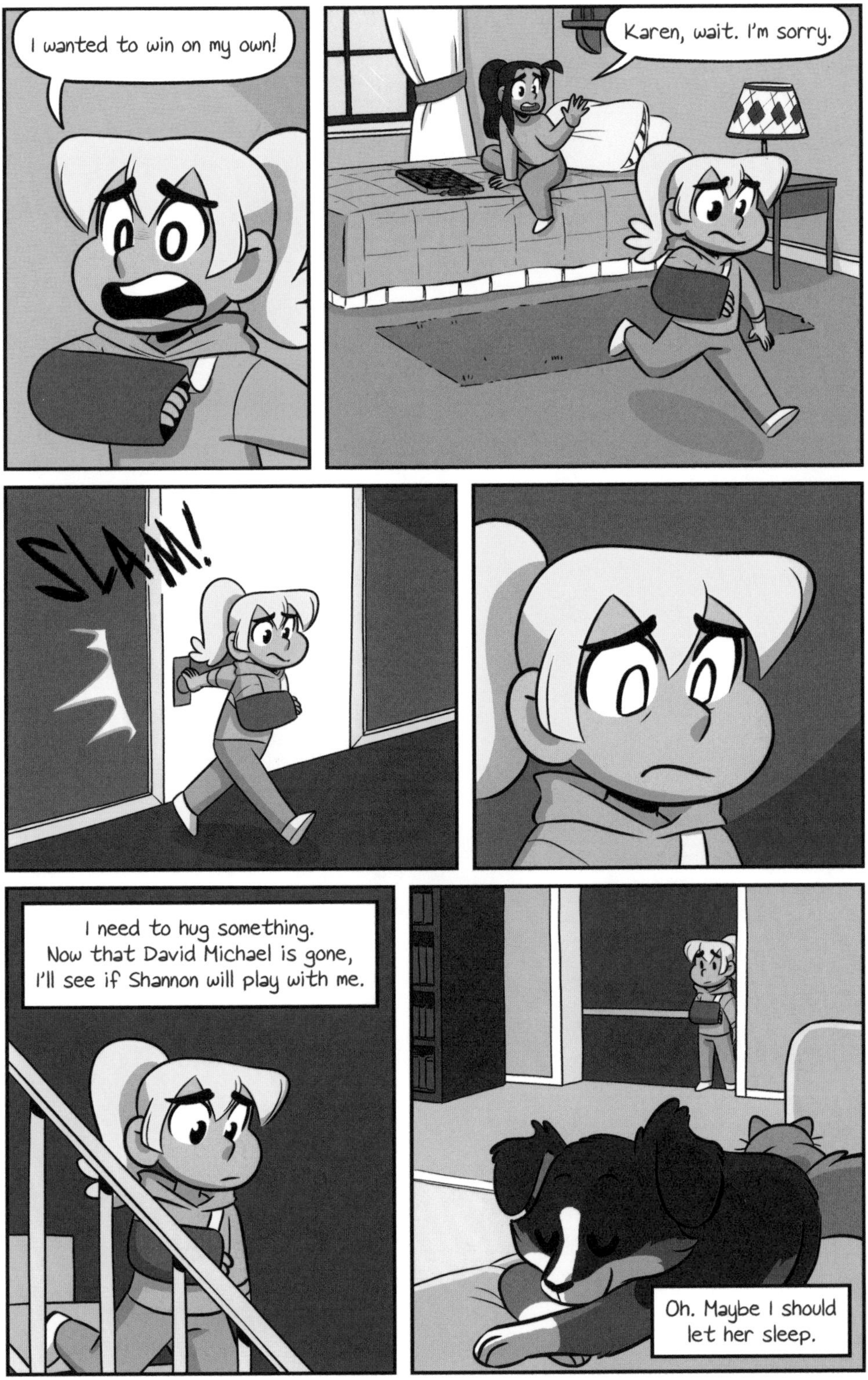
I wanted to win on my own!
Karen, wait. I'm sorry.
SLAM!
I need to hug something. Now that David Michael is gone, I'll see if Shannon will play with me.
Oh. Maybe I should let her sleep.

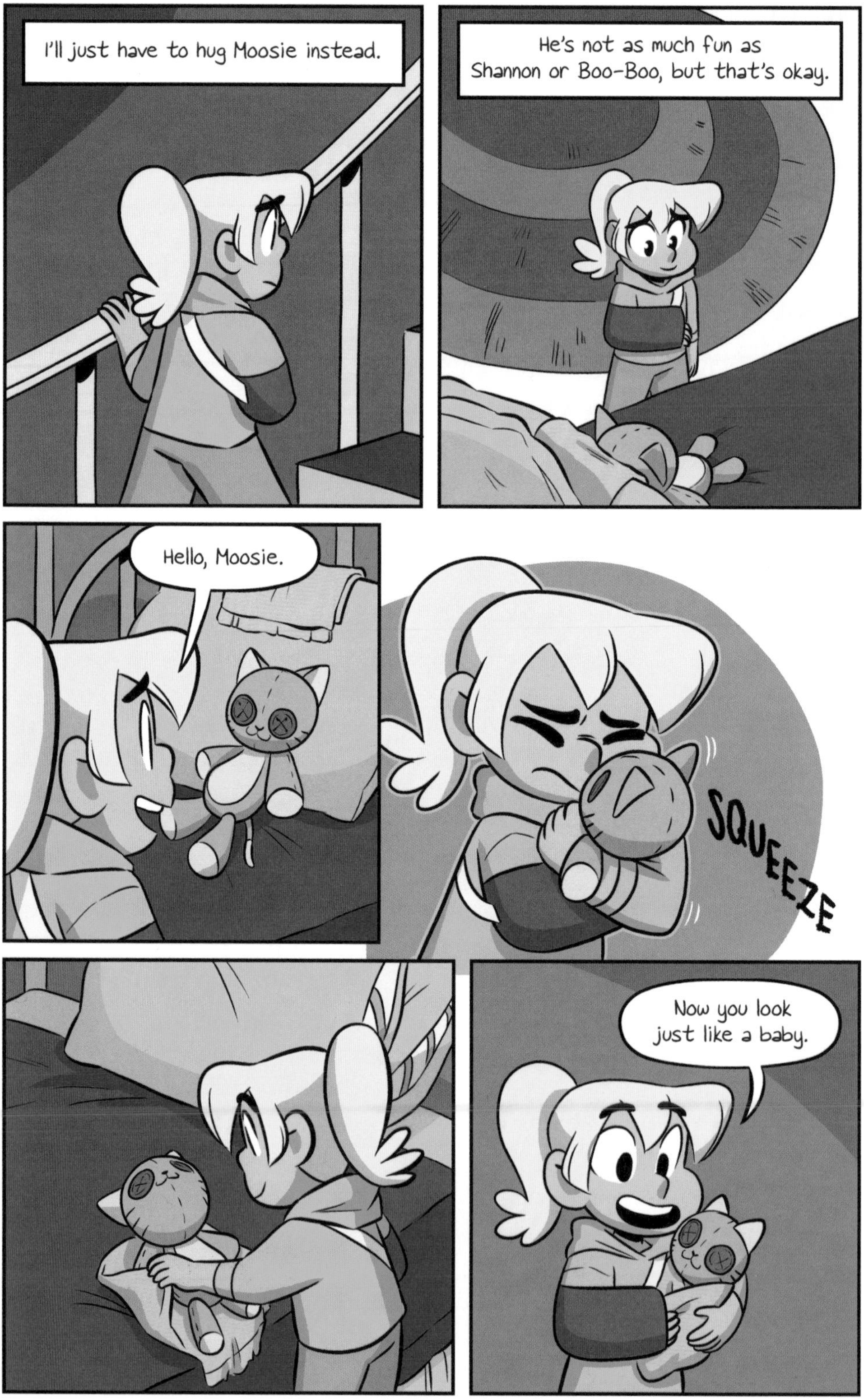

I'll just have to hug Moosie instead.
He's not as much fun as Shannon or Boo-Boo, but that's okay.
Hello, Moosie.
SQUEEZE
Now you look just like a baby.

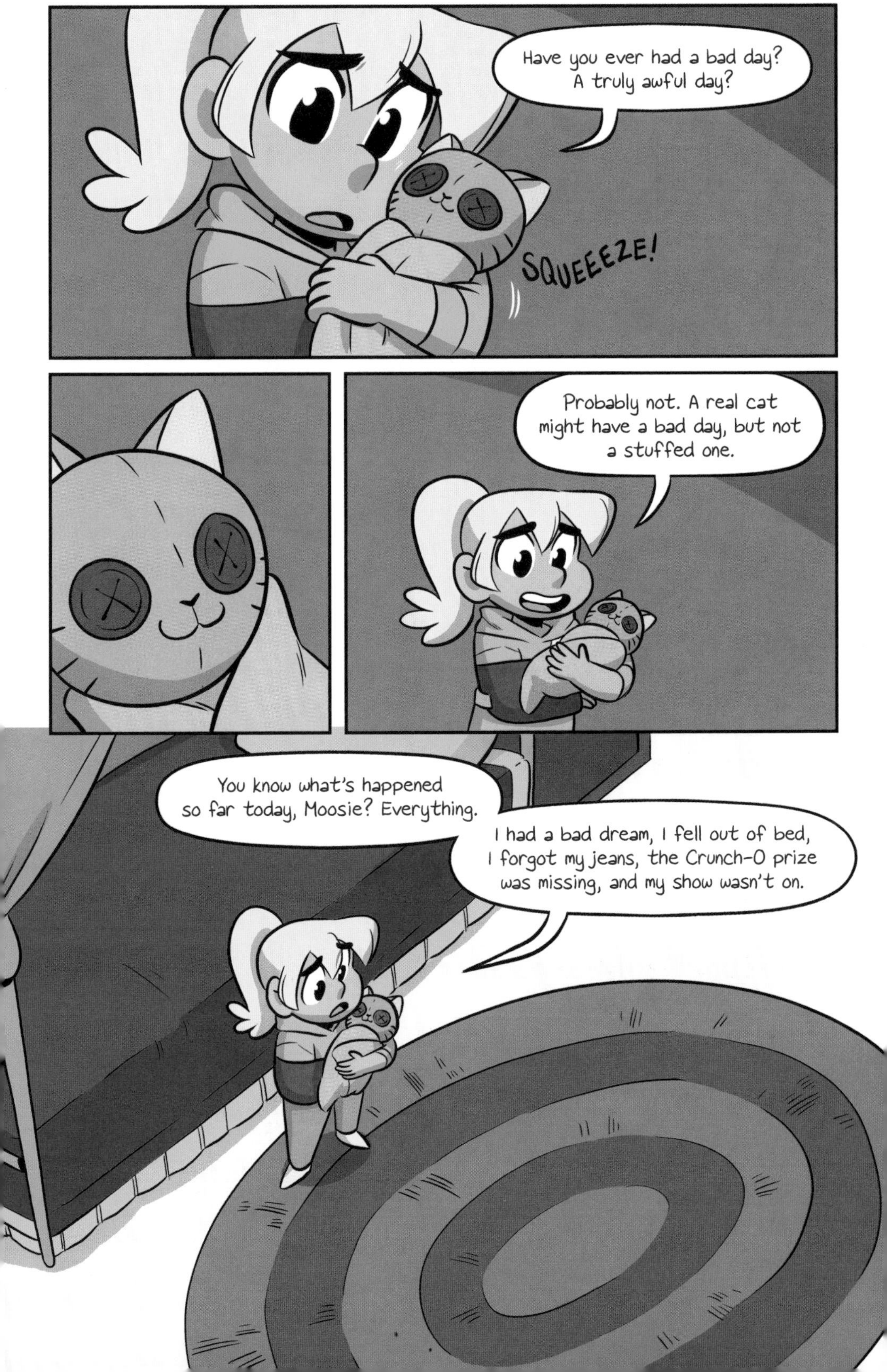
Have you ever had a bad day? A truly awful day?
SQUEEEEZE!
Probably not. A real cat might have a bad day, but not a stuffed one.
You know what's happened so far today, Moosie? Everything.
I had a bad dream, I fell out of bed, I forgot my jeans, the Crunch-O prize was missing, and my show wasn't on.

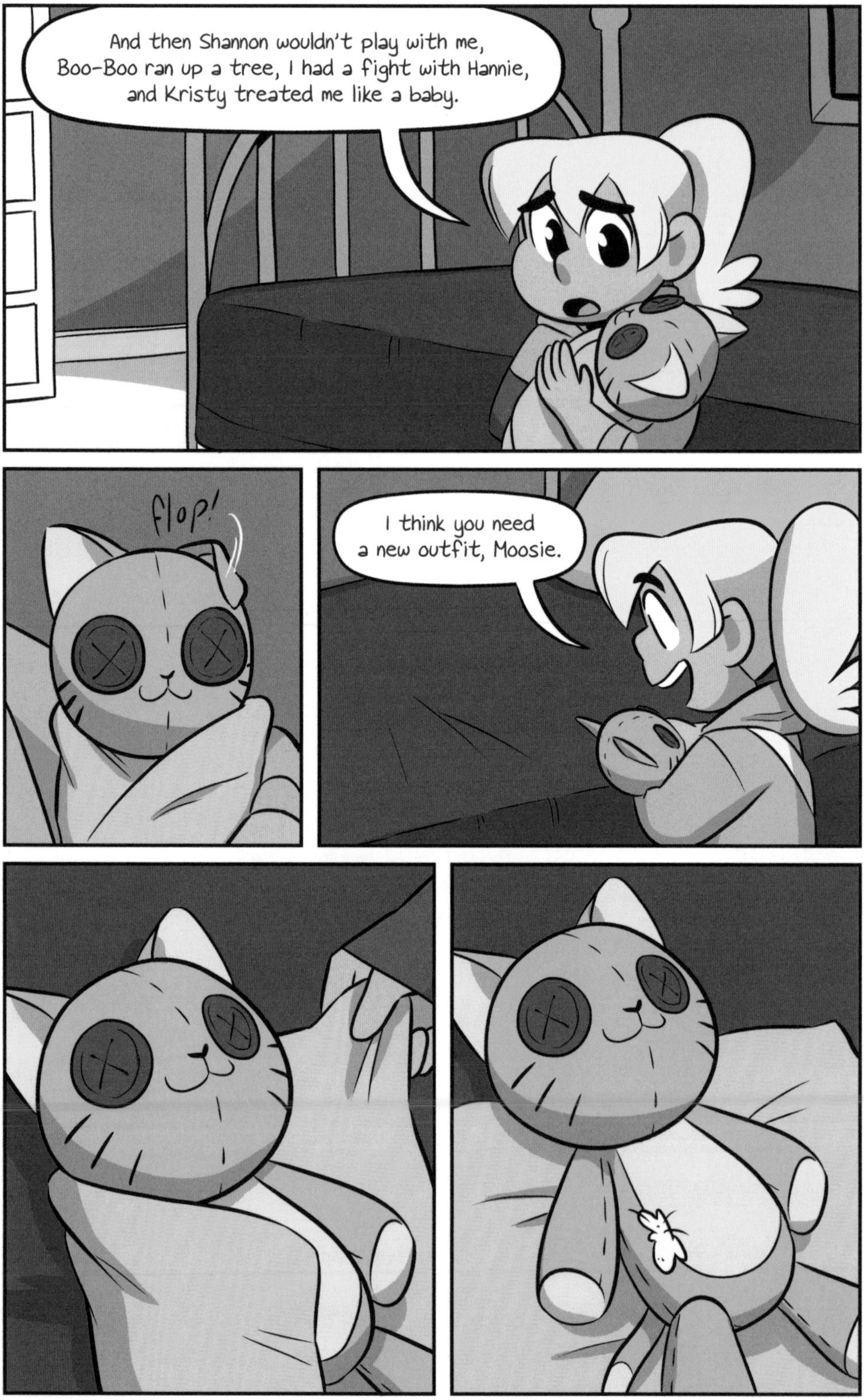
And then Shannon wouldn't play with me, Boo-Boo ran up a tree, I had a fight with Hannie, and Kristy treated me like a baby.
flop!
I think you need a new outfit, Moosie.

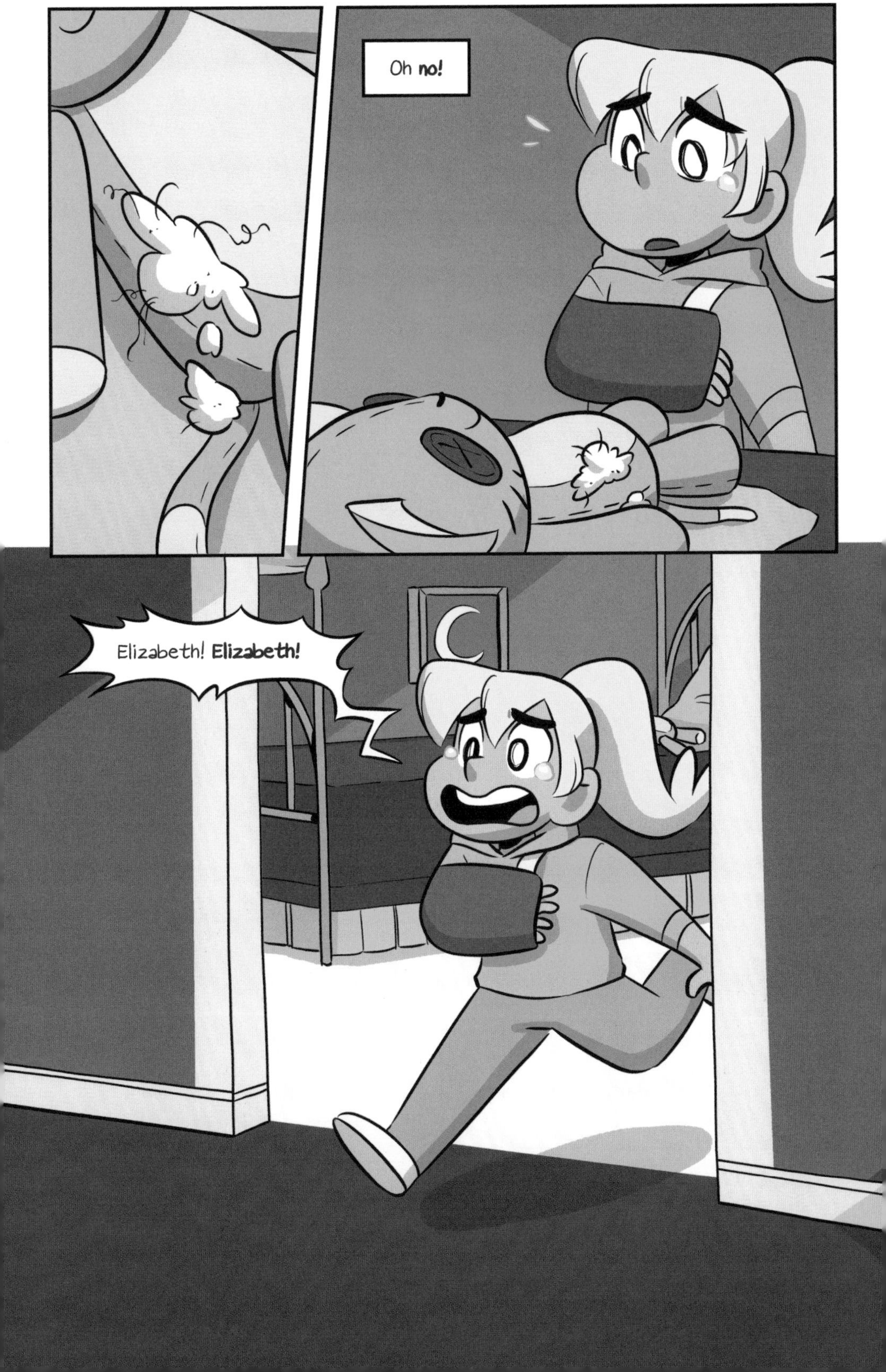
Oh **no!**
Elizabeth! **Elizabeth!**

CHAPTER 6

Karen, what's the matter?

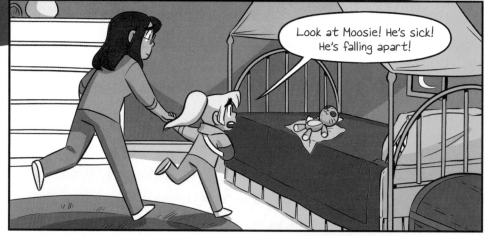

Look at Moosie! He's sick! He's falling apart!

Hmm...

POKE POKE

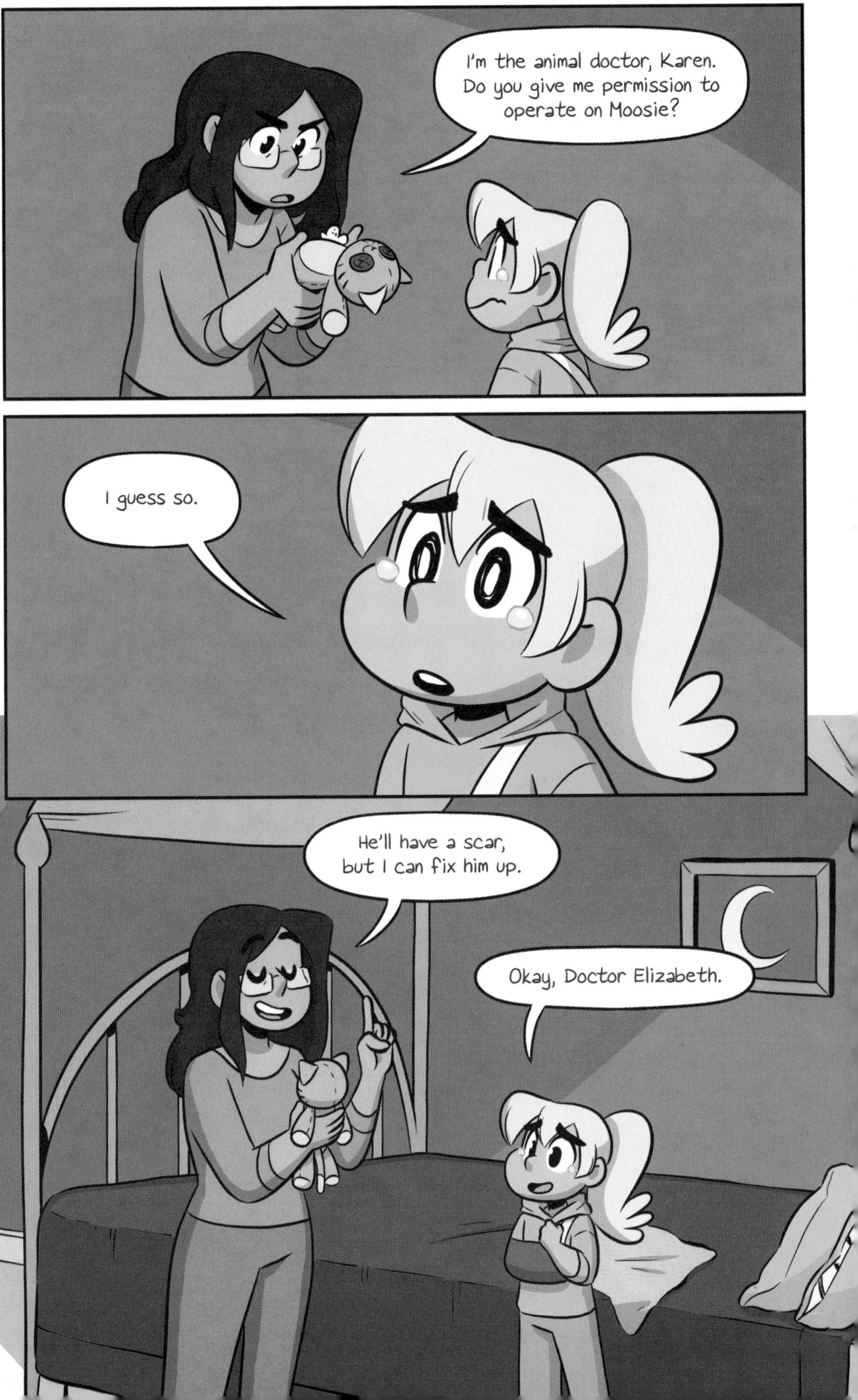
I'm the animal doctor, Karen. Do you give me permission to operate on Moosie?
I guess so.
He'll have a scar, but I can fix him up.
Okay, Doctor Elizabeth.

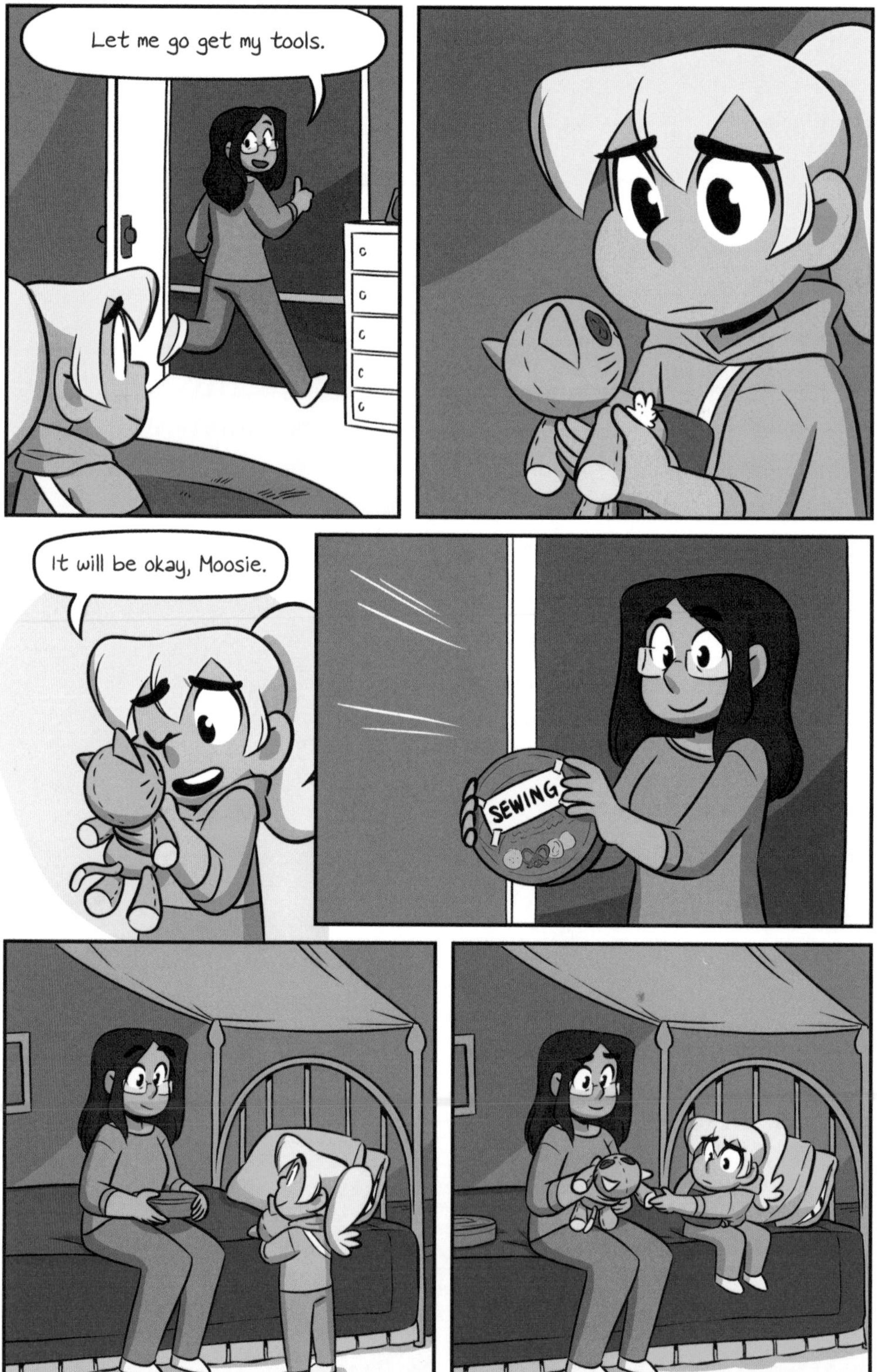
Let me go get my tools.
It will be okay, Moosie.
SEWING

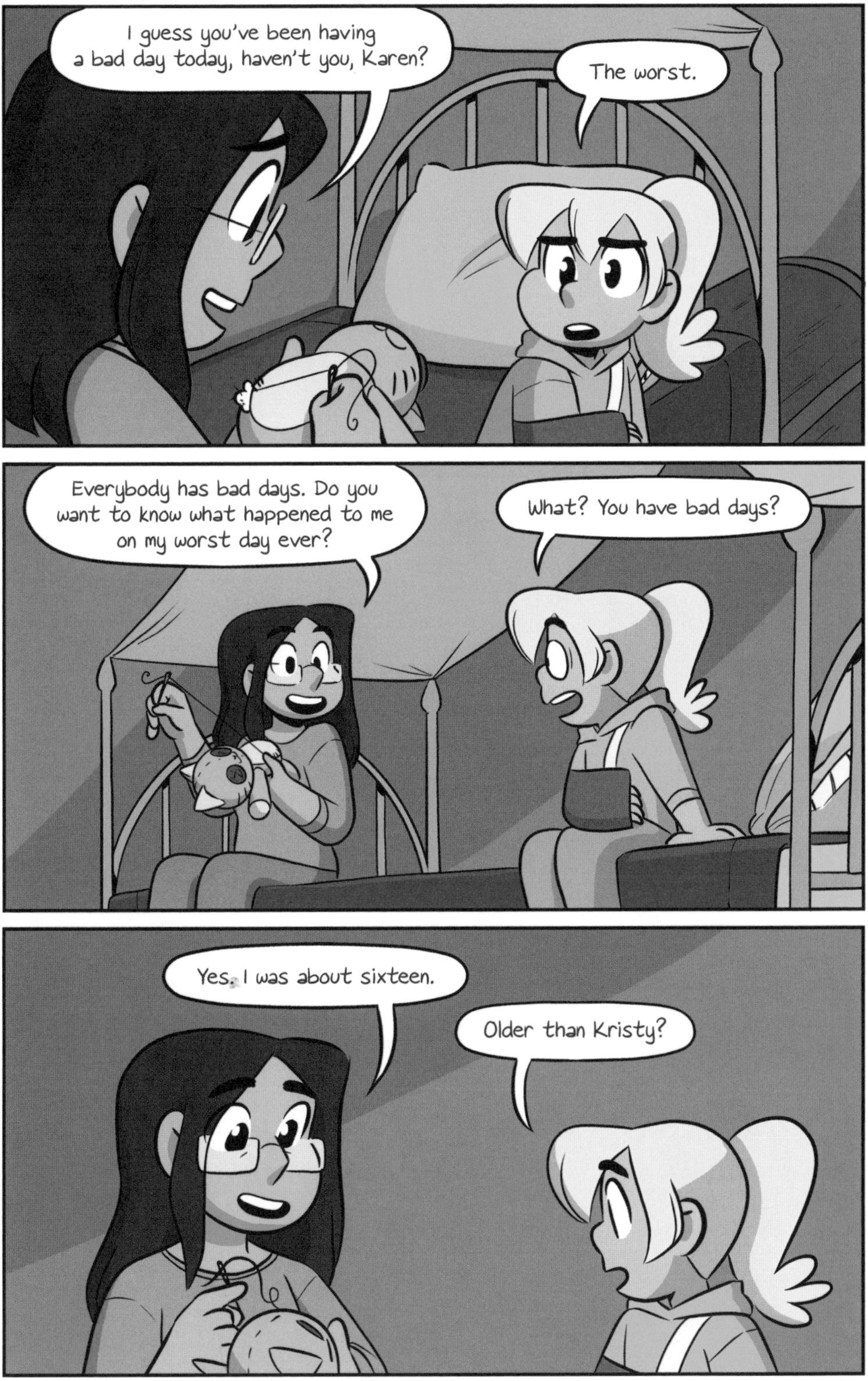
I guess you've been having a bad day today, haven't you, Karen?
The worst.
Everybody has bad days. Do you want to know what happened to me on my worst day ever?
What? You have bad days?
Yes. I was about sixteen.
Older than Kristy?

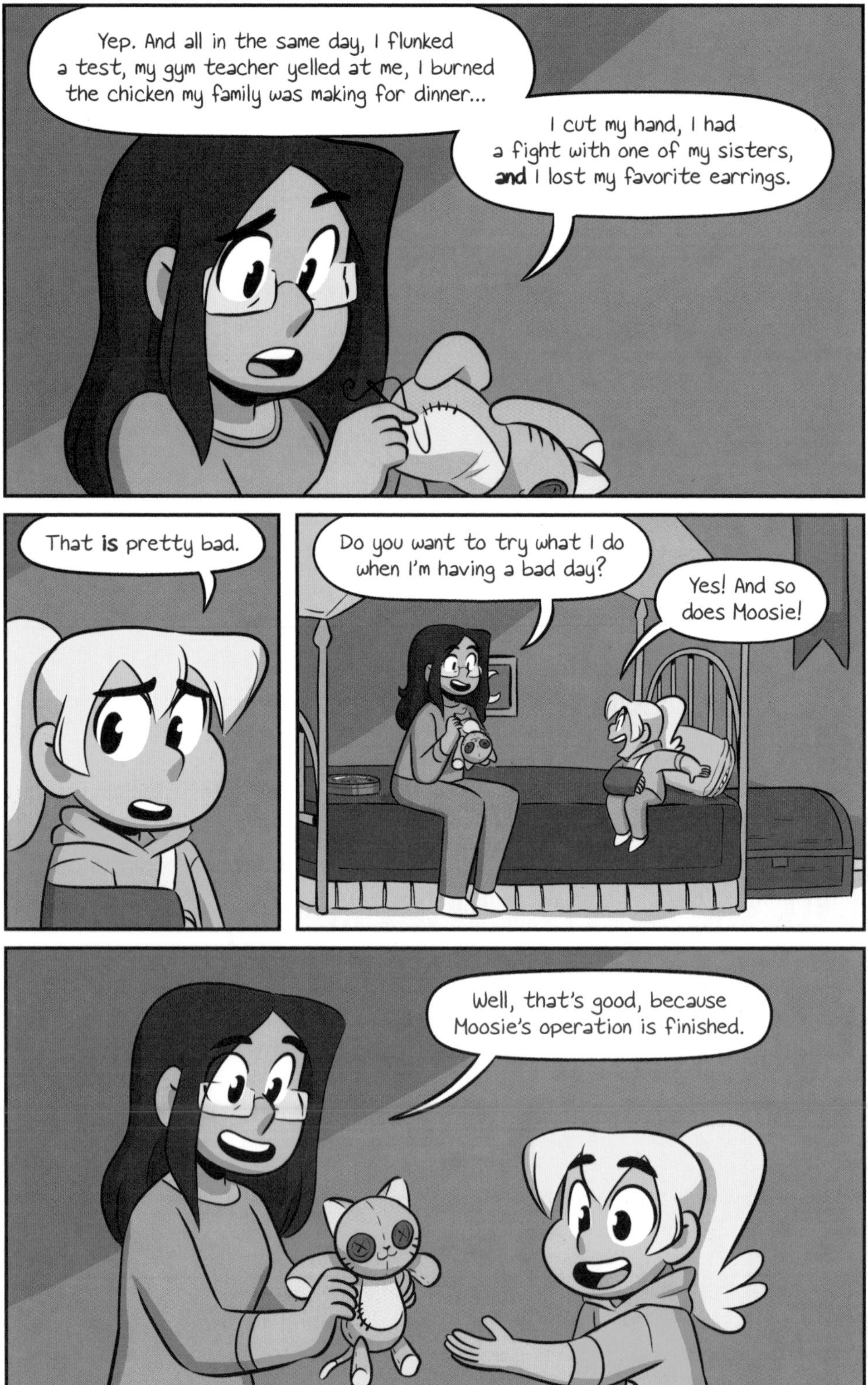

Yep. And all in the same day, I flunked a test, my gym teacher yelled at me, I burned the chicken my family was making for dinner...
I cut my hand, I had a fight with one of my sisters, **and** I lost my favorite earrings.
That **is** pretty bad.
Do you want to try what I do when I'm having a bad day?
Yes! And so does Moosie!
Well, that's good, because Moosie's operation is finished.

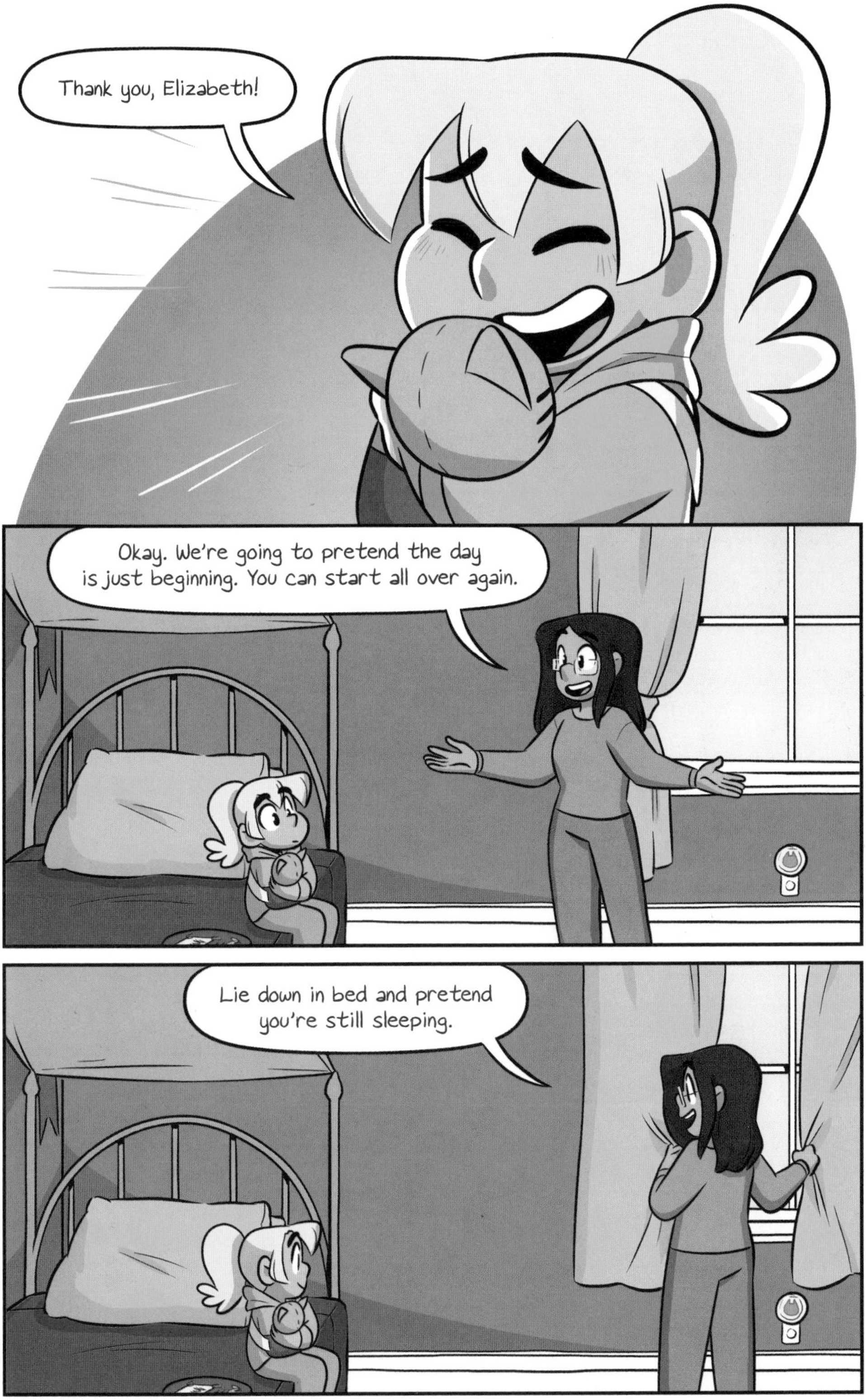
Thank you, Elizabeth!
Okay. We're going to pretend the day is just beginning. You can start all over again.
Lie down in bed and pretend you're still sleeping.

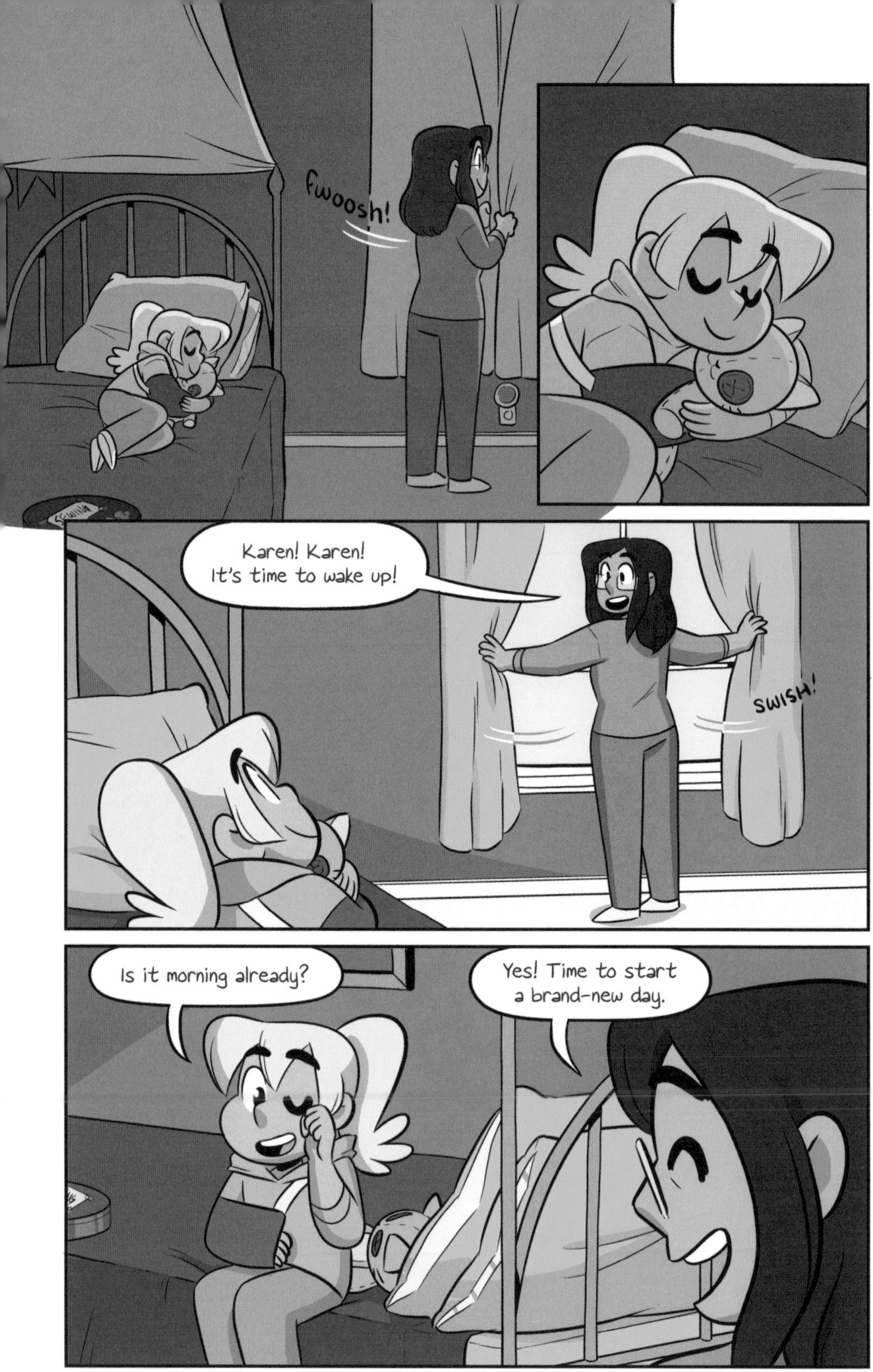
FWOOSH!
SEWING
Karen! Karen!
It's time to wake up!
SWISH!
Is it morning already?
Yes! Time to start
a brand-new day.

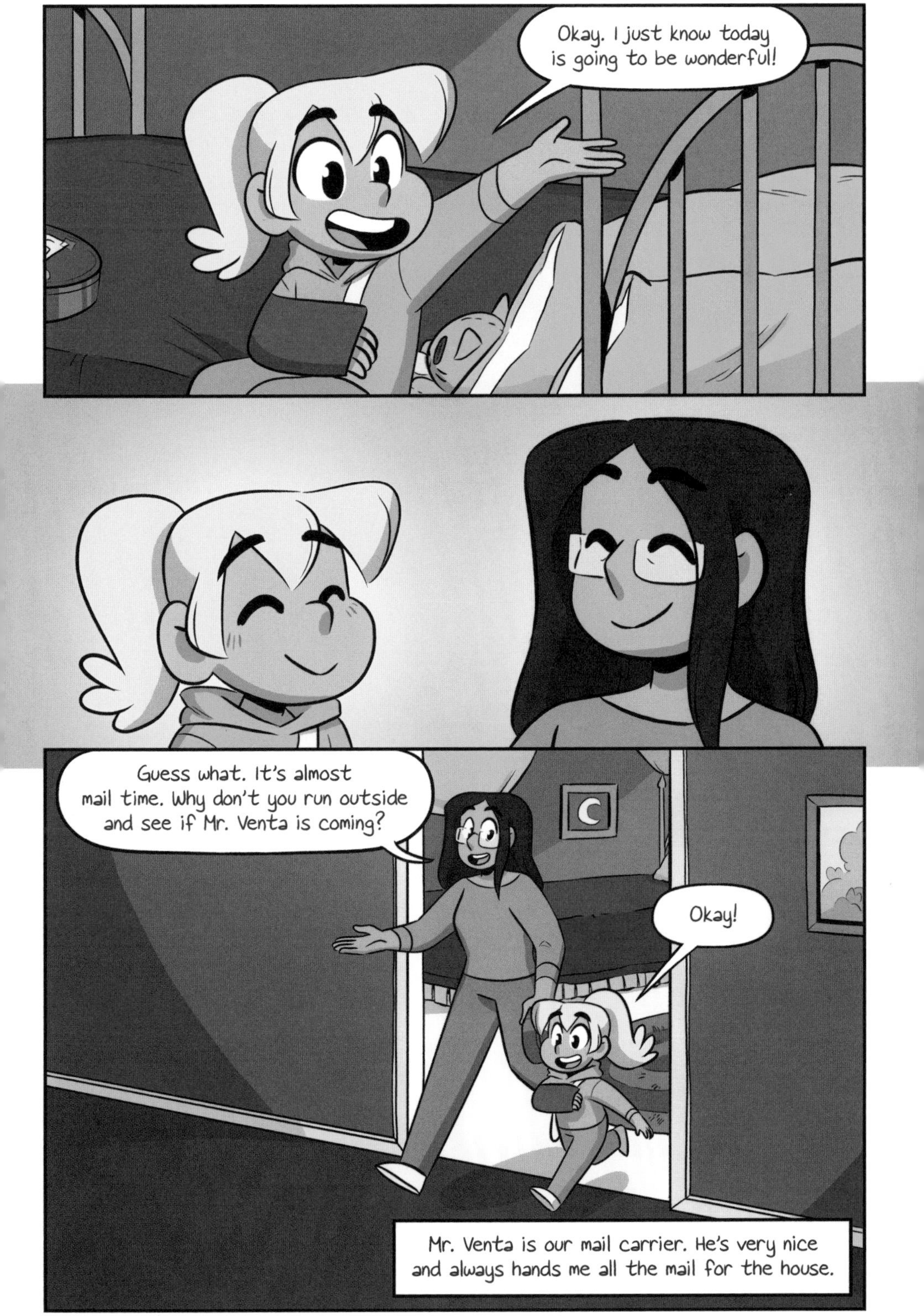
Okay. I just know today is going to be wonderful!
Guess what. It's almost mail time. Why don't you run outside and see if Mr. Venta is coming?
Okay!
Mr. Venta is our mail carrier. He's very nice and always hands me all the mail for the house.

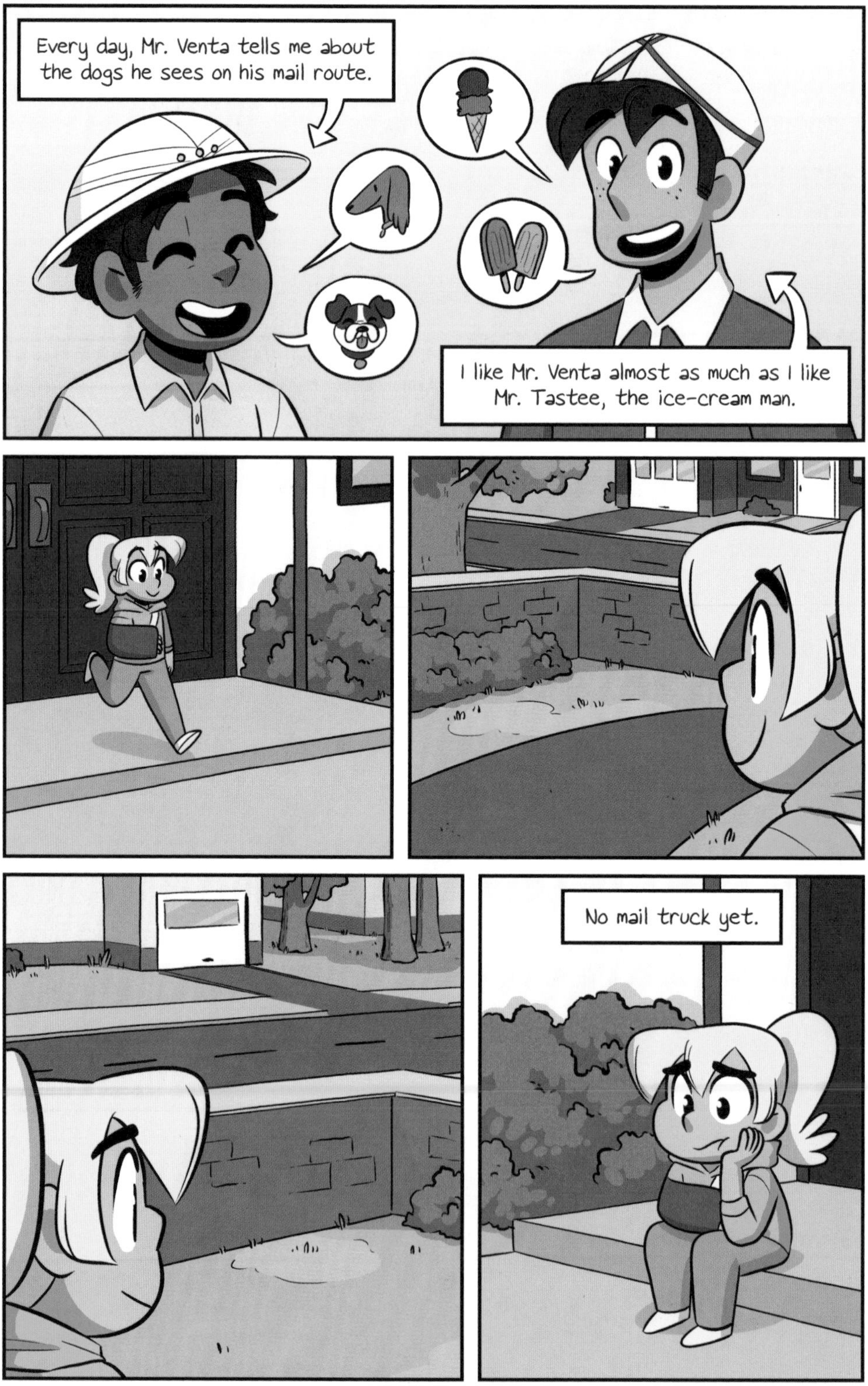
Every day, Mr. Venta tells me about the dogs he sees on his mail route.
I like Mr. Venta almost as much as I like Mr. Tastee, the ice-cream man.
No mail truck yet.

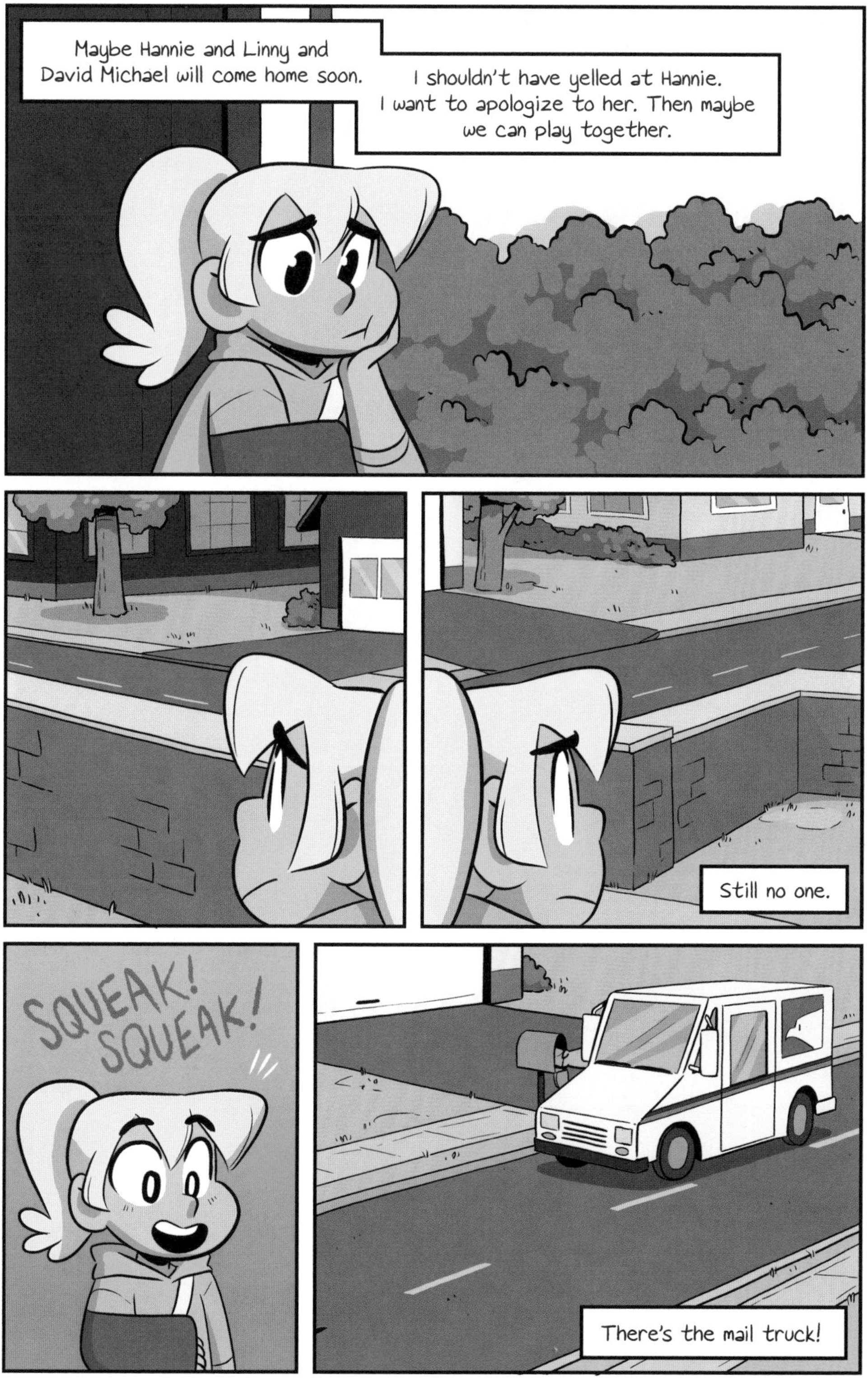

Maybe Hannie and Linny and David Michael will come home soon.
I shouldn't have yelled at Hannie. I want to apologize to her. Then maybe we can play together.
Still no one.
SQUEAK! SQUEAK!
There's the mail truck!

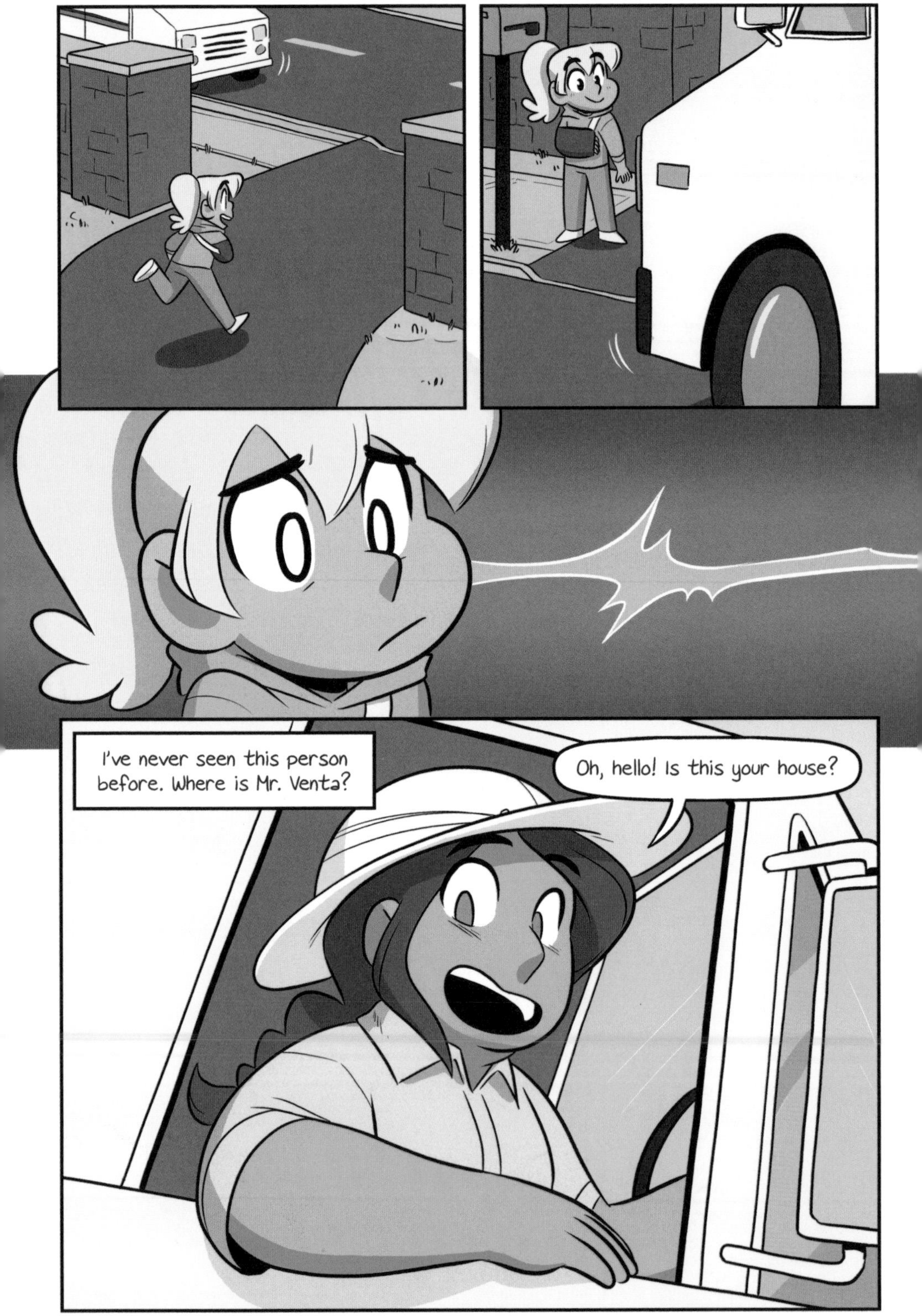
I've never seen this person before. Where is Mr. Venta?
Oh, hello! Is this your house?

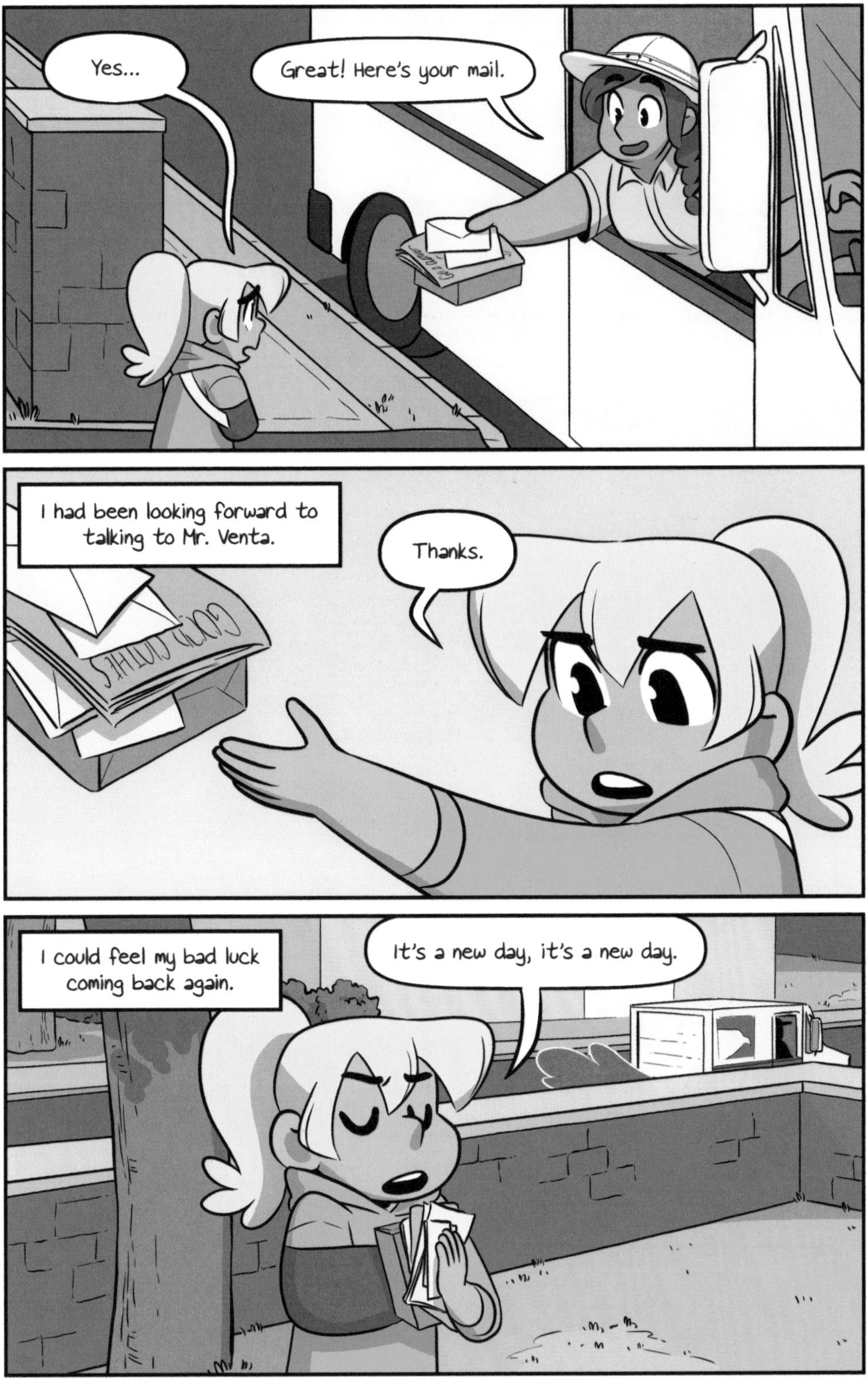
Yes...
Great! Here's your mail.
I had been looking forward to talking to Mr. Venta.
Thanks.
I could feel my bad luck coming back again.
It's a new day, it's a new day.

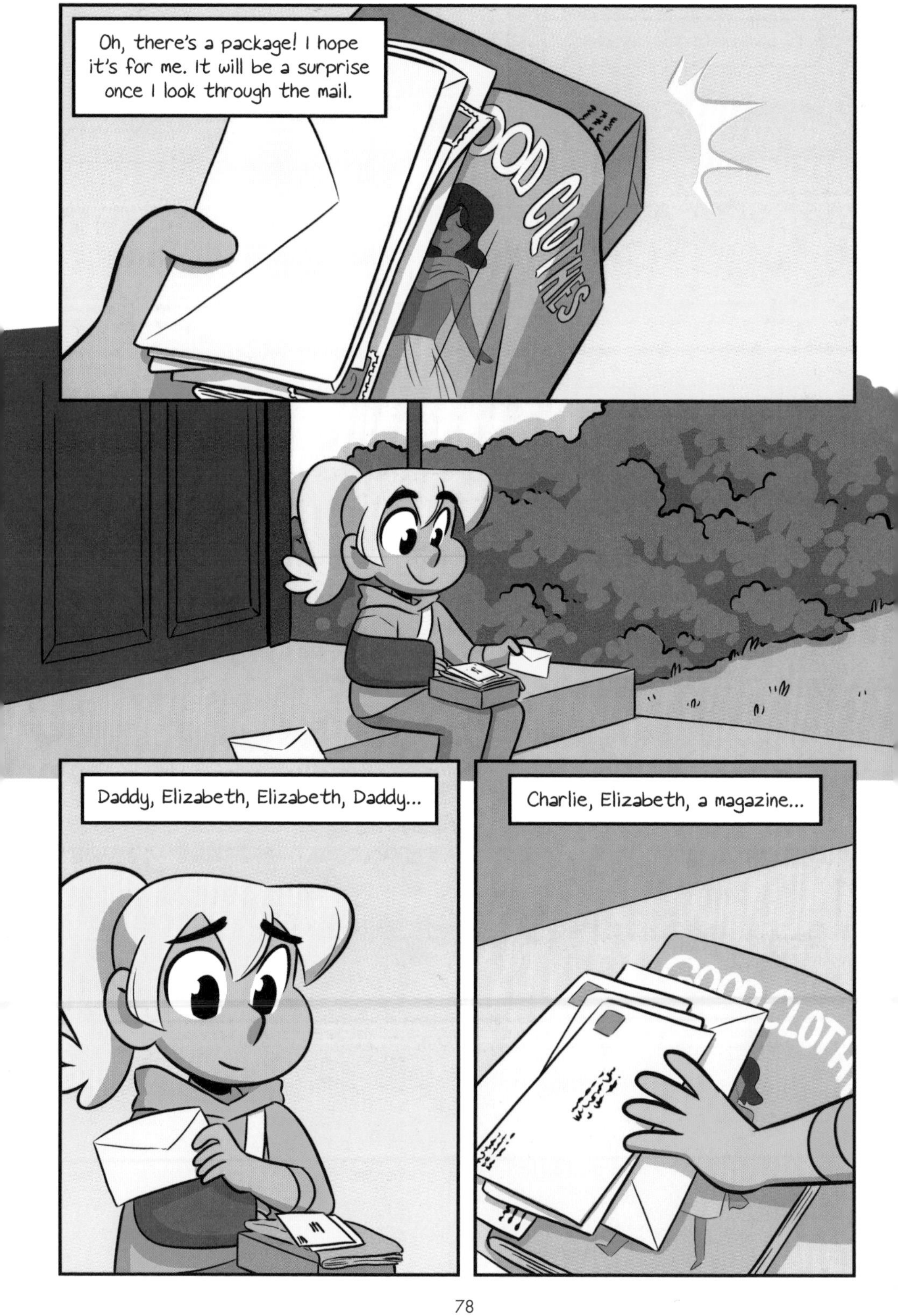
Oh, there's a package! I hope it's for me. It will be a surprise once I look through the mail.
GOOD CLOTHES
Daddy, Elizabeth, Elizabeth, Daddy...
Charlie, Elizabeth, a magazine...

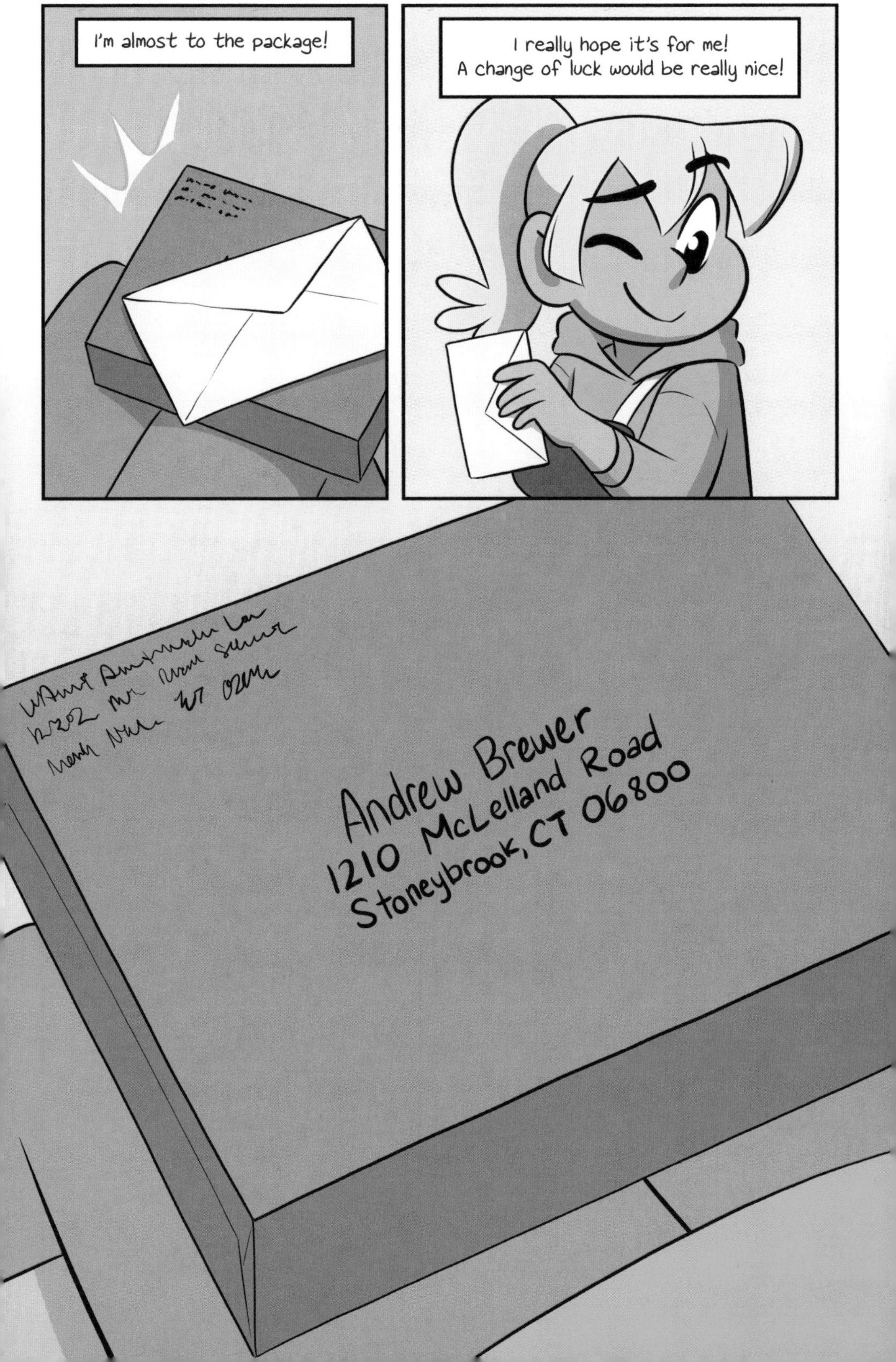
I'm almost to the package!
I really hope it's for me!
A change of luck would be really nice!
Andrew Brewer
1210 McLelland Road
Stoneybrook, CT 06800

CHAPTER 7

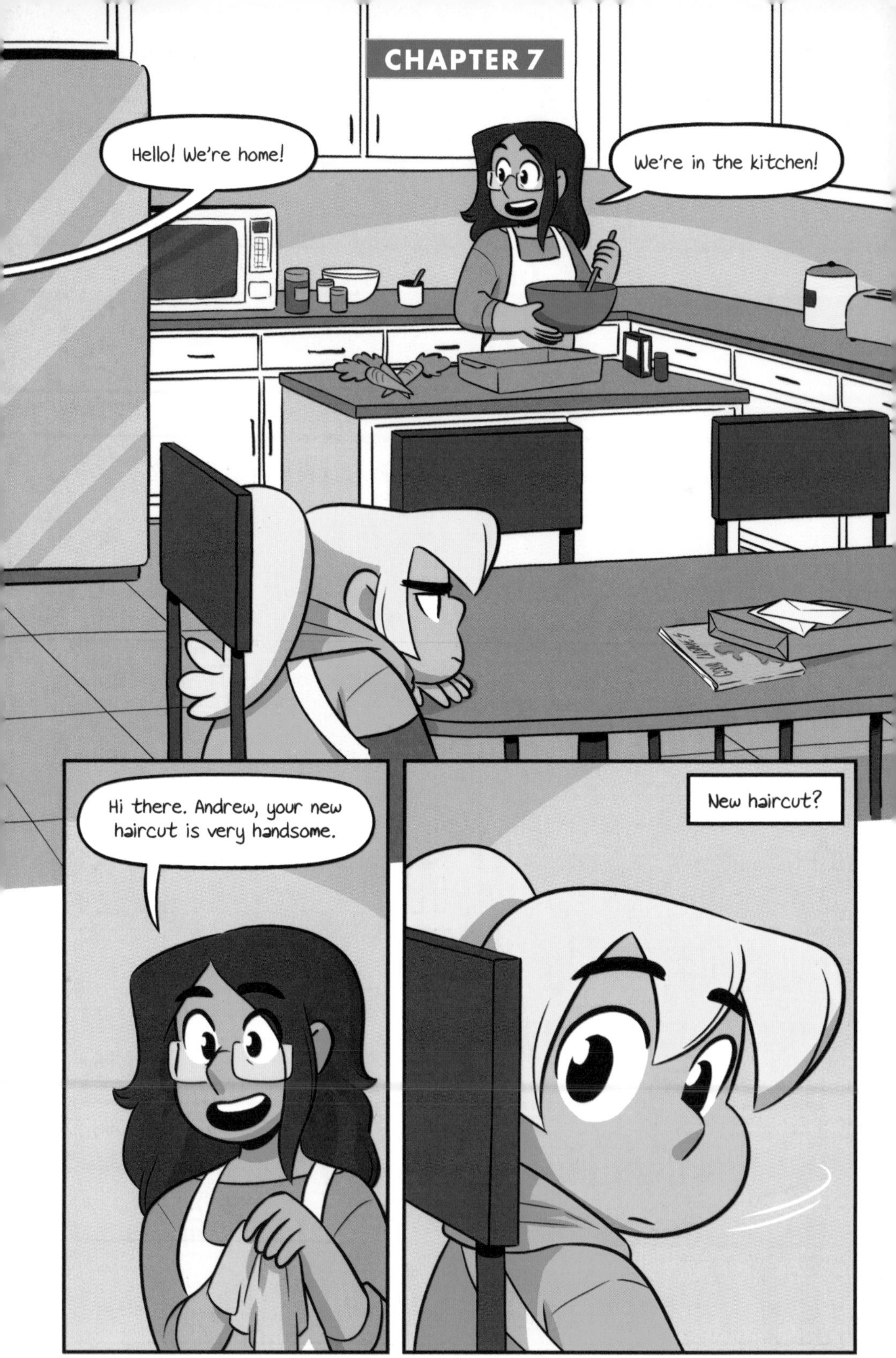
Hello! We're home!
We're in the kitchen!
Hi there. Andrew, your new haircut is very handsome.
New haircut?

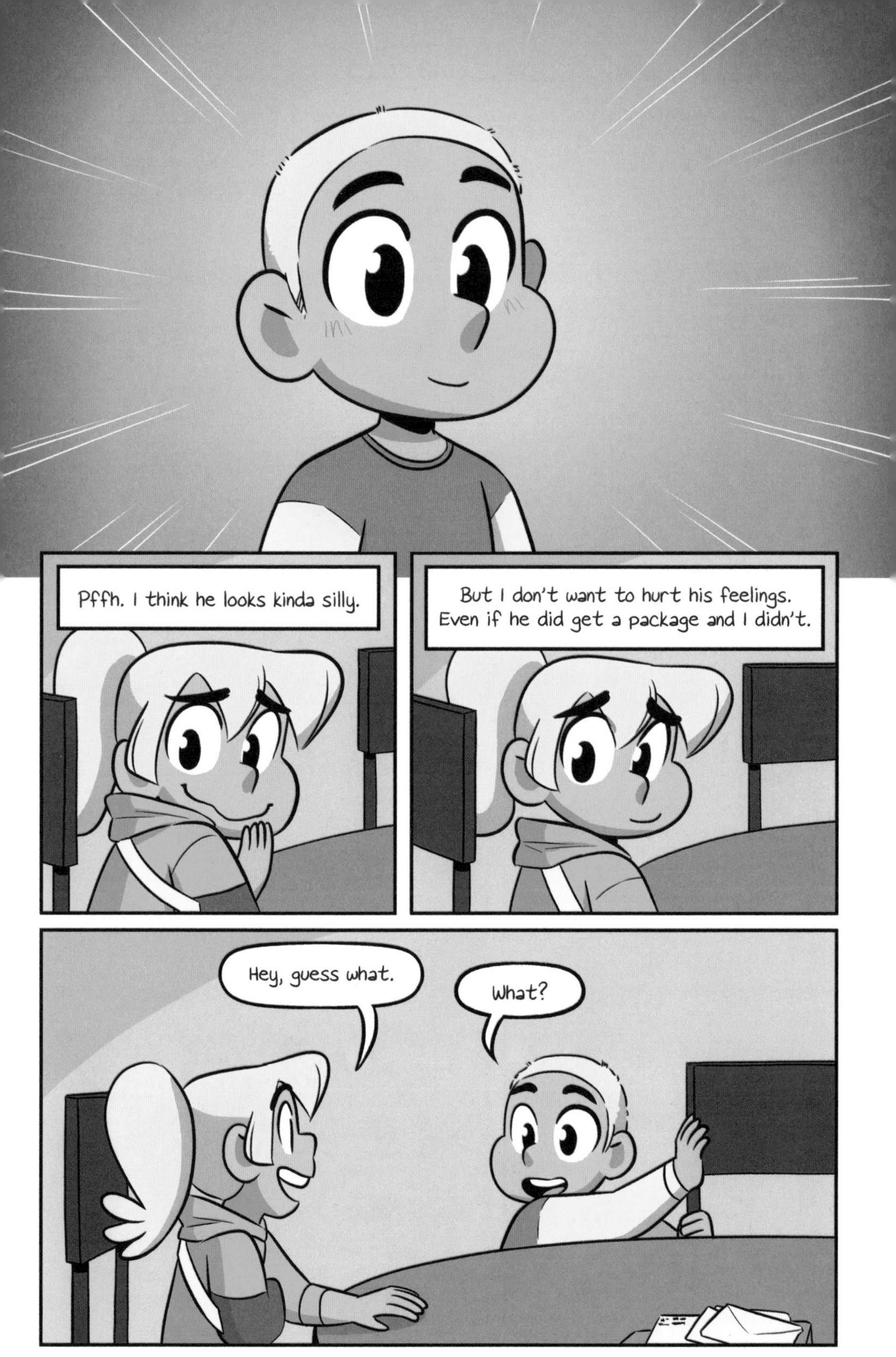
Pffh. I think he looks kinda silly.
But I don't want to hurt his feelings. Even if he did get a package and I didn't.
Hey, guess what.
What?

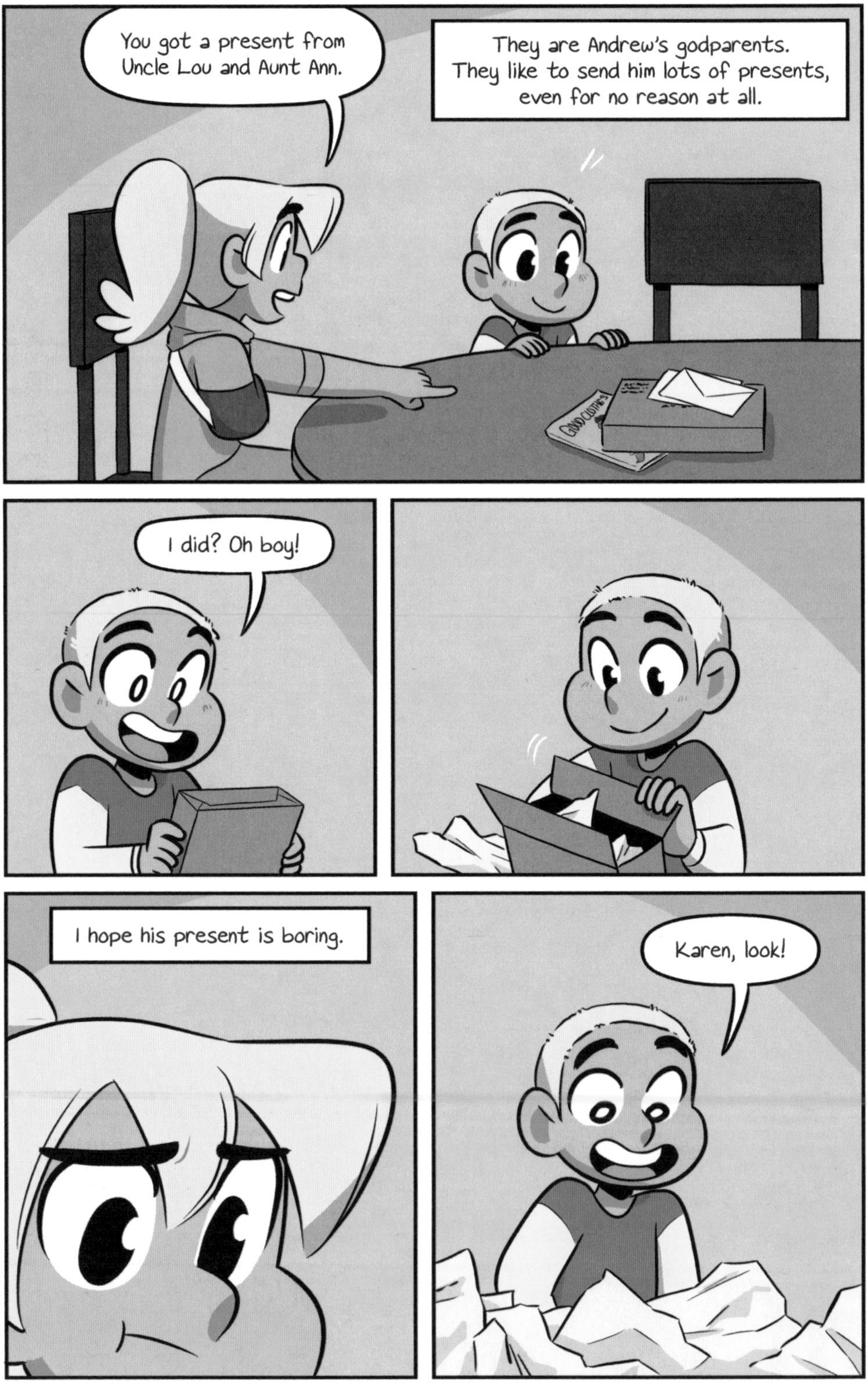
You got a present from Uncle Lou and Aunt Ann.
They are Andrew's godparents. They like to send him lots of presents, even for no reason at all.
I did? Oh boy!
I hope his present is boring.
Karen, look!

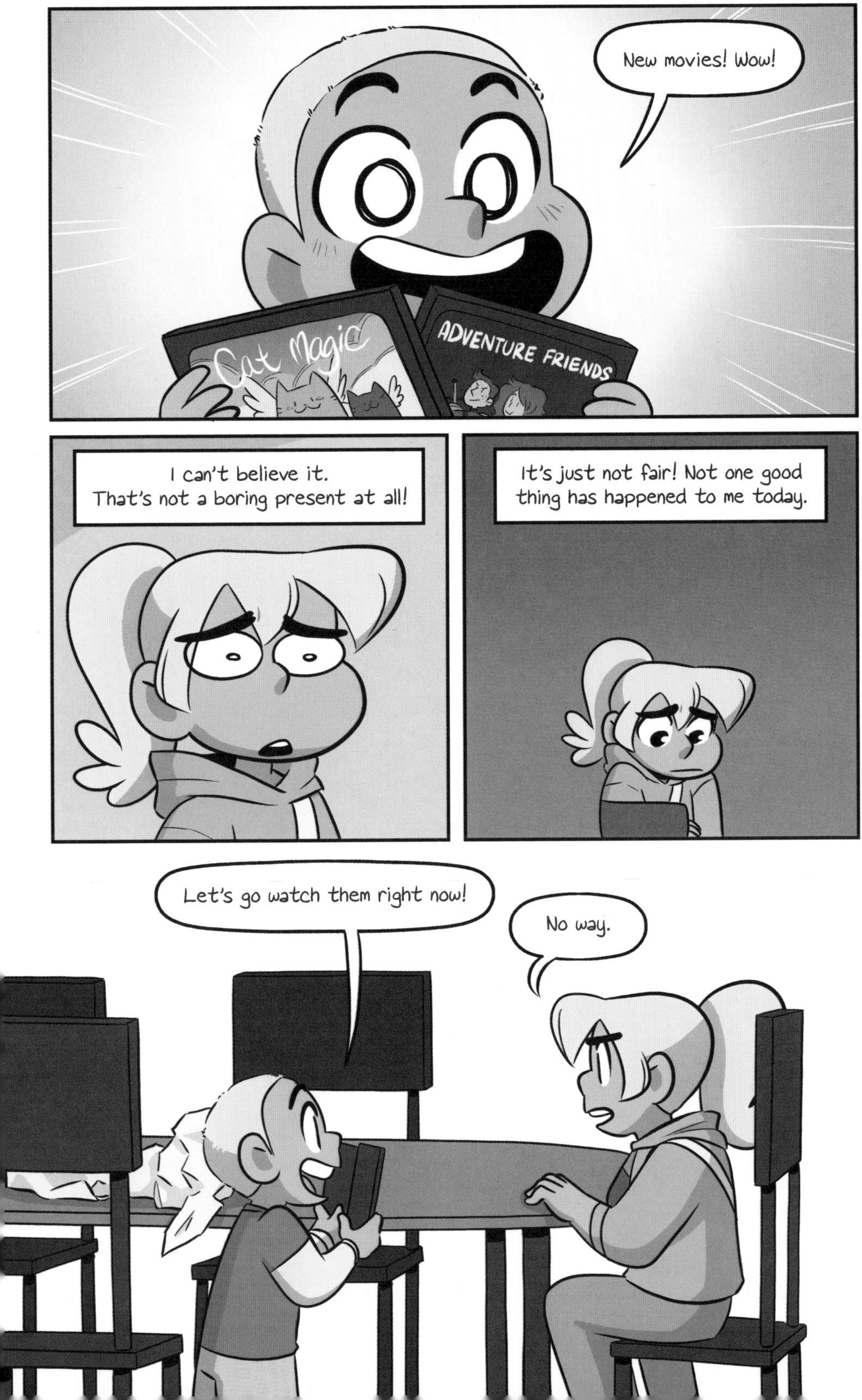
New movies! Wow!
Cat Magic
ADVENTURE FRIENDS
I can't believe it. That's not a boring present at all!
It's just not fair! Not one good thing has happened to me today.
Let's go watch them right now!
No way.

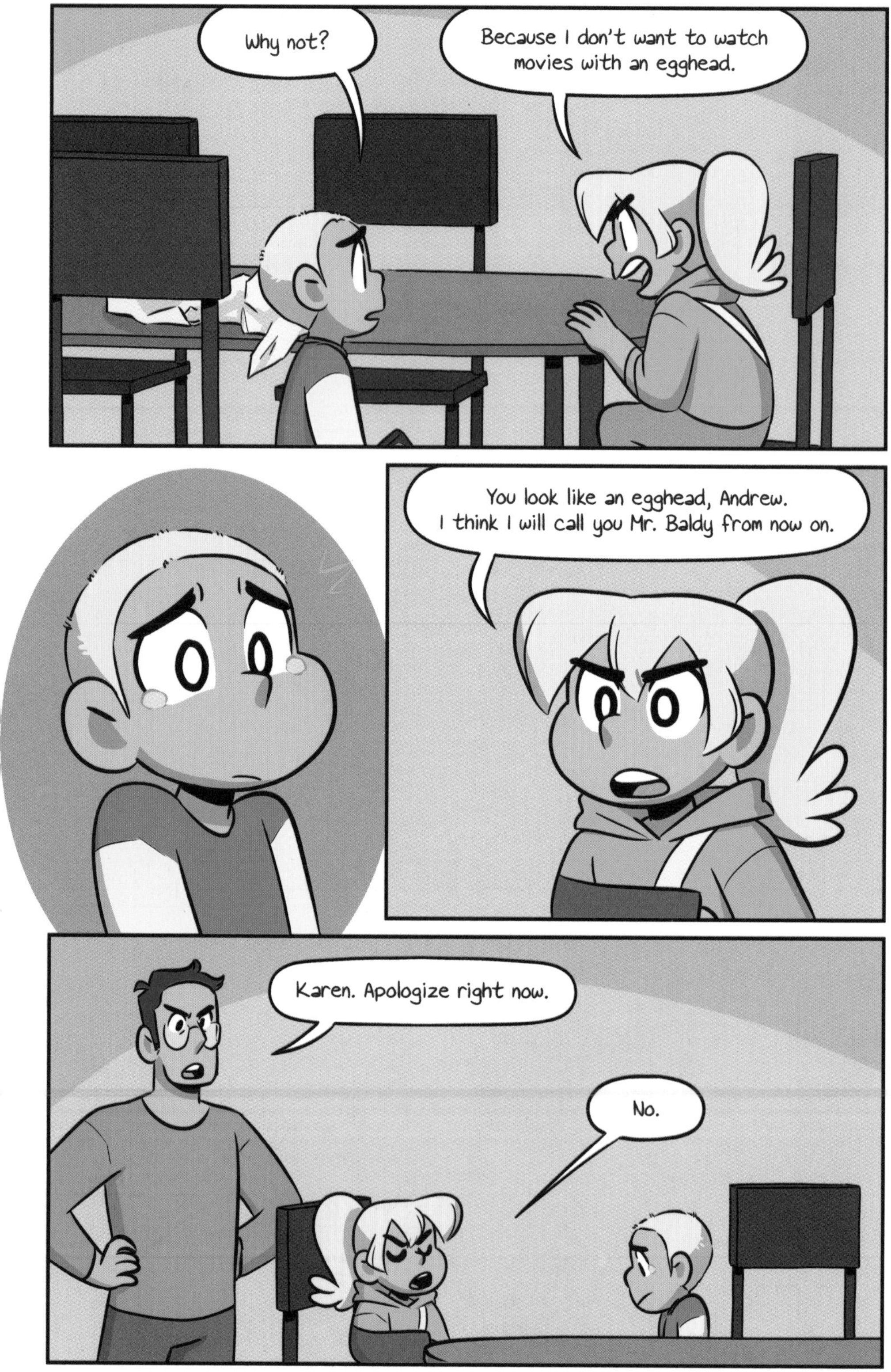
Why not?
Because I don't want to watch movies with an egghead.
You look like an egghead, Andrew. I think I will call you Mr. Baldy from now on.
Karen. Apologize right now.
No.

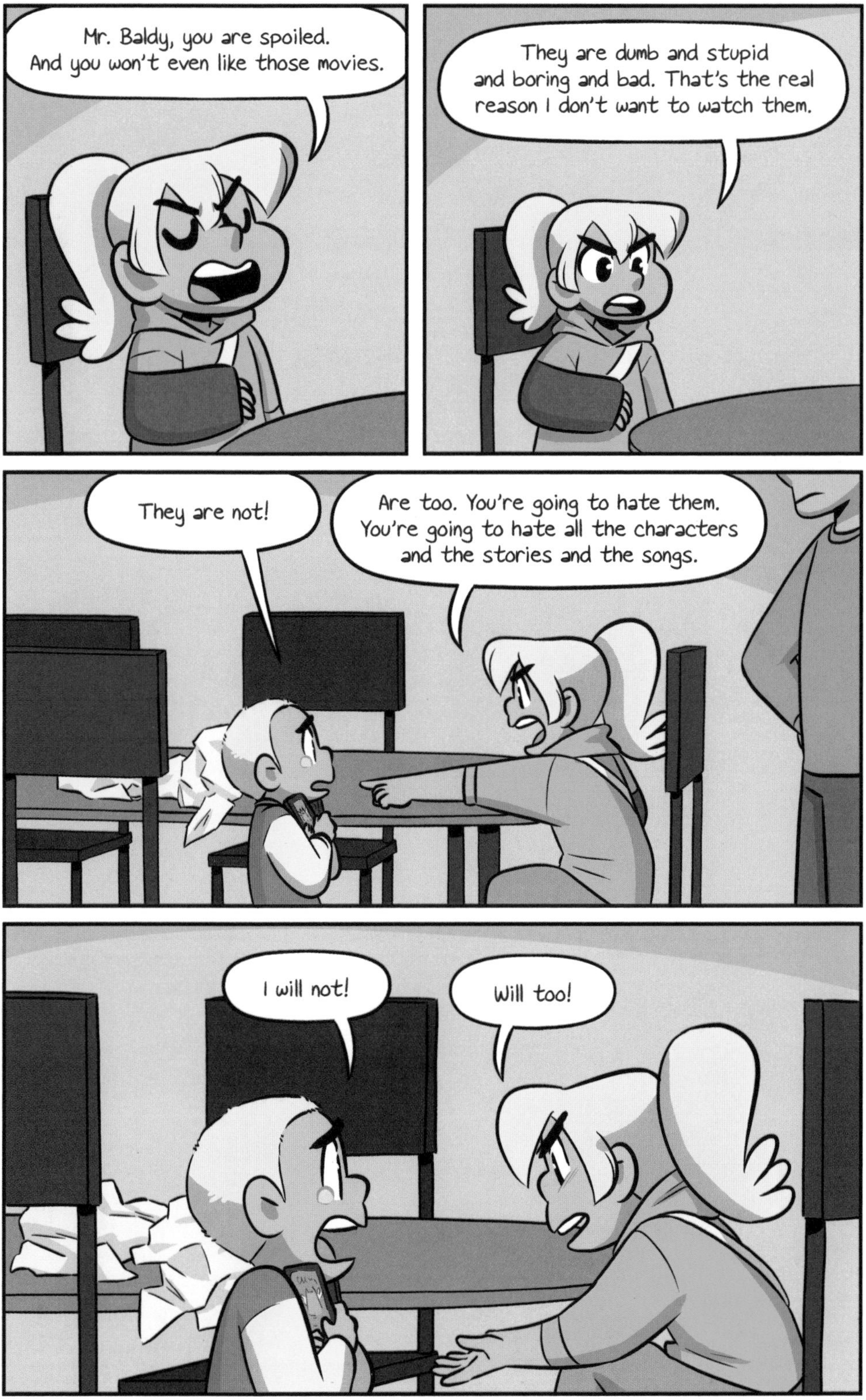
Mr. Baldy, you are spoiled. And you won't even like those movies.
They are dumb and stupid and boring and bad. That's the real reason I don't want to watch them.
They are not!
Are too. You're going to hate them. You're going to hate all the characters and the stories and the songs.
I will not!
Will too!

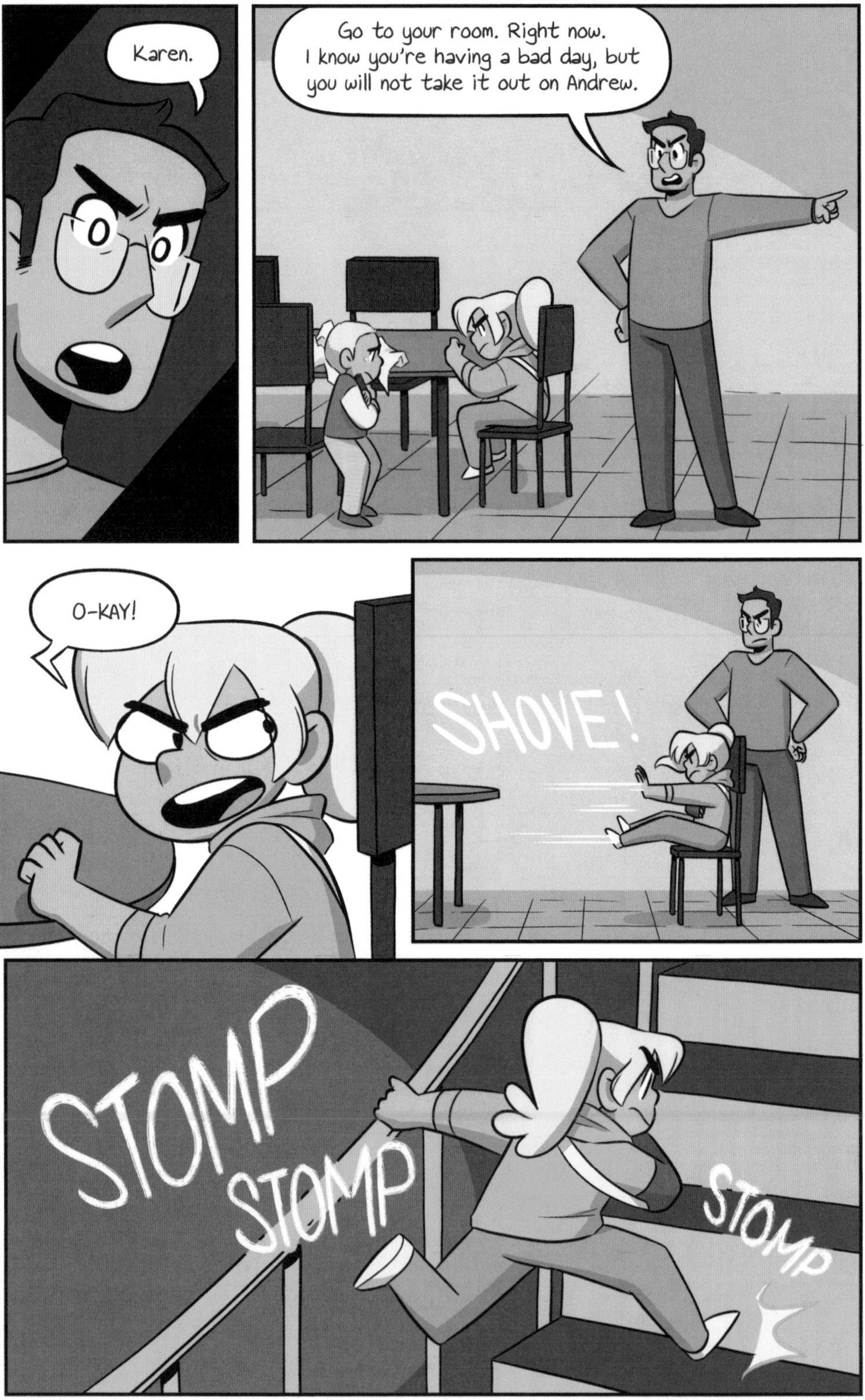
Karen.
Go to your room. Right now. I know you're having a bad day, but you will not take it out on Andrew.
O-KAY!
SHOVE!
STOMP
STOMP
STOMP

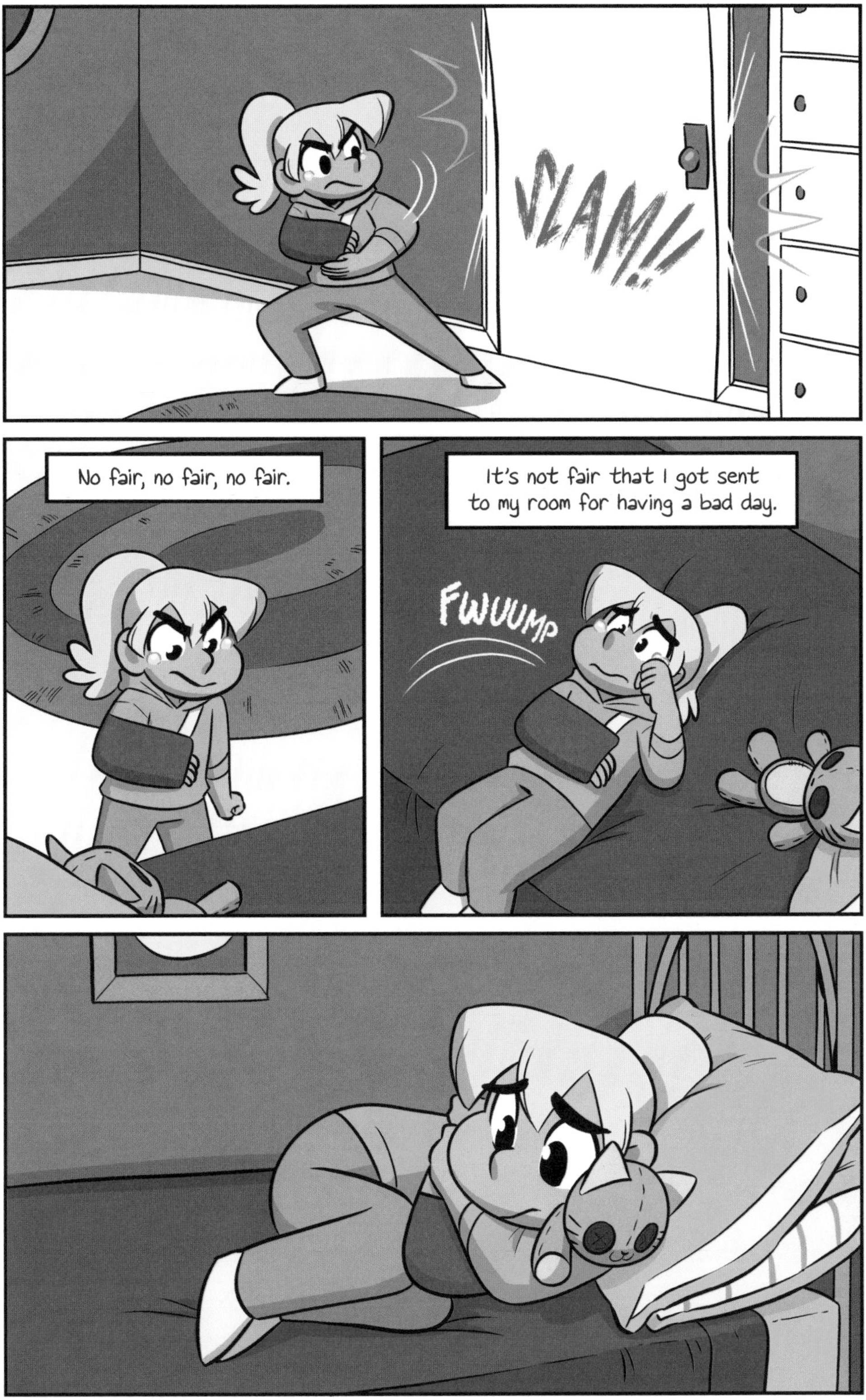

SLAM!!
No fair, no fair, no fair.
It's not fair that I got sent to my room for having a bad day.
FWUUMP

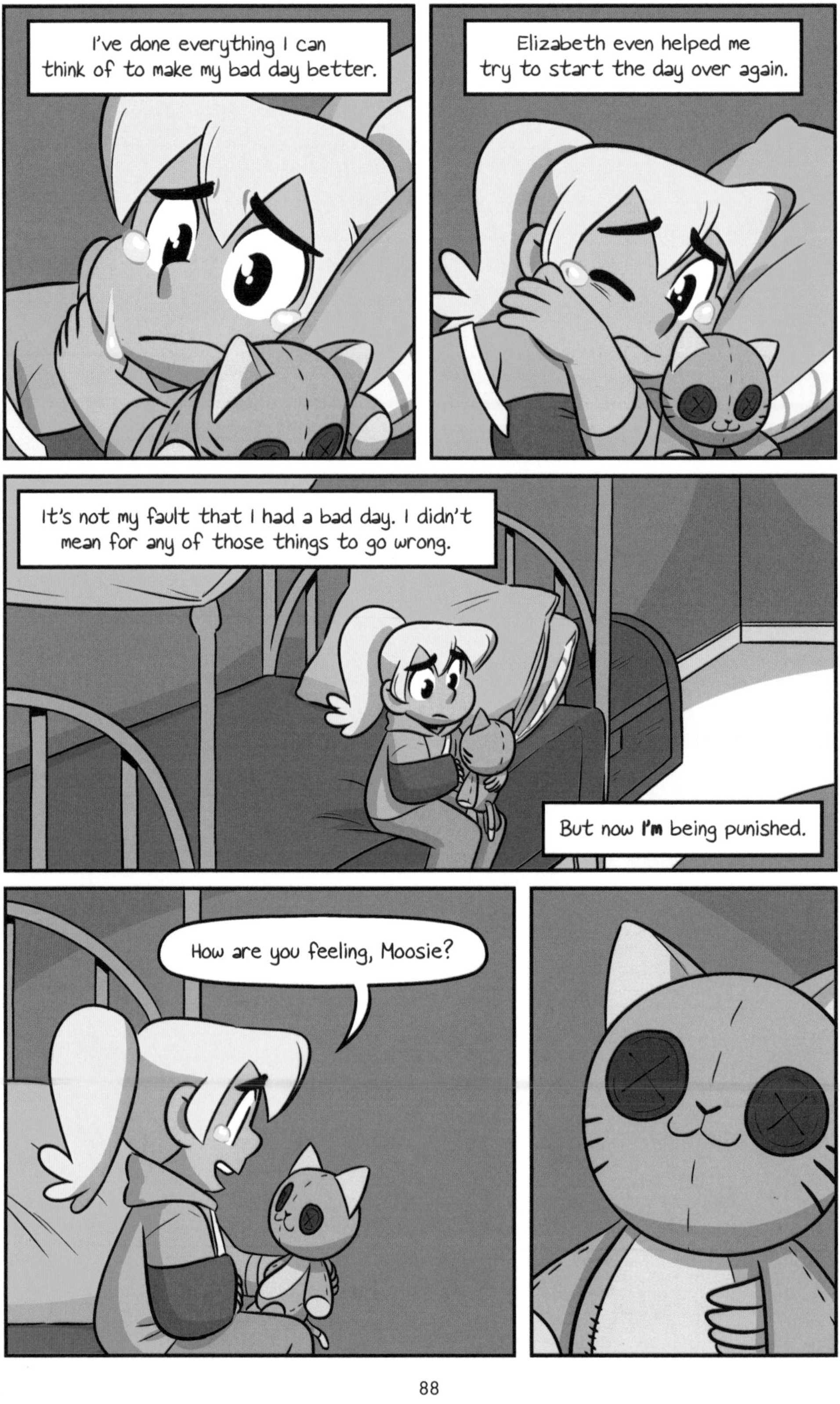
I've done everything I can think of to make my bad day better.
Elizabeth even helped me try to start the day over again.
It's not my fault that I had a bad day. I didn't mean for any of those things to go wrong.
But now **I'm** being punished.
How are you feeling, Moosie?

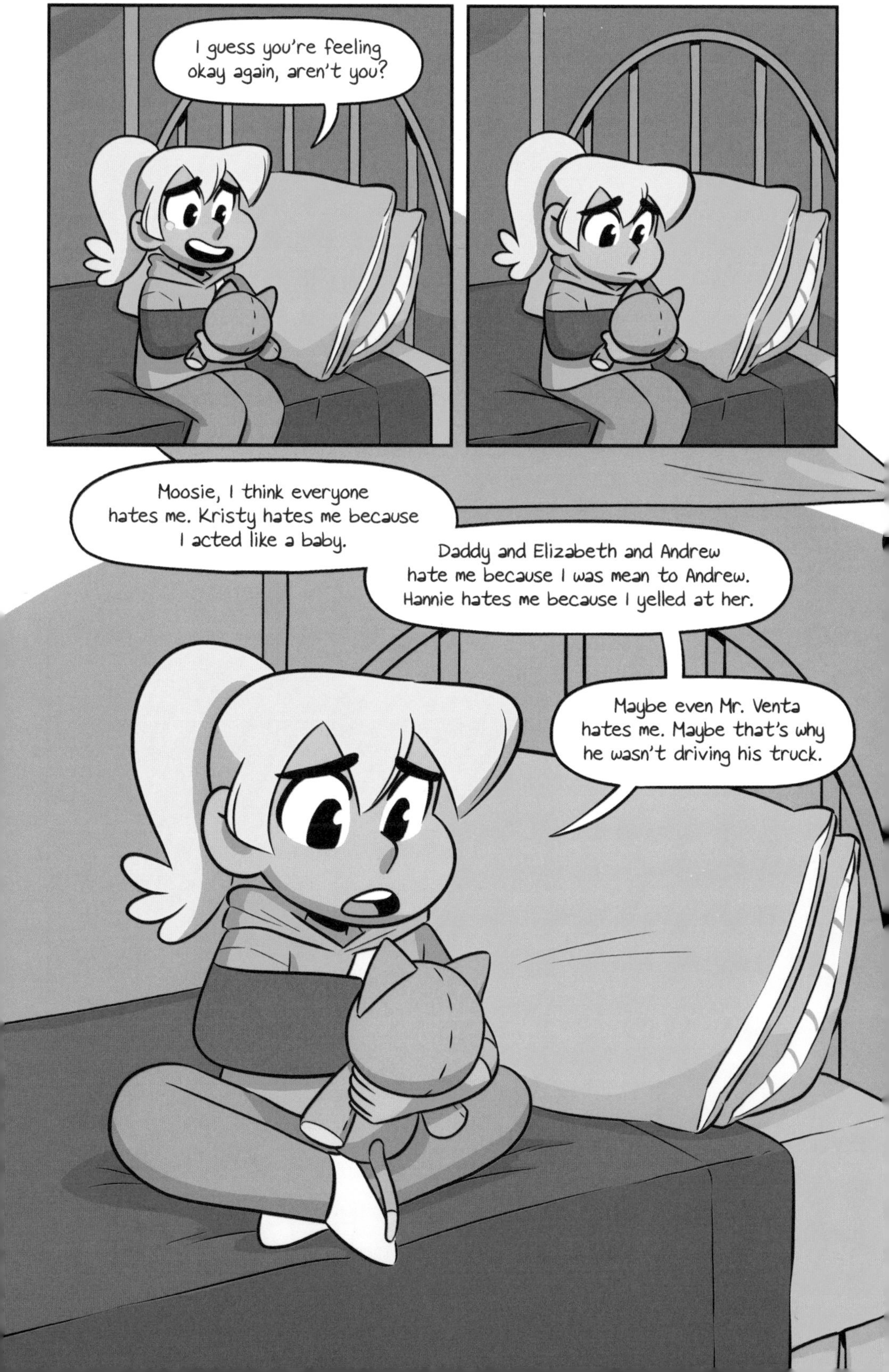
I guess you're feeling okay again, aren't you?
Moosie, I think everyone hates me. Kristy hates me because I acted like a baby.
Daddy and Elizabeth and Andrew hate me because I was mean to Andrew. Hannie hates me because I yelled at her.
Maybe even Mr. Venta hates me. Maybe that's why he wasn't driving his truck.

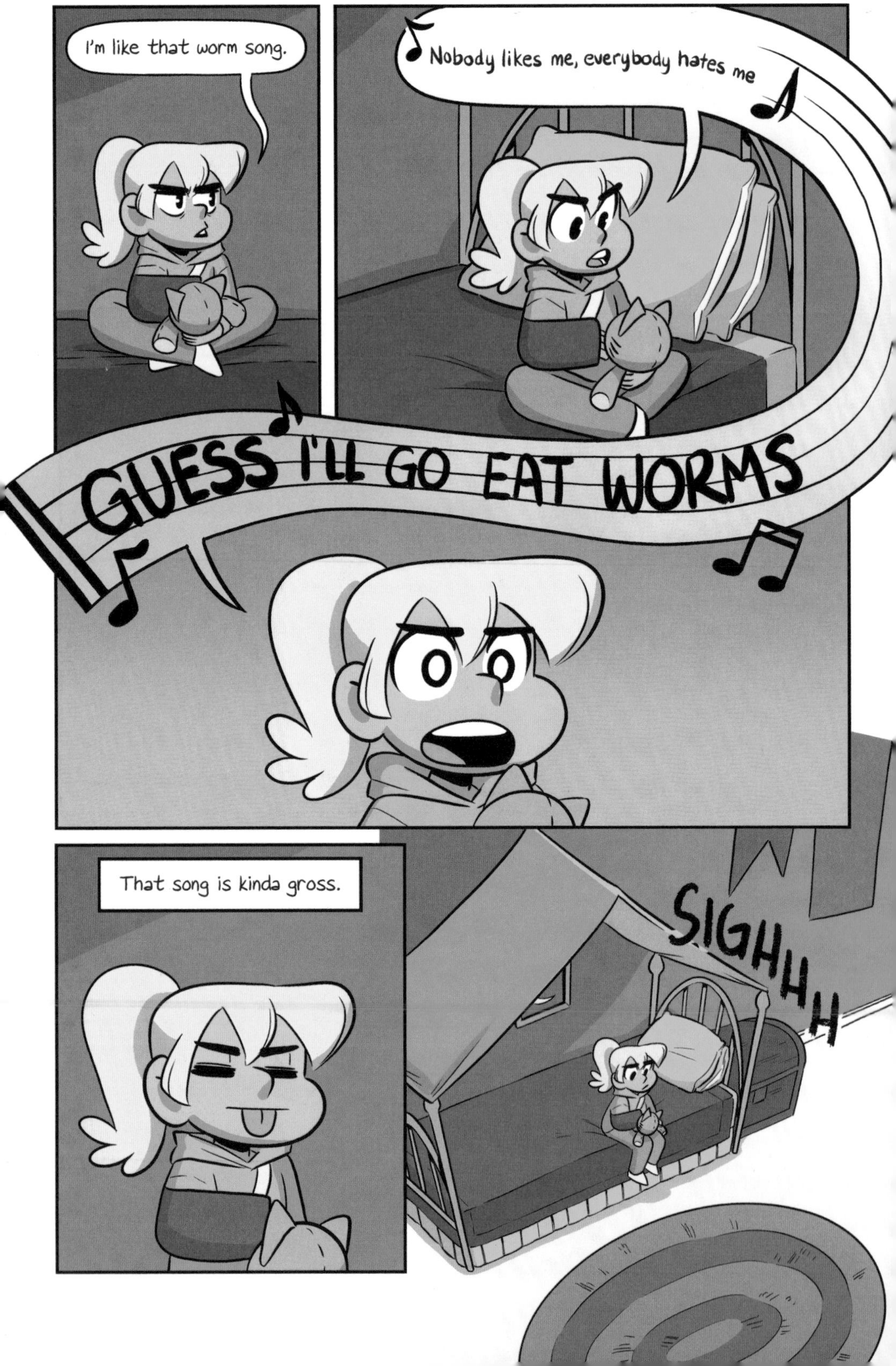
I'm like that worm song.
Nobody likes me, everybody hates me
GUESS I'LL GO EAT WORMS
That song is kinda gross.
SIGHHHH

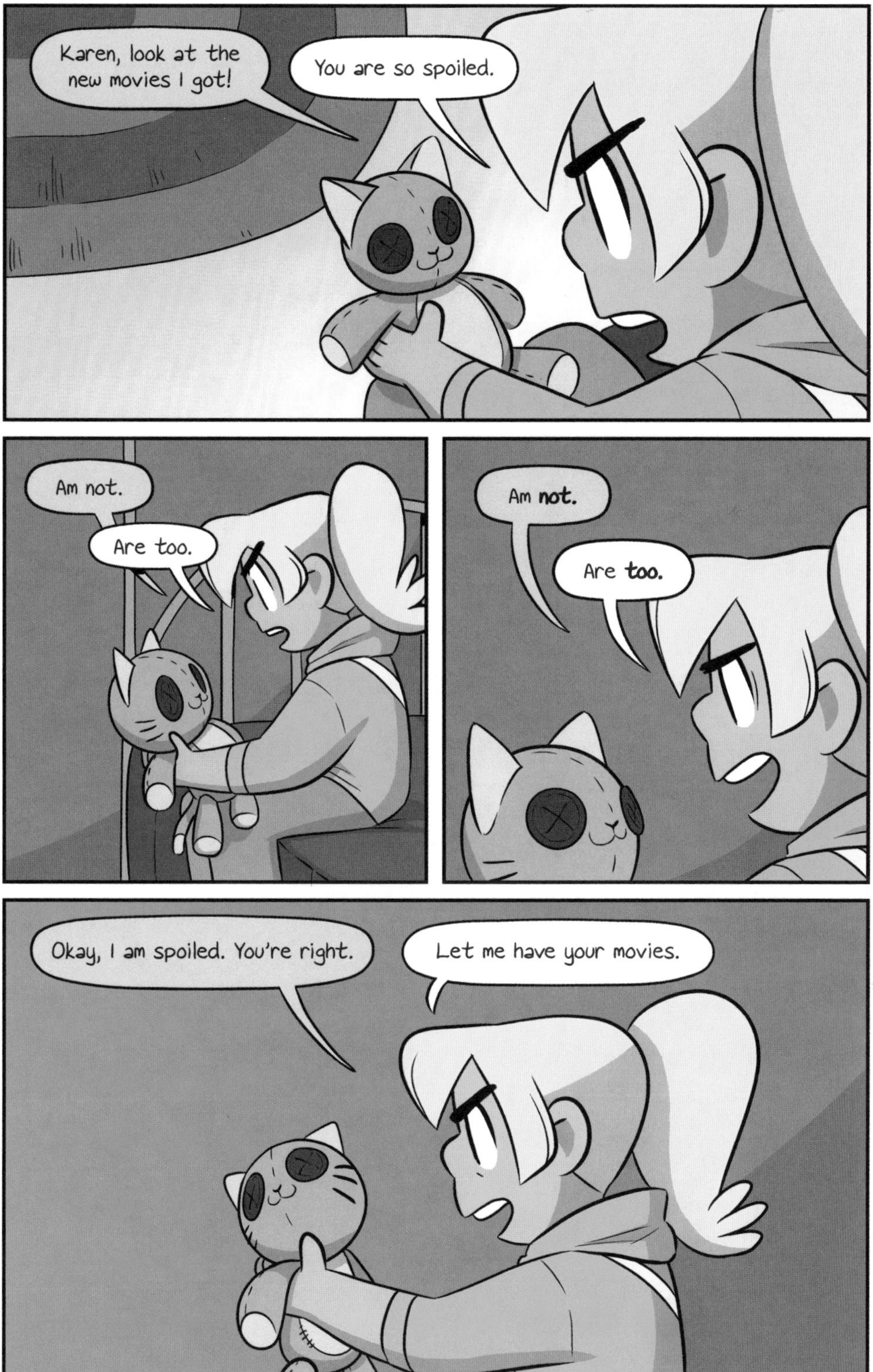
Karen, look at the new movies I got!
You are so spoiled.
Am not.
Are too.
Am **not.**
Are **too.**
Okay, I am spoiled. You're right.
Let me have your movies.

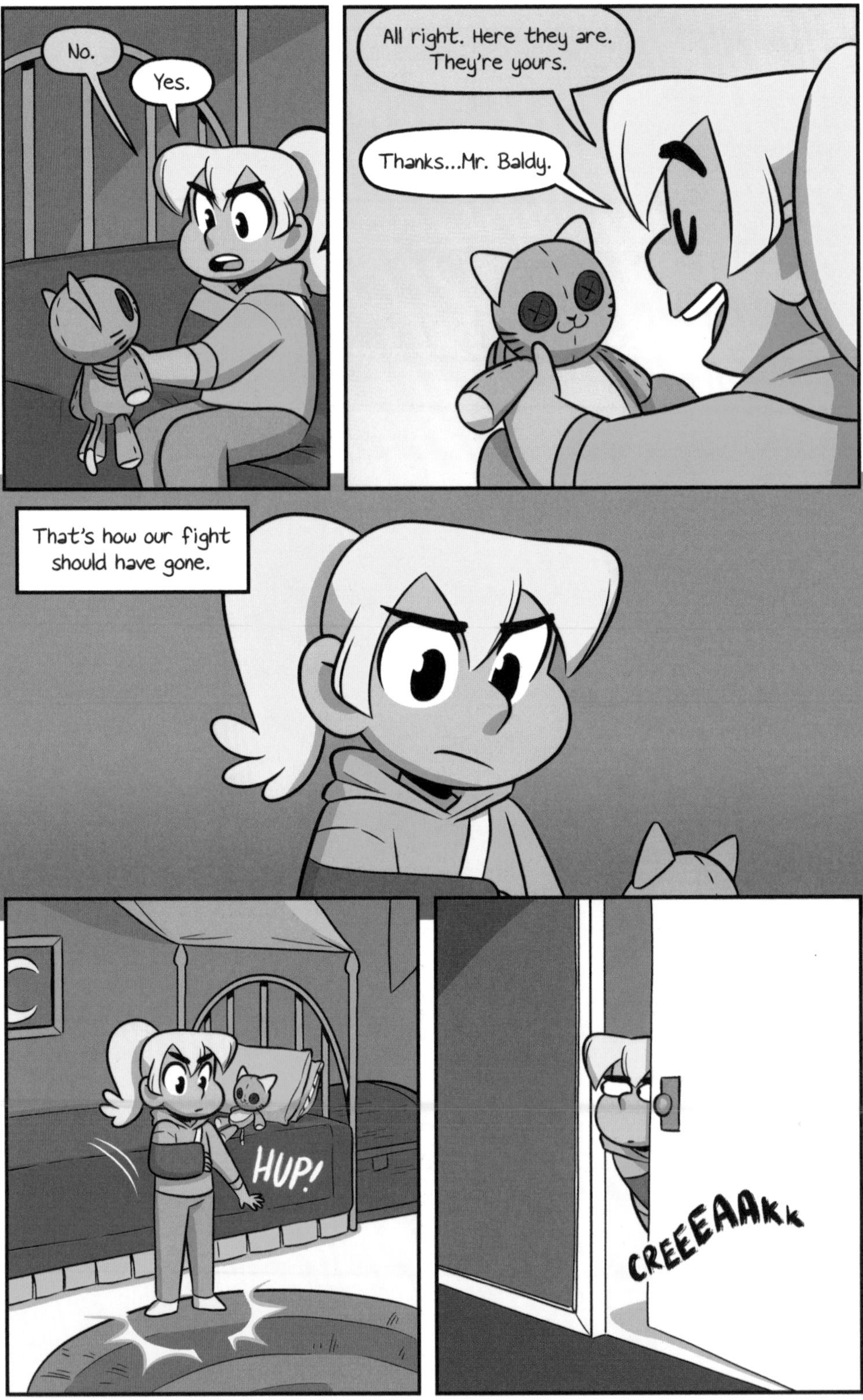
No.
Yes.
All right. Here they are. They're yours.
Thanks...Mr. Baldy.
That's how our fight should have gone.
HUP!
CREEEAAKk

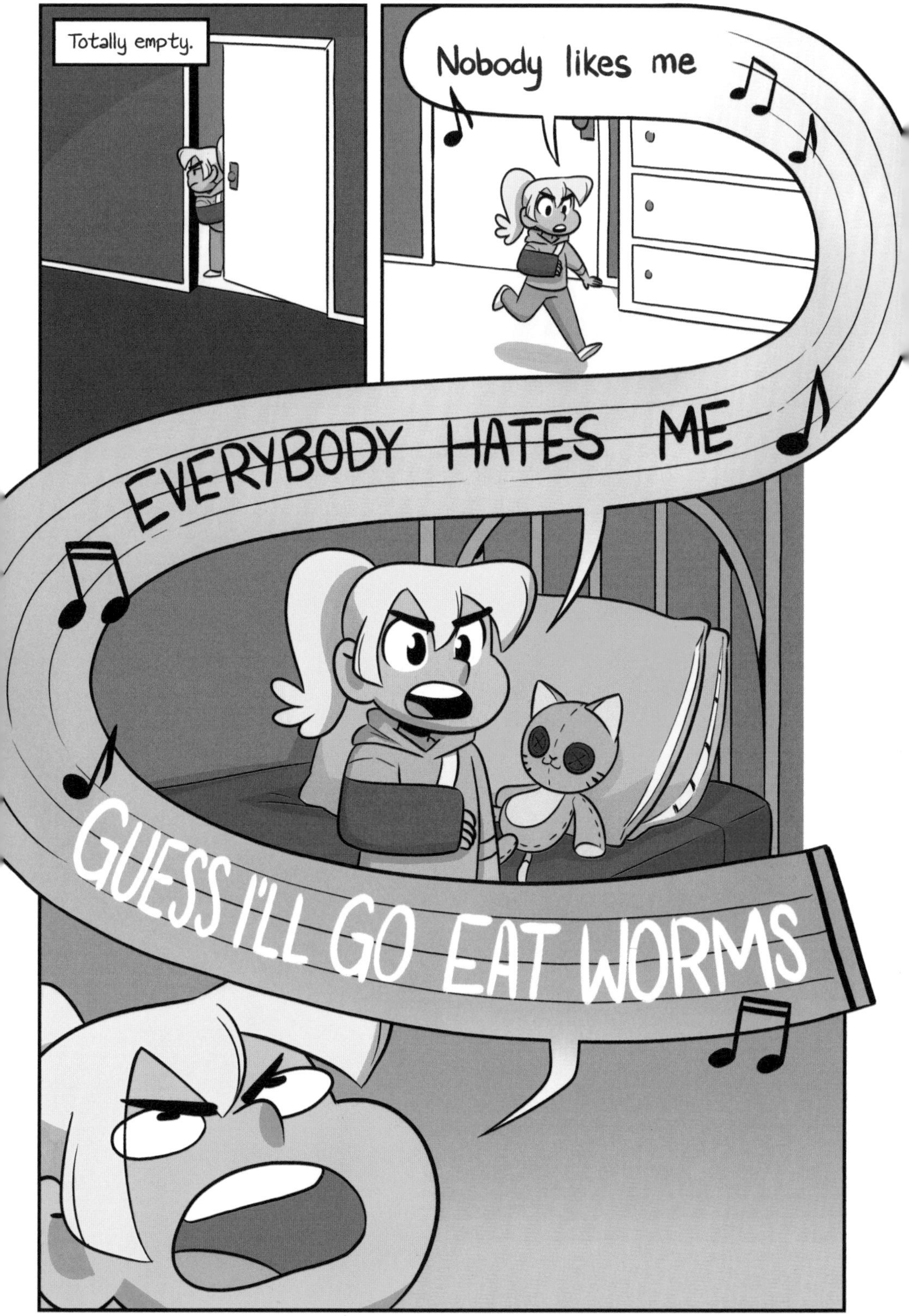
Totally empty.
Nobody likes me
EVERYBODY HATES ME
GUESS I'LL GO EAT WORMS

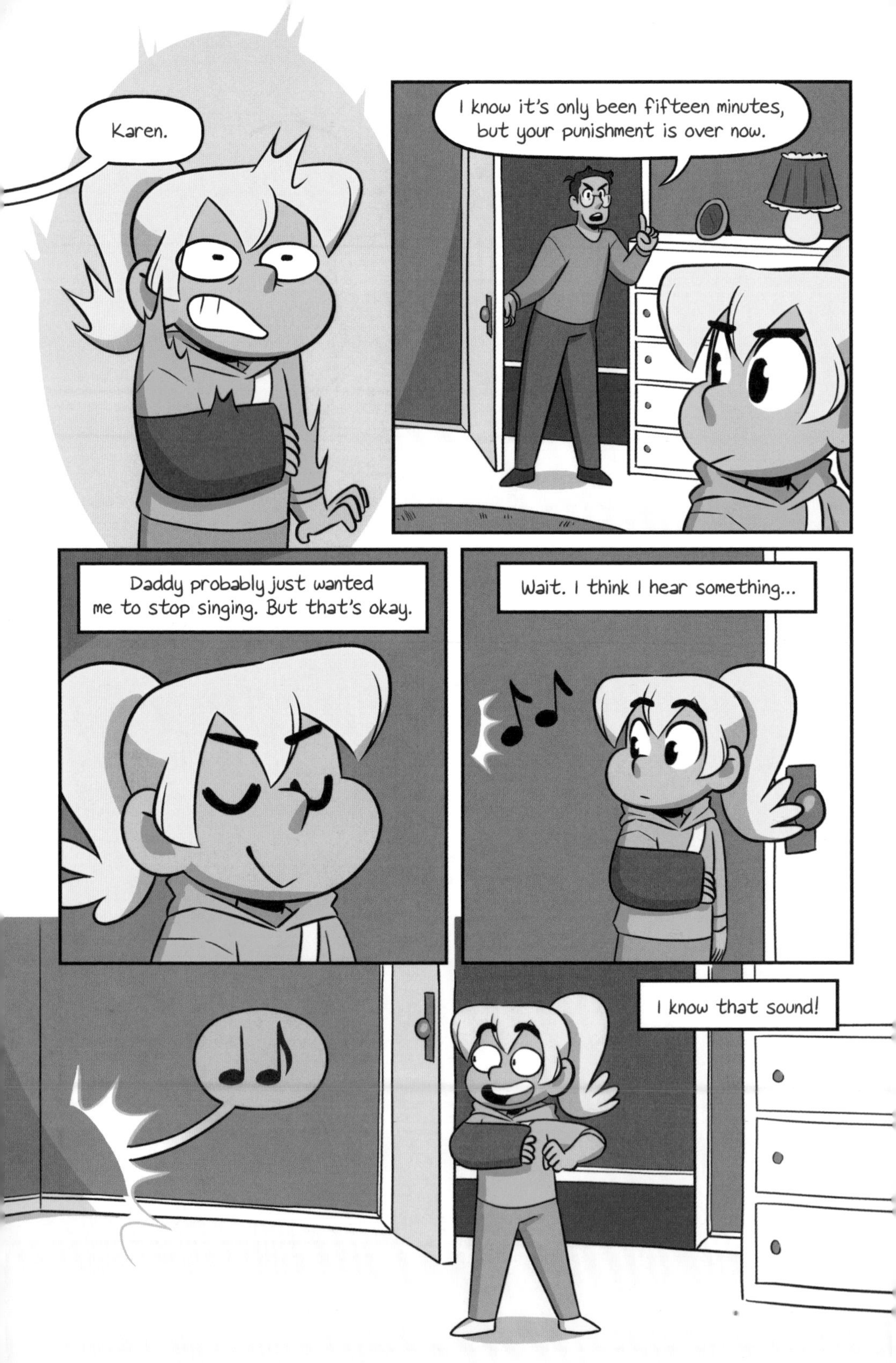
Karen.
I know it's only been fifteen minutes, but your punishment is over now.
Daddy probably just wanted me to stop singing. But that's okay.
Wait. I think I hear something...
I know that sound!

CHAPTER 8

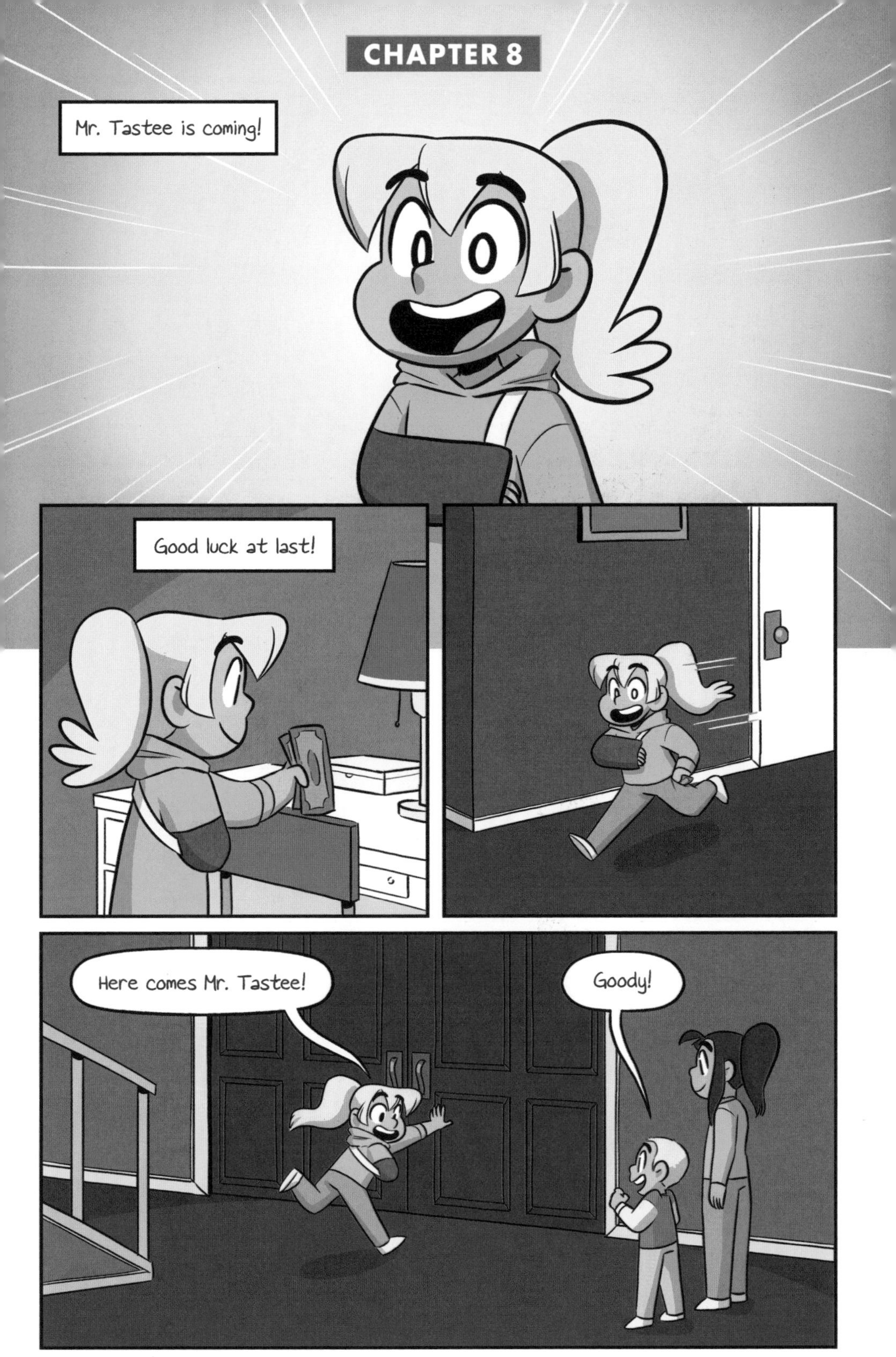

Mr. Tastee is coming!
Good luck at last!
Here comes Mr. Tastee!
Goody!

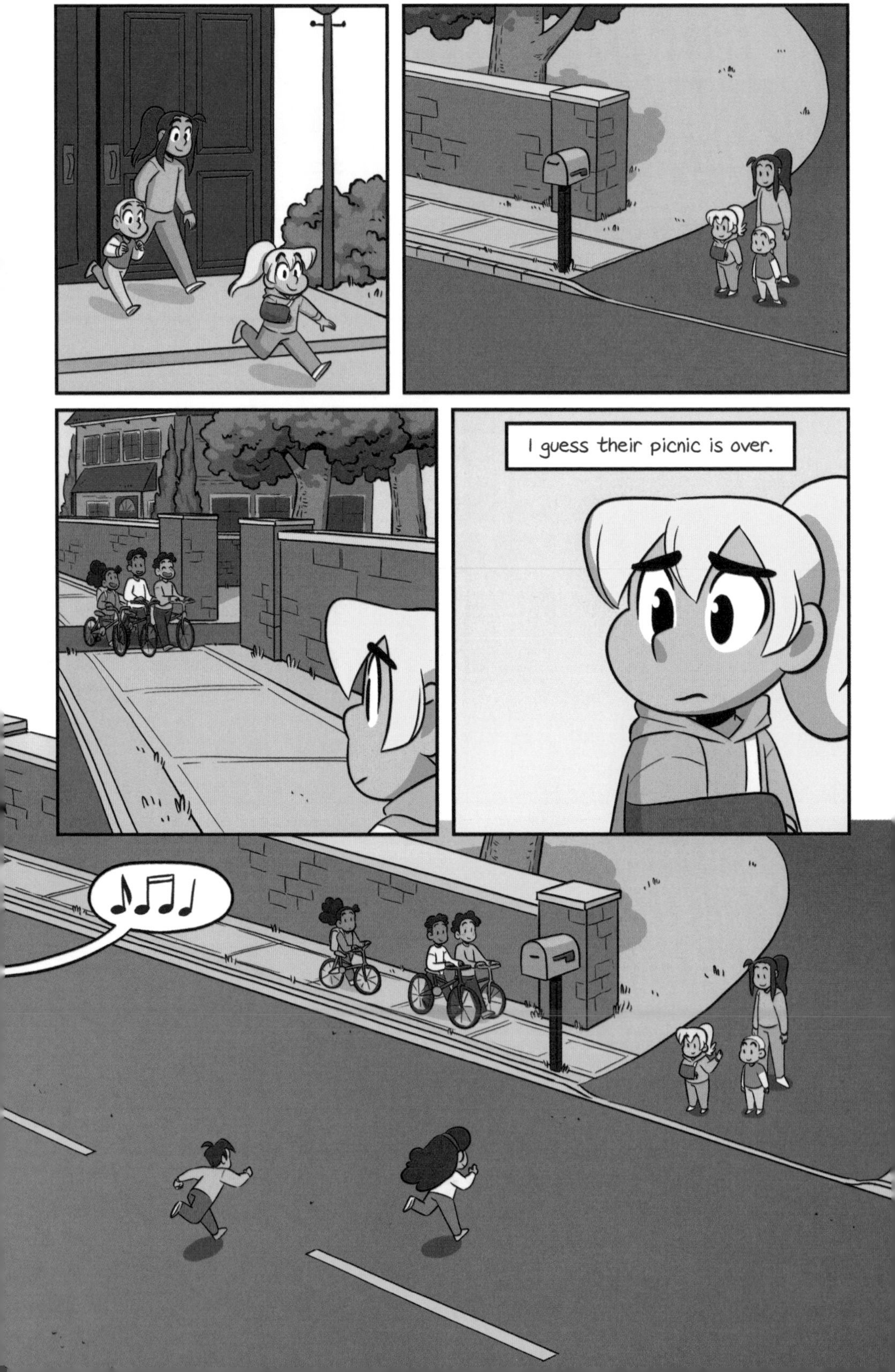
I guess their picnic is over.
♪♫♩

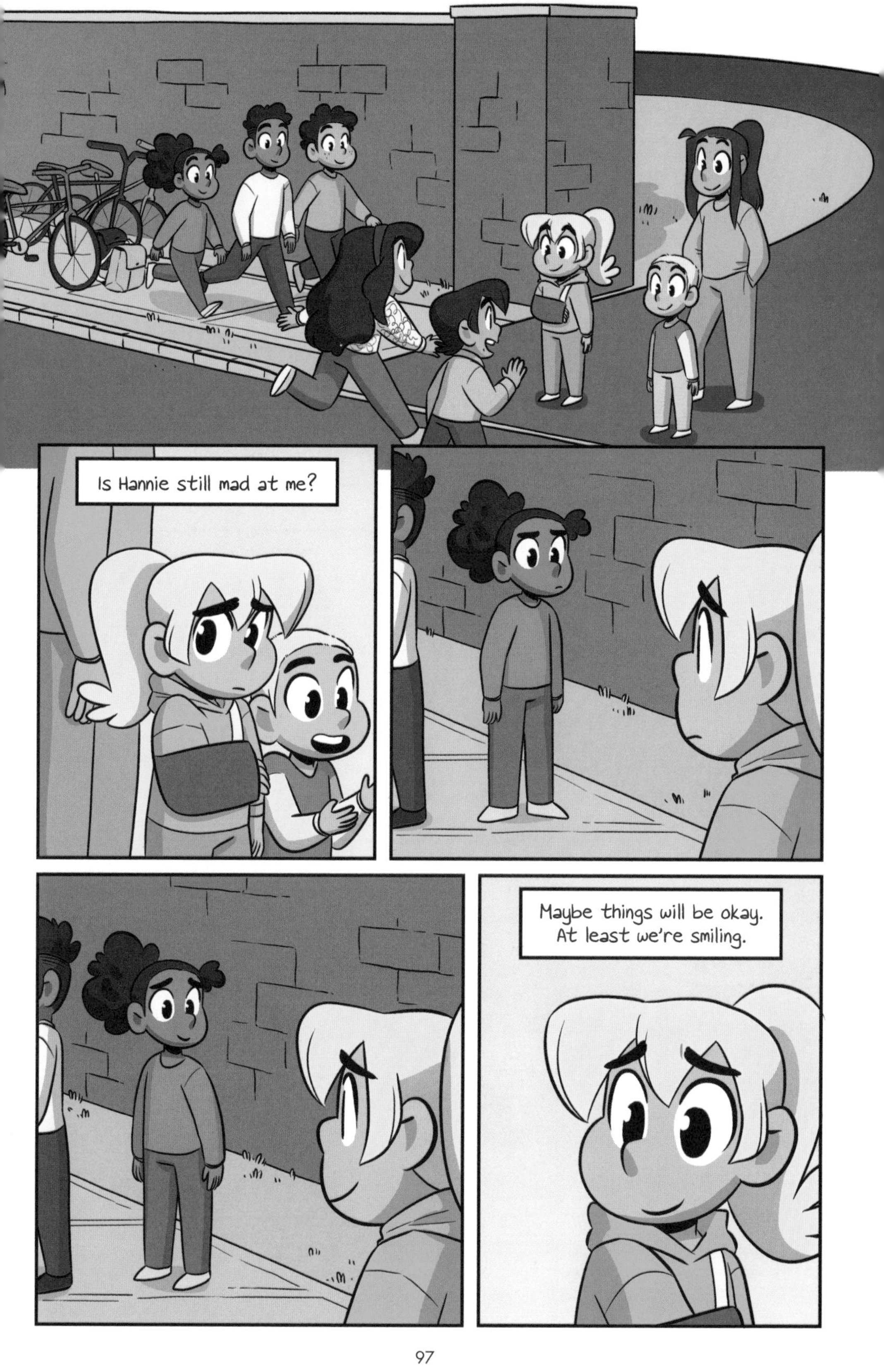
Is Hannie still mad at me?
Maybe things will be okay. At least we're smiling.

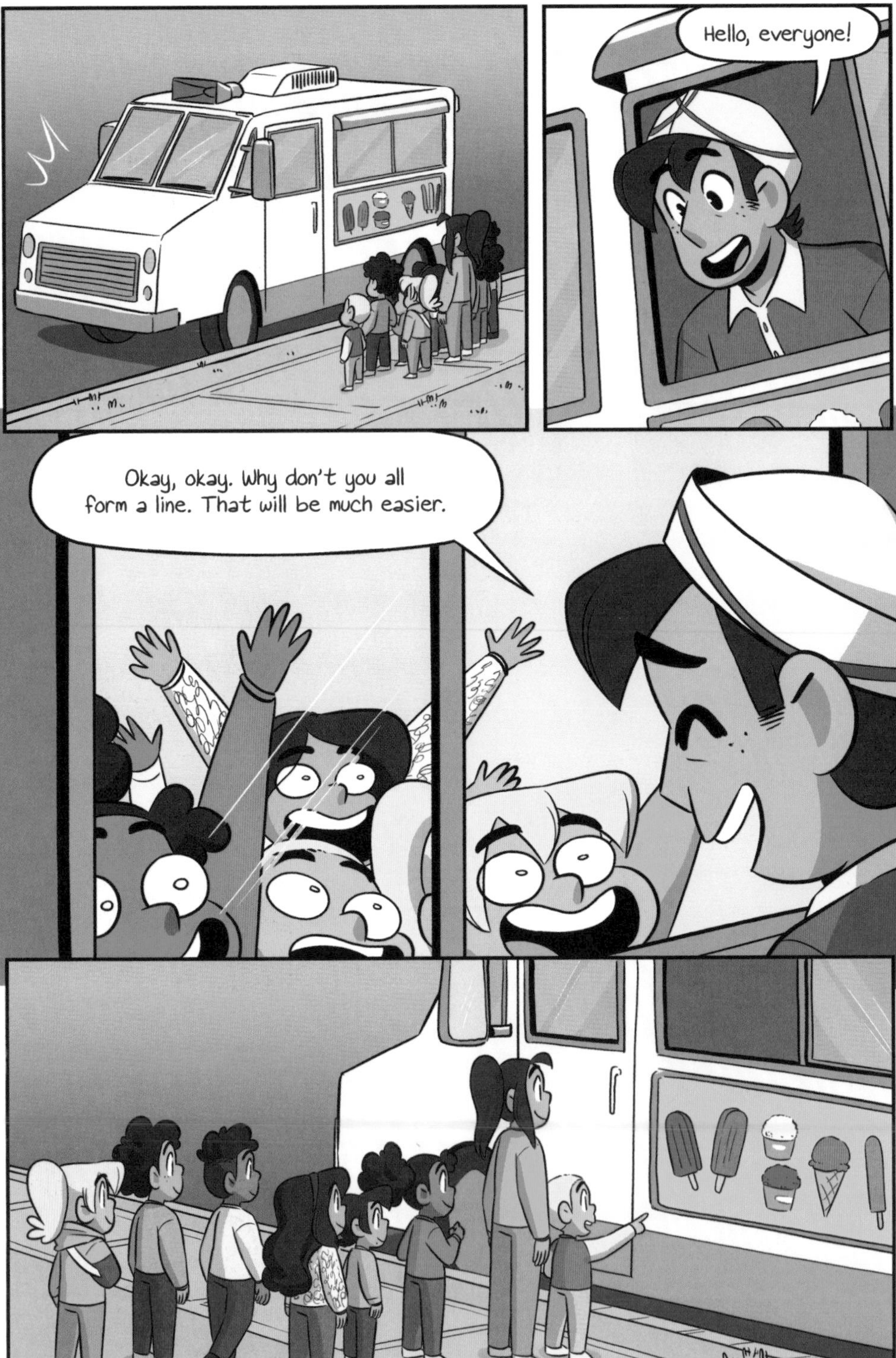
Hello, everyone!
Okay, okay. Why don't you all form a line. That will be much easier.

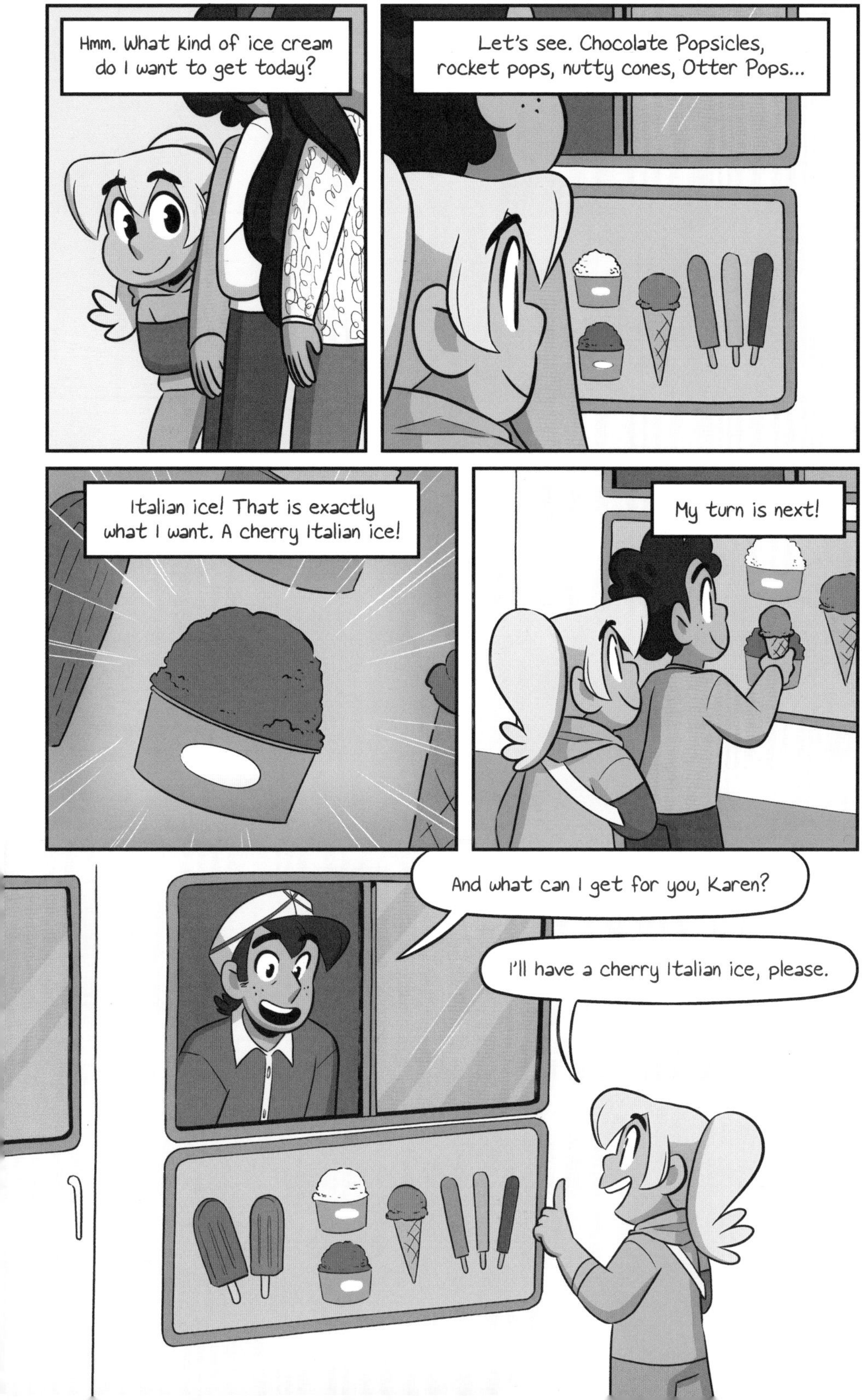
Hmm. What kind of ice cream do I want to get today?
Let's see. Chocolate Popsicles, rocket pops, nutty cones, Otter Pops...
Italian ice! That is exactly what I want. A cherry Italian ice!
My turn is next!
And what can I get for you, Karen?
I'll have a cherry Italian ice, please.

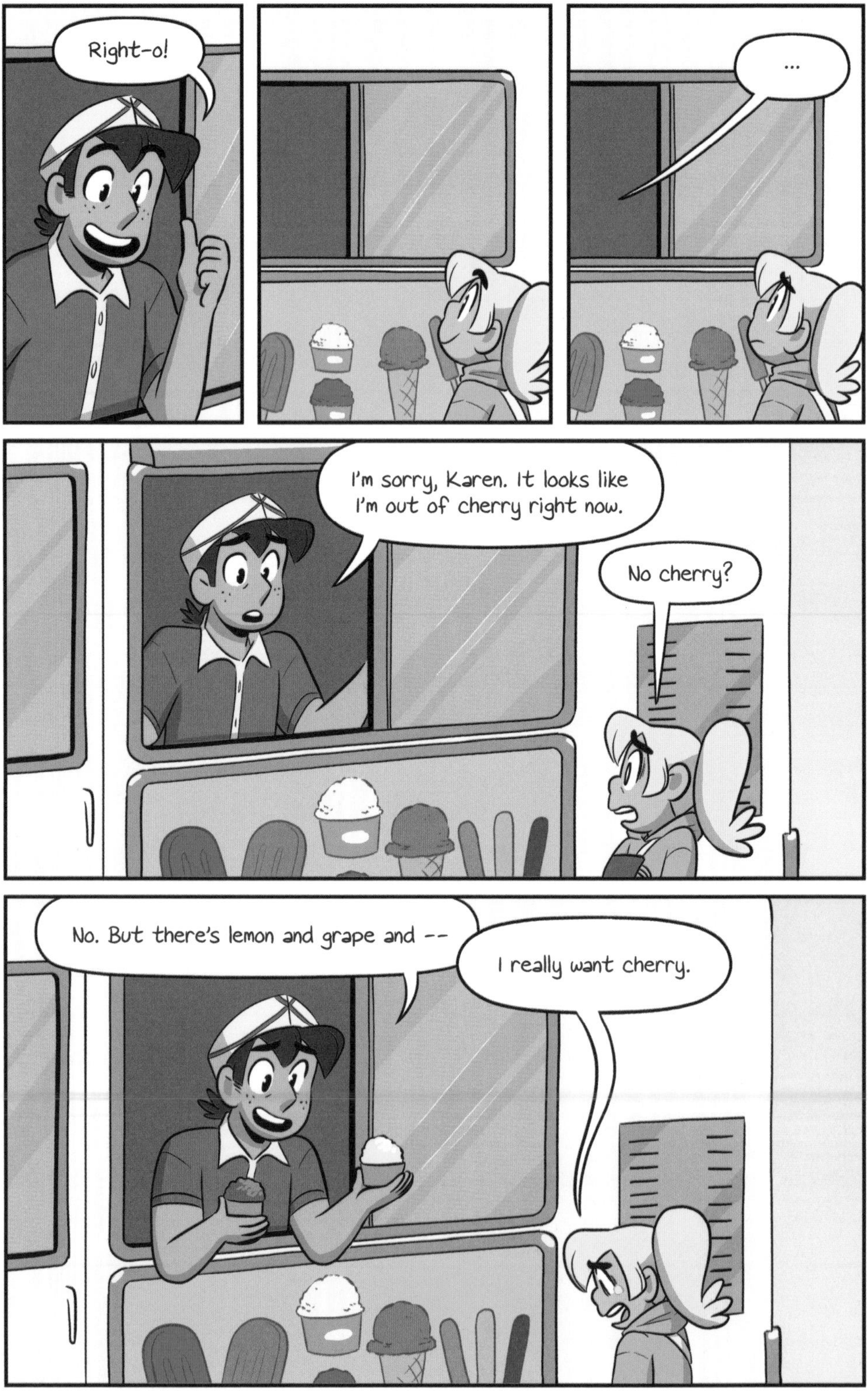
Right-o!
...
I'm sorry, Karen. It looks like I'm out of cherry right now.
No cherry?
No. But there's lemon and grape and --
I really want cherry.

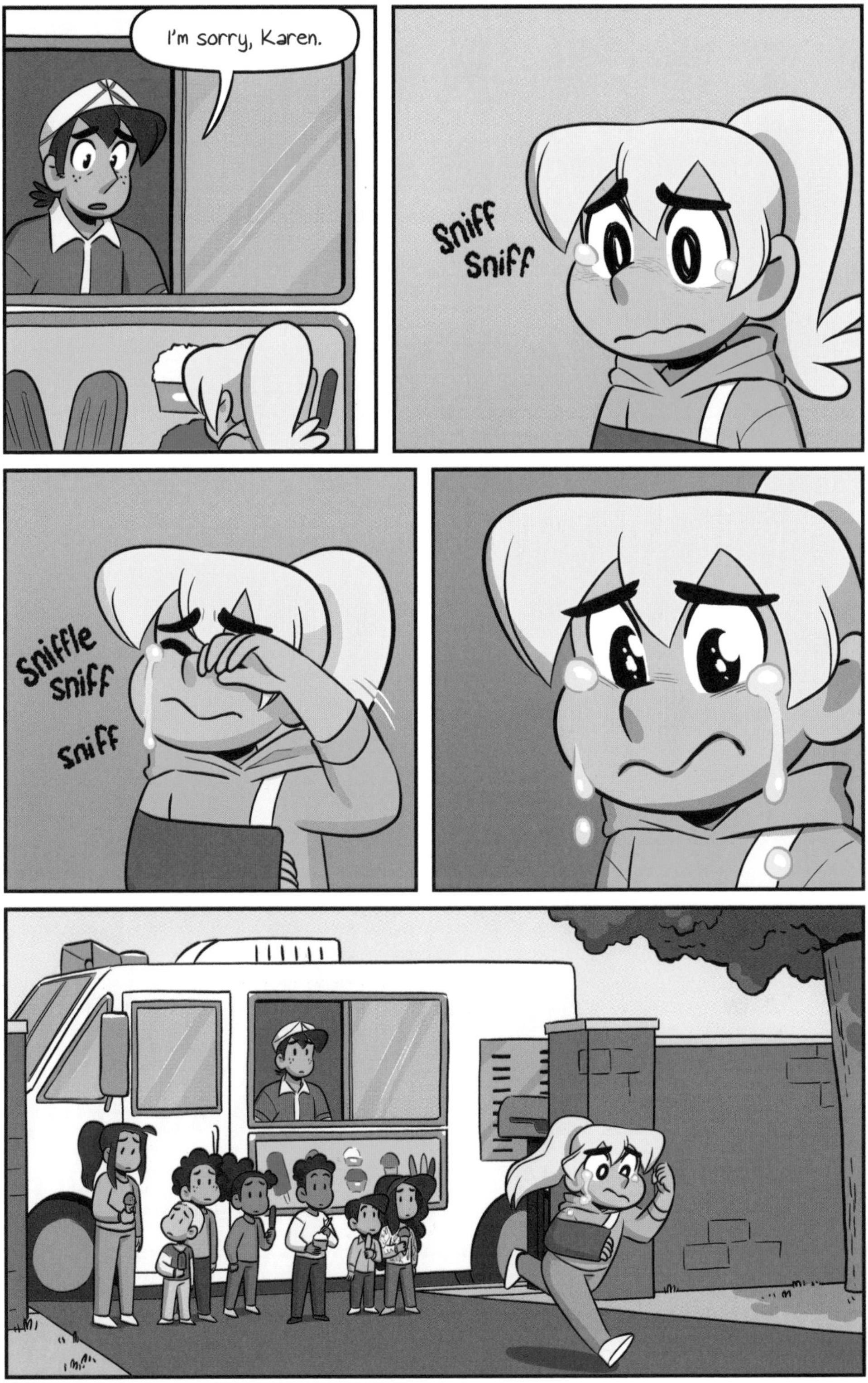
I'm sorry, Karen.
Sniff
Sniff
Sniffle
sniff
sniff

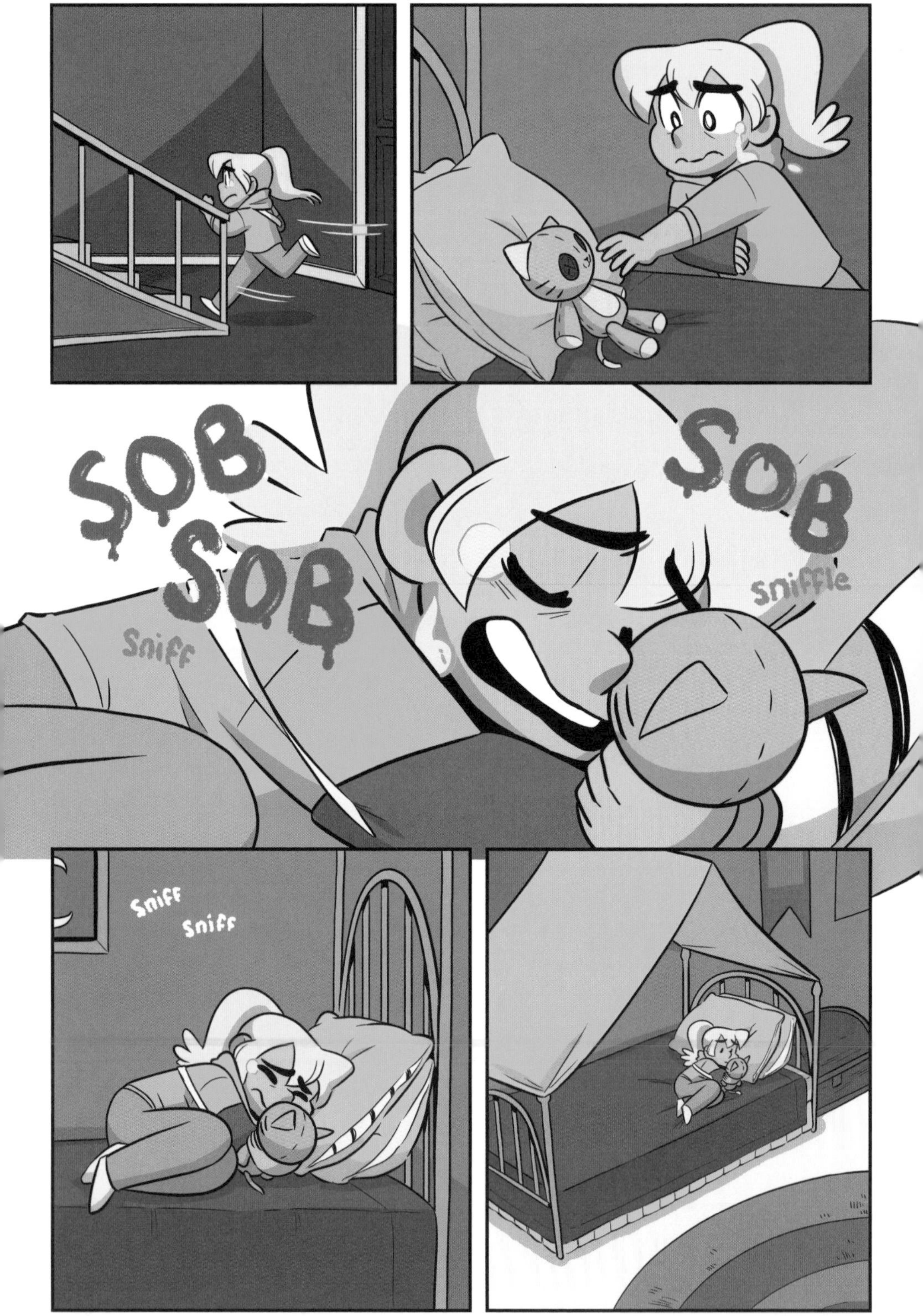
SOB
SOB
Sniff
SOB
sniffle
Sniff
Sniff

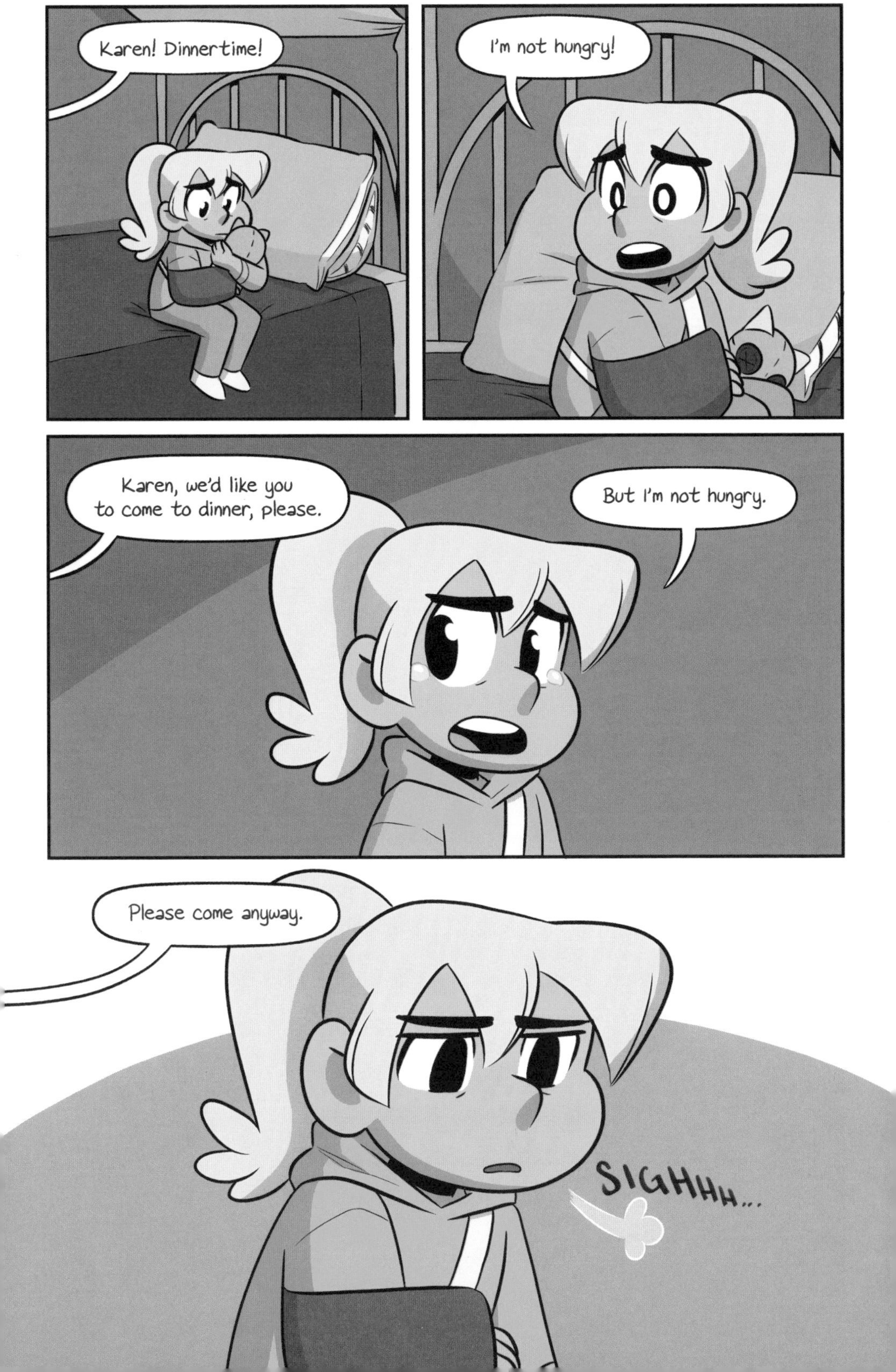
Karen! Dinnertime!
I'm not hungry!
Karen, we'd like you to come to dinner, please.
But I'm not hungry.
Please come anyway.
SIGHHH...

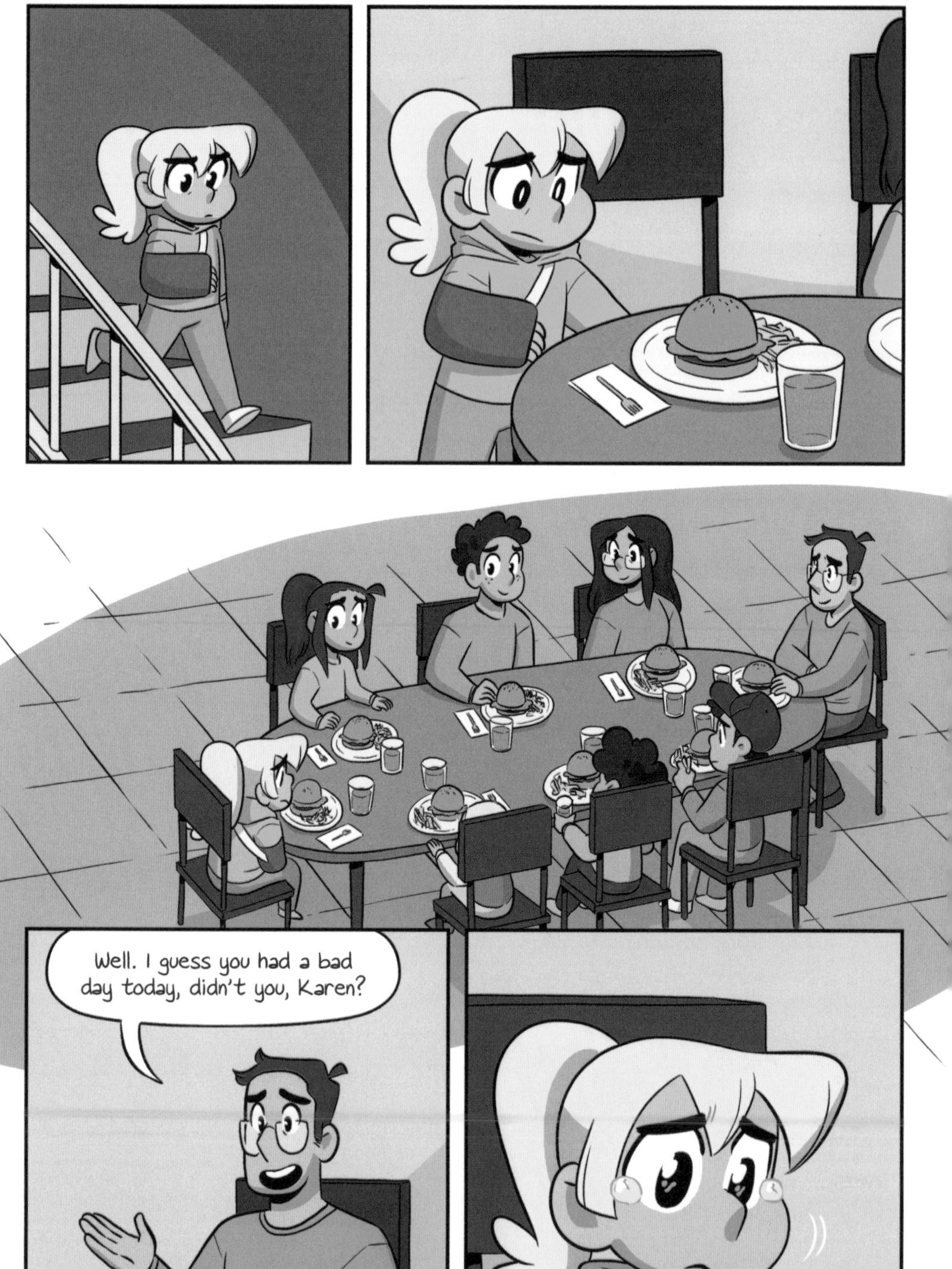
Well. I guess you had a bad day today, didn't you, Karen?
Nod Nod

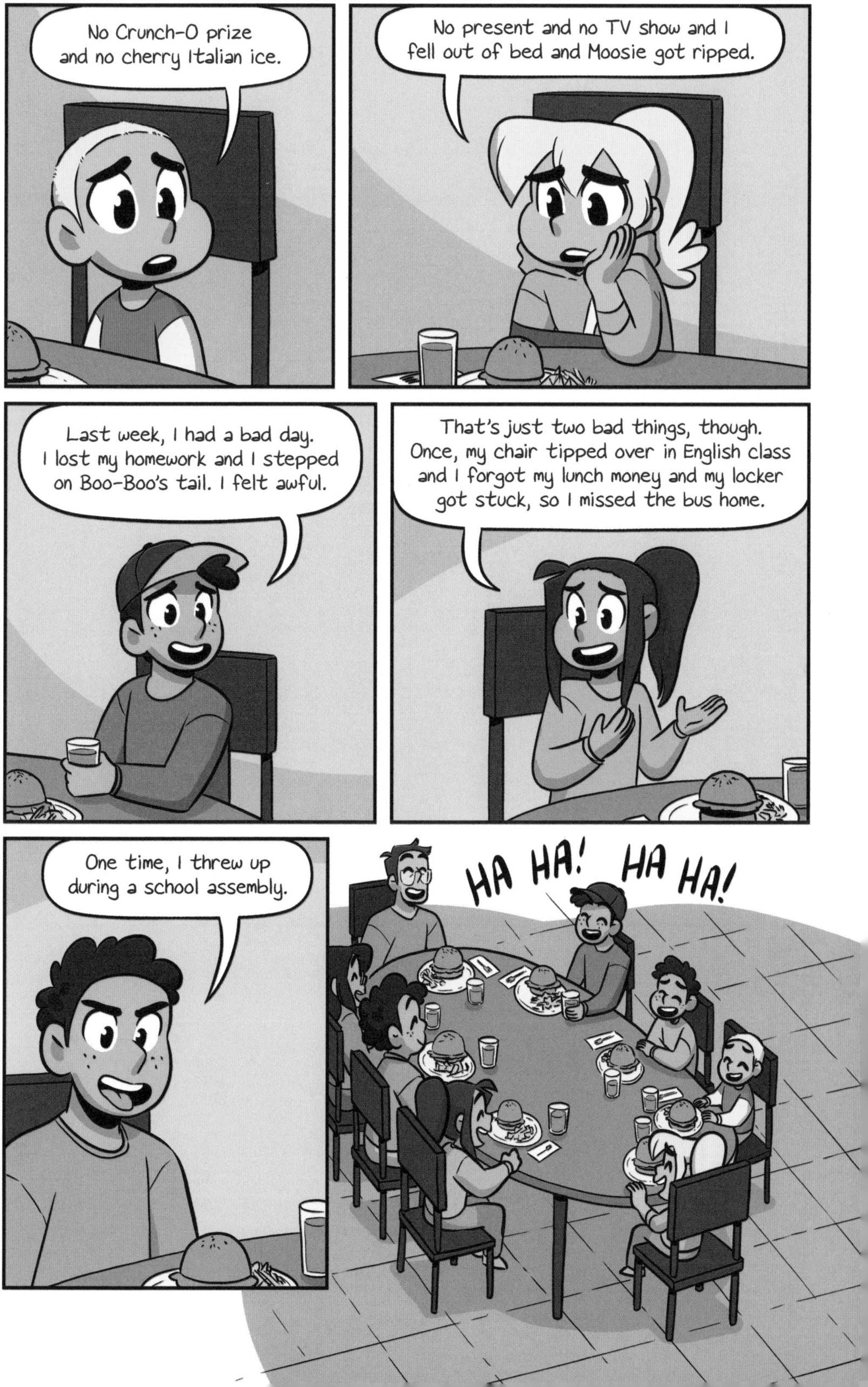
No Crunch-O prize and no cherry Italian ice.
No present and no TV show and I fell out of bed and Moosie got ripped.
Last week, I had a bad day. I lost my homework and I stepped on Boo-Boo's tail. I felt awful.
That's just two bad things, though. Once, my chair tipped over in English class and I forgot my lunch money and my locker got stuck, so I missed the bus home.
One time, I threw up during a school assembly.
HA HA!
HA HA!

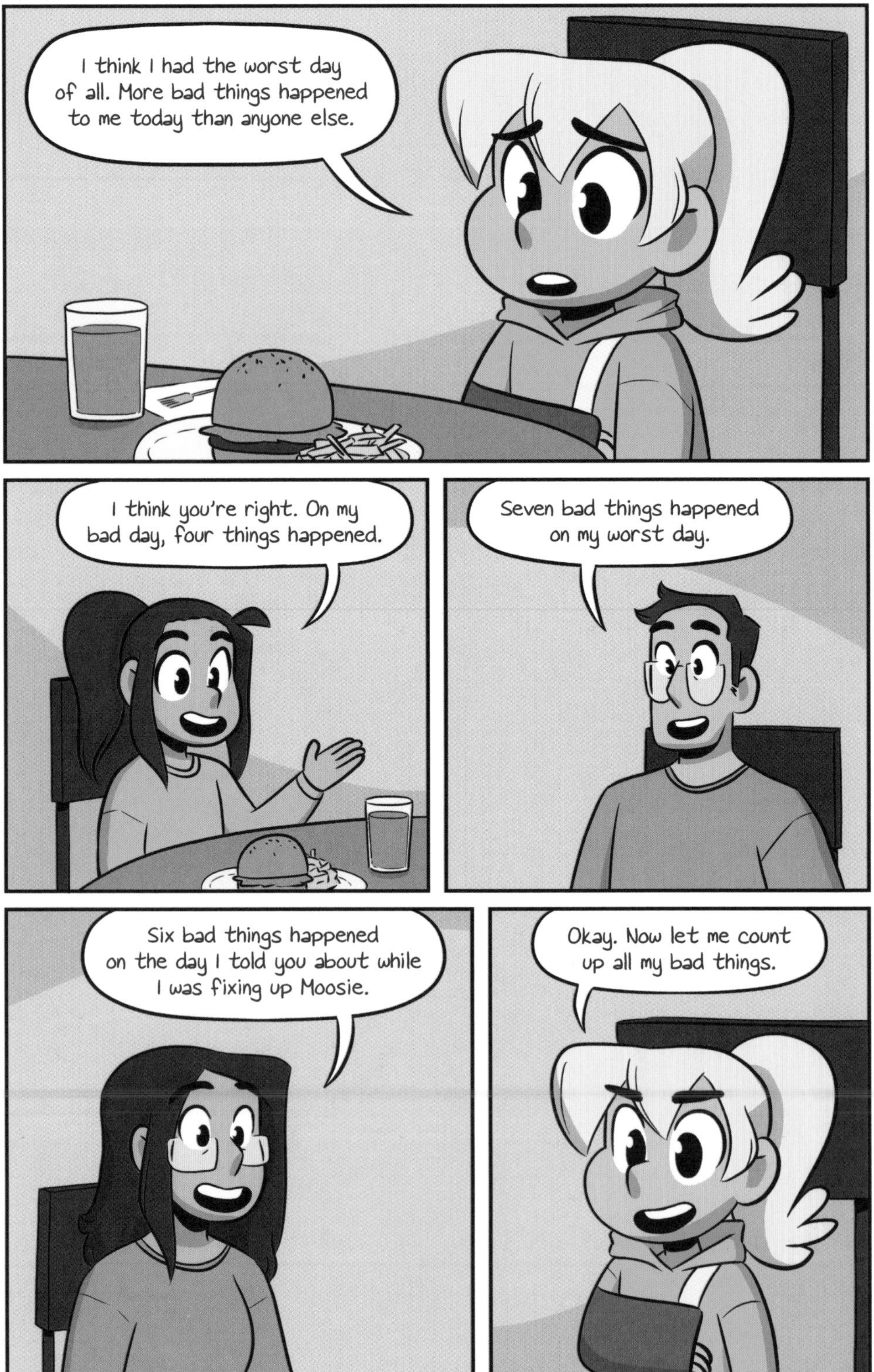
I think I had the worst day of all. More bad things happened to me today than anyone else.
I think you're right. On my bad day, four things happened.
Seven bad things happened on my worst day.
Six bad things happened on the day I told you about while I was fixing up Moosie.
Okay. Now let me count up all my bad things.

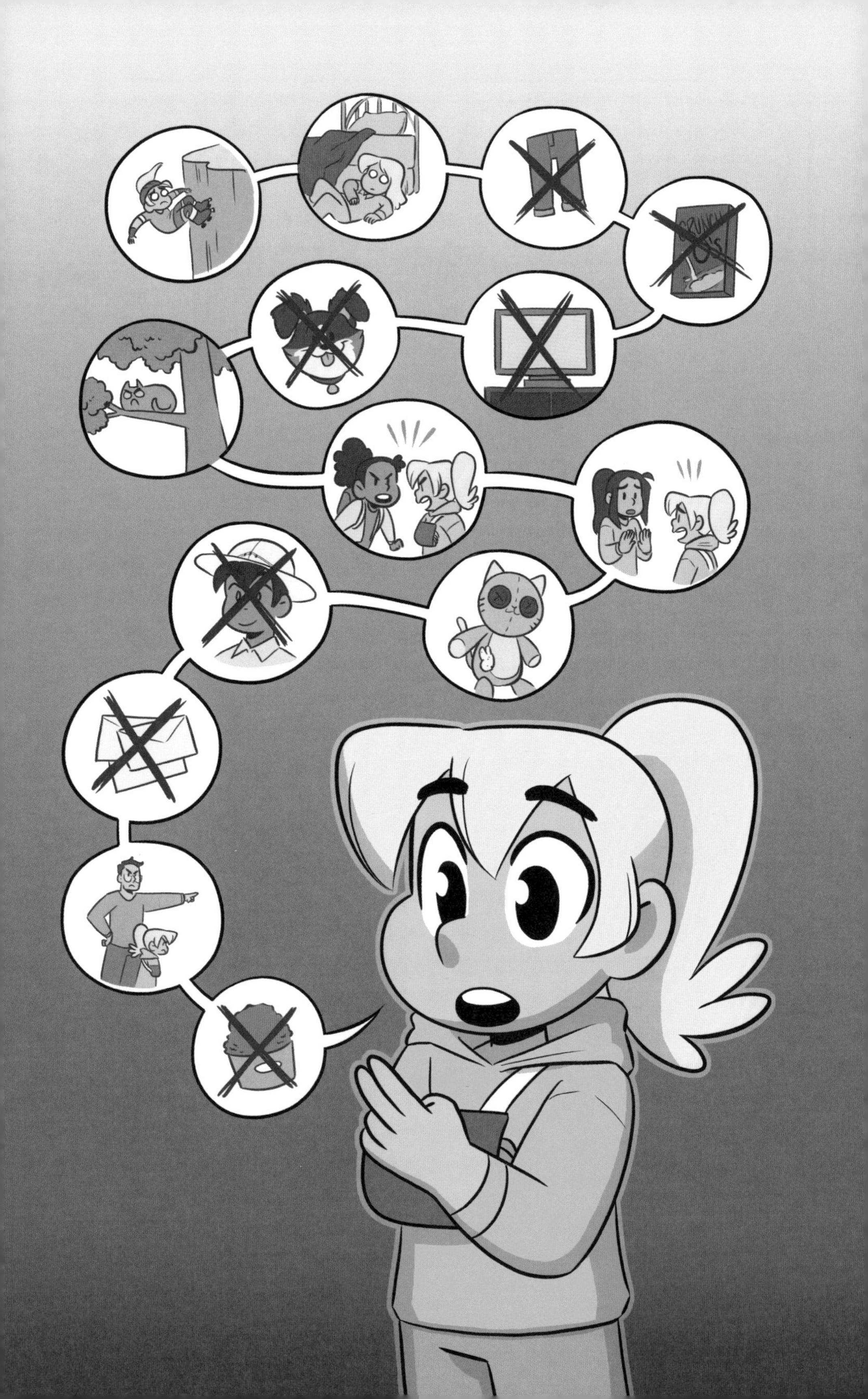

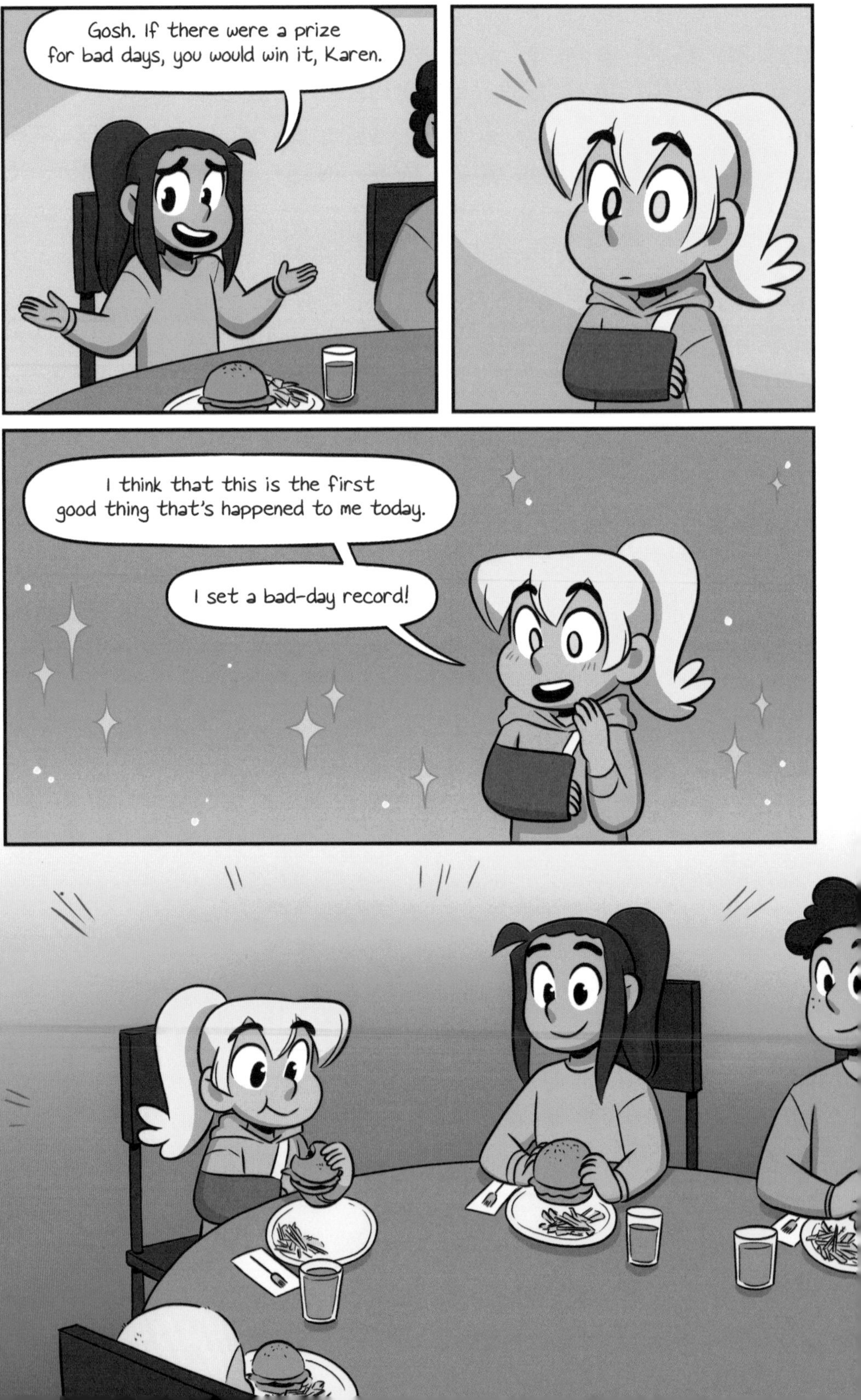
Gosh. If there were a prize for bad days, you would win it, Karen.
I think that this is the first good thing that's happened to me today.
I set a bad-day record!

CHAPTER 9

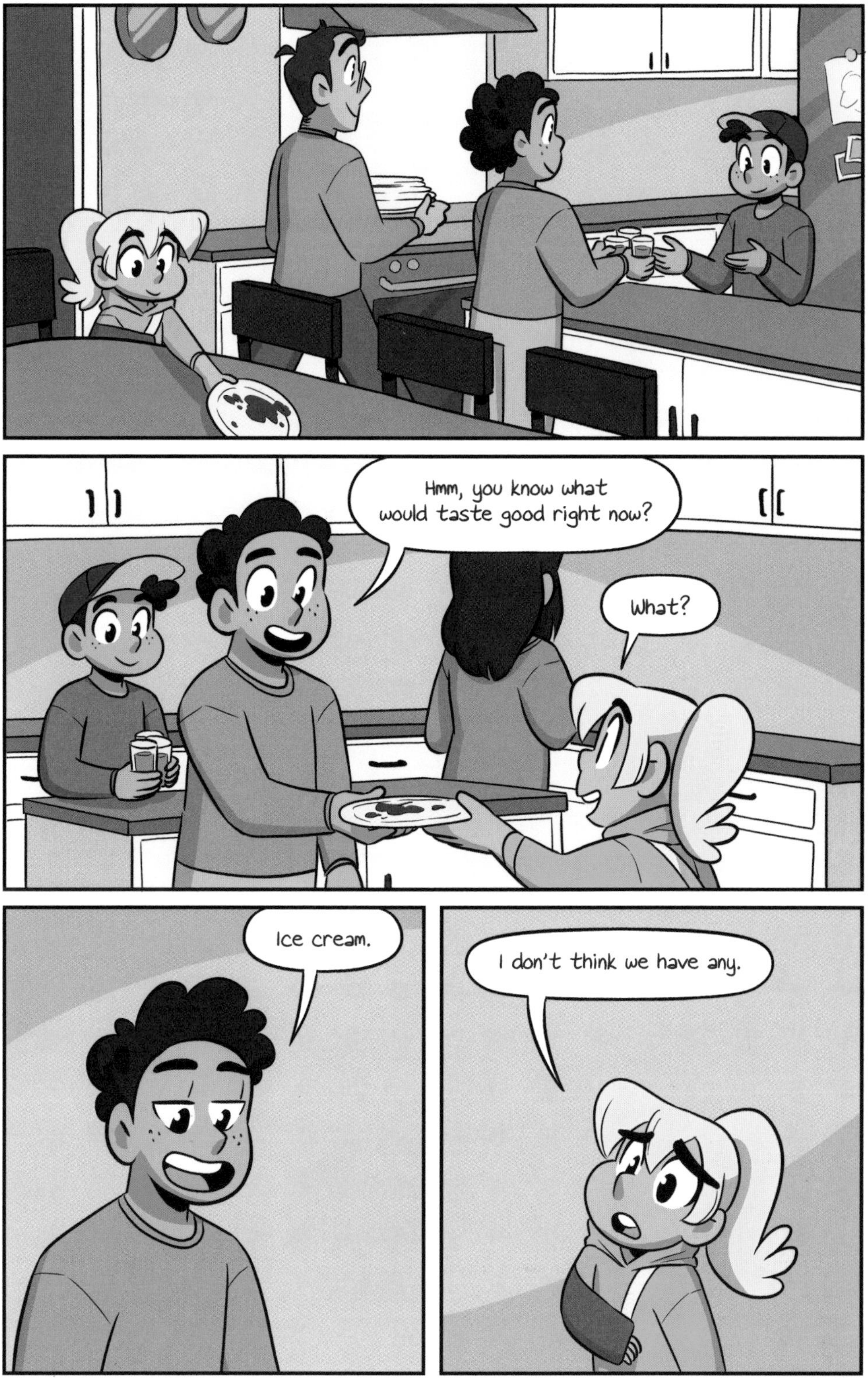
Hmm, you know what would taste good right now?
What?
Ice cream.
I don't think we have any.

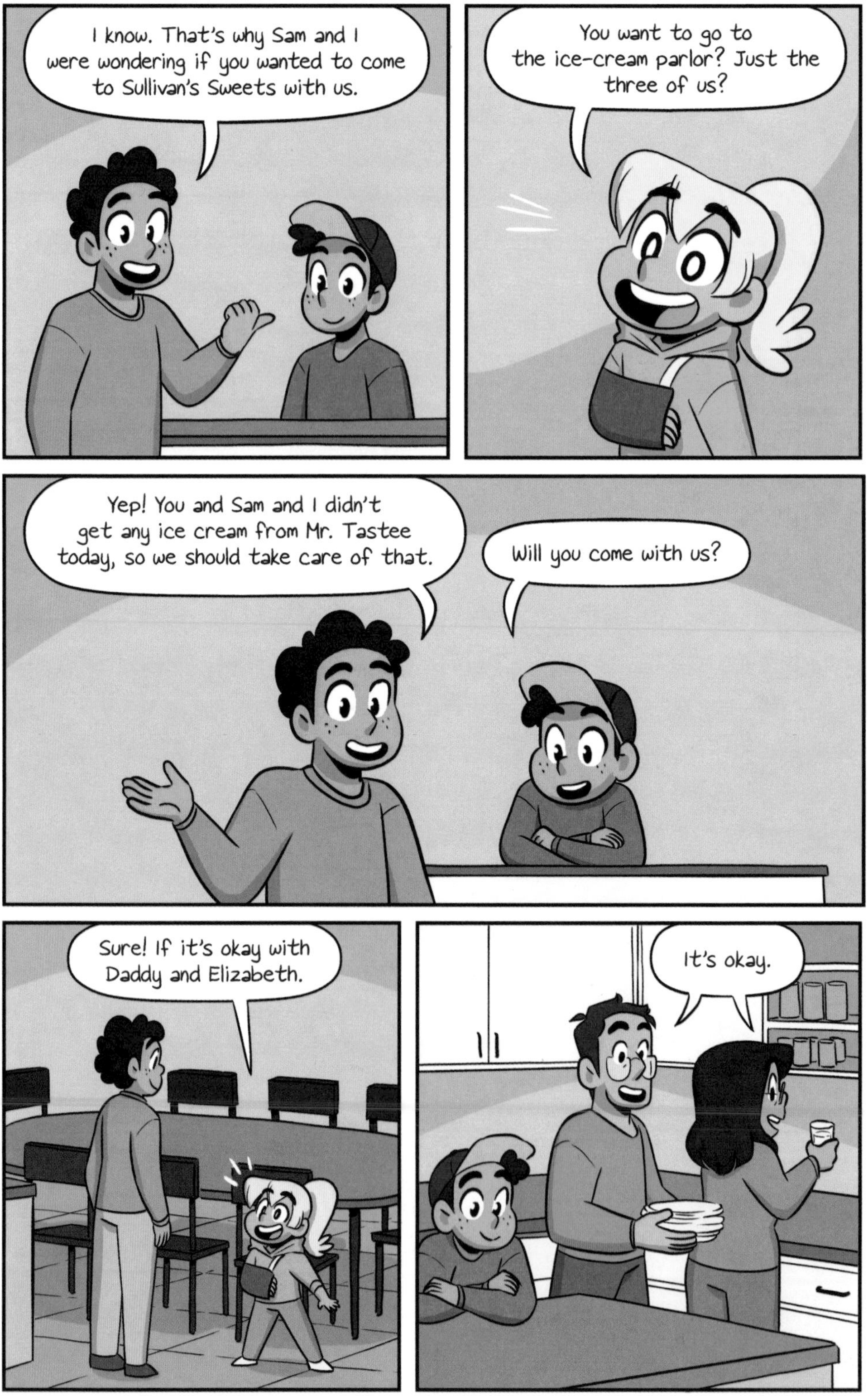
I know. That's why Sam and I were wondering if you wanted to come to Sullivan's Sweets with us.
You want to go to the ice-cream parlor? Just the three of us?
Yep! You and Sam and I didn't get any ice cream from Mr. Tastee today, so we should take care of that.
Will you come with us?
Sure! If it's okay with Daddy and Elizabeth.
It's okay.

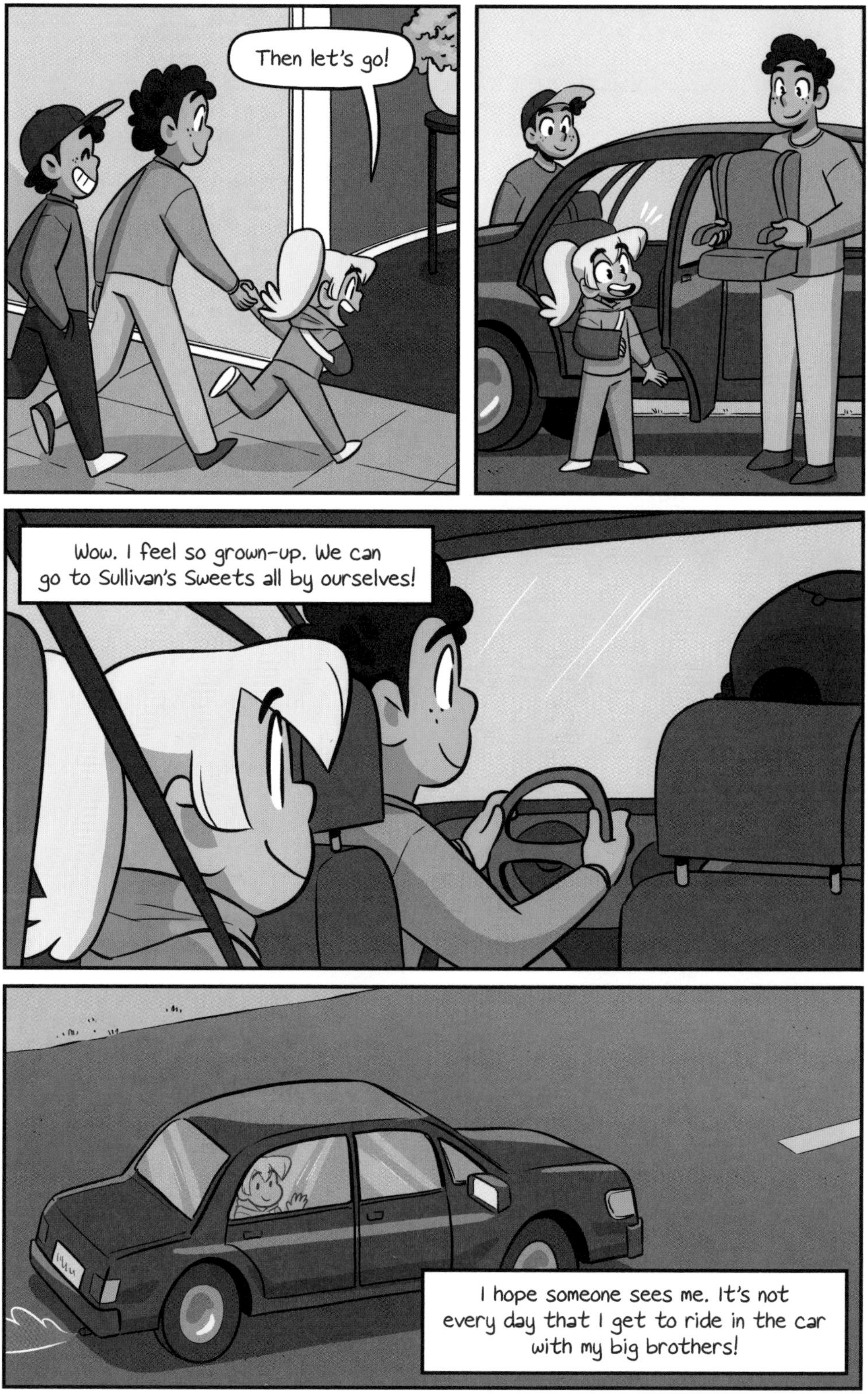
Then let's go!
Wow. I feel so grown-up. We can go to Sullivan's Sweets all by ourselves!
I hope someone sees me. It's not every day that I get to ride in the car with my big brothers!

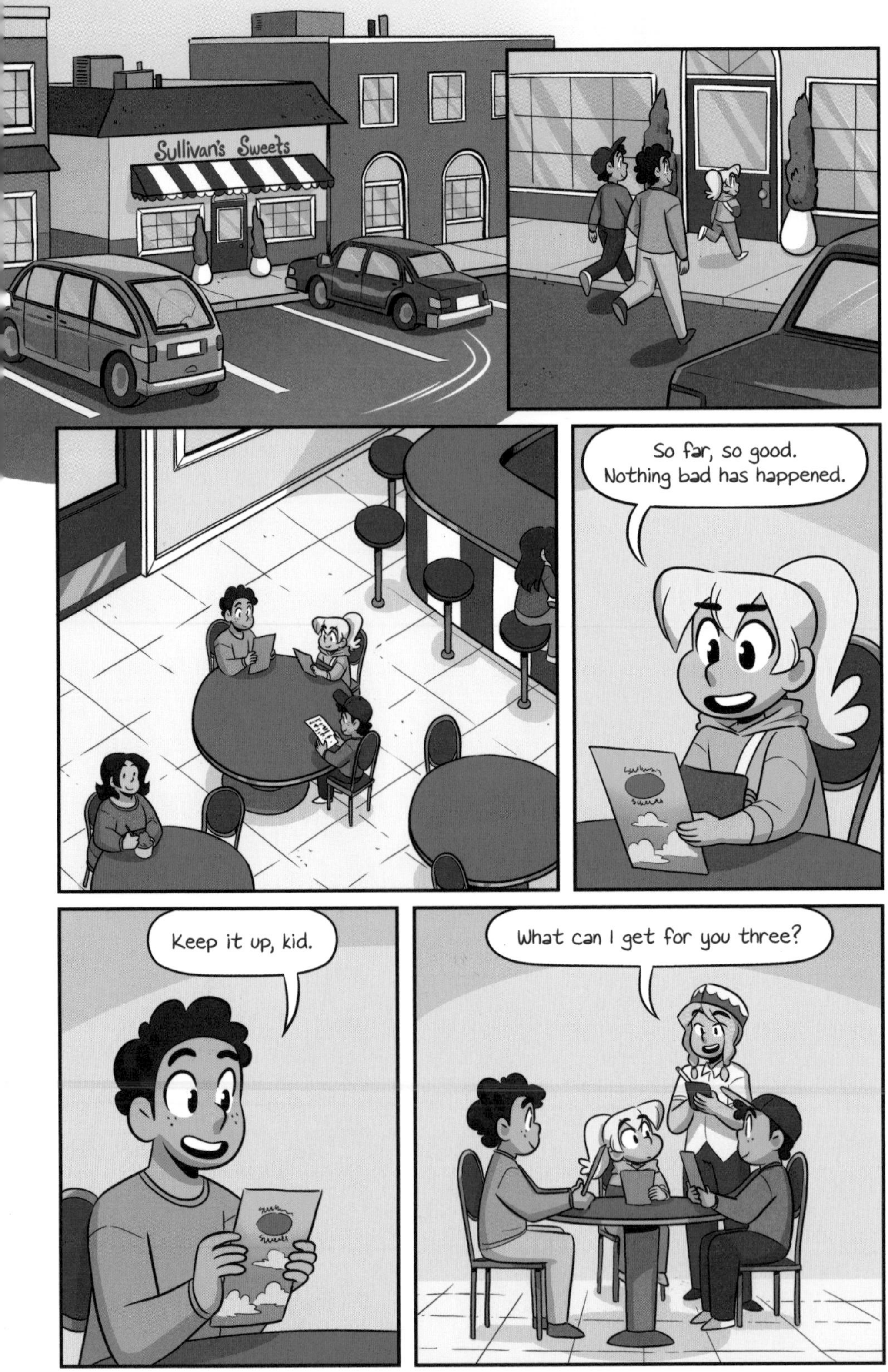
Sullivan's Sweets
So far, so good. Nothing bad has happened.
Keep it up, kid.
What can I get for you three?

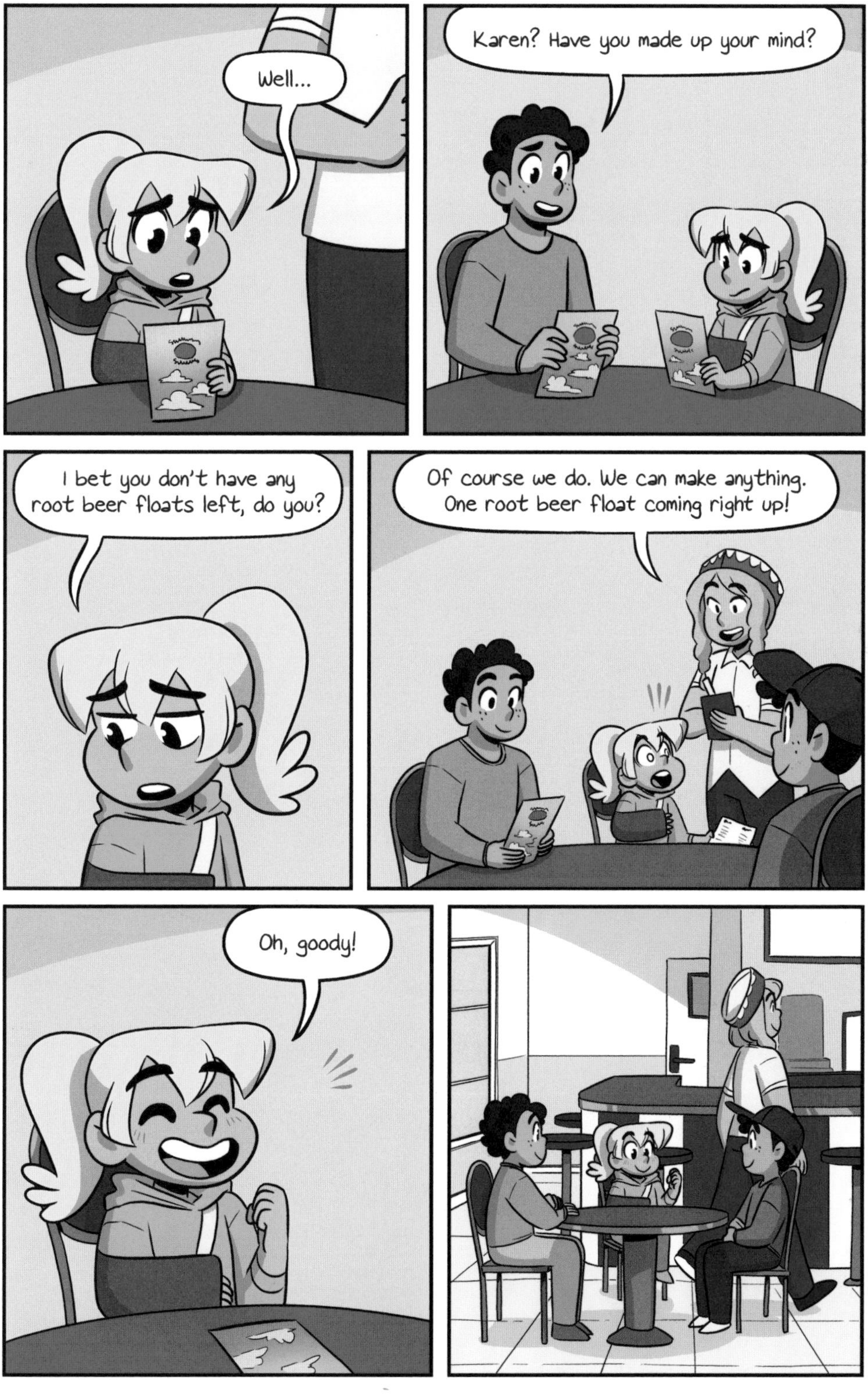

Well...
Karen? Have you made up your mind?
I bet you don't have any root beer floats left, do you?
Of course we do. We can make anything. One root beer float coming right up!
Oh, goody!

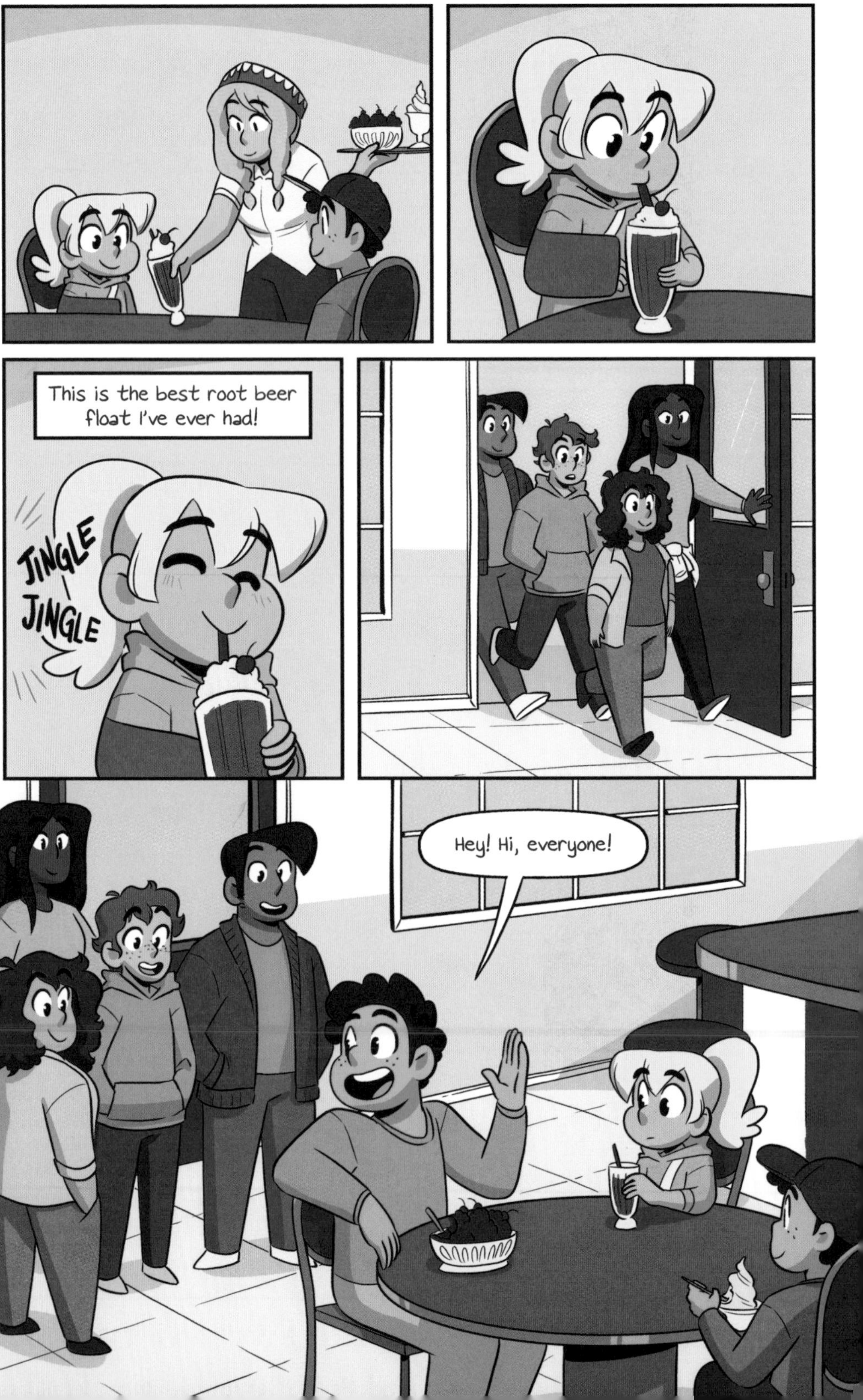
This is the best root beer float I've ever had!
JINGLE
JINGLE
Hey! Hi, everyone!

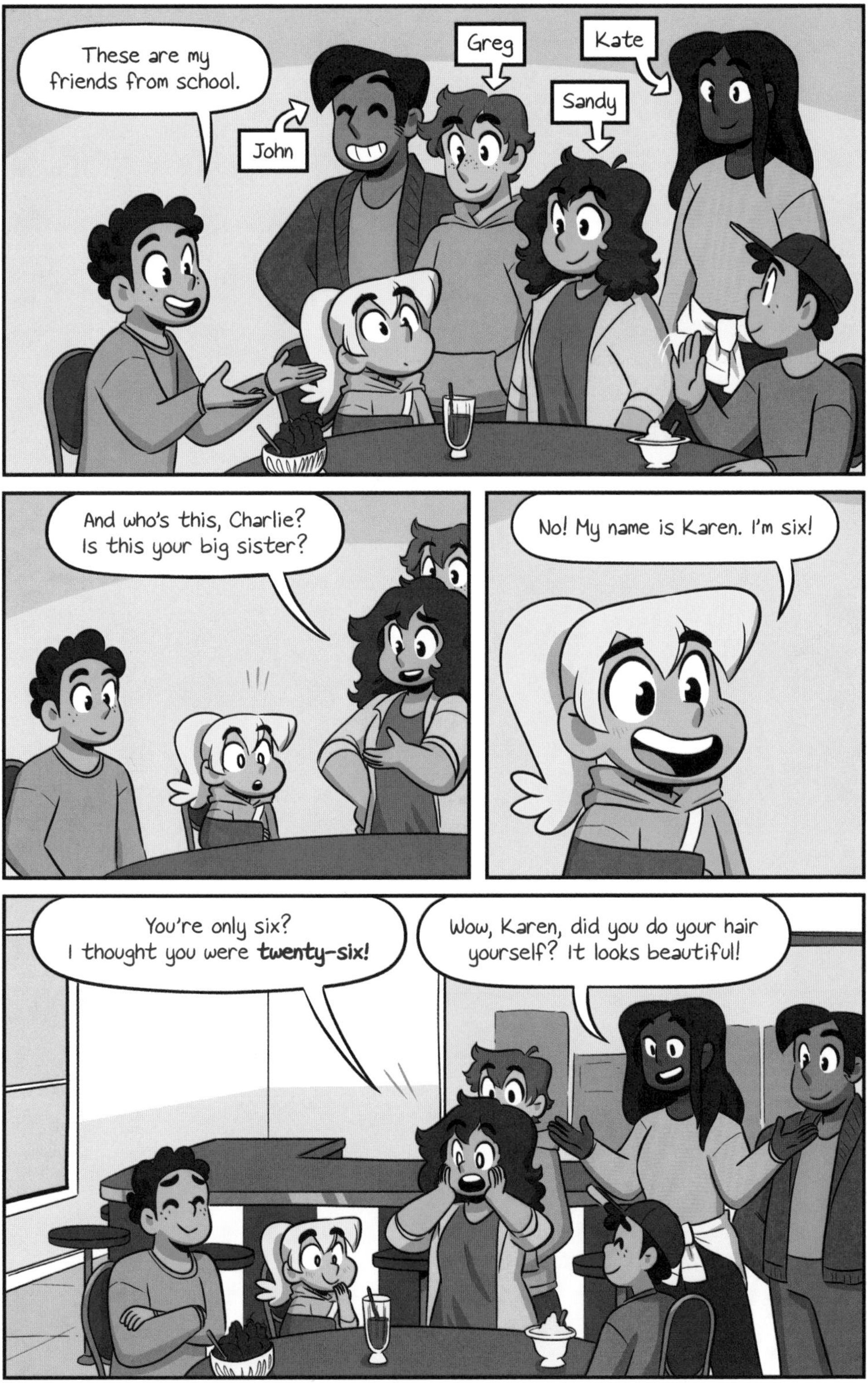
These are my friends from school.
John
Greg
Sandy
Kate
And who's this, Charlie? Is this your big sister?
No! My name is Karen. I'm six!
You're only six? I thought you were **twenty-six!**
Wow, Karen, did you do your hair yourself? It looks beautiful!

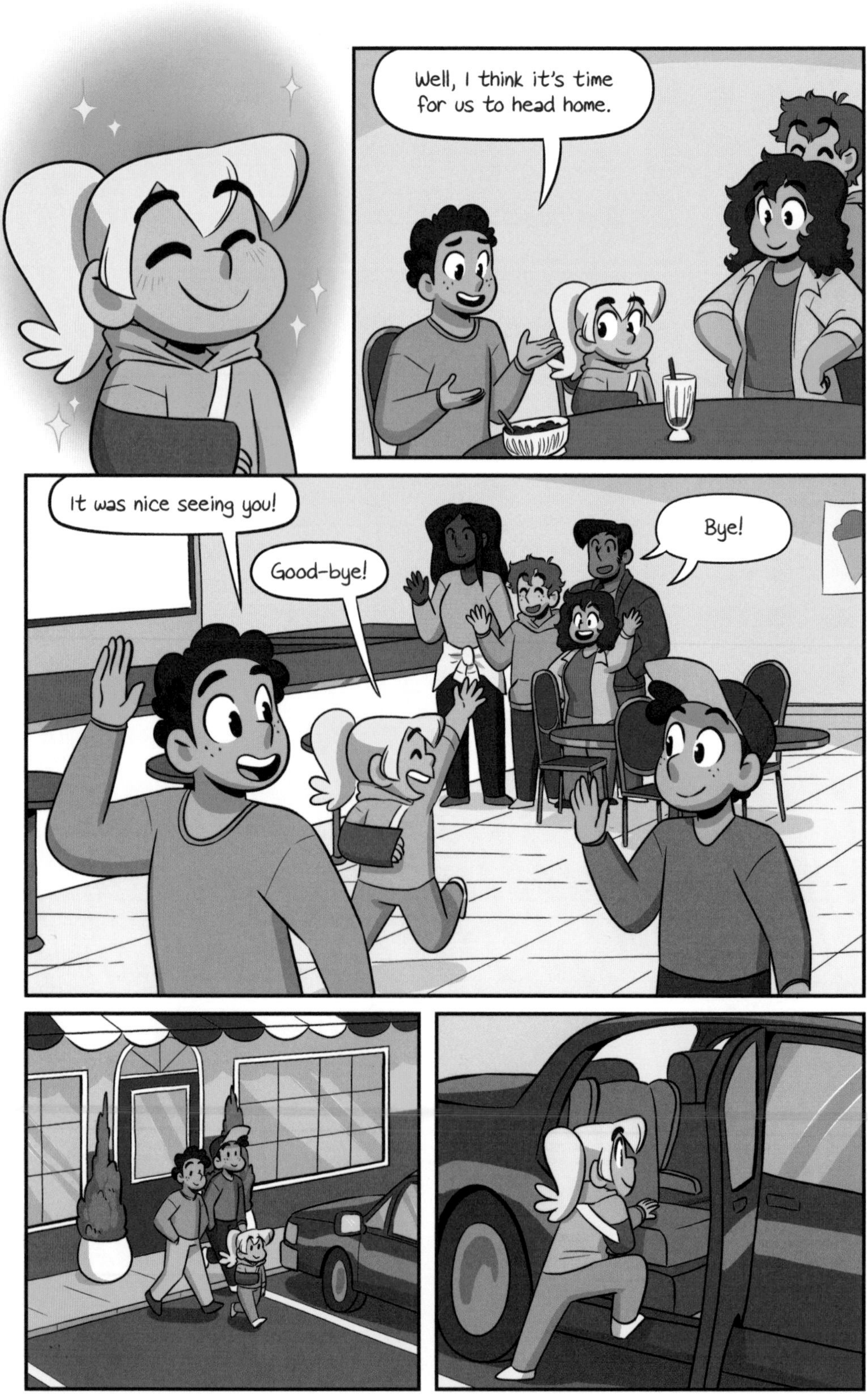
Well, I think it's time for us to head home.
It was nice seeing you!
Good-bye!
Bye!

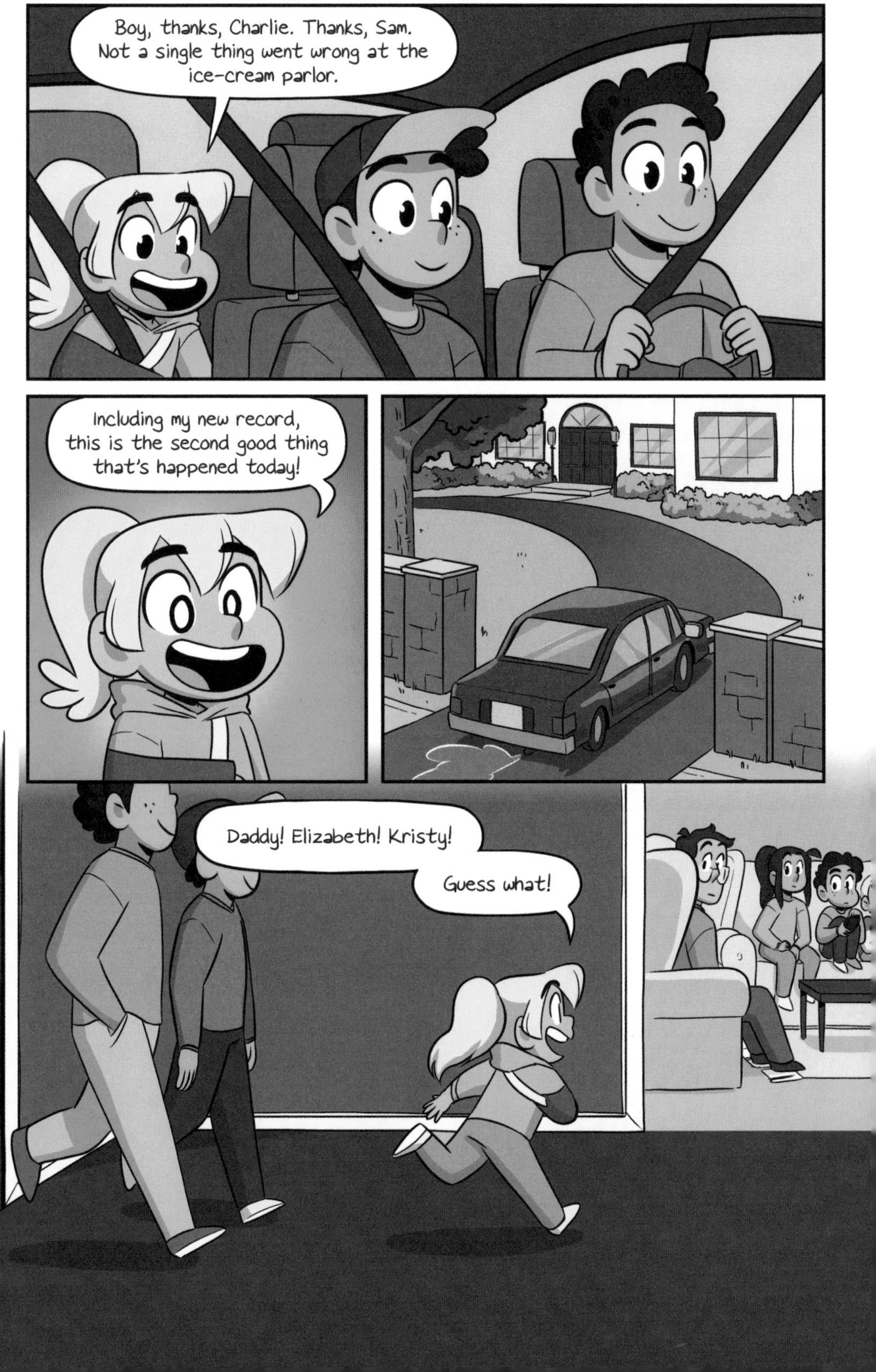
Boy, thanks, Charlie. Thanks, Sam. Not a single thing went wrong at the ice-cream parlor.
Including my new record, this is the second good thing that's happened today!
Daddy! Elizabeth! Kristy!
Guess what!

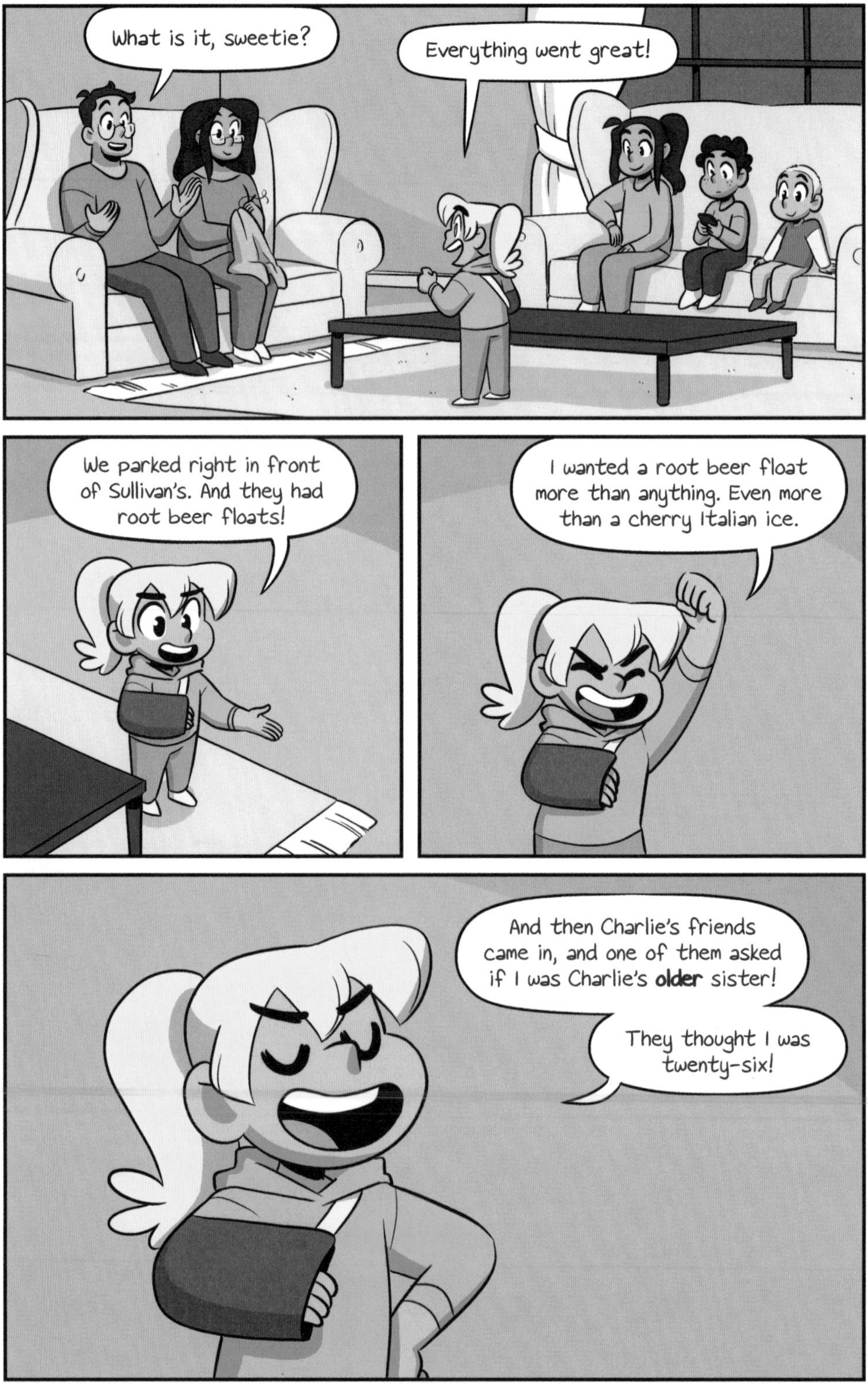
What is it, sweetie?
Everything went great!
We parked right in front of Sullivan's. And they had root beer floats!
I wanted a root beer float more than anything. Even more than a cherry Italian ice.
And then Charlie's friends came in, and one of them asked if I was Charlie's **older** sister!
They thought I was twenty-six!

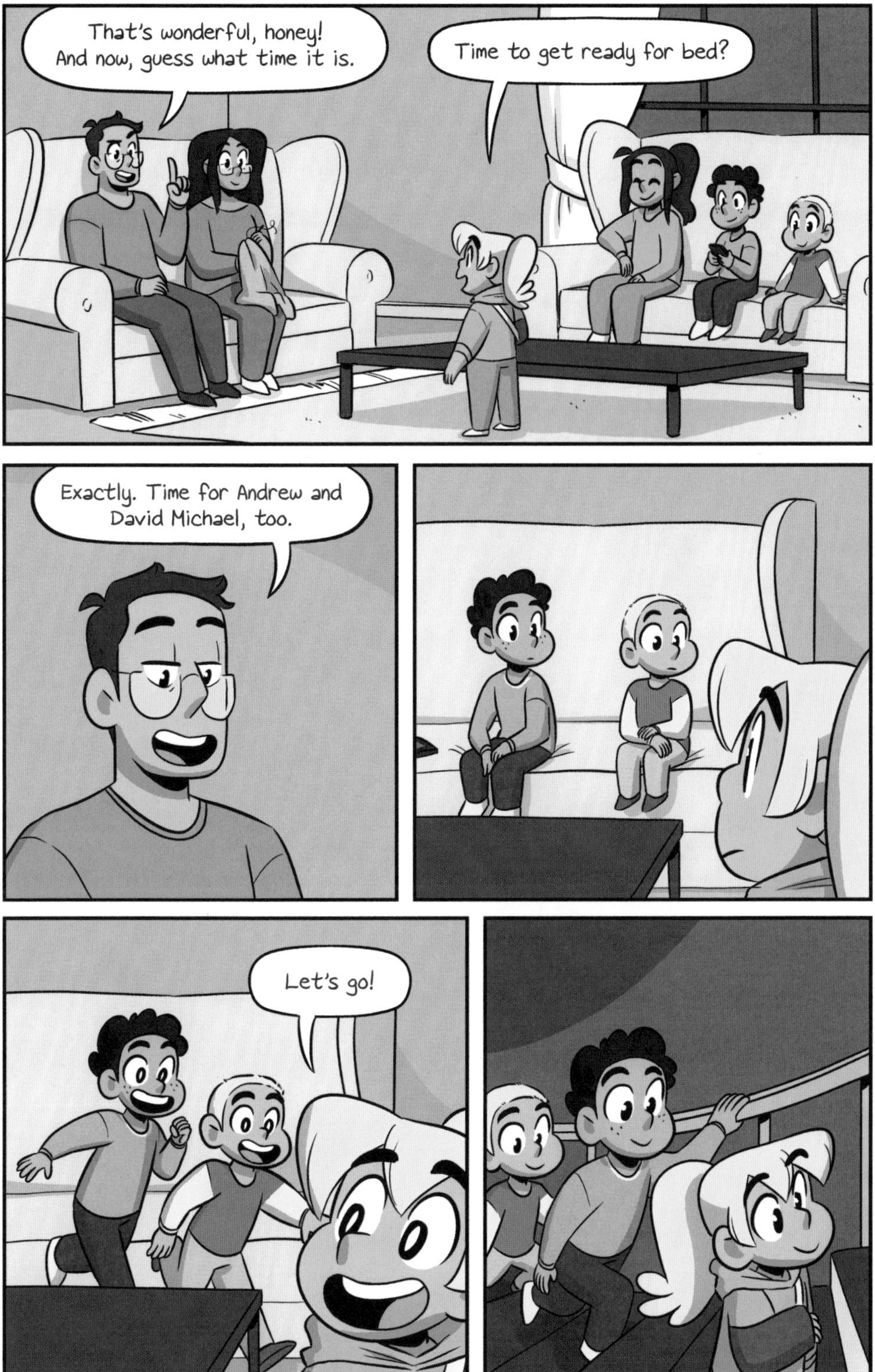
That's wonderful, honey!
And now, guess what time it is.
Time to get ready for bed?
Exactly. Time for Andrew and
David Michael, too.
Let's go!

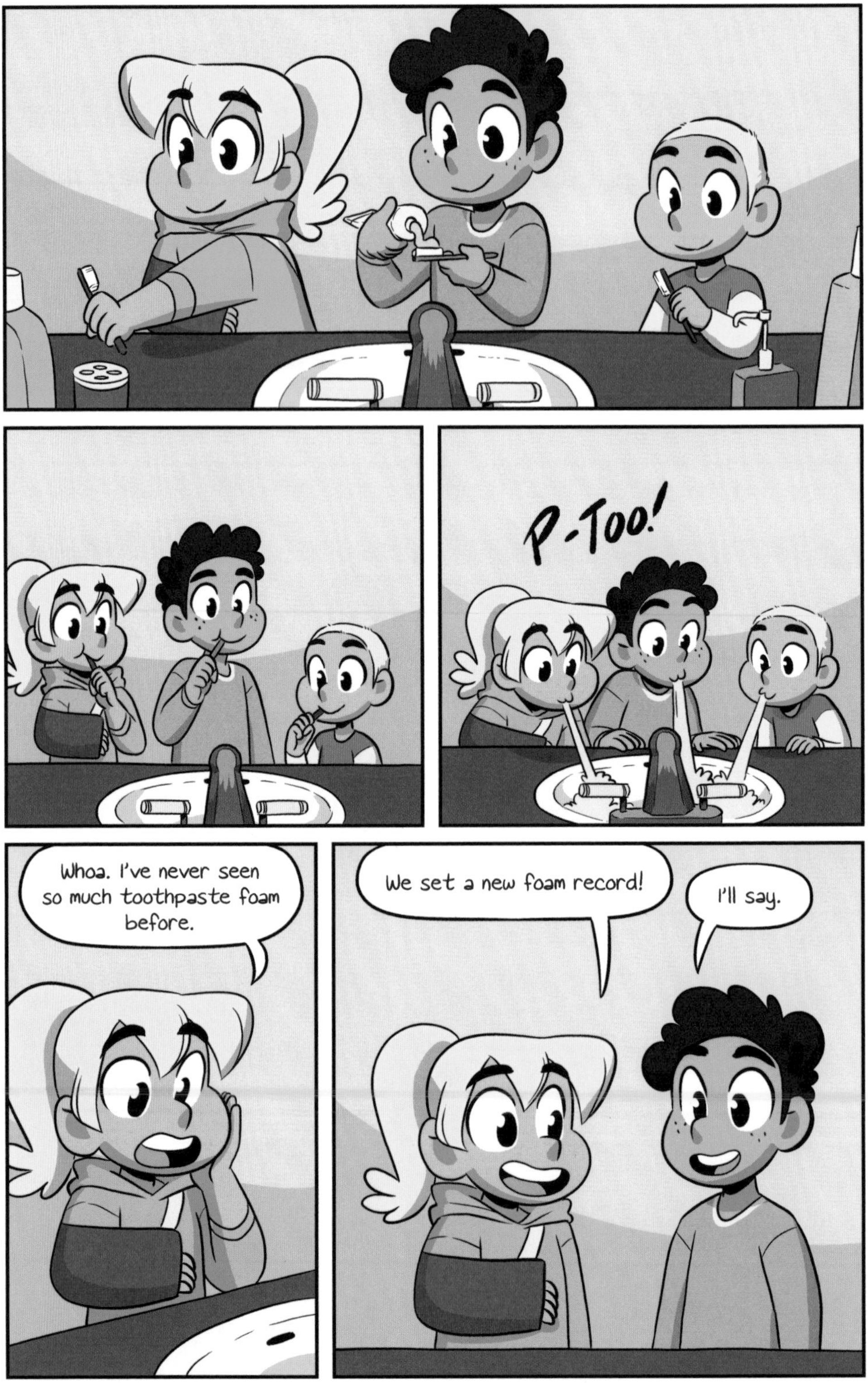
P-TOO!
Whoa. I've never seen so much toothpaste foam before.
We set a new foam record!
I'll say.

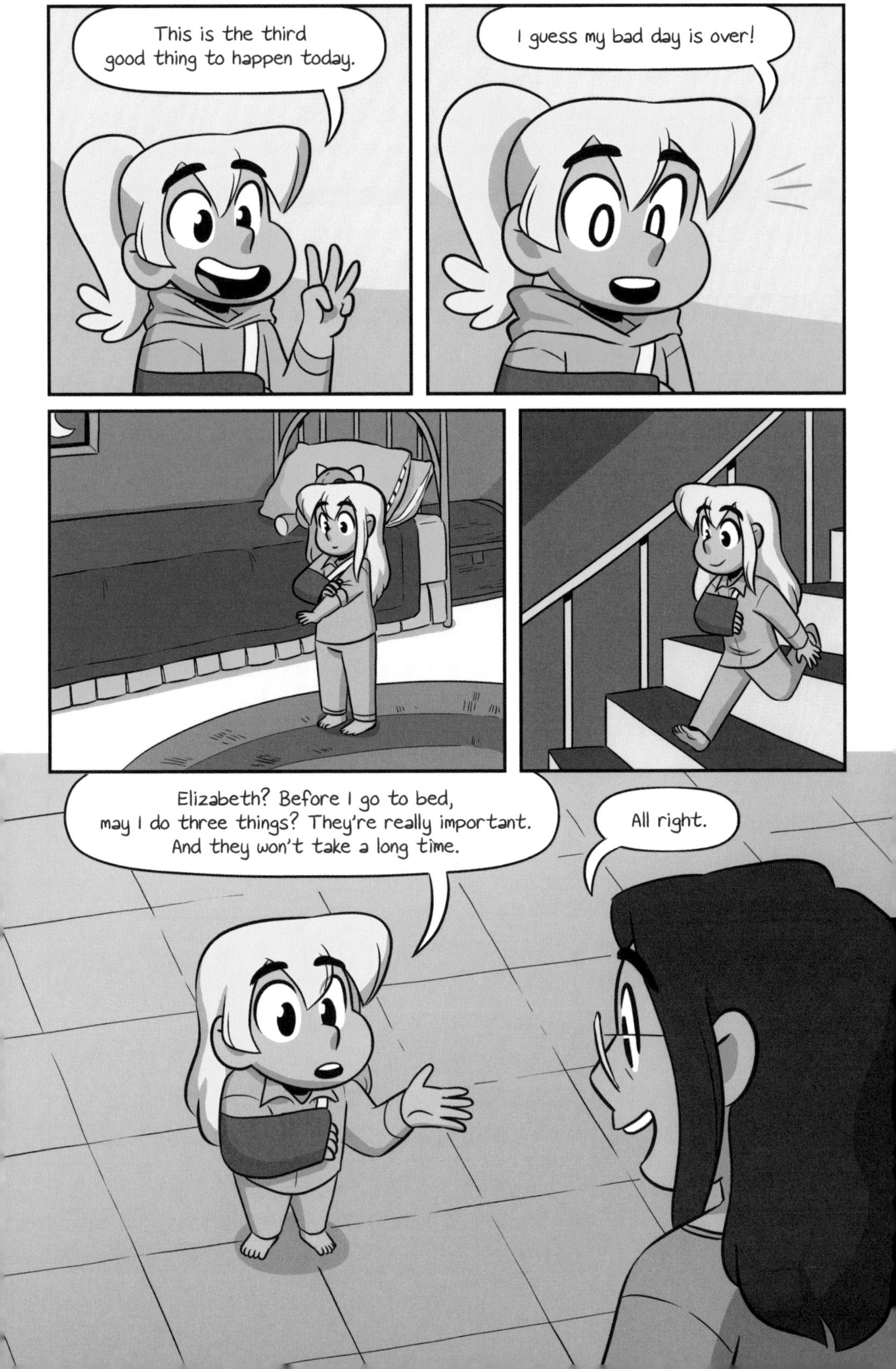
This is the third good thing to happen today.
I guess my bad day is over!
Elizabeth? Before I go to bed, may I do three things? They're really important. And they won't take a long time.
All right.

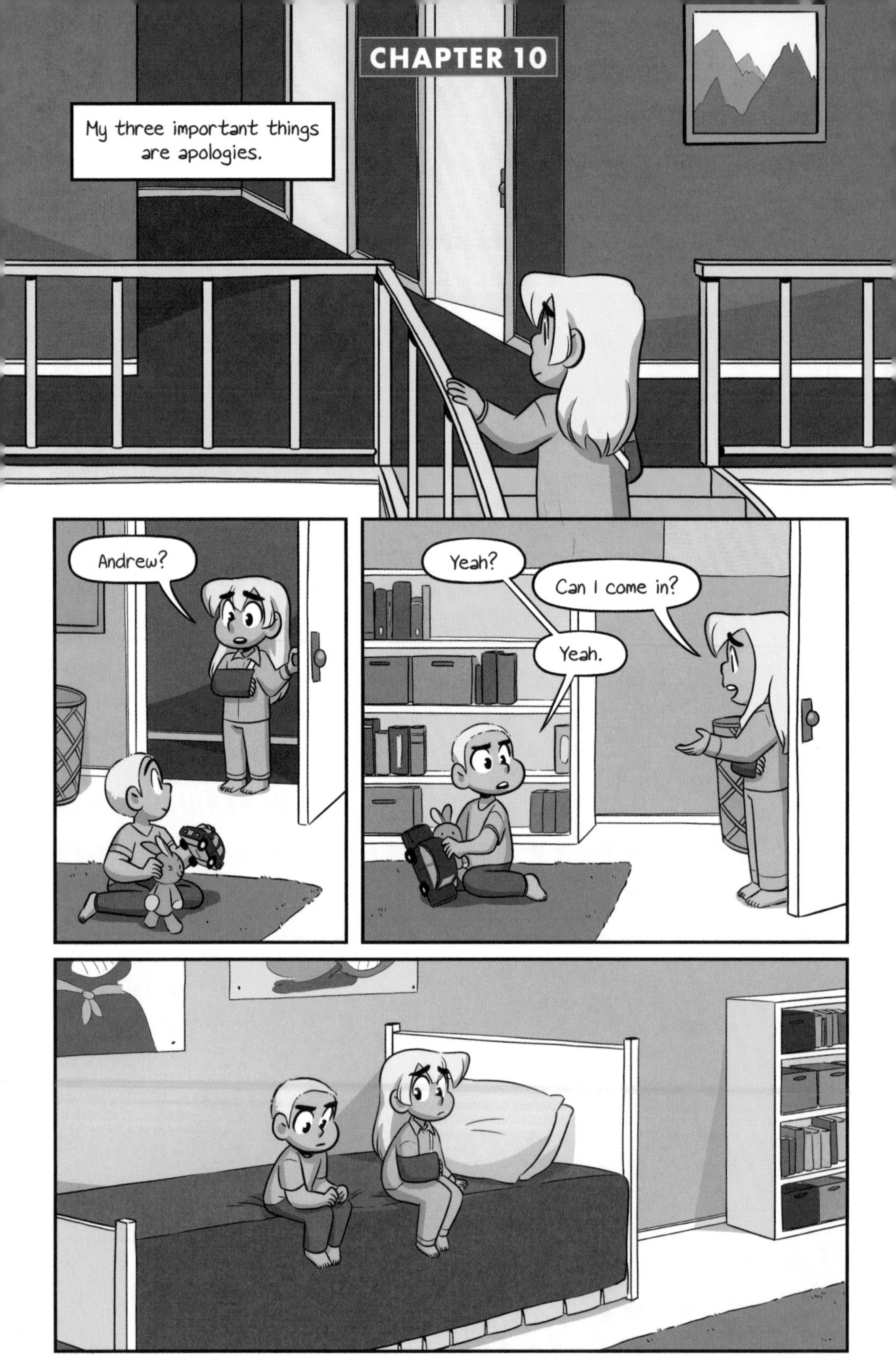
CHAPTER 10
My three important things are apologies.
Andrew?
Yeah?
Can I come in?
Yeah.

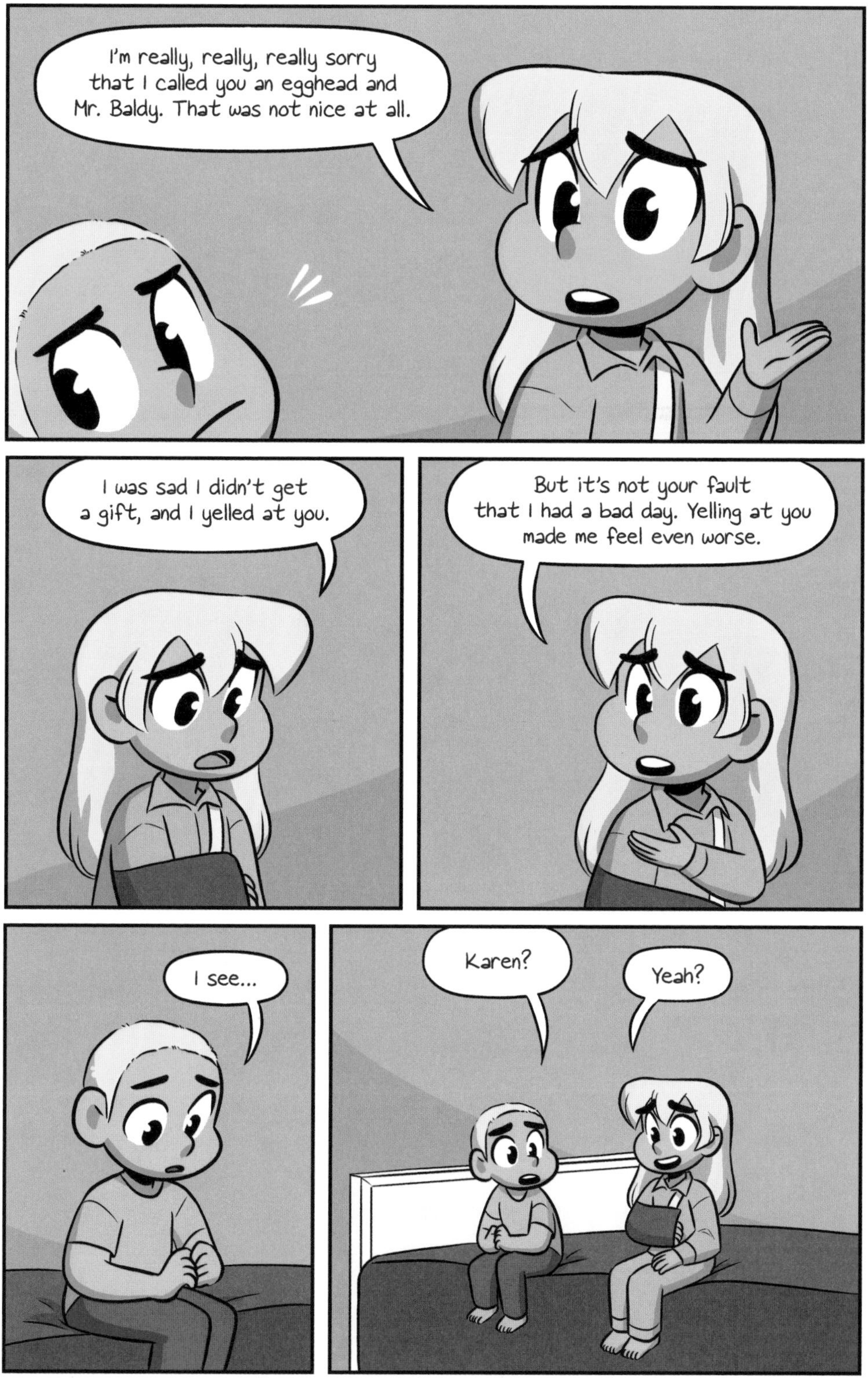
I'm really, really, really sorry that I called you an egghead and Mr. Baldy. That was not nice at all.
I was sad I didn't get a gift, and I yelled at you.
But it's not your fault that I had a bad day. Yelling at you made me feel even worse.
I see...
Karen?
Yeah?

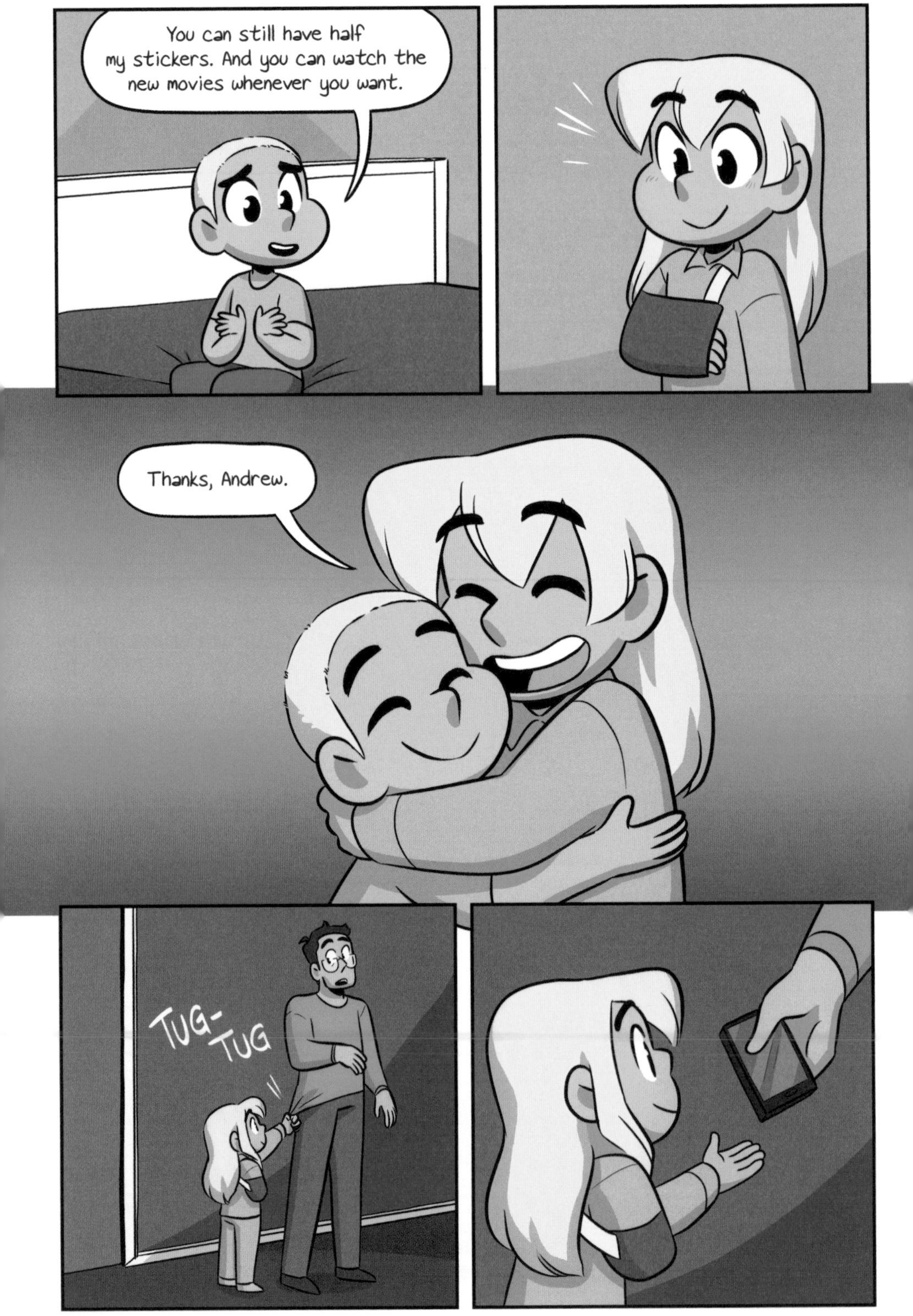
You can still have half my stickers. And you can watch the new movies whenever you want.
Thanks, Andrew.
TUG-TUG

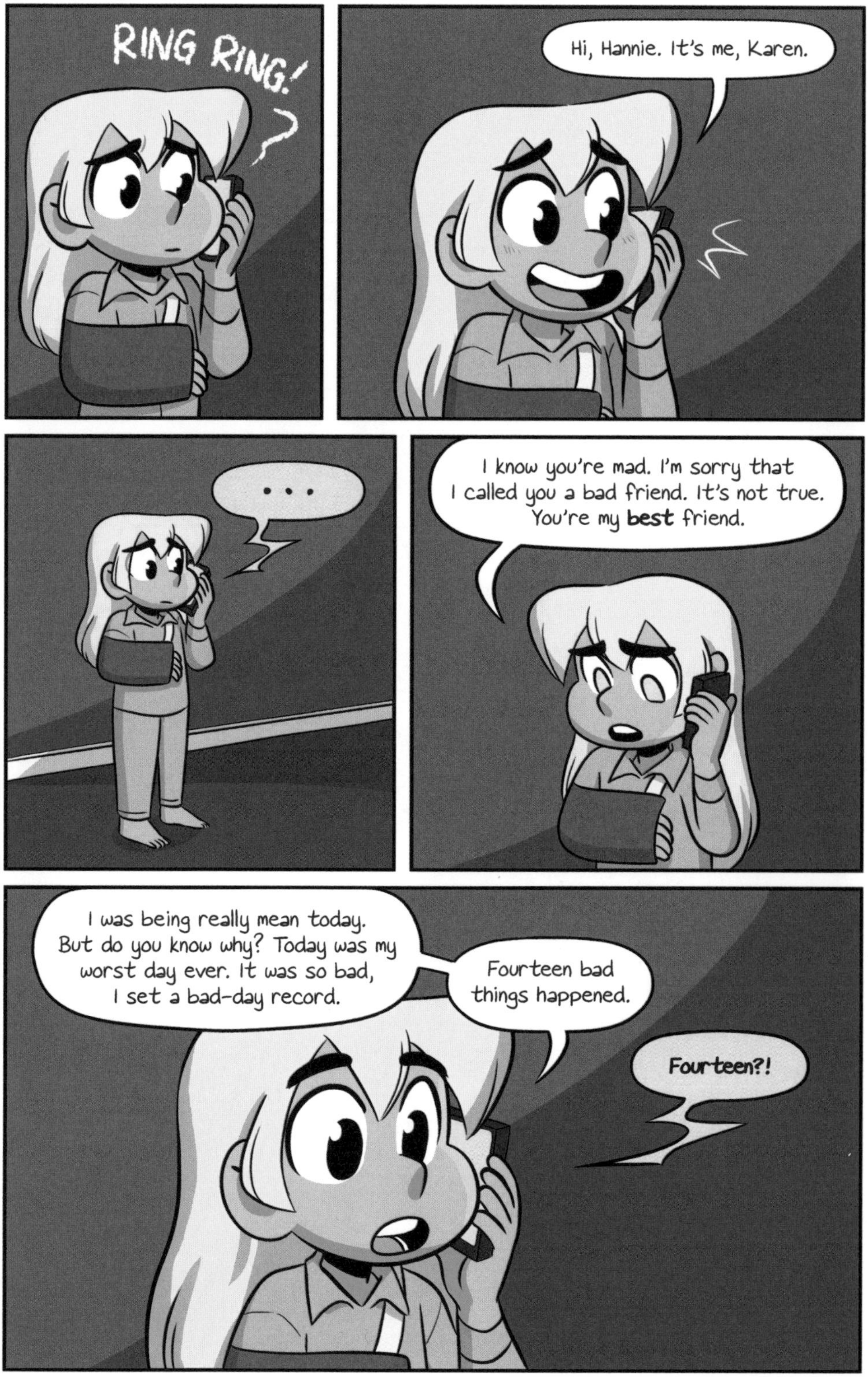
RING RING!
Hi, Hannie. It's me, Karen.
. . .
I know you're mad. I'm sorry that I called you a bad friend. It's not true. You're my **best** friend.
I was being really mean today. But do you know why? Today was my worst day ever. It was so bad, I set a bad-day record.
Fourteen bad things happened.
Fourteen?!

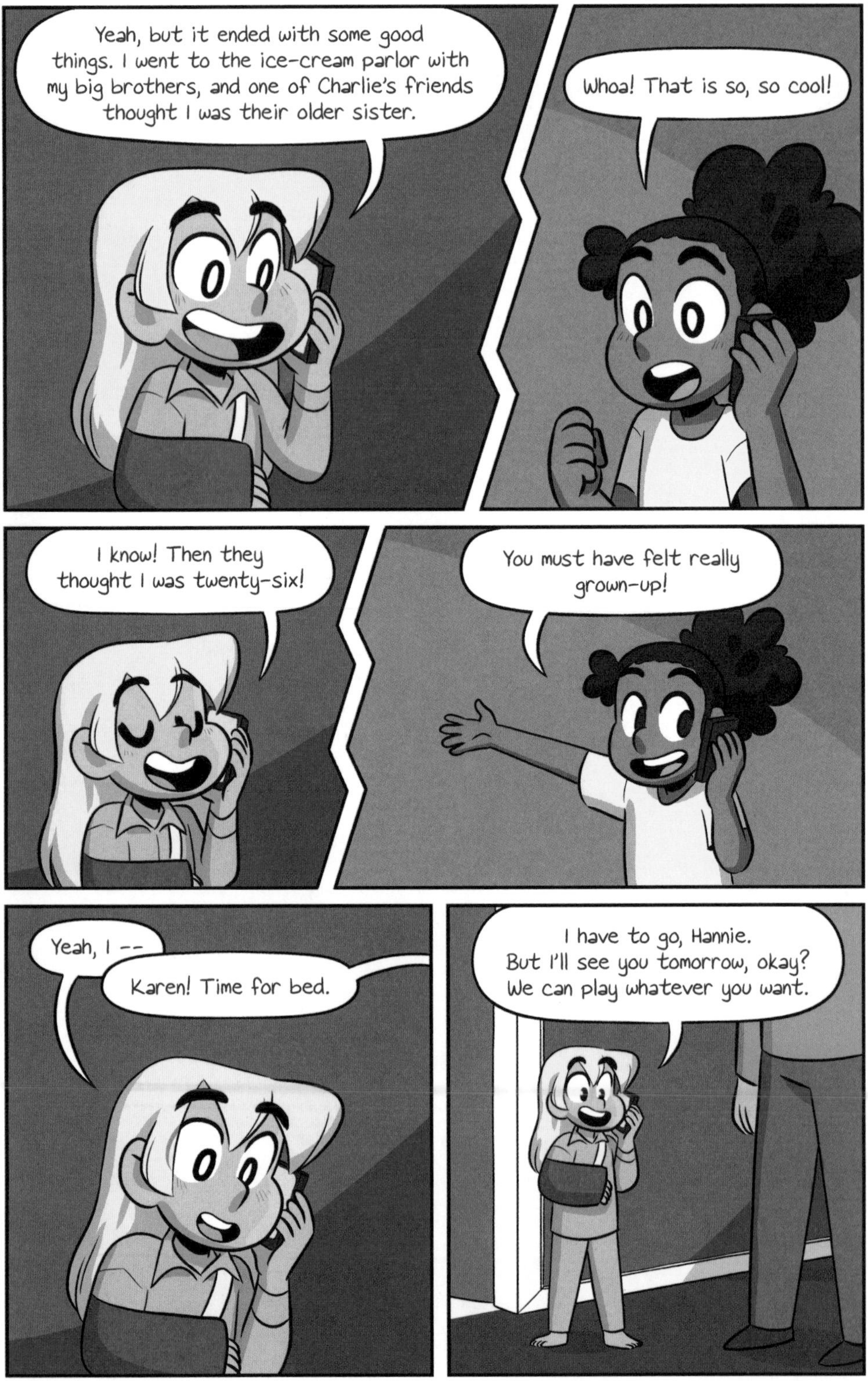
Yeah, but it ended with some good things. I went to the ice-cream parlor with my big brothers, and one of Charlie's friends thought I was their older sister.
Whoa! That is so, so cool!
I know! Then they thought I was twenty-six!
You must have felt really grown-up!
Yeah, I --
Karen! Time for bed.
I have to go, Hannie. But I'll see you tomorrow, okay? We can play whatever you want.

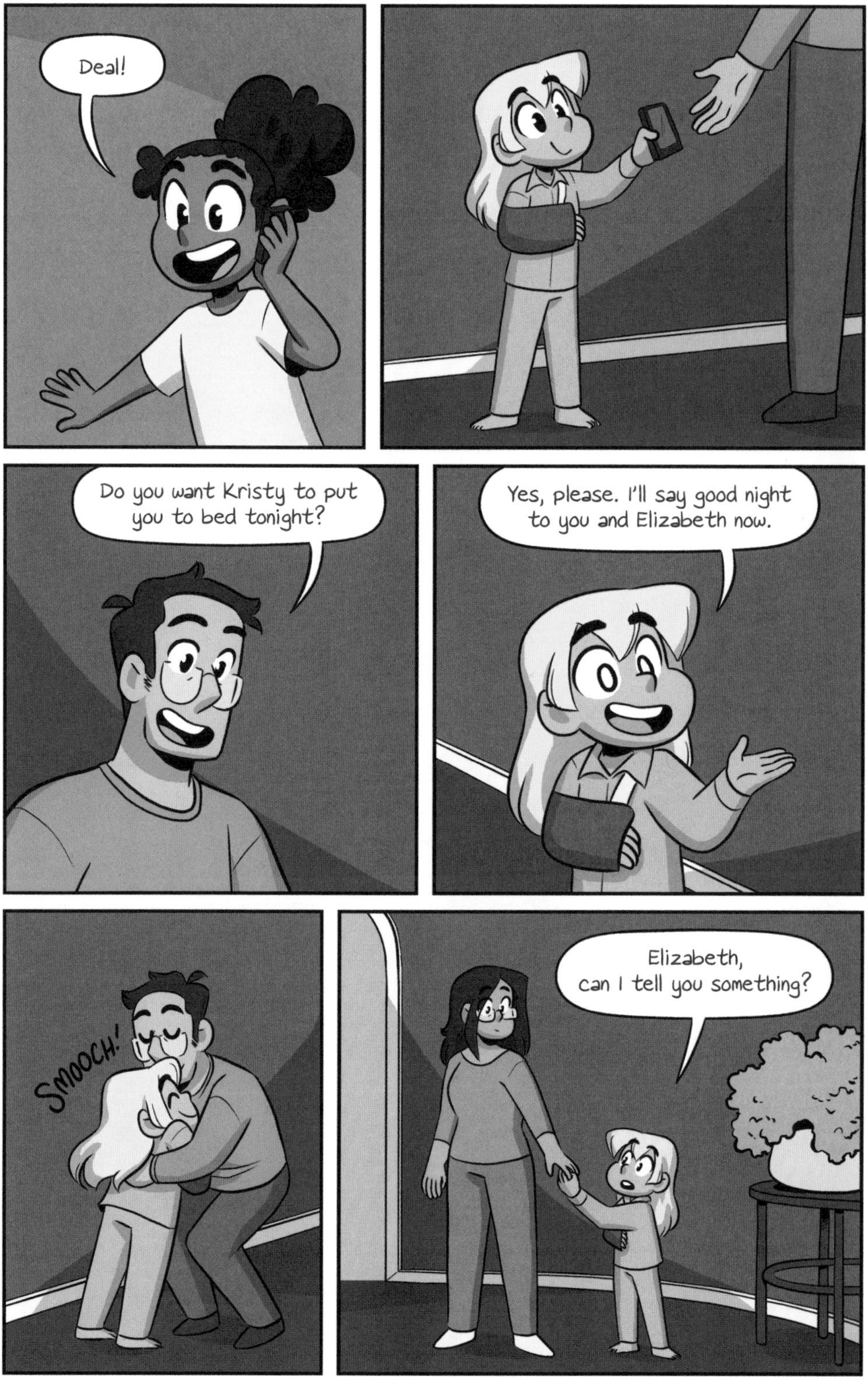
Deal!
Do you want Kristy to put you to bed tonight?
Yes, please. I'll say good night to you and Elizabeth now.
SMOOCH!
Elizabeth, can I tell you something?

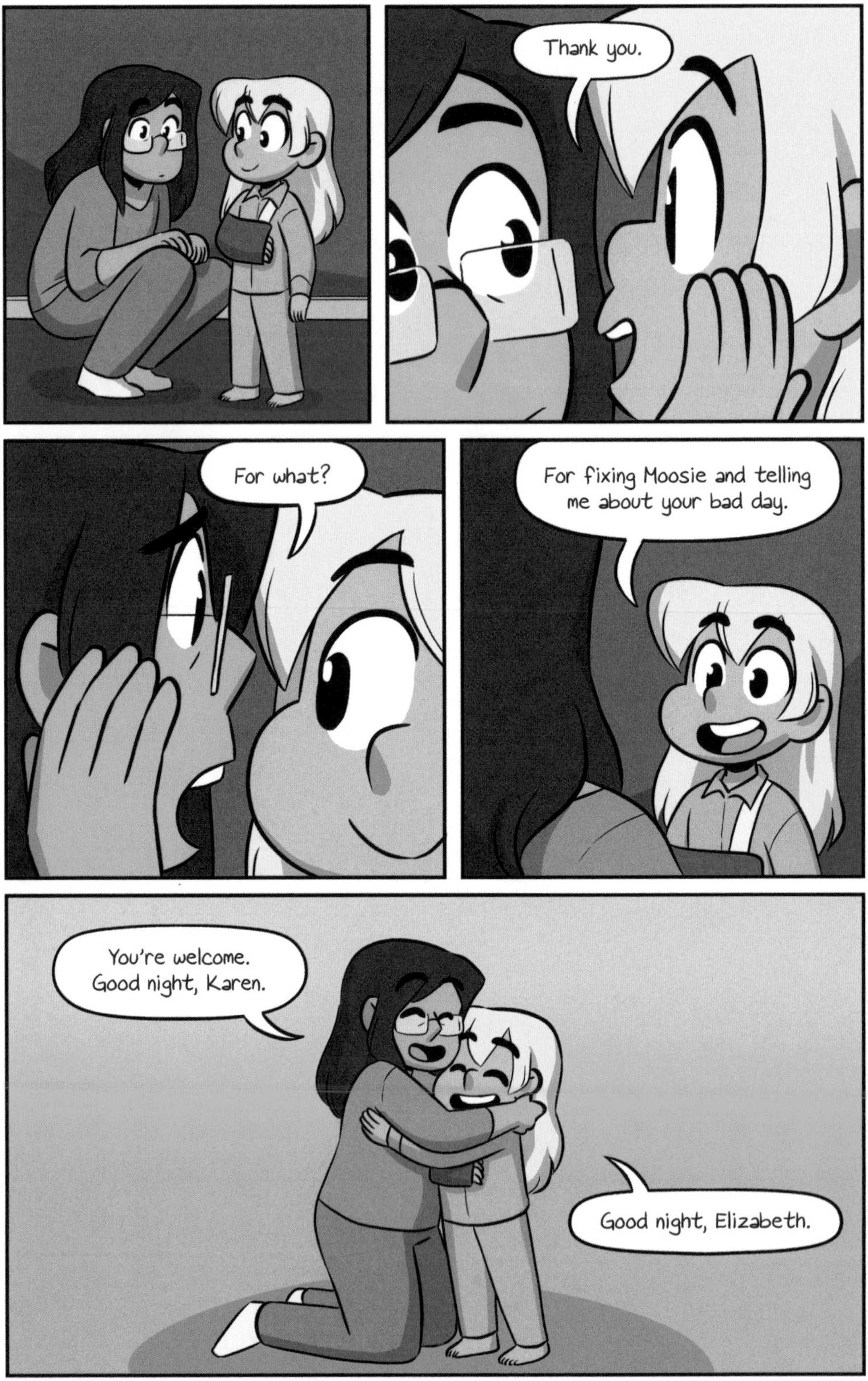
Thank you.
For what?
For fixing Moosie and telling me about your bad day.
You're welcome. Good night, Karen.
Good night, Elizabeth.

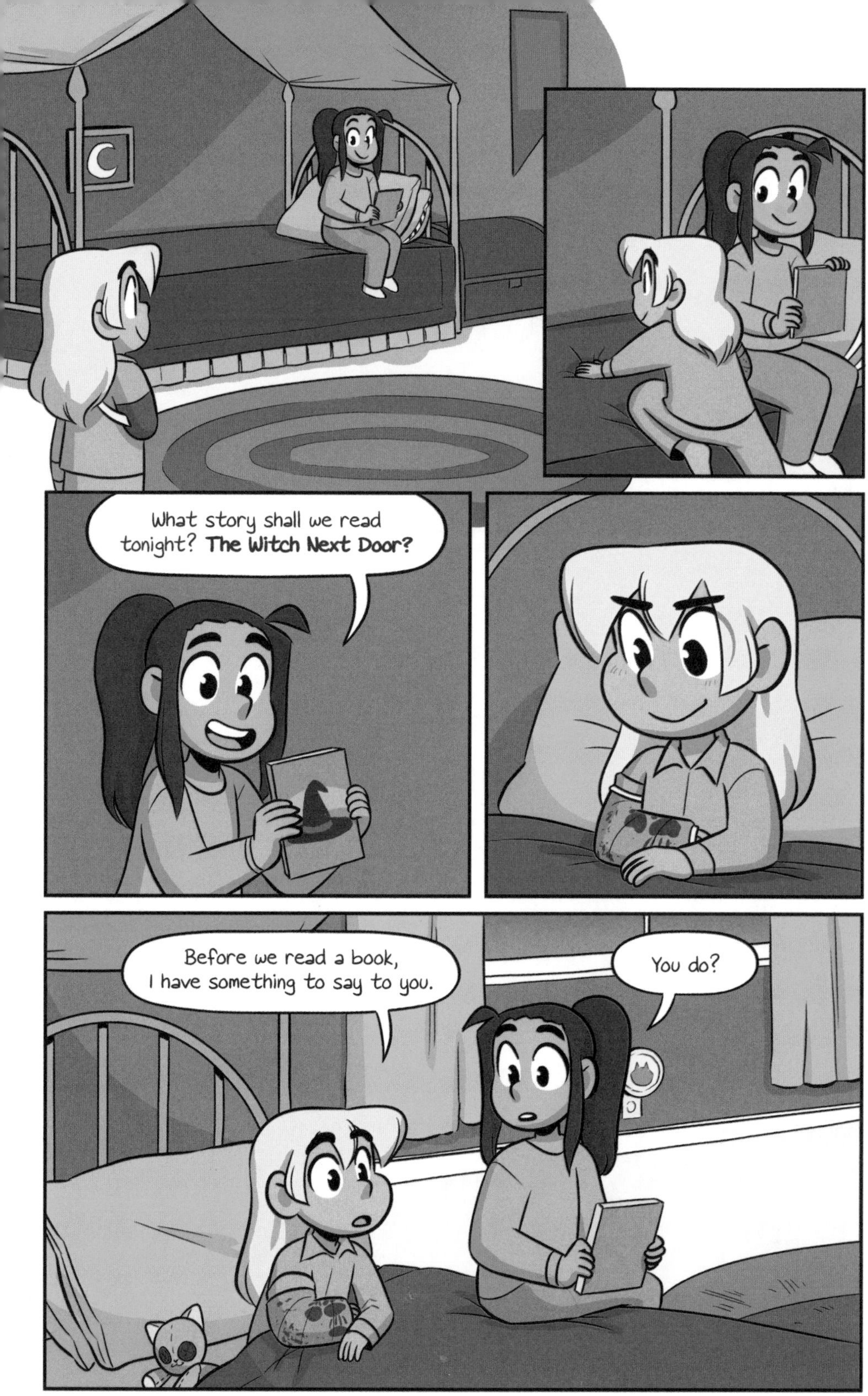
What story shall we read tonight? **The Witch Next Door?**
Before we read a book, I have something to say to you.
You do?

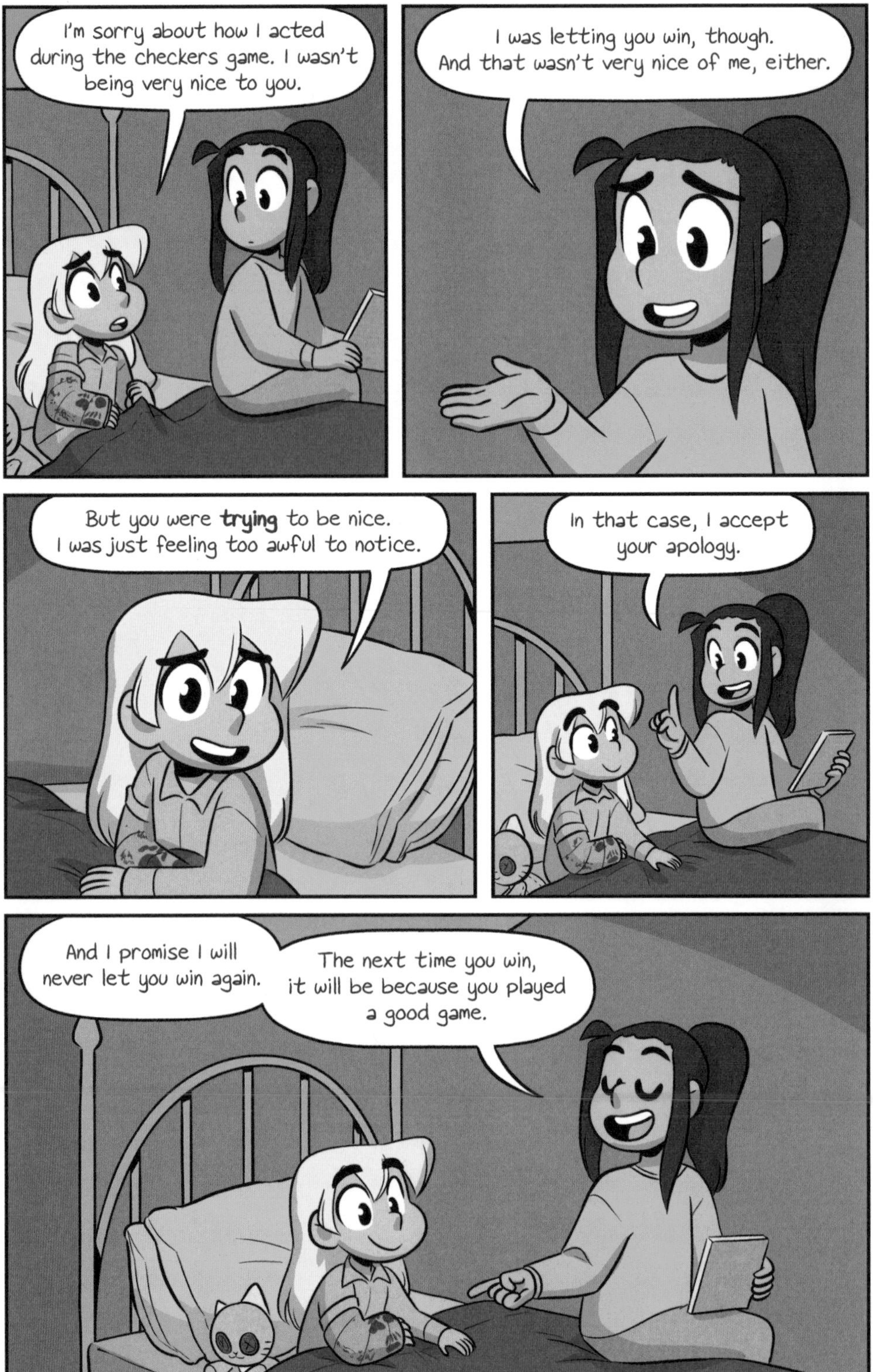
I'm sorry about how I acted during the checkers game. I wasn't being very nice to you.
I was letting you win, though. And that wasn't very nice of me, either.
But you were **trying** to be nice. I was just feeling too awful to notice.
In that case, I accept your apology.
And I promise I will never let you win again.
The next time you win, it will be because you played a good game.

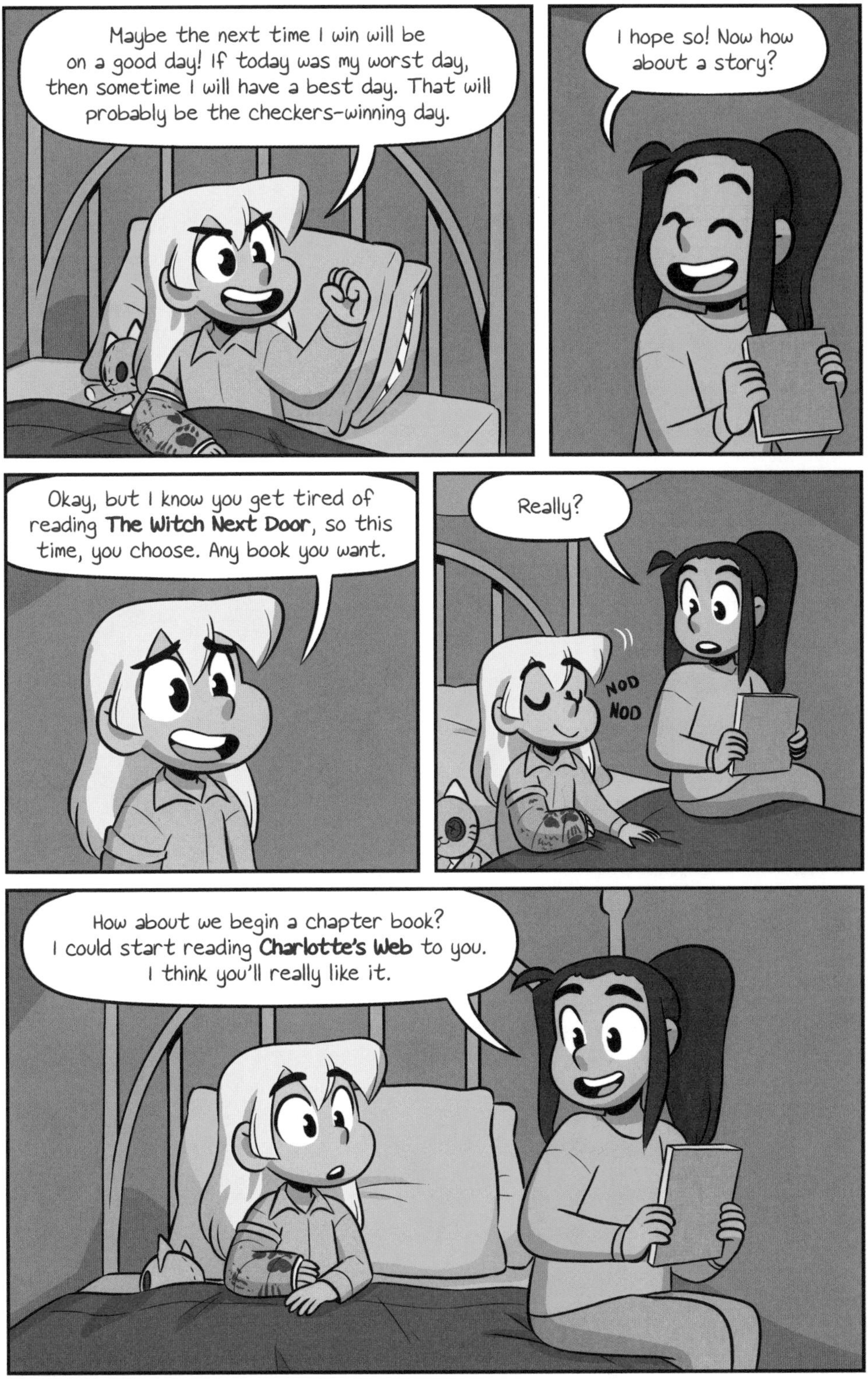
Maybe the next time I win will be on a good day! If today was my worst day, then sometime I will have a best day. That will probably be the checkers-winning day.
I hope so! Now how about a story?
Okay, but I know you get tired of reading **The Witch Next Door**, so this time, you choose. Any book you want.
Really?
NOD
NOD
How about we begin a chapter book? I could start reading **Charlotte's Web** to you. I think you'll really like it.

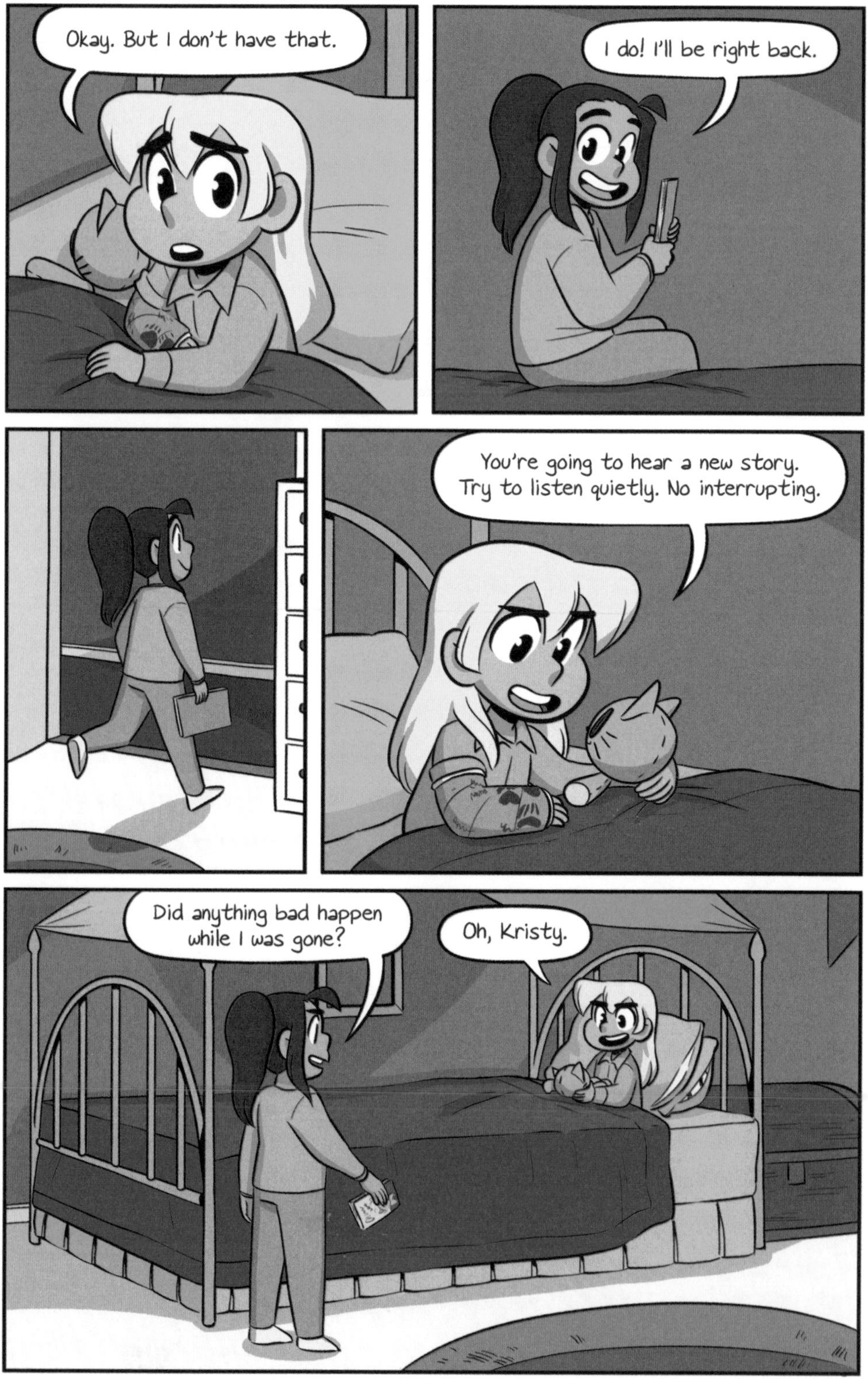
Okay. But I don't have that.
I do! I'll be right back.
You're going to hear a new story. Try to listen quietly. No interrupting.
Did anything bad happen while I was gone?
Oh, Kristy.

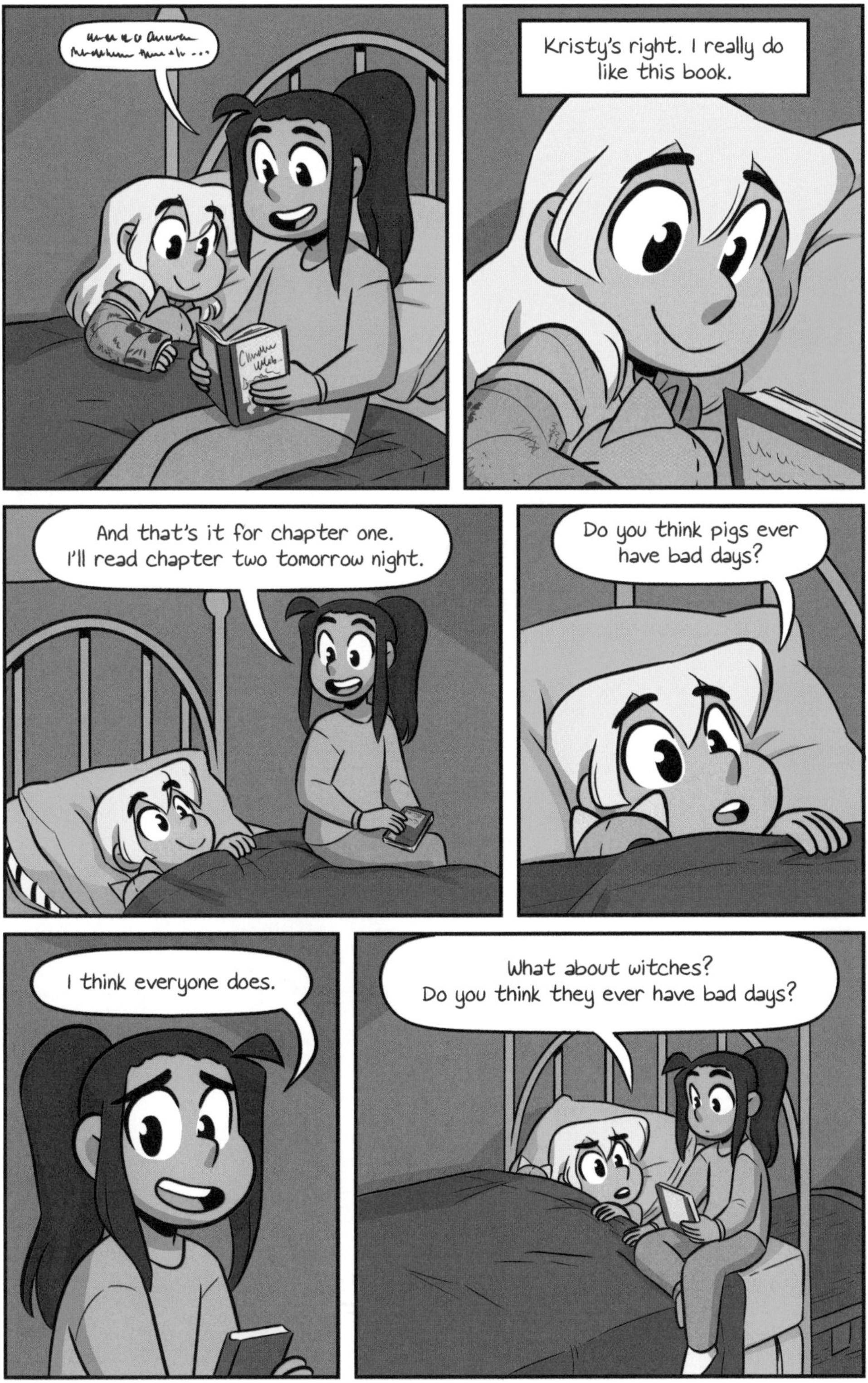
Kristy's right. I really do like this book.
And that's it for chapter one. I'll read chapter two tomorrow night.
Do you think pigs ever have bad days?
I think everyone does.
What about witches? Do you think they ever have bad days?

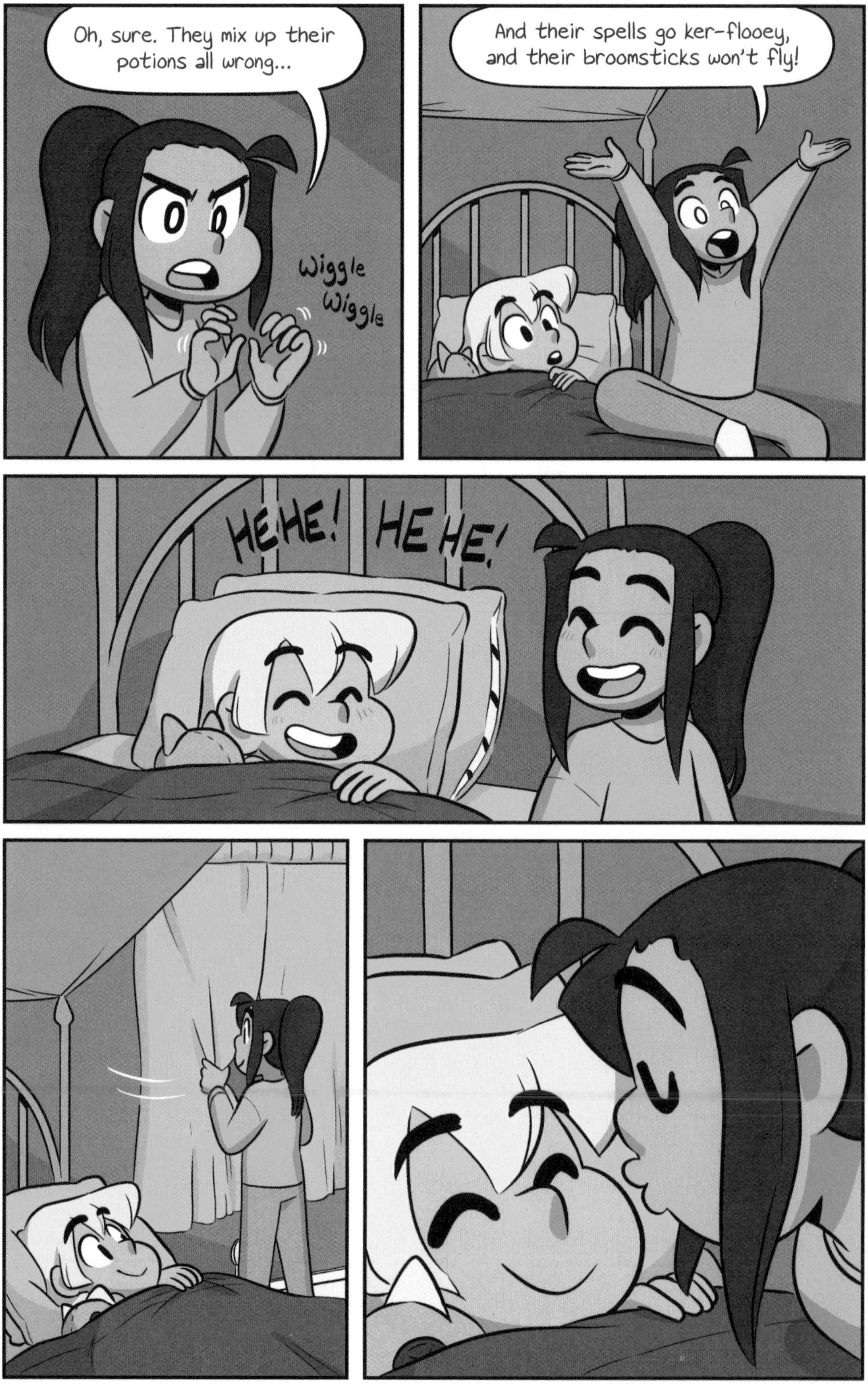
Oh, sure. They mix up their potions all wrong...
Wiggle Wiggle
And their spells go ker-flooey, and their broomsticks won't fly!
HE HE! HE HE!

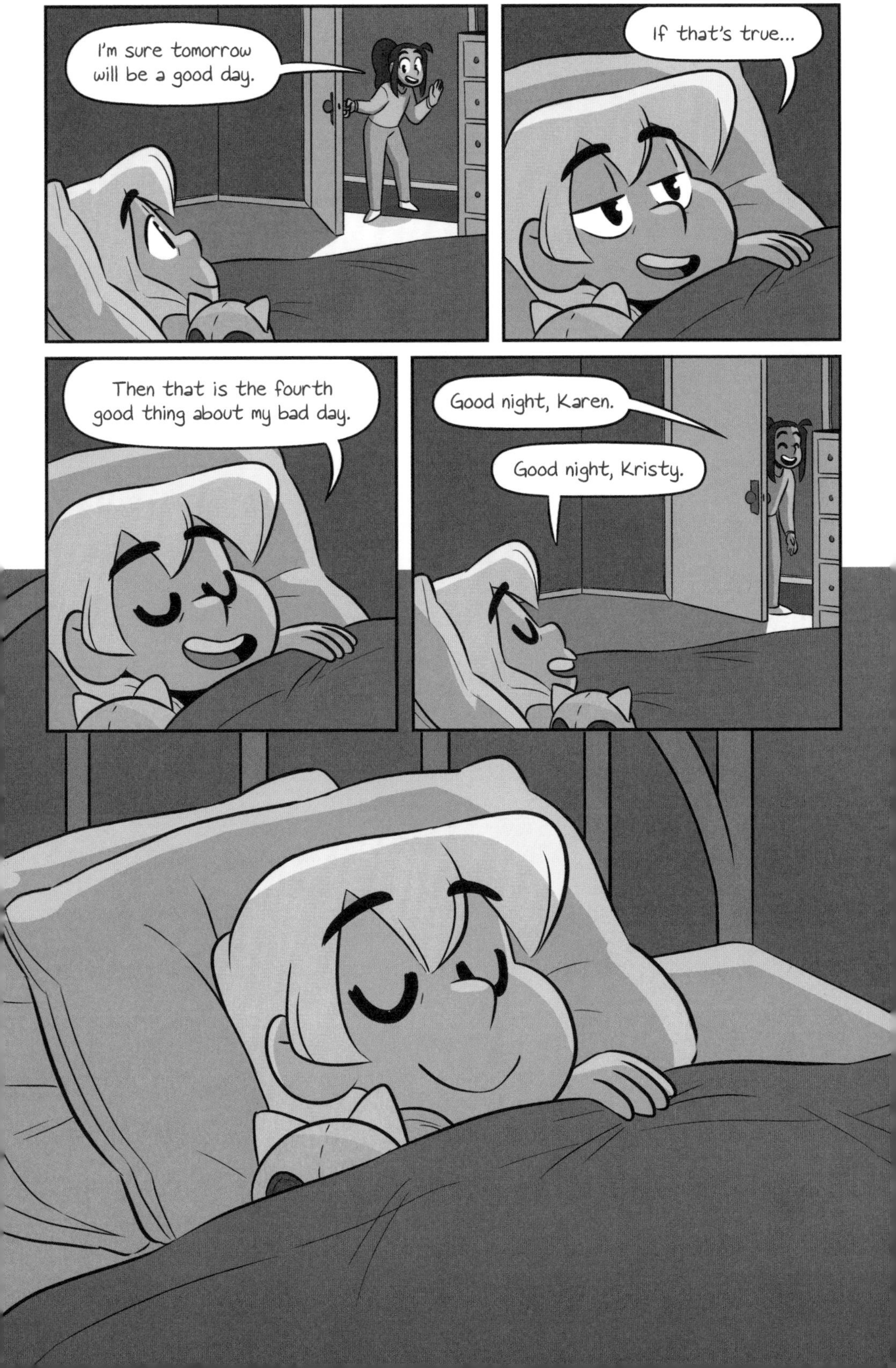
I'm sure tomorrow will be a good day.
If that's true...
Then that is the fourth good thing about my bad day.
Good night, Karen.
Good night, Kristy.

ANN M. MARTIN'S The Baby-sitters Club is one of the most popular series in the history of publishing — with more than 180 million books in print worldwide — and inspired a generation of young readers. Her novels include *Belle Teal*, *A Corner of the Universe* (a Newbery Honor book), *Here Today*, *A Dog's Life*, and *On Christmas Eve*, as well as the much-loved collaborations, *P.S. Longer Letter Later* and *Snail Mail No More*, with Paula Danziger, and *The Doll People* and *The Meanest Doll in the World*, written with Laura Godwin and illustrated by Brian Selznick. She lives in upstate New York.

KATY FARINA is the creator of the *New York Times* bestselling graphic novel adaptations of *Karen's Witch* and *Karen's Roller Skates* by Ann M. Martin. She has painted backgrounds for *She-Ra and the Princesses of Power* at DreamWorks TV and has also done work for BOOM! Studios, Oni Press, and Z2 Comics. She lives in Los Angeles. Visit her online at katyfarina.com.

DON'T MISS THE OTHER BABY-SITTERS LITTLE SISTER GRAPHIC NOVELS!

A GRAPHIC NOVEL BY
KATY FARINA
BABY-SITTERS LITTLE SISTER®
KAREN'S WITCH
BASED ON THE NOVEL BY
ANN M. MARTIN

A GRAPHIC NOVEL BY
KATY FARINA
BABY-SITTERS LITTLE SISTER®
KAREN'S ROLLER SKATES
BASED ON THE NOVEL BY
ANN M. MARTIN

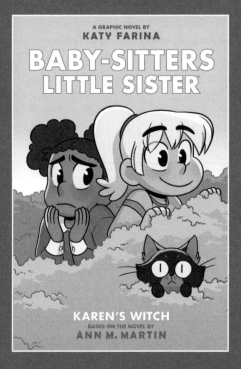

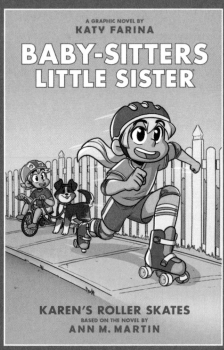